Ghoul

Ralph McGeary

Cover and maps drawn by Kevin McDonough
Cover design by Kevin McDonough

ISBN-13: 978-1477589137

ISBN-10: 1477589139

Also available as a Kindle eBook

First Edition: August 2012

To Andrea, who reads everything.

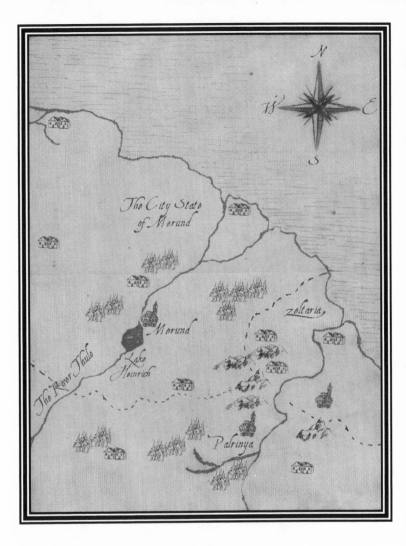

Map of the East

City map of Merund

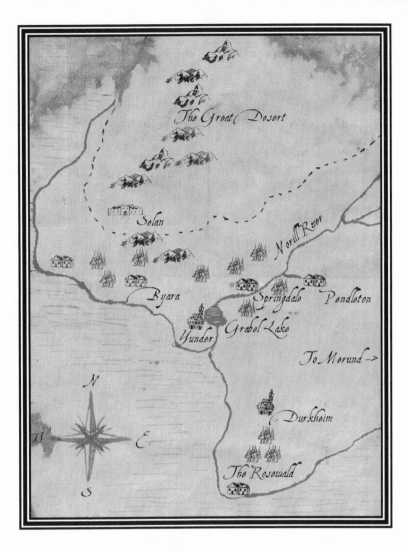

Map of the West

Prologue

There was nothing particularly strange about the alley to a casual observer. Merund, after all, was a city of alleys, the tiny pathways serving as countless spokes to interconnect the main roads into a massive, asymmetrical spider's web. Certainly Langham Alley was longer than many of those others: when one looked down it, the end seemed distant, as though miles away.

The alley's length appeared greater for the tremendous size of the buildings on either side of it. On the east was what had once been the Merund trade house. In a way it still was that; certainly the ancient building still hosted its fair share of small shops peddling various wares. Where it had once been the shopping place of the richest of the City-State, however, now it was trafficked by a smaller crowd, solitary figures who skulked from stall to stall, their eyes scanning the illegitimate goods from deep within bottomless hoods.

On the west, Langham courthouse, part of the thriving center of Merund's government more than half a century prior. Statues of angelic beings that towered over the broad entryway of the courthouse, once perfect, shining sentinels, were now worn down to almost unrecognizable lumps of stone, picked apart over the years by a lack of upkeep and the profiteering of thieves and souvenir hunters. Court hearings had long ago been moved to the newer, smaller courthouse in the Northern District of the city, leaving the Langham building officially abandoned. Nevertheless, city officials had never seen fit to have the building repurposed or demolished, and public murmurings suggested that this had something to do with substantial kickbacks being paid out from those less than reputable individuals who had moved into the courthouse since.

If the sort of individual who now occupied the courthouse itself was of an illegal and unsavory nature, such individuals seemed upstanding citizens when compared to those that lurked in the alley that ran along behind it. The narrow cobbled path running between the derelict courthouse on one side and the many back doors of the trade house on the other was home to the worst kind of person in Merund, or in any other city.

It was a reputation known better to some than to others. While most laborers and artisans could ignore the alley's very existence, few were the Guardsmen in Merund who had not imagined themselves dying there. Stabbed in the back, perhaps, while trying to break up a scuffle, or even stabbed in the front for so much as looking down it. If a Guardsman was going to die of unnatural causes in Merund, Langham Alley was a rather unoriginal place to do it.

Alois Gustav would normally have been immune to eerie premonitions of such a fate, being a Police Chief who within rights could stay in the station at all times if he saw fit to do so. Nevertheless, Alois had among his few strong principles a feeling that a leader should try to provide an example, and so, begrudgingly, he occasionally led raids on the alley, thus boosting the chances that he would meet his end there, as so many had before him. He knew this as well as anyone else did.

So, then, Alois would not have been terribly surprised if he were able to look into the future to the night that he lay dying in that very alley, his back propped against the courthouse wall, the blood soaked through his tunic mingling with the rain that was pouring from the black sky and slowly flooding the gutters on the street. What Alois might have found more surprising would be that he had, in fact, been stabbed blocks and blocks away from Langham Alley, and had used the last few minutes of his life to stumble and drag his ruined body to the very site where it now lay. Alois had gone out of his way to be where he was. He had come to see a man.

4 | Ghoul

Part I:
The Chief Constable

6 | Ghoul

Chapter 1

"Shouldn't you go home, Chief? Your shift is over, isn't it?"

"My title is Constable, Moltke."

"Constable it is, Chief. You gonna go home, though?"

"What answer do I give you every night when you come to take over the watch?"

"I believe it's 'not until I'm sure that everything is in order,' Chief."

"Look at that, he can learn."

"And it only took me four years! How about that?"

Alois grunted and began aimlessly rearranging the papers on his desk.

"If you really want, Chief, you could stay and head up the night watch as well. I wouldn't say no to a couple more hours of shuteye."

"Scamper off, then," Alois said, putting his pen to paper and carefully signing his name at the bottom of a report. He frowned when this did little more than make a slight inkless imprint against the paper. He held the pen in front of his face and shook it, as if to encourage it. "Leave your badge, though. I'll give it to Klein."

"Aww, Chief, Klein? He started, what, two days ago?"

"Three weeks. And I already like him better than you. What do you think that says about your job performance?"

Moltke gave him an extremely well-practiced toothy grin. "You put it that way, Chief, I think I will stay for my shift. You, though, you should go home and be with the family."

"We're starting to go in circles, I'm afraid," Alois said, trying the pen again without success. He sighed and dropped the thing back into the old ale stein sitting at the corner of his desk, as though it might start working again in time. "I've got to get a blasted enchanted pen. The mechanical ones break in a day."

"Who're we waiting on, anyway?" Moltke asked. "They're pretty damn late."

"Schmidt," Alois said calmly, and he knew that Moltke was right. The whole of the night watch had already come in, armored up, and went out on patrol, leaving just the clerks and a few Guardsmen in the front area, and just he and Moltke in the back rooms.

"Schmidt? He doesn't usually go out all that far, does he? Shouldn't he be back by now?"

"Yes, probably."

"Aren't you worried?"

"Yes," Alois said, fishing his quill and ink pot out of his desk drawer, "probably."

"Aww, Chief. I didn't know you had it in you."

"Joke all you like, but I'm not leaving until Schmidt comes back."

"Where was he patrolling?"

"Langham."

"Hmm."

"Yes."

"Let's hope he comes back in possession of his entire body."

Alois shot him a dirty look. "Let's hope."

"Let's hope what?"

Alois and Moltke jerked their heads up to the figure that had appeared in the office doorway. It was Schmidt, his chain shirt rustling noisily as he walked to an unoccupied desk and fell gracelessly into the chair.

"Schmidt! Not dead! I guess I owe you dinner, Chief."

"Moltke, shut up. Schmidt, why are you late? Is everything all right?"

"Everything's fine, Chief. I just got drawn into an argument and lost track of time."

"An argument."

"Yeah."

"And are you planning," Alois said, trying to be patient, "on being paid for the time you spent shooting the breeze with one of your buddies?"

"You misunderstand, sir! It was an argument with a law-breaker."

"Uh-huh. And you're aware that you do have authority to arrest people whether or not they think it's a good idea, correct?"

"Arrest would have been a bit harsh, Chief. It was just a little old man."

"Lord, not the one from last week, with the squeaky voice?"

"The very same."

"I was sure he understood that he had to clear out."

"He's just a corner magician, sir; he's not doing any harm."

"Magic that's not sanctioned by the Wizard's Guild is illegal, Schmidt. And anyway, clearing him out of there is as much for his own protection as for anyone else's. The thieves and rogues that hang around back there will eat him alive. It's a miracle that you didn't find him dead and stripped of everything but his skivvies."

"Well, don't worry, sir, he was clearing out when I left him."

"He was clearing out last time we left him, too. This is two strikes, now. What does he look like?"

"Don't you know?"

"No, it was dark, and I couldn't see his face because of those stupid robes."

"Well, yeah, me neither, actually. Those things are far too big for him. His head is practically lost in the hood."

"Say, wait a minute, I know that guy!" Moltke interjected happily. "Those robes! Have you ever seen anything more pathetic, with all those sparkles on them? Someone needs to tell him that buying the best pair of sparkly robes that the costume shop has doesn't actually imbue you with magical powers."

"That's a good point, actually," Schmidt said. "I've never seen him do any magic. Not even make stuff float or anything."

"Not doing something blatantly illegal in front of an officer of the law? You don't say," Alois said dryly. "I'm sure he's got some magic, wouldn't be much point to being a street magician otherwise. Anyway, I hope you're right about him being gone, or tomorrow you're going to have to go back to the alley and bring him in here until we can find a shelter or something to stick him in."

"Erm, Chief… tomorrow I'm off duty."

Alois sighed. "Fine, fine. I can have Severson do it."

Schmidt smiled as he undid the laces on his boots. "You're the best, Chief!"

"Heart of gold, Chief!" Moltke added.

"Shut up, Moltke. I'm going home."

"G'night, Chief!"

"Say hello to the missus and the girls for us!"

"I will, I will. Good night, boys."

Alois pulled his cloak off the rack in the hallway and walked through the large open area where the Guardsmen filed paperwork and took their breaks. A few of the night staff waved to him, still looking tired and disgruntled, and Alois nodded farewell as he pushed out the oaken double doors and onto Thule Street. The sun had set, and carriage traffic was minimal, so he was able to walk down the cobblestones without the fear of being trampled to death that was a usual feature on Thule Street during the daylight hours. Fat pigeons scurried out of his way as he passed.

As a higher official in this part of the city, many knew him, and people nodded cordially to him as he passed. The baker at Thule and Bismarck, closing up shop for the night, shoved a baguette into Alois' hands, as he did whenever he saw the Chief Constable. Alois wasn't entirely comfortable with this kind of patronage, but it made the wife happy, and that made his life easier, so he always took it gratefully without ever actually giving the baker any special treatment. The baker didn't seem to notice.

It was, he felt, a very nice city, and certainly the largest that he knew of—he'd never been further than fifty miles away from it, and none of the farming hamlets spread about the City-State's dominion came even close to Merund itself in terms of size. It was a modern city, made of brick and stone. Crime, of course, was a problem; increasingly so in the Central District, over which Alois had dominion. His boys did their best with what they had, anyway. It would have been easier if so many damn things hadn't been illegal.

Alois' two-storey house, which sat in the residential area on the southern edge of the wealthy Northern District, was nestled among many other houses like it, though some were far grander. It was a few miles from the Guard's Station in the Central District, and typically he took a carriage, though today he was leaving late and it wasn't worth the trouble of trying to find one. The exertion of the occasional walk home was largely the only exercise that the big man ever got, which apparently wasn't enough to reduce his widening middle. Unlike the patrol officers, he no longer wore the normal uniform of chainmail under a city watch tunic, opting instead for a plain, button-down shirt under a dress coat. He did, however, still carry his saber, a gilded ceremonial piece that had never drawn blood. It had been given to him just a year prior, to celebrate twenty-five years of service. The sword that he had used in his early days in the Guard—and in the border wars—was kept in the attic at home.

By the time Alois had reached his front steps, the sky had turned from dark blue to black. The light of the stars was blotted out by dull brown rain clouds that loomed overhead, waiting to burst and drench the city. He worked late often, and wasn't surprised to see the windows of his home unlit as he approached; his family had already gone to bed.

He was considering having something to eat as he climbed the steps and reached for the knob. Abruptly, he stopped, staring down. The door was open, just a crack. His wife, Elizabeth, sometimes left the front door open on warm summer days, but it was still early on in spring, and nighttime besides. He pushed the door the rest of the way open and took a step into the antechamber. A single candle cast a dim light on the floorboards. He didn't take off his boots, but stepped further into his home, and saw a familiar oil lamp lying at the foot of the stairs. It was shattered.

"Elizabeth? Cassie? Juliet?" he bellowed, running into the darkened house, his bag and the baguette dropped forgotten on the floor. The kitchen and parlor were empty, and as he came back to the stairs he pounded up them, not even short of breath when usually even the front steps winded him. He reached the top of the stairs, and had to put a hand against the wall for support as his worst fears were confirmed. His wife laid there, blood pooled around her head. And over her—over her stood a man in black, what looked like a dingy kitchen knife in his hand. It was clear that he had been drawn back to the hallway by Alois' bellowing. He didn't even have time to ready the knife as the giant Police Chief threw himself at the invader, pushing him to the ground, grabbing a bronze candelabrum off the nearest end table and clubbing the man in the head with it until a bloody dent was apparent through the coarse brown head sock he wore.

Up again, Alois charged to the room of his eldest daughter, Cassandra. The door swung open as he was reaching for the knob, barely giving him time to think as another masked assailant rushed forth, stabbing with a short cutlass. Alois shouted with rage, stumbling back and drawing his sword before charging the man with no thought of defense, taking him through the neck, the sharp, pristine blade of his sword slicing through artery and tendon, nerve and flesh.

Into the room as the second assailant fell, and Cassandra lay dead on the floor, scarlet staining her night dress, her stomach opened. Eyes clouded by fear and rage, Alois turned to run to Juliet's bedroom, but a sound stopped him: a soft, delicate whimper came from under Cassandra's bed, and Alois dropped to the ground and threw up the dust ruffle. There lay Juliet, tears streaming down her face, a gasp escaping her lips.

"Papa…"

Alois dropped his saber and reached in, gingerly taking his twelve year-old daughter in his arms and pulling her out from under the bed, cradling her in his lap.

"Juliet, beloved. I'm so glad that you're…"

But she wasn't. His hand had become slippery and wet where it gripped her around the middle. He dared to look, and saw that it was not a superficial wound.

"Stay… stay still, beloved," he moaned, "I'll take you to the doctor's."

"It'll be okay, papa. Don't worry…"

"Yes, my dear, that's right." He lifted her slowly. Cassandra and Elizabeth were dead. He had seen enough murder victims to know. Surely God would not allow for him to lose Juliet as well. So sure was Alois that he would be able to save Juliet as he carried her out of Cassandra's room that he didn't even notice the blood that was now trailing from her mouth.

"It'll be okay, Papa. Don't worry…. but Papa…"

"Yes, beloved?"

"But you're hurt, Papa."

"What? No, I…"

Her eyes slipped shut.

"Stay with me, Juliet. You must stay awake."

She was motionless, and he stopped at the top of the stairs, where he knelt down, cradling her. "You must stay awake, Juliet. Listen to your papa. It is very important."

Alois was still sure that God would not take her away from him, and so his shock when he felt for her pulse and did not find it was absolute. He slowly slid to the floor, his back against the wall. He did not weep, because he still could not believe what was happening. He could only stare at the fragile thing in his arms that had been alive a moment ago and was now only a body, still as warm as if nothing had changed. The doctors could do little in the best of cases, and they could surely do nothing now. He gently placed his hand on her chest. It had fallen still. He rose up and carried her to where he could sit between Cassandra and Elizabeth and mourn there together with his family. This seemed the correct thing to do.

He was unsure how long he sat there, cradling his dead daughter's body against him. Soon enough, though, the fog of anger that had turned to fear and then to shock slowly began to lift, allowing his senses to operate. He was able to feel for the first time the trickle of warm blood that had soaked his tunic and was now dripping even into his trousers. He knew that the blood from Juliet's body should not be flowing so fast, without any heartbeat to pump it. Without thought, he reached to his own stomach, and there his fingers found a tear even worse than the one that had just claimed the life of his youngest daughter. He had been stabbed, at some point.

Fitting, perhaps, that he should die here with the rest of them. They could all be reunited only minutes after they were parted.

Yes, he thought, shutting his eyes, leaning back slowly, a hand absently stroking Juliet's golden hair. Die together, meet again...

But.

But God had taken them from him. Why should he then turn around and see fit to reunite them? What sort of perverse world would this be then, a happy reunion after an unjustified atrocity, something that could have been prevented, something that should have never happened in the first place? How could God allow such a thing? Didn't he know what was happening? Couldn't he stop it?

But of course he knew: he was Delar, the Forever Seer. He had written the Divine Book of the Time at the beginning the world, and all things were set. God knew the fate of everyone who had ever lived or would ever live. God had written out what was happening at every moment.

God, Alois thought, not angry, not even horrified, too many new thoughts exploding in his mind to leave room for either emotion, had conspired to kill his family.

It was that... or it was something else. Something that, beyond all reason, was somehow even worse. For, even given all the evidence, Alois could not believe that the God of his childhood would do this—would do this to the poor thing in his lap. Delar must not have seen. And if Delar, the Forever Seer, had not foreseen this, then what was Delar at all?

Alois began to feel a looming dread that perhaps the words he had exchanged with Juliet had been the last that he would exchange with her. He might truly never see her again, or speak to her again.

Indeed, because of his wound, he might never speak to anyone again. He would die here. The other Guardsmen would talk of his fate in lowered voices. They would attend the funeral wearing black garb and somber faces.

That was how it should have been. But what could ever be as it should be, anymore?

Somehow, Alois couldn't stand it. It couldn't end there. He had no goals now, no dreams, nothing but a desire for his end not to be at the top of the stairs. That was something far too noble for what he had just seen done. Far too noble to exist in such a world.

Alois came to his feet. He carried Juliet to his bed and laid her down, and then gently retrieved the body of his wife, laying her to rest beside her. He finally rested Cassandra on the other side, placing his hand briefly on her forehead. Then he turned away and walked to the stairs.

He would have to go to the government doctors. They had only a rudimentary ability to fix wounds, and he had almost no hope, but surely it was better than nothing. Except that Alois was a police officer, and he had seen many badly injured people be taken in by the city doctors. He had heard of great medical advances in distant nations, but there had been none in Merund. The treatment of Merund's doctors, for one with a wound such as his, was neither better nor worse than nothing. It was exactly the same as nothing.

So, as he clambered down his front steps, the wound in his side now suddenly shrieking in pain, making it difficult even to walk, he did not turn right, to head north to the municipal hospital. Instead he headed south, towards the old part of town; the Central District. He had only one chance of being healed now.

Healing magic had been outlawed by the Church many decades ago as a part of the Declaration of Piety. Such intervention in death and disease was viewed as a blatant affront to the will of Delar the Seer, and hence any magic that might counteract God's will in terms of who lived and who died was forbidden. While most magic could only be practiced by licensed Wizards, curative magic could not legally be practiced by a single soul in all of Merund.

And so, with a total lack of any moral dilemma (a fact that a few hours before would have left him shocked), the dying Chief Constable found himself, like many before him, seeking out an illegal street magician to cure his wounds. It was not a hopeful search. A magician who could cure a wound as critical as his was rare, and finding one who was willing to help a Police Chief who had been such a burden to the illegal magic industry would be even more difficult. Further still, there was nowhere in particular that one could go to find these magicians, as they were constantly moving to avoid arrest.

Except, of course, for one magician, a little old man with a squeaky voice who wore baggy, sparkling robes. Someone who had apparently not figured out the importance of staying on the move to the livelihood of a magician's career. It had begun to rain when Alois turned onto Hound Road, the buildings around him growing gradually dirtier and more disused as he neared Langham Alley.

Thus, Alois Gustav, Chief Constable of Merund's Central District, sat in the pouring rain, drenched through with equal parts filthy water and his own blood, his back pressed against the wall of the derelict courthouse. He felt light-headed, and his limbs lay heavy as though cast from lead. Every movement now was painful, and the rain blurred his vision so that he could barely see.

"Magician!" he called out. "I know you must be here! Come out, magician! I need you!"

Nothing. Alois groaned. If there was no magician here, it would have been easier to have just died on his front steps.

"Please, magician! I can pay! Any amount!"

Slowly, a black shape emerged, like a blotch of ink splattered on his eye, growing bigger against the almost equally black surroundings of the alley. An odd glow seemed to come from the cuffs and hem of its robes.

Suddenly, part of the alleyway was lit up as the figure opened its robes and revealed a glowing lantern. Now, even soaked through with water, those robes nearly blinded Alois as the glimmering dust enmeshed with the cloth brightly reflected the lantern light.

"Old man!" Alois yelled to be heard through the storm, "I am wounded. Please, heal me. I can pay, I can."

The figure took a step back. "Old man?" he spat indignantly, barely understandable over the rain.

Alois grunted. "Fine, fine, distinguished fellow, whatever you prefer!"

"I am not a fellow!" His arms rose up, small hands emerging for the first time out of the massive cuffed sleeves of the robe. Those hands grasped the edges of the massive hood and pulled it back, revealing a small, smooth, dark-skinned face. Auburn hair was pulled back into a ponytail that wrapped over her shoulder and disappeared into the top of her robes. "I am a girl, thank you!"

"A girl!?" Alois blubbered, "But... but..."

"Yes?"

"But girls can't be magicians!"

She glared at him. "No one without a small fortune and a fancy Wizard's diploma can be a magician according to you, but we seem to manage nonetheless."

"I... but..."

"But what? What are you even doing here? Did you really come out here in this rain to tell me to go away? I have to admit, I didn't expect such dedication!"

"Well... can you actually do magic?" he sputtered, wiping rain from his eyes, trying to get a better look at her.

"Can I actually do magic? Wouldn't be much point being a magician if I couldn't do magic, would there?"

"But... how old are you, twelve?"

She glared. "I'm fourteen! And if you're going to insult me, I'm leaving!" She turned around haughtily.

"Wait!" he cried out. "I'm sorry. I need your help."

"Oh, I get it. You threaten to lock me up if I don't clear out of here, and now suddenly you want a floating cuckoo clock or something and you decide we can do business."

"No, I... please, just look."

He indicated his stomach, and she held out the lantern, casting light on the tear in his flesh. They both gasped. His clothes were so soaked through with blood that they'd barely been able to take on any rain water.

"This looks really bad. You want me to cure this?"

"Yes..." he moaned. His eyes had begun to drift in and out of focus.

"Hey, listen, I would help you, but I'm really not a curative magic user."

"Please... you have to..."

"I really want to, but... I can't. I'm sorry..."

"No, listen, anything... please... I just.... don't want to die..."

"Oh."

The rain poured down, harder than ever.

"Well, why didn't you say so?"
It was the last thing he heard.

Chapter 2

An excerpt from An Introduction to Magical History, by Pontius Sleighman

Chapter 1 – The Nature of Magic

There are many reasons not to practice magic. After all, while the magical arts may help us greatly in nearly all of our endeavors, rarely can they produce results of either the quality or quantity to make up for the sort of hard work that farmers, laborers, and artisans do every day. Not everyone practices magic because not everyone *has* to practice magic; the world only needs so many Wizards, just as it only needs so many tailors, butchers, or even farmers. After all, farmers are important, but if everyone is a farmer, who shall act in our theaters? Who shall make our candles, distill our liquor, or rent us a place to stay when we're out of town? Farmers are important, but the world needs more than just them. Wizards are important, but the world needs far more than Wizards, as well.

There are many reasons not to practice magic. There is not, however, a single good reason in existence for not understanding magic. Far, far too many common folk look on magic as a force with neither method nor even explanation; they see Wizards as wild practitioners of a chaotic, lawless ability with unknowable causes and unguessable results. It is, of course, not so. Magic, while certainly a very unique and impressive art, is an art all the same; it can be practiced, perfected, and most of all, it can be understood.

Magic comes not from without, but from within. And yet, neither does it exist in a vacuum. To boil its principle down to the most basic, magic is a process that allows humans to change reality through little more than sheer will. It is more than will, though, certainly, or else any man who furrowed his brow could produce a gout of flame or a bouquet of flowers. Using magic requires patterning the mind in a very specific way, depending upon the result that one hopes to achieve. A Wizard must key his mind to the resonating frequencies of the world around him, and through this can change a small part of that world, be it by making a tin coin into a gold one, or turning a dragon into a shrew. "Frequency" is not the right word—sound has nothing to do with it—but the word will serve as well as any for my intention here.

Keying to the frequency is a process almost impossible to explain; it must be experienced to be understood. What can be said is that it is very difficult, and that it is an almost infinitely complicated process, specific to a desired single end. The process of tuning in to the frequency and changing it is what we call magic. Specific techniques for tuning in to specific frequencies are what we call spells.

A spell is simply a process that is formulated especially to allow the mind to key in to a specific frequency. Sometimes, no other process would work; other times, the specific process that is used is one of many that would function, but is favored out of tradition, or for some other reason. Most spells require a number of subtle hand gestures, and nearly all require a string of words be spoken. These words are almost always in Arcanic, which, though a dead language that is cumbersome to converse in, is spoken by nearly all those who practice magic. Whether the words must be in Arcanic for the spell to be fully effective, or if they could be in any language, is a topic that is still debated to this day.

Casting a spell is not so easy as merely learning the verbal and physical components. These are simply a guide to patterning the mind to the desired end; they must be practiced over and over again with careful focus, under the tutelage of one who has mastered the spell themselves. Thus, magic is an art that is taught. Those who will become Wizards begin their education often as early as age five, and certainly always in childhood. Like speech, magic is a skill that can only be learned by the developing mind. If a child is not taught how to cast their first spell by the time they reach puberty, they will lose their aptitude for magic forever. However, once the fundamentals are ingrained, the mind can continue learning new magical techniques far into adulthood— though with increasing difficulty.

"Hey, I think he's coming around. Can you hear me, Chief?"

"Oh, lord, Moltke," Alois groaned, eyes shut, "if this is Heaven, I'm going to need to talk to someone in charge about your being here."

"Chief! Hey, everybody, he's woken up!"

"Everybody?" Alois grumbled, blinking his eyes open and allowing his surroundings to come slowly into focus. He was indoors now, and as he swiveled his head he saw just about everyone he worked with, which made the room a rather tight fit. He patted the surface under him, which confirmed that he wasn't on the hard cobblestones of the street anymore, but rather lying on a bed. Further, someone had changed his clothes, and he was now wearing a shirt and pants made of clean, dry white linen. There wasn't a speck of blood in sight.

"She did it!" he proclaimed happily, smiling at his guests. They stared back blankly.

"Who did what, Constable?" ventured Viv Kohler, one of the girls who worked on the morning shift. Alois mentally chided himself for his stupidity. He was in a room full of City Guard personnel, and he'd just nearly admitted to committing a felony.

"Nothing, nothing," he said, shaking his head. "Just still a bit groggy, I think."

"Well, sure, Chief, after what you've been through. Imagine, dragging yourself all the way to the Station with that stomach wound."

"Police Station? That's where you found me?"

"That's right, Chief. We figured you were looking for help after you came home and... well... we've already heard what happened at your house. We all..." he trailed off as Alois groaned softly, clamping his eyes shut.

"Oh, Lord, Elizabeth and the children..."

"God, Chief, I thought you knew! I didn't mean to..."

"No, no, I knew, I just... I guess I just..."

"It's all right, Chief. It's probably been taking all your will power just to keep yourself alive," someone in the back ventured.

"Yes, that's quite true," Alois said. His gaze flicked around the room, tracing the faces for some sign of judgment. He wondered whether his choosing not to die there with his family made him a bad person. He didn't feel like a bad person, but that didn't prove much. God knew he had locked up plenty of men who had no conception that they'd done anything wrong.

They'd found him at the Guard's Station. That was fortunate, as it was far easier to explain than being found at Langham Alley, and yet Alois couldn't fathom how that girl could have moved him. She could have used magic, he supposed, but it wasn't as though she could have levitated his body and floated it through the streets without being noticed—though the storm may have aided in that. He'd have to try to find her, so he could thank her, and ask her how she'd done it.

"I'm at the hospital, is that right? The one near the Capitol building?"

"That's correct, Chief Constable," Kohler said. "We took you here straight away. They cleaned you up, but said there wasn't much they could do for you. I think the doctors were all quite surprised that you lived through the night, but now they say that you'll probably be fine."

Alois frowned. That wasn't good. If the doctors thought something unnatural was going on, he might be in serious trouble. Suddenly suspicious, he turned his head to the slightly opened door, through which he could hear voices.

"What's going on out there?"

"Oh, it's just the Church Inquisitor debriefing your doctor. Don't worry, Chief, you know how standard that is."

Alois grimaced. A Church Inquisitor? Already? The Church was probably trying to make it clear that they were in charge by showing that even government officials weren't above suspicion of heresy. If they found out what he'd done...

"I... I don't think I'm feeling well enough to see him just now," Alois tried.

"Actually, Chief, the worse you're feeling the better with these types. If you start to feel better you'll just have to fake it to get him off your back."

Kohler shoved Moltke playfully in the shoulder. "That's not terribly legal advice, Guardsman."

"What the hell has legality got to do with police work, young lady?"

They all laughed. Alois threw in a chuckle to be polite, though he didn't much feel like it. He'd gotten himself out of one terrible situation, but here he was in a new one. If things went poorly, there would be a lengthy trial to strip him of his position. He'd almost certainly end up having to retire in disgrace, and be denied his pension. Worse, if the Church was feeling especially assertive... they could try for a penalty of imprisonment or torture.

The door swung open, and a bespectacled man, wearing the standard-issue red jerkin of a city doctor, led in the Church Inquisitor. A tall, thin man in midnight blue vestments, the Inquisitor was perhaps Alois' age, but had a clean-shaven face and thinning hair. A bronze circlet perched delicately on his head identified his Church rank, though Alois had never gotten the hierarchy figured out.

"All right, everybody, clear on out," the doctor said, "you'll be able to see Mr. Gustav again soon."

With a chorus of farewells, the crowd of people slowly filed out of the room. Moltke went last, miming to Alois that he should press his forehead against the oil lamp hanging next to the bed. Alois faked a disapproving glare, even though all he really felt was a plummeting sensation in the pit of his stomach.

Well, he couldn't exactly leap for a daring escape out the window.

"Hello, Deacon," he said to the Inquisitor, using the generic term for a member of Merund's High Church. The Inquisitor nodded back.

"Chief Constable. I'm sure I won't find anything out of the ordinary here."

The doctor crossed over to Alois' bed and slowly lifted Alois' white linen shirt, revealing his stomach, which Alois noticed was looking exceptionally pale where it was visible. Where it wasn't visible it was being obscured by a large white bandage, placed over where his wound had been. Alois stared at the bandage. There was no blood, and he had a terrible suspicion that the curative magic would have finished its work as he'd slept. There would be no wound there at all when the bandage was pulled up.

"Well, Doctor, can't you just tell him how badly you saw me hurt last night? It must have been clear that I hadn't had any curative magic cast on me."

In Alois' experience, Merund's doctors were concerned first and foremost with avoiding the wrath of the Church, and this one did not disappoint his expectations.

"That's certainly true, Chief Constable, but the fact that you lived after receiving such a brutal wound is in itself quite extraordinary. I'm not accusing you of anything, of course. Merely following procedure."

"Of course," Alois thought to agree, "The procedures are there for a reason." His eyes lingered on the bandage as the doctor's hands reached towards it and gripped its edge. He gritted his teeth as the bandage was pulled away from his stomach.

It is safe to say that all three men were surprised at what they saw.

"Goodness," the doctor murmured.

"Well," the Inquisitor said, analyzing the inflamed and oozing knife wound in Alois' stomach, "I've studied the perverse art of curative magic extensively in order to fulfill my role in the Church, and I can firmly say that there aren't any healing spells that heal the man but leave the wound."

"Yes," the doctor said, "The wound doesn't look any better than it did when he was brought in last night... there's no scabbing at all, and yet no blood flowing from it either."

"I'm sure that you and the other doctors will have a fine time postulating what could explain such an occurrence, but I know what doesn't explain it, and that's all I am concerned about." The gaunt man leaned over and firmly grasped Alois' shoulder. Alois greatly wished to flinch away. Whether out of fear or disgust, he was not sure.

"It was not part of God's plan that you should die of your wound, Chief Constable Alois Gustav, and you are not suspected of any heretical behavior." Alois thought he noticed a hint of disappointment in the Inquisitor's voice. The Inquisitor promptly released Alois and turned his lanky stride to the door, disappearing through it.

"God be with you, brothers."

"God be with you," Alois and the doctor echoed back, as though they were having a competition to see who could be less enthusiastic about the sentiment. The doctor began patting the bandage back down. "Well, is there any pain?"

"No," Alois murmured, watching the horrid wound disappear back under the white cloth. "No pain at all."

Within a few days, Alois was discharged from the hospital. They sent home in a hospital carriage, and the moment he had stepped out, the thing was off down the street at a trot. He stared at his house from the edge of the lawn, his eyes lingering on the door. For a moment he thought it was open a crack, but he quickly realized that this was merely a trick of the mid-day shadows. The door was shut, left that way by the police investigators who had examined and cleaned up the scene.

The scene. It was not a word he would have ever wanted applied to his home. He began walking up the path toward the door, and made it as far as the front steps. He stared down at the small burgundy dots trailing down them. They'd be there for some time, he knew. Once blood had dried into stone, it was very difficult to get up.

He reached for the door knob, but paused short of touching it. Through the small windows on either side of the door, he saw that it was dark inside.

He withdrew his hand, and carefully took a seat on the top step. He didn't mind that there was blood soaked into the stone. It was all his, after all. Inside the house, it would be a different matter.

Eventually, he got up and walked back down the steps, heading up the lawn and turning out into the street. His wound was stitched up now, but still didn't seem to be making any effort at closing itself. Its edges had turned an unsightly black, the skin fading to purple a few inches away from the wound before blending back into the pale white of the rest of him; he'd never regained his pinkish luster from before the accident. Alois knew that he looked terrible, and felt as though he should be tired, weak, and perhaps barely mobile. However, he didn't feel that way.

Not at all, in fact. He felt just about as energetic as he ever had. There was no pain in his wound, but it was more than that. There was no pain anywhere. None of the pains he had begun to feel as he'd aged. No aching in his back or his feet; no tight feeling in his chest. He felt fantastic, in terms of the physical. As he walked, he passed by a corner tavern he'd often frequented, and realized that he hadn't eaten since breakfast at the hospital—and even then he had barely picked at his food. He did feel quite hungry now, though, and he turned towards the tavern. He could get something to eat, and at the same time throw off anyone who might be trailing him. Alois had had enough encounters with Inquisitors to know that they didn't always give up easily, the believable verdict of the Deacon notwithstanding.

He pushed the door of the tavern open and slid inside. Thin beams of sunlight arcing through the thick, blurred glass windows were the only source of light. The barmaid, a young woman named Theresa, looked up at the sound of the bell at the door. Upon seeing Alois, she crossed over to him and gave him a gentle hug, softly cooing reassurances and regrets to him, things containing "I'm so sorry" and "in a better place" that he was becoming very familiar with. A few others sitting nearby, most of whom he knew or at least recognized, nodded to him morosely. He did not know what to say, but in the past few days he had found that staying silent was appropriate. Everyone seemed to assume he was too aggrieved for words.

Was he, though? Had he even thought of his wife and children much since the event? Other things had been on his mind, it seemed. Nevertheless, hating to disappoint them, he went silently to his seat before quietly requesting a plate of pork belly and fried eggs.

He sat quietly as he waited, running a finger up and down an old wine bottle sitting on the table that now held a couple of slightly wilted daisies. The magician had done her work well, that much was clear. Not only had she healed his mortal wound, she seemed to have cured him of all the ailments of middle age, leaving him feeling perfectly fit. Perhaps, he thought, a new idea occurring to him, she had even healed his mind, and that was why he was not consumed by grief over the loss of his wife and children, as he should have been.

But if she had healed him, why was the wound still there? Why did he look like hell? And why didn't the Inquisitor immediately detect the influence of magic? The three oddities had to be connected. Alois had been incredibly lucky, and had ended up going to, surprisingly, quite an adept magician. Not only was she a very advanced healer, she seemed to have mastered a technique that the Church, at present, couldn't detect. By making his wound appear open and yet curing the damage to him, she had made a complete mockery of the law. He was alive, employed, and un-jailed because of that girl in those tacky, sparkling robes. And she hadn't even taken any of his possessions as payment while he was unconscious, an act he certainly would have understood and begrudgingly accepted.

He had to thank her, but he had no idea how to find her. Perusing the station's files on unlicensed magicians wouldn't be much help, as he was sure they'd never taken the girl in, and he didn't even know her name. He knew only that her tan skin tone suggested that she—or her ancestry, at least—was not local.

If he was going to find her, there was only one place to look, really. After he ate, he'd return to Langham Alley.

His meal was placed in front of him, a heaping plate of greasy egg and bacon, and he had already sliced open an egg yolk with his knife before he realized that nothing could seem less appetizing. His hunger vanished as he stared down at the food.

"Hrmm," he muttered. Could it be that the healing magic had removed his need for food? He wasn't sure he liked that. That couldn't be, though; he had been quite hungry when he came in. He decided that it must have been shock—something akin to the battle fatigue suffered by soldiers after experiencing a trauma.

Cleaning his mouth carefully with a napkin, he prepared to get up to leave. If he were a baker or some other sort of artisan, he'd leave without paying and then owe the café owner a loaf of bread, or some other piece of craft, at a later date. As a government official, though, he had no tangible goods that he could legally offer. Typically he'd pay with paper currency awarded per his hours worked, but he currently had none. Luckily, it was typically accepted that Guardsmen ate free, as it was considered bad for business to get on the Guard's bad side. Alois headed as discreetly as possible through the kitchen of the tavern to the back door, which exited into a dank little alley. No one had followed him into the tavern, so if anyone was tailing him, they'd be waiting for him to come out of the front door. Satisfied that he'd lost any unwanted religious attention, Alois headed south, towards Langham.

As he went, he pondered the fact that he was so actively breaking religious and city law. As the Chief Constable of a city district, this was no small matter. And yet, while he knew he had acted selfishly, he couldn't see that he had done much wrong. Surely the magics of a young girl couldn't subvert the will of God? Couldn't it be true that Alois being healed was a part of God's plan all along, and Alois had merely helped to fulfill destiny? This argument had, in the past, been used by many swiftly excommunicated Church figures, and certainly by many heathens on their way to the gallows, but it had always seemed a somewhat hollow one. By making the idea of destiny so slippery, such ideas had irritated Alois. Yet, now...

He pondered this for some time as he walked before finally reaching his destination. He approached the alley, peering down it. It wasn't empty; several figures skulked in the shadows, shying away from the strip of sunlight running parallel between the walls. It wasn't just a cramped lane. Dozens of side alcoves branched off it, their contents totally hidden from view.

Alois strode in. After what he'd been through, suddenly it didn't seem so dangerous anymore. The first figure he passed, while hooded, was much too tall to be the girl, so he continued on. He heard the man break into a run towards the alley mouth a few seconds later, and Alois remembered that he was wearing his badge—and even if he hadn't been, he rather *looked* like a policeman. He didn't bother to look back, but merely continued onwards.

The person he found next lay in the gutter, clutching a liquor bottle in both hands. It was an old man, face covered in filthy stubble. Again, Alois continued on.

There was one other figure in the main alleyway, small, wearing black, half lurking in an alcove that led to a barred-up backdoor to the courthouse. As Alois approached, the figure spun into the light, though it took a step back in surprise as Alois deliberately diverted his path towards it. It recovered quickly, and the dull blade of a knife appeared out from under the dingy black cloak. The hand that held it was knotted and pale.

"Ah," Alois said, disappointed. Not her, then.

"All right, old man, let's see you empty your pockets," the man barked.

"Hrmm," Alois said, "Is that any way to speak to a police officer?" and, surprising himself perhaps as much as his assailant, he swung his heavy arm around and backhanded the figure in the face, knocking him soundly into the wall. Hissing, the thief, whose hood fell away, grabbed his nose in pain, allowing Alois to easily snatch his knife, tossing it to the cobblestones.

The assailant roared, brushing his matted red hair out of his eyes as he threw himself at Alois, swinging his bony fists in a fury. Alois took a hit square in the chest and stumbled backward, not really surprised when his chest didn't hurt at all from the blow. He reached out, grabbed the man by the collar, and pulled hard to the side. Now Alois *was* surprised. The man was flung into the courthouse rear wall as though he'd been catapulted, hitting it with a resounding thud so loud that it provoked a yammering of gibberish from the old man down the alleyway. The thief's body crumpled into the gutter. Alois stared down at it.

Apparently, healing magic did all sorts of wonderful things to a person.

He left the alley, disappointed. He hadn't found what he was looking for. He was strong, though—stronger than he used to be. It didn't really seem like it mattered. On top of that, he was behaving somewhat brashly, but he didn't think the magic had anything to do with that.

On his walk home, on which he didn't bother being evasive, he found a corner watchman and told him to go arrest the unconscious man in Langham Alley. He was still a Chief of Police, after all. The watchman didn't seem too thrilled at the assignment, but he trotted off anyway. As for Alois, he went home, wondering if he'd make it further than the front steps this time.

Chapter 3

An excerpt from An Introduction to Magical History, *by Pontius Sleighman*

Chapter 7 – Magical Schools

As has been noted in the previous chapter, most common people in Merund do not know very much about magic or those who practice it, and generally view Wizards and magicians with fear, mistrust, or both. The commoner's view of magic is a simple one, and it does not make distinctions between different types of magic users. While all but the dimmest of the peasants are generally aware that Wizards are licensed University graduates while magicians are semi-trained and often illegal operators, they are usually totally unaware that there are many different schools of magic. A respectful commoner would buy a drink for both a diviner and an alchemist without being aware of the difference between the two.

There are, in fact, six schools of magic, and it is important to have at least a partial grasp of each one in order to understand magic as a whole. It may be easiest to start at the end.

The most recently developed school of magic is Alchemy. This is perhaps the best-known school, due to the impact it has had upon recent history. As some may still be old enough to remember, for many generations, precious metals such as silver and gold were used as currency everywhere in the known world, Merund being no exception. The advent of Alchemical magic changed this. Wizards have been attempting Alchemy since perhaps the earliest days of magic, and by the time it was finally realized, many had given it up as a lost cause. When a few Wizards finally perfected the art of transforming one substance to another, they immediately began making huge amounts of gold, and it was not long before they were enormously wealthy. More and more Wizards began to train as alchemists, and it was not long before the market of every town and city had been so clogged with gold, silver, and the like that these precious and yet functionally almost worthless materials soon lost nearly all value.

Thus, it is because of Alchemical magic that the currency system of old has disappeared, and the current system of bartering and work credits is largely used in its place. The complex items most highly valued today, often containing intricate clockwork or other mechanical workings, cannot be reproduced by Alchemy, which can only turn a piece of one substance into a piece of something else. In some places, metal alloys such as steel and bronze are now used as currency—Alchemy is not able to produce such mixtures; only substances made up of identical molecules.

As a result of these developments, Alchemy has now been relegated to a lesser school of magic. Most view it as a field that very quickly peaked and then became entirely useless. Should gold ever become valuable again, no doubt many will quickly dust off the Alchemical guide books and destroy the economic system once again. Until then, however, Alchemy is a school of magic with few remaining followers and virtually no advances in technique since its advent a few decades ago.

Alois' family was buried in a large plot in Grafton Cemetery, the largest graveyard in the city. Almost everyone from the Central District Guard station came to the funeral. The grave marker itself was quite large, a granite slab carved with the name, birth date, and death date of Elizabeth. A large blank space left open next to it was presumably meant for Alois. He had allowed his workmates to pick out the marker for him, as they assumed he would not want to deal with such reminders of his grief. He wondered if they thought that a better husband would already have his name and date of death chiseled on the blank half of the marker. "Devoted wife and mother," the stone read under Elizabeth's name. What would they carve under his?

To the right and left of the large marker where two smaller ones, each bearing a carved motif of holly leaves garlanded around its top. They marked the names, ages, and birth dates of Alois' daughters.

Alois had married Elizabeth at the age of a twenty, a young man in the Guard. It was nearly a decade later when Cassandra was born, and he was away at the front at the time, serving as a Lieutenant in the Third Border War. He had only finally met his first daughter when she was five months old, and had often wondered at the time if he'd missed something that he could not get back.

Juliet, four years later, had been a surprise. He and Elizabeth had great difficulty conceiving Cassandra, and a second child was not expected. Money was tight, for a time, but five years after Juliet's birth, Alois was appointed Chief Constable of the Central District, and they'd been able to move to their home in the Northern District. The appointment was surprising to everyone— Alois had never been a terribly ambitious man. Elizabeth had said at the time that it was this which made the Magistrate comfortable giving him the position.

After that they'd fallen into a routine, and it seemed that little had changed for eight years. He spent more and more time at work, and his relationship with Elizabeth had begun to cool.

That routine had been broken, as all routines eventually are.

The ceremony was a standard one, presided over by a funeral minister sent by the Church. He gave the standard eulogy, which aimed to remind the crowd that God always had a plan, and that it was good for the world to fit with that plan, even when it seemed a heart-breaking and savage one. God, they were reminded, worked in mysterious ways, and all would be put right at the end.

Alois, for his part, did not pay attention, instead staring at the grave markers and wondering if he felt sad enough. He had a sinking feeling that he did not. He missed them, surely. He had loved them. But he didn't feel useless or helpless without them. He didn't feel like he couldn't go on. He had gone to quite some trouble to make sure that he did go on, actually.

It was surely the girl's fault, for healing him too well. She had even healed him of the grief that should have been overwhelming him. He wasn't sure now that he felt so grateful towards her; after all, it had been several days since the tavern, and he still couldn't eat.

Yet, there, at the funeral, he felt incredibly hungry—hungrier than he ever had in his life. His stomach growled and churned, but somehow the thought of a plate of food still wasn't appetizing. Alois simply did not know what to do about it, but there was little he could do just then anyway. So he stared at the grave markers, and now he wondered what the girl in the sparkling robes had done to him.

On his first night out of the hospital, he'd eventually managed to venture back into his house. His men had seen to it that all the blood was cleaned away—only the absence of the lantern that had shattered, the relocation of some of their valuables, and the missing linens on his bed gave any indication of what had happened.

Nevertheless, the wooden floor in the hallway felt sticky with blood under his boots.

He now slept in the parlor on the first floor, where he was sure there wasn't any blood. In the mornings he cut slices from the loaf of bread he'd brought home on the night of the event, which was stale by now, and tried to make himself eat. He didn't manage it. Anything he managed to chew and swallow soon came back up—and yet his stomach still growled ferociously.

The day after the funeral, he returned to work. Things were almost back to normal, soon enough, but it still seemed off. People were gentler with him, and even Moltke was attempting to tone things down a notch. The men often invited Alois out to lunch with them, but he always refused, opting to take a walk instead. He thought it would concern them if they noticed his lack of appetite. Or, anyway, his lack of eating.

Two weeks after the murder, the investigation was closed. Alois was sitting behind his desk when Oliver, a detective at least a decade older than him, came and sat down across from him.

"Well, Chief Constable, it looks like everything's just about wrapped up."

"Oh? Yes?"

"Yes, sir. We've checked into multiple angles, and it looks like the men who did the deed were freelance burglars. They were just there to steal, though they were more than willing to kill when the opportunity arose. They had hit another house on the north side just a few weeks prior, but Ambassador Samuels and his family were on holiday when they struck, thank God. Maybe they thought your family was gone too, for whatever reason. It's a nice house, Chief, you know? Who knows what they thought they'd find inside."

"Ah, I see," Alois said calmly. Just thieves. Alois knew for a fact that there wasn't anything in his house worth killing three innocent women over, much less losing one's own life in the process. What a disgusting waste. What a terrible plan.

But it wasn't their plan, was it? That wasn't what the Church taught.

"I'm sorry that there's not much more I can tell you, Chief. I don't think there's a larger organization involved, and if there is we have no leads thus far, so it's unlikely we'll be able to find it. But you did the world a favor when you killed those two bastards, I can tell you that. I hope that's at least a bit of comfort."

Honestly, he hadn't really thought about it. "Yes, thank you, Oliver. You've done a bang-up job on this. I very much appreciate it."

"Sure, Chief."

"Just... just random, really. Just a random act of aggression, motivated by greed and chance. Not even planned, the murders."

Oliver's face fell. "Chief, you know how it is... sometimes terrible things happen to good people, and no matter how hard you look, there's no deeper reason for it."

"Doesn't our religion teach that there's a deeper reason for *everything*?"

Oliver paused. When he spoke again, his voice was guarded. "I'm not a Deacon, Chief, but I'm sure that if you spoke to one he'd be able to help you with what you're feeling."

What he was feeling. Shouldn't it be loss, incredible loss? Or at least incredible anger? He felt chagrined, and little more.

"No, no. I'm sorry, Detective; I shouldn't take my... feelings out on you. Thank you for looking into this so thoroughly."

"Any time, Chief. Oh, and me and Twilling are heading out soon to grab some sandwiches. How about you come with?"

"Thank you, Oliver, but I think I'll pass this time."

"All right. But we'll rope you in eventually, Chief."

"I don't doubt it."

Alois shuffled papers around until Oliver had left, then got up and headed into the corridor, walking around to the back door to take his walk. He'd learned not to go out through the front door. Too many lunch invitations.

Soon he was outdoors, glad to have the anonymity of the streets. Despite his relatively important position, Merund had a high enough population that the vast majority of citizens didn't know or care who Alois was, and he was glad for their ignorance. Everyone who knew what had happened to him seemed to be expecting something of him now, and he didn't know how to provide it.

He went where his feet took him, crossing the River Thule and heading through the business district, trying to ignore the sensation of his stomach writhing and gnawing on itself, begging him to consume something. The healing magic, he suspected, was starting to wear off, as aches and pains had returned to his body. Everything ached at least a bit as he trod along, even more so than it had before he'd been stabbed. He wished that he had a better idea of how it all worked, but knew he was lucky so long as his still-dreadful wound didn't start to spout blood again. Lord knew it had done enough of that on the night it was created.

Lost in thought, he wandered for some time. Eventually, he noticed that the thrum of pedestrians around him had subsided. He looked up.

"Dammit."

He'd done it again. Unintentionally, without even thinking about it, he was here. Grafton Cemetery. This was the third time in as many days that he'd ended up at Grafton without knowing he was doing it. It would appear he missed his family after all. Sighing resolutely, he headed towards the gate and undid the latch, walking slowly into the grassy, pleasant place. He strode over the slab-studded gentle hills to the site of the large granite slate that marked the grave of his family, and knelt down in front of it.

As a child, his mother had taught him to pray at the graves of departed family.

"God..." he began, but trailed off. He'd never been much for praying, but now it was harder than ever. "Lord Delar," he tried again, "Thank you, in your infinite wisdom, for... seeing fit in your plan... to kill my family." He groaned and stood back up. That sort of prayer wasn't going to do anyone any good, he suspected.

It had been a long walk, and his lunch break would soon be over. He turned and walked away from the grave, toward the gate, trying in vain to ignore his stomach, which had chosen that moment to act up more fiercely than ever. He had made it halfway back to the gate when he heard it.

"No, Alexander! Not there, you're getting dirt on my robes! Alexander! Over there! Yes, that's better. Good!"

That voice. He knew that voice. It was *the* voice. He turned and strode resolutely towards it. It was coming from beyond a small, hilltop grove of elms, of which the cemetery contained many.

As he reached the trees and looked through them, he saw her. She'd apparently taken off her robes in the midday sun and was dressed in a faded yellow sundress and brown leather boots that came halfway up her calves. Her dark, reddish-brown hair was tied in a ponytail, and she was gesturing to a large man wearing a shirt and pants made of thick, tattered black material. The man had a great, messy mop of brown hair, and was dutifully using a shovel to unearth mound after mound of soil, which he was piling next to the girl. Nearby her robes lay discarded, some dirt spread over them. The man's face, bent low, was difficult to see.

In front of the rapidly deepening hole was a tombstone that looked to be at least a few years old.

Alois stared through the tree trunks at the two figures, illuminated clearly in the midday sun. He thought about calling out, but wasn't quite sure what he would say. "Say, you there, stop that grave robbing at once!" would have been the traditional choice, but having colluded with the girl to commit a crime only a few weeks before, the hypocrisy of hauling her into the station was not lost on Alois.

Nor, of course, was the fact that if she was put in front of his coworkers, she might start singing like a mocking bird about what he'd done.

Sighing resolutely, he stepped through the trees, the leaves brushing his hat and shoulders, and started down the hill, treading slowly in the soft grass to keep from losing his balance. The girl had her back turned toward him, but the man with the shovel, still dutifully digging, could no doubt already see Alois. Alois expected that the man would call out, but he didn't. Nor did he so much as look up, or break pace for even a moment.

The Constable snorted as he reached the bottom of the hill. The man was so confident that Alois was no threat that he wasn't even making any attempt to hide his actions. Was it too much to expect that criminals would at least *pretend* to respect the law?

Reaching the girl's crumpled robes, the sound of his approach masked by the scraping of shovel blade against the hard earth, Alois brought up a hand and poked the girl right between her exposed shoulder blades.

She shrieked, spun around, and fell over, her body taking an unfortunate turn and ending up directly in the pile of dirt that had been accumulating. Bemusement all over her face, she looked up at Alois.

"Oh, it's only you. You scared the living daylights out ofMHHMMFFF!"

Alois' eyebrows raised high as a shovelful of dirt was thrown directly into the girl's face. A cloud of silt drifted away in the sun while she bent over and coughed profusely. The tall man, meanwhile, was digging into the hole for another shovel-load.

"Uhm, I say fellow, maybe you'd ought to cut that out." Alois tried, but the man made no sign of hearing him, swinging around his freshly heaped shovel.

"Alexander, stop!" The girl yelled, breaking down into a coughing fit as soon as the words were out. Alois was about to lunge forward to pull her out of the way, but the man with the shovel had, indeed, stopped. In fact, he was now standing perfectly still, the shovel held in both hands. He looked like a painting, feet cocked as though he'd been frozen in time.

Alois stared at the man's arms. They weren't shaking at all. Even a strong man would have quickly tired from holding up a loaded shovel, but this one…

"Oh, fine, that's all right," the girl sputtered, trying to wipe dirt off her face but succeeding only in rubbing it around, "don't help me. I'm perfectly fine by myself."

"Erm, my apologies," Alois blustered. He felt on his belt for his canteen, which of course wasn't there. He always found it strange how his memories of the war never really left him.

"I'm afraid I don't have any water," he said.

"There's a water skin in my robes, you can go fill it up at the spring over the next hill," she coughed, spitting profusely into the grass immediately afterwards.

"Erm, right." Alois went to the girl's robes and scooped them up, feeling them for weight. He was surprised by how loaded down with items they seemed to be; the girl must have lived out of them. Their glittery surface glinting in the sun gave the robes the effect of an oily beast slithering through his hands. They were really quite nice, he realized, and would have been absolutely perfect for the kind of magician who did card tricks for tips at a medium-quality tavern.

He decided not to mention that, reached into a pocket at random, and felt around. His hand closed over the worn leather of what seemed to be a book cover, and then moved on to the rough but yielding suede of a water skin, which he pulled out of the robes and carried off over the hill.

The spring was where she said it would be, glittering with perfectly clear water that looked profoundly refreshing, though Alois doubted how many people actually drank from it. People were funny about cemeteries, really. Which wasn't to say that he *wasn't* funny about them.

"Here you are," he said, handing the skin over once he'd returned to the hole in the ground. She grabbed it from him, held it over her face, and squeezed a gout of water into her waiting mouth. Immediately after this she was doubled over again, sputtering and coughing. "It looks like there's a bit less dirt in your spit now," Alois said, trying to be helpful.

"Yes, I'm making great progress," she muttered, taking another swig, gargling it thoroughly, and spitting. She didn't spit out her next gulp but swallowed it gratefully before taking several deep breaths.

"All right. That's better," she said, shutting her eyes. Her face was practically black with dirt, her brown skin only showing around her ears. "I suppose a little dirt never killed anyone."

"No," Alois agreed, "but a lot of dirt tends to."

She laughed. "You'd be horrified by just how often that actually happens."

"Huh. Erm, here, let me have that for a moment," Alois suggested, taking the water skin out of her hands. He removed his handkerchief from his back pocket and dribbled some water onto it before reaching out and using it to wipe her face off. She flinched away at the touch, but then sighed and sat still, allowing him to finish.

Her face, while still very smudged, was looking much cleaner as he put his now-blackened handkerchief away.

"All right," she said. "So."

"So," he said, nodding. He glanced at the man with the shovel, who had been standing in exactly the same position for several minutes. "Is he going to move?"

"No," she said, matter-of-factly. Standing up and making an effort at dusting off her dress before giving it up as a lost cause, she looked Alois up and down, then slowly walked in a circle around him, her eyes narrowed into slits. Alois had the distinct feeling of being in the company of a blacksmith who was taking a long, hard look at a set of horseshoes.

"A little pale," she said finally, "and thinner than I remember you. Have you been eating?"

He smiled. She seemed to know exactly what he wanted. Perhaps healing magic was an imprecise art, and a follow-up appointment was standard procedure.

"Well, no! I'm hungry… well, not quite. I'm starving, actually… literally, I think. But I just can't bring myself to eat anything. It's actually rather indescribably awful."

She frowned. "You can't eat? Hmm. I'm not sure what to do about that… where've you been getting your meat?"

"Hmm? Oh, from the usual places, you know. The butcher shop, the tavern, sometimes from the little grocery on the corner of Lun—"

He trailed off when he noticed that she was now staring at him incredulously.

"The butcher shop," she said. "Are you making fun of me?"

He frowned. "I'm afraid I've now lost track of this conversation."

She shut her eyes and clasped her forehead with one of her small, filthy hands.

"I can't believe this. All right, just wait a couple of minutes. Alexander II!"

The big man with the shovel suddenly lurched back to life, though he kept the shovel held nearly exactly as it had been. He turned his head toward her, his greasy hair swaying slightly.

"Alexander, let's take a break on Mr. Wiede. Go over to…" She scanned the nearby graves before bringing up a hand and pointing to one a few plots away. "That one, the one that says 'Könnig.' Let's get that one dug up, please."

The man with the shovel dropped his load of dirt onto the ground in front of him, slowly turned, and shambled toward the grave she'd indicated.

"Erm, listen, I can't really have you digging up graves like this…"

"What are you complaining about? Alexander II is doing you a favor."

"What in blazes do you mean, he's doing me a favor? And it's junior, by the way!"

"I'm sorry?"

"In Merund," Alois continued, somewhat flustered, "when a man is named after his father, he is typically referred to as 'junior'. You don't start with the numbering until you get to three."

"Oh, well, I wouldn't imagine that Alexander's father had the same name as him."

"Then why—"

"And what is your name, anyway?"

"What? Oh, I'm sorry; I've never properly introduced myself."

"Well, that's all right. If I ever get stabbed, I'll probably have other things on my mind, too."

"Yes. Well, I am Alois Gustav. It is a pleasure to meet you." He held out his hand before remembering how caked in dirt hers was, but could hardly do anything to stop it as she grabbed his much larger hand and pumped enthusiastically.

"It's nice to meet you, Mr. Gustav."

"You may call me Alois, I think."

"Alois, then. And my name is Lina."

"It is a pleasure, Lina, and thank you. You saved my life."

"Well, in a manner of speaking," she said.

Before he had time to figure out what that meant, she had turned away and begun walking toward Alexander, who had by now produced a very substantial pile of dirt next to the Königg grave. Alois noted that the date on the tombstone was only a few weeks prior.

"That's good enough, Alexander, thank you," Lina said, and the man promptly stopped digging, now standing stock-still over the hole. Lina, glancing down into the pit, bent over to reach her boot and pulled out a small knife in a suede scabbard, which she promptly unsheathed. Its serrated edge shined brightly before she jumped into the hole, disappearing from sight.

Alois frowned. He was grateful for what she'd done for him, certainly, but there was only so much he could allow. Tomb defacement was perhaps a victimless crime, but that didn't mean that Alois advocated it. He strode tentatively toward the Könnig grave, from which emerged a sound very similar to that of a coffin being pried open.

As he came over a slight rise and was finally able to look into the hole, what he saw confirmed his fears; the coffin was wide open. Before he could notice anything else, Lina, crawling up the side of the hole, filled his view, a small bundle held tightly under her right arm.

"Now, listen," he tried, but she ignored him, coming to a crouch in front of him and unwrapping the bundle. He stared down. The bundle itself looked to be made of part of a man's shirt, and inside was the small serrated knife. Next to it sat something oddly leathery, an ugly pale chunk of meat with rough edges and—

Alois gasped as he realized what it was.

"Delar in Heaven," he moaned, "You sliced a piece off of—"

He was cut off as she came to her feet and thrust the bundle directly into his face. He recoiled in horror, bringing his arm up to try and strike the horrible thing away. Except...

Except that it smelled more delicious than anything else in the world.

Alois could no more stop what happened next than a starving man who had crawled through the desert could stop himself after coming upon a banquet meal. He snatched the hunk of flesh away from her, and, turning away and crouching down, he devoured it, unable to focus on anything but the sensation of his stomach being filled, aware that it was disgusting and yet finding both the texture and flavor completely wonderful.

It was only after he was finished that he was able to fathom what he'd just done. Staring down at the crumpled piece of shirt in his hands, he began shivering. The truth hit him hard. He began coughing, willing himself to regurgitate, but in truth his stomach felt quite settled.

Finally, he put his face in his hands and moaned.

"What did you do to me?"

"You know what I did to you."

"You... you didn't heal me. You turned me into... into... a zombie."

"Don't be ridiculous," Lina said, a bit of sympathy in her voice. "I turned Alexander into a zombie. I turned *you* into a ghoul."

Chapter 4

Continued: an excerpt from An Introduction to Magical History, *by Pontius Sleighman*

Chapter 7 – Magical Schools

Alchemy, then, is well known by many if only because of its fairly recent heyday. Perhaps the second most recently-developed branch of magic (though by now it is centuries old) is one near and dear to the heart of all citizens of the land of Merund. It is the art of Divination.

Until now, I have described magic as the process that allows men to change reality. The problem with using a simple description such as this, unfortunately, is that magic is not simple. Divination is unique from the other schools is that it is not used to change anything. Rather, divining, which is a process that is time-consuming and difficult to master, lets one resonate with the frequencies of reality for entirely different reasons.

Divination magic is the blanket term covering any and all magic that grants knowledge of the present or, even more impressively, predicts the events of the future. Such magic covers many practices: the gazing of seers into balls of glass and crystal, pools of water, and mirrors; the ecstatic dances and tongue-speaking of oracles who channel the very thoughts of God to be interpreted by we humble mortals; and, as perhaps is most common in Merund, the disciplined meditation of diviners in order to ascertain special knowledge of the future. While this knowledge often comes in the form of visions that are difficult to interpret, these visions are always at the very least recognized as prophetic when the events they foretell come to pass, proving the great power of Divination.

Divination is, perhaps, the most important branch of magic in Merund. In many foreign lands, where savage magic-users worship harems of heathen gods, Divination is not practiced, nor even regarded as a serviceable form of magic. Even some supposedly great Wizards from the more civilized foreign lands have argued that attempting to divine the future is a misguided practice that yields no results. That these men continue their objections in the face of such obvious evidence (and the superiority of Merund's culture itself) speaks to their stubbornness and ignorance.

In Merund, however, Delar, God of Gods, who wrote the book of time at the beginning of all things and who above all wishes to see his story fulfilled, is worshipped by one and all. In our land we respect the importance of fate, and we are pious and reverent in our attempts to see to it that the fate intended by God is the one that is carried out. Many of our laws are built around such attempts (as will be discussed later), and the city of Merund contains far more diviners than any other city on the face of the world due to our diligence.

The Magical University located in Merund's heart hosts a multitude of diviners in one of its highest towers. Here, expertly trained practitioners of the subtle art of foretelling learn of things to come, and give their inspired knowledge to Church leaders so that they might act in the best interest of Delar's divine plan.

Albert Krupp was a slender man of average height, and a young one at that, having passed his civil service exam with flying colors only two years previously. His hair was black and his skin pale, and his dress was formal, befitting a man of his position. He was seen each day all through

Merund's Capitol building, carrying messages back and forth. People smiled when they saw him, because Krupp spoke for the Magistrate of Merund, and people liked the Magistrate.

Krupp liked the Magistrate, too. Enough that he'd taken the position of aide despite the climb up a long, spiraling staircase that was required of him dozens of times a day. He'd always expected that working directly under the head of the city would impress his friends and relatives, but it hadn't ever worked out that way. His father had wanted him to become a Priest, and his mother had always been disappointed that he did not enroll at the Magical University. Taking the Civil Service Exam, which Krupp thought would be a good compromise, ended up satisfying no one.

Except, as it turned out, himself. Because, as Krupp quickly discovered, the Magistrate was not the friendly but powerless figurehead that everyone thought he was. He was much, much more, and Krupp might have been the only person in the city who knew it.

He was on the staircase for the seventh time that day, only slightly out of breath as he reached the top. Past Magistrates had worked out of normal, ground floor offices, or even out of their homes, but Schiller had insisted upon being moved up to the high tower of the Capitol. No one was quite sure why he'd made the change. Krupp suspected he liked the view.

Schiller was at the window when Krupp opened the door and stepped into the highest room in the city of Merund, five hundred feet skywards. Even from this vantage, the city was large enough that the expansive window pane merely gave a nice view of the Capitol Plaza and a lot of rooftops. Schiller seemed to be regarding his public fondly whenever he looked out the window, and it was an appropriate sentiment, as the people of Merund admired him in return. They rooted for him as the underdog, apparently dwarfed by the juggernaut figures that were the Dean and the Archbishop. Many of them weren't even aware that the man's name was Schiller; everyone referred to him simply and affectionately as the Magistrate.

It was not the only thing that the people were poorly informed about. It was no longer the case, as it had been for decades, that the Magistrate was second to the Dean and the Archbishop. The pendulum of power had swung back again, as it always did, and the Magistrate was, of late, the most powerful man within hundreds of miles.

And Krupp was the man who ran his errands.

"What's the good word, Albert?"

"It's a slow day, Magistrate. Just the typical business."

"Good. Any word from the Dean?"

"He's still furious about your proposal of lightening the restrictions on street magicians. He's sent several messages. Some of them are extremely colorful."

"I'd expect nothing less. Take a letter in response, won't you?"

Krupp walked to the desk and pulled a sheaf of paper out of a drawer, sitting down in the Magistrate's chair and dipping a quill in an open ink pot. This sort of behavior would have been unthinkable when he'd first begun the job, but he had quickly learned that the Magistrate expected a certain informality of behavior. Schiller, meanwhile, still stood at the window. He hadn't looked at Krupp yet today, though that wasn't entirely unusual.

Krupp put the quill to parchment and began by neatly writing the date, breaking the silence with the quiet scratch of nib on paper.

"Always with that quill. Why don't you use one of my pens? There's a mechanical one in the right drawer, and an enchanted one in the left."

"I've always been more comfortable with a quill, sir."

"That's what you were brought up with?"

"That's what everyone's brought up with, sir. Quality mechanical pens are worth too much to actually write with, and enchanted pens can't be found anywhere."

"No big loss. Even the one the Dean gave me gets ink everywhere. Incompetent bunch of bastards."

"I'll take it that this isn't dictation, sir?"

"Excellent deduction, Krupp. Let's start now, though, shall we? Most exalted Dean."

Krupp went to work with the quill.

"Thank you for informing me of your objection to my most recent proposal. Your guidance is always appreciated, and has ever been my most useful source of information when I attempt to determine what is best for the city."

The Magistrate waited until the scratching had finished, meanwhile watching a blackbird flutter by a few stories below.

"Now that I know how strongly you feel on the issue, I of course withdraw the decision of deregulating unlicensed magicians. I have been made to see—why have you stopped writing?"

"I'm sorry, sir, I'm just surprised. You're backing down?"

"I was always going to. I just wanted him distracted for a few days while I reorganized the bureaucracy. Anyway, now he'll feel like he's the one in power, and perhaps even like I've done him a favor."

"I see. Don't you worry he'll know what you're up to?"

"I have no doubt that Dean Baldermann has the wiles to do so, but he's usually too preoccupied with magic to devote much consideration to governance. If and when he does devote the due consideration, he's usually blinded with rage, as is his penchant. If you haven't deduced by now what I'm doing, it is unlikely that the anger-drunk Dean will have done so. This is one of the things that make you so helpful. You make it clear when my plans are too obvious."

"Thrilled to serve as your example idiot, sir."

"Oh, Krupp, you know how highly I respect your opinion. But perhaps we could go back to writing?"

"Of course, sir. I have been made to see…"

"I have been made to see that you were quite right regarding the chaos that would be caused by allowing unlicensed magicians to practice in Merund. Such individuals would be a danger to themselves and others, and their sloppy, illicit acts of so-called magic would only serve to lower the Wizarding profession in the eyes of the public. I am—you've stopped writing again, Krupp?"

"Sorry, sir. I'm just wondering… how did you know that those were the complaints he'd raised? You didn't read the letters."

"I don't need to bother; every letter he sends me now is largely the same words combined differently. In fact, I'm pretty sure he's not even writing them himself anymore— it's probably just his assistant regurgitating the policy that has been in place for the last… six decades now, is it? Besides, what else was he going to say was the problem with unlicensed magic? That it created new job opportunities, or made useful magical services more widely available?"

"I see, sir."

"You see, but can you write?"

"Yes, sir. I am…"

"I am glad that you were able to clarify for me the reason that unlicensed magic is illegal in the first place. I hope you will not find me too foolish for not seeing it immediately. Please give my regards to the rest of the University Board. Very truly yours, etcetera etcetera."

Krupp hurriedly finished writing, then opened a desk drawer and took out the stamp bearing the Magistrate office's crest, which he pressed to an ink pad and depressed at the bottom of the letter. Fishing out a second stamp with the same sigil, he pressed this one into the dish of red wax sitting suspended over a candle on the edge of the desk, and, folding up the letter, he sealed it for delivery.

"There we are. Give that to the delivery boy sometime today, will you?"

"Yes, Magistrate."

"So, that takes care of the University for the day, I think. Any word from the Church?"

"Nothing terribly important, sir. Oh, though I have gotten word that they've finally closed the case against Alois Gustav. He's been cleared of any wrong-doing."

"I'm a bit surprised to hear that. Do you think that the Church is mellowing with age?"

"If they haven't mellowed after several hundred years, sir, I doubt another year or two has made much of a difference."

"Good point. Hmm... it's good that Gustav is a free man. He's a relatively competent administrator. Crime has been down in the Central District since he took over."

"Do you know him personally, sir?"

"I've met him once or twice at state functions. He's a fat fellow with a mustache. Probably a bit of a wet blanket, but I suppose the world needs them as much as anyone else."

"Do you think the Church is right? That he's innocent?"

"From the initial report, I thought it sounded pretty cut-and-dry like he got an illegal healing performed. I'm surprised that their Inquisitor disagrees. He must have seen something that dissuaded him in person."

"I've always wondered, sir. Do you agree with the Church's views on the illegality of healing magic?"

This was another act that would have been unthinkable when he'd started out. Krupp himself was not terribly religious, and rarely attended Church. The Magistrate, on the other hand, was devout in his devotion to Delar, which Krupp found surprising, considering how willing the Magistrate was to pull the fleece over the Church's eyes when the situation called for it.

"You know, I'm not sure. The sacred texts are so vague... we know there is an absolute divine plan, but how can we be sure of what does or doesn't violate that plan? I'm not certain that the opinion of the Church is always correct in those matters."

Krupp raised an eyebrow. Neither was he, but that was quite a claim for a religious man to make, much less the Magistrate of the city.

"It seems to me that, since fate is Delar's plan, it must be entirely unchangeable, and hence the practice of healing magic has its own place in that plan."

"Hmm. That doesn't mesh terribly well with... well, anything the Church teaches."

"Perhaps. I'm still undecided on the healing issue, though, and for as long as I am, I'm forced to agree with the Church."

"Not that you'd disagree publicly even if you did privately."

"Of course not. When a society is not broken, Albert Krupp, one should not endeavor to fix it."

Alois kept expecting the vomit to come, but it just wasn't happening. Nevertheless, he sat over the hole that was once the Wiede grave, crouched down on his knees, occasionally whimpering, confident that his body would eventually catch up to his brain and realize what it had just done.

"Mr. Alois? What are you doing?"

He shut his eyes, ignoring the voice. It was always possible that she would just go away.

"Mr. Wiede has been dead for too long, Mr. Alois; he's just going to be bones. There's plenty left on Mr. Könnig if you'd like more to eat. Here, I'll go ahead and cut you som—"

"No!" Alois shouted, sitting up and turning to look at her. "No, I'm fine!"

"You didn't eat terribly much, Mr. Alois. You may as well have some more while you're here." She put her hands on her hips and stared at him disapprovingly, like he was a naughty toddler who refused to eat his vegetables.

"Now you listen, young lady," Alois said, coming to his feet, "I will not be lectured by a child. And further, I will not be made to desecrate the dead! I insist you reverse the black magic that you've inflicted upon me!"

She frowned. "Don't call it that. It's not black magic. There's no such thing as black magic."

Alois growled and thrust a finger at the still body of Alexander. "If the enslavement of a human corpse is not black magic, then I do not know what is!"

"Then we're in agreement. You don't know what black magic is."

"That's not what I—"

"Mr. Alois, you asked me to help you, and I did. You're alive, aren't you?"

"Well… yes. I suppose I am alive…"

"Yes. I mean, well, sort of."

Alois glared. "And what is that supposed to mean? Am I alive, or not?"

"Well," she said, biting her lip, "technically you're undead, but that just means you're not deceased, right? And anything that's not deceased must be alive, right?"

"I am neither a physician nor a linguist, young lady. But I talk and I breathe."

"And eat."

He glared harder.

"Also," she added, "you actually don't breathe."

"What in God's name are you talking about?" he growled. "Of course I damn-well breathe!"

"No, you don't. Your heart doesn't beat, either. I mean, it's excusable that you didn't notice. Everything's working fine, so you never really thought about it. It's like when someone's leg is chopped off and they feel like it's still there."

He frowned. "Does that happen?"

"Doesn't it? Well, I mean, if it does happen, it's like that."

"Hrm. And how exactly am I still walking and talking, if my blood isn't being pumped?"

"The magic I imbued you with is keeping you going. Normally a body needs a functioning heart and lungs, but the magic sort of fills in for them."

Alois frowned and sat down heavily on a flat grave marker. As many of the guards at the station had figured out, and used to their advantage, a bit of confusion tended to do wonders at dulling Alois' anger.

"How in the world does that work?"

"I'm not really sure."

"What do you mean, you're not sure?"

"Hey, just be happy it worked!"

"How do you cast a spell without even knowing what it does? Aren't you saying what it does when you cast it?"

"The spell was in Arcanic!"

"Yes, but you still—hold on, now. Arcanic? What's that?"

"It's the language they use in old spell books. The language of dragons."

Alois guffawed. "Dragons! My dear girl, dragons do not exist!"

"No," Lina said, frowning at him as though he'd said something very foolish, "of course they don't. They're extinct."

"Extinct? Dragons have never existed!"

"What makes you say that? Have you been around forever?"

"No. But I do know that most of the wonders from fanciful stories end up not being real."

"You mean like zombies?"

"That," he said dryly, "is a rare exception."

"Look, Arcanic is the language of dragons, okay?"

"Let's just agree that it's a language. So, where were we? Ah, yes. You cast the spell, so how can you not know what it does?"

"I said the words. That doesn't mean I understood them."

Alois blinked rapidly. "Hrm. Is it common for Wizards to not understand the language of the spells they cast?"

"Sure," she said confidently. This was not technically true, although neither of them knew any better.

"All right, fine. But… listen, how can you… do things like this? It's unnatural!"

Her face crinkled into a scowl. "Why do people always say that? It's not unnatural! Maybe I think being a stupid Chief Constable or whatever it is you are is unnatural, what then?"

He frowned confusedly. "Well, I guess I'd ask that we clear up our definition of 'unnatural'."

"That's right! And I say that nothing is unnatural, not so long as we can do it. We're natural, aren't we? And so how can we do anything that's not?"

Alois groaned, rubbing his head. "All I know is that this... this is not what I meant when I asked you to help me."

"Well, this is pretty much what I do, so..."

"Is this really all you can do? That doesn't strike as particularly useful."

"Hey, it was useful enough to keep you alive and get you to the police station!"

"You mean 'sort of alive'."

"Well... yeah."

"Hrm. And how exactly did you get me to the Station, anyhow?"

"Oh, I had Sebastian VIII take you."

"Sebastian VIII."

"Yes, that's right."

Alois sighed resignedly. "And who might he be?"

"He *was* a skeleton. Speaking of which, Alexander, back to work on the Wiede grave, please."

Alois watched nervously as the large man—or, large zombie—groaned softly and went back to work with the shovel.

"Shouldn't we be worried about getting caught at this?" Alois asked, wondering immediately after he said it exactly when this had become an affair of "we".

"No, no one checks here during the day, and any mourners will think that we work here. I mean, granted, we might not be able to come back after today, considering the state we've left these graves in."

"Hmm. Can't you just refill them?"

"Yes," she said sarcastically, "but replanting the grass would tend to take a bit more time than I'd care to commit Alexander to."

Lina looked up at the sound of clanging from the Wiede grave. Alexander's shovel was hitting the casket.

"That will do, Alexander," she said happily, walking over. As she passed, she gave the frozen zombie a pat as high up as she could reach on his back. Then she hopped down into the hole, disappearing from view.

Tentatively, Alois stood from the tombstone and walked over to the hole. As he approached, he could hear a low chanting coming from within: mumbled words that he could not understand. Looking down into the pit, he saw the opened pine box, which had several holes rotted through it, and the macabre brown skeleton contained within, dressed in the tattered remains of a garment that could no longer be identified. Lina's voice rose in volume and pitch, and she extended a small hand and pressed it to the skeleton's wide sternum.

Immediately, the bones seemed to be shot through with a brilliantly fluorescent violet light, the sort of incredible and sudden flash that Alois had only before experienced at fireworks displays. The light was gone within a fraction of a second, leaving behind bleached streaks on the dirt walls as the only sign that it had ever existed.

Of course, there was one other, somewhat more obvious sign. The skeleton's neck creaked unpleasantly as its head turned from side to side. It then planted its hands firmly on the wood under it and pushed itself up into a sitting position. It glanced at Lina, who smiled encouragingly. The skeleton's long legs bent back and launched it straight up into a standing position and further still a few inches into the air, where it grabbed onto the grassy edge of the grave.

With another swift action of bone, it heaved itself out of the hole, leaping up high and landing on its feet in the grass a few yards away from Alois. He stared at it in shock and it stared back, grinning broadly. Granted, it didn't exactly have much choice.

"Sorry about him," Lina said, crawling out of the hole. "My skeletons have always been a bit eccentric."

Alois glanced at the stock-still zombie, then back at the skeleton, which was now rocking slightly back and forth on the balls of its feet, creaking like a rocking chair and seeming to enjoy it.

"You mean they're not supposed to be like this?"

"I'm not really sure. I'm starting to have trouble imagining them any other way, though."

"You don't seem to know terribly much about Necromancy, for a necromancer."

"Hello!" Lina said to the skeleton, ignoring Alois completely. "You are Sebastian IX!"

The Skeleton cocked his head and stared at her, but made no other sign of understanding.

"Doesn't he speak?"

"No, dummy, he hasn't got a tongue!"

Alois considered pointing out the fact that Sebastian seemed to have no trouble standing without muscles, but he decided not to bother.

"And how exactly is the magic keeping *him* alive? He hasn't got much to be kept," he asked instead.

"It works differently. For the same reason that you and Alexander work differently."

"Ah, so that's why I have free will and Alexander doesn't?"

"Yes, that's right. And there's also the difference in diets."

"Oh? What does Alexander eat?"

He knew immediately from her face that he'd said the wrong thing, though he could not fathom exactly why she seemed to become so upset. She turned away from him.

"Something else," she said quietly.

"I'm sorry. I did not mean to upset you."

"No," she said, "no, it's not your fault... I've just been so stupid... I can't believe that I..."

"Erm," Alois said, approaching her and patting her on the shoulder, "There, there, my girl. I'm sure it isn't your fault. Whatever it is."

He had expected her to brush him off, but instead she let out a deep breath, crossed her arms over her chest, and finally looked up at him. "Do you really think so?"

"Yes, of course I do." Alois was not a master of a great many things, but comforting young girls who were upset over things that he did not understand was something that his experiences as a father had left him well prepared for.

"So," Alois said, trying to change the subject, "Why Sebastian IX? What happened to Sebastian VIII?"

She sighed, arms sliding back down to her sides. "Sebastian VIII didn't make it home from the police station the night you died."

"Ah, yes," Alois said, a piece of the puzzle snapping into place, "so he was the one who took me there. Where in the world were you hiding him? I didn't see anyone there with you that night."

"Oh, I made him after I made you. There were bones under the water in one of the rain gutters. Isn't that creepy?"

"No. That's just Langham."

Chapter 5

Continued: an excerpt from An Introduction to Magical History, *by Pontius Sleighman*

Chapter 7 – Magical Schools

It seems only pertinent that following a discussion of Divination magic and its importance in the City-State of Merund, a related subject should be discussed. Curation magic, which is used by its practitioners to close wounds, cure diseases, and generally return others to health, is perhaps as reviled in Merund as Divination magic is loved. The High Church of Merund has outlawed curative magic entirely, and therefore not even fully educated and licensed Wizards may practice the "art" of healing through magic. Officially, curative magic is listed as the second most profane and perverse form of the mystical arts.

An entire branch of the High Church, the Inquisitorial Council, has been formed with nearly the sole task of rooting out any and all in the city who practice healing magic or consent to have it practiced upon them. Indeed, curative magic is among the most profitable of the underground magical industries, as people who require healing magic are often willing to part with anything—even, I regret to say, their sense of morality—in order to obtain it for themselves or loved ones.

While Curation is forbidden by the Church, the opinions of others are of course more varied. Few are those who have not had a family member who was wounded or otherwise fell ill, and such occurrences are always a cause for rumblings that healing magic should be allowed in Merund. It is well known that in other lands, curative magic is practiced quite successfully, and has far outpaced the mundane medical arts. Indeed, in some foreign places, it is healing magic, not Divination, that is known as the magic nearest and dearest to the clergy and to divinity itself.

Unpopular though the Church's edict on the matter of Curation may sometimes be, there are very good reasons for it. Interpretations of the ancient texts by sages strongly support the belief that to avert death through healing magic is to interfere in God's plan. If a person is too badly wounded to be cured by normal human intervention, it is felt that they should be allowed to pass on to the next world in accordance with Delar's wishes.

Other Church fathers have noted that the practice of healing magic could instill in the citizenry a disregard for their own health that would be ill-advised, and that soon people would expect that they should be immortal. While even the most powerful healing magic has never been able to stop the degradation brought around by old age (and certainly it has never done anything near to raising the dead), it is certainly easy to see how it may encourage people to pay less heed to caution in terms of their health.

Healing magic is of late a controversial subject in Merund. Nevertheless, the Church is guided only by a drive to please Delar, and has never before bent to the will of the public. I hope that the citizenry of Merund will come to understand that death, aging, and diseases, while unpleasant, have their place in God's order.

It was not a very good job, Radcliff had to admit. While many children, for instance, hoped one day to be the Dean of Merund's Magical University, or perhaps the Chairman of its Divination Department, probably exactly zero had ever desired to be the University Adjunct to Municipal Law Enforcement. This was due not a little to the fact that the vast majority of people in Merund, and probably a good chunk of faculty at the University, were not aware of the existence of this position.

The current University Adjunct to Municipal Law Enforcement, who was usually called the Adjunct in the rare instances that anyone needed to refer to him, was named Radcliff Falkenhayn, and he did the majority of his work alone in a cramped office located at the very rear of the University's Department of Magical Theory. The office, which did not have a window and was poorly lit by two puny oil lamps, barely had enough room for Radcliff's spartan desk and chair. The space issue was not made any better by the number of wooden file cabinets in the room; they totally covered one wall, stacked three high, many drawers sticking open with sheaves of parchment stuck half in and half out. More piles of papers covered Radcliff's desk and littered the floor immediately in front of the file cabinets.

Radcliff was petitioning for some new file cabinets, and a bigger office. Failing that, he was petitioning for the ability to get rid of all the archives he was hanging on to, which would free up plenty of room. He found difficulty even in this, however, as the University Treasurer seemed quite surprised every time that Radcliff informed him of the Adjunct Department's existence. Hence, Radcliff was stuck with the files for the time being, just as he was stuck with his job. As it was, the year was progressing fairly well for him. He was only a few weeks behind in his analysis of the crime reports.

Radcliff's job was at once extremely simple and devastatingly complicated. Police departments all over the city of Merund, and indeed all over the entire state of the same name, prepared reports on all the crimes and unusual events that occurred in their localities. Any such crimes or unusual events that even hinted at involving magic were bundled up and sent off to the University, where they were carried by the letter boy to Radcliff's department.

On the one hand, Radcliff, who had graduated from the University six years prior with grades that were neither particularly impressive nor exactly terrible, had a pretty easy time of determining when a case did not involve magic. For example, when the municipality of Bernham in the east, population 114, reported that the same black cat was seen in two different parts of town at the same time, Radcliff confidently chalked it up to what he usually referred to officially as "non-magical circumstances" and unofficially as "unmitigated stupidity."

Unfortunately, in the few cases when the reports on Radcliff's desk did seem to indicate that magic had been performed, his job became quite difficult and frustrating. To begin with, it was almost impossible to figure out what spell, or even what school of magic, might have been used based on the extremely vague and often second-hand reports of Guardsmen who were completely uneducated in the magical arts. As a result, Radcliff's verdicts often contained the word "unknown" quite a bit, which made offenders difficult to prosecute.

That, of course, was another problem. Illegal magic was a pervasive scourge in Merund, and Radcliff got the feeling that even when he was able to positively confirm magic use and send a report to the Guard's Station in question, his recommendations were totally ignored. At the end of the day, he found that it was difficult to figure out what the point of it all was.

Nevertheless, there was always more work to do, and keeping his mind busy was a good way to avoid considering his consummate lack of legacy or importance. In Merund's Western District, he was currently reading, a card cheat was seen to throw a dust-like substance to the ground upon being caught, escaping in the resulting plume of sparks and smoke. Radcliff scrawled *"likely purchase of illegal magical 'trick' goods from apothecary"* in his untidy hand at the bottom of the report and moved it into the "finished" pile on the edge of his desk, which, he noted with pleasure, was gradually growing.

Flipping to the next report, from Merund's Central District, Radcliff began reading. After a few sentences, he blinked, stopped, and started over.

Cab driver reports a collision with a pedestrian at approximately 4:40 AM on the fourteenth day of the third month. According to cab driver, the pedestrian was headed away from Maxim Street and in the general direction of the old municipal seat. Additionally, pedestrian was reportedly a human skeleton. Skeleton is said to have flown to bits upon being hit by cab after running into street. Bones were indeed found on street upon investigation.

Radcliff stared, rubbing his fingers through his pronounced stubble. This was a bit more extreme than the cases he was used to analyzing. At any rate, it seemed very unlikely that anything but magic could have been responsible for such an occurrence. Such an odd report called for an unusually thorough response, Radcliff knew. The fact was, it was probably just a rogue enchanter having a bit of fun, as often turned out to be the case. However, he had a nagging suggestion that it might be something else.

He stood, grabbed the report, tiptoed around the file cabinets, and exited the room, entering the far better ventilated and more brightly lit atrium that housed the Department of Magical Theory. Hedged on all sides with offices much bigger than the virtual storage closet that Radcliff worked in, the atrium itself was filled with many writing desks paired with book cases, each set portioned off from the rest by a pane of thin wooden walls that rose halfway to the ceiling.

Radcliff hurried down the row between the partitions and turned left into one that contained a Wizard who was leaning back in his chair, smoking a pipe with one hand and holding a large grimoire open in front of him with the other. He was as young as Radcliff, but certainly more handsome, and, as Radcliff was bitterly aware, better paid as well.

"Merkel," Radcliff said.

"Yes, I see you there, Falkenhayn. What's going on?"

"I've got something pretty big. I wanted to ask your opinion."

Merkel lowered the book and used his pipe hand to pull his glasses down his nose so he could look over them at Radcliff.

"Something big, eh? Not the enchanted gardening trowel again, I hope."

Radcliff snorted. "That's nothing compared to this!"

"I'm sure that's true, but to be fair, that report was nothing compared to pretty much anything. So? Shoot."

"Animated complete human skeleton spotted in Central Merund. Blown to smithereens after a collision with a carriage."

Merkel blinked. "Huh. That is a bit more spectacular than I expected."

"See? I never disappoint."

"Well, yes you do, but this time not so much. Let's see. Animating bones is easier than animating, say, a statue, of course, since the bones can move independently. Granted, you'd have to use a number of separate spells to keep the bones together, and you'd have to be pretty accomplished to even get it to walk in the right direction. Of course, considering that it ran into a carriage, maybe the magician didn't really manage that part."

"Right. So you're thinking a mid to high level enchanter?"

"Yes, I suppose. Could have been one of the higher-level University students out for kicks. There are always a few who can't get enough object animation."

"Yeah, I'd considered that…"

"Well, I think that's your most likely culprit. So, there you go."

"Yes."

Merkel turned back to his book, taking a brief puff of his pipe. Radcliff loitered in the entryway, biting his lip, trying to figure out what he wanted to say.

Eventually, Merkel sighed and looked up. "Out with it, Falkenhayn."

"Well, Merkel … after all, there is another way to bring a skeleton to life…"

Merkel snorted. "Come on, Falkenhayn; don't let your imagination run away with you. That kind of thing hasn't been practiced in Merund for… well, centuries, as near as anyone can tell. It was just normal object animation. It could have been a human figure made out of teacups and worked the same way. This fellow just happened to use bones."

"Ah, well. I guess you're right, then."

Merkel smiled. "I'm always right, my good man! But this one was actually pretty interesting. Maybe I should come down there and visit you in that office of yours sometime."

"Don't bother," Radcliff said, rolling his eyes. "With both of us in there, I don't think we'd be able to get the door closed."

He walked back down the aisle to his office, more slowly this time, the report dangling in his hand. Merkel was right, of course. With a report this vague, there was no reason to assume the occurrence of something very unlikely when there was a far more rational explanation.

Back in his office, he scrawled down *"Enchantment: object animation. Possibly committed by University students."* If it *had* been students, and in the extremely unlikely case that they were found, they'd only get a slap on the wrist. While technically not licensed, higher-level University students had nearly a free hand at using magic. Unless, of course, they used Curation magic. Then they'd have the Inquisitors to deal with, who would probably bring their wrath down all the more heavily upon students of the Magical University.

Placing the report in the finished pile, Radcliff went back to work, writing his opinion on one tedious statement after another. He dealt with a man selling mysterious potions, a man that seemed to turn into a woman (Radcliff had a feeling that the culprit in that case was far more mundane than magic), and someone who was being compelled to slap themselves repeatedly in the face. It was hours later, when he was nearing the bottom of the pile, that his heart rate shot back up again.

Merund Northern District, The tenth day of the third month, 5:35 in the evening. A man on his way home from work was involved in a scuffle with another man on the street. Man who filed report was walking along when other man, passing on his left, lunged forward and bit him in the shoulder. Assailant described as extremely strong though small in frame, and to have made a loud groaning noise during encounter. Assailant was accompanied by a short figure in garish Wizard-style robes. Sole witness, a pastry vendor across the way, reported that the attack ceased when the robed figure grabbed the assailant, who then reportedly exploded. Human remains were found strewn around the street and on the wounded man.

Magician currently wanted for questioning and probable incarceration. Please advise as soon as possible."

Radcliff read the report again after finishing, and then read it a third time, before reaching a shaking hand toward the finished pile and digging through it, feverishly throwing reports on the ground and through the air until he found the one about the skeleton, which he placed on his desk next to the one he'd just read.

As he began crossing out what he'd written earlier, Radcliff's mind raced. This needed to be reported to a higher authority. It should be the Inquisitors, but as a University graduate, Radcliff didn't feel an undue amount of love for the Church. No, these would go straight to the Magistrate. The Magistrate would know what to do.

Radcliff smoothed out the report about the skeleton, and placed the tip of the pen in an empty area. He only wrote one word. It was all that was needed.

Chapter 6

The sun had begun to set by the time Alexander II had finished messily filling in the graves, at which point Lina pulled on her robes, shaking them out first to try and dislodge some of the dirt. She turned to the big ghoul with the mustache—Mr. Alois, she had to remember to call him—and said a friendly farewell, then turned to leave, ordering Alexander to follow as an afterthought. She didn't bother giving Sebastian such a simple order, as she found that skeletons could usually figure that kind of thing out for themselves. His presence behind her was marked only on occasion when his foot bones clacked against a flat tombstone.

Of course, while the skeleton had little else to do than follow her, she wasn't quite clear on why the ghoul was.

She looked over her shoulder at Alois, who was trailing along after Alexander.

"Uhm...."

"Yes?" he asked, as though nothing was wrong.

"Don't you need to go home, or something?"

Alois stood silently for a minute before shaking his head. "No, I think I'd rather prefer not to."

"Oh. What about work, don't you have work?"

"They'll assume I got caught up mourning. They're always very happy to assume that."

She wasn't sure what that meant, but decided to ignore it. "Hmm. Well, I guess you can come with me, if you want."

"I thought I would. There's still some more I wanted to ask about."

Lina rolled her eyes. Zombies were so much easier. They never asked any questions. And skeletons, well, she didn't know if she would call them easy, exactly, but at least they didn't wear out her ears.

"All right, you can come with. I guess it's only fair, my having made you undead."

"Yes," he said, a little too quickly for her liking.

She sighed, pushing the graveyard gate open and exiting onto the street. It wasn't rush hour yet, though there were still a good number of carriages and pedestrians heading back and forth down the road. She turned right, humming softly to herself.

"Excuse me, Miss Lina."

"What is it now?" she groaned.

"Don't you think we'd better do something about… erm… Sebastian?"

She was about to ask what he meant, but then she figured it out for herself. "Oh, I guess you're right. Magic is illegal here. I keep forgetting."

"It is if you don't have a University degree. I won't even bother asking if you have one."

"Good idea. Here, into this alley."

They quickly crossed the street and turned into a small, winding path between two buildings, occupied by a few rats and some garbage pails but little else.

"All right, wait here. I'll be back."

She heard Alois begin to voice a protest, but ignored it and turned back out into the street. She began reading the names on the shops. She'd never been to this part of town before, and certainly had never been clothes shopping here.

She soon found a second-hand store. It was poorly lit inside, full of racks of old clothing and shelves covered in pots, pans, and other well-used mundane goods. The woman at the counter was starting at Lina's robes. Lina smiled to herself. They *were* pretty impressive.

She wandered about the shop, grabbing articles of clothing off racks on impulse and holding them up to check size. After a few minutes, arms loaded down, she crossed to the front of the store and piled all her purchases on the counter, then began digging around in her pockets. She produced a small velvet bag, which she emptied on top of the clothes. A handful of bronze ingots fell out.

The cashier stared at the ingots, then made an attempt to glare at Lina, though it is difficult to glare at someone whose face you can't see.

"What's this supposed to be? We don't take these here," the old woman said.

"Oh," Lina responded. She hadn't actually tried to buy much in Merund. She dug around in another pocket and came out with a cloth satchel, the contents of which she unceremoniously dumped on the counter next to the pile of clothes. Among the things that fell out were a ball of yarn, a pocket watch, some knitting needles, a small set of books tied with a leather band, a hair brush, a number of small knives made of various materials, and several vials of colorful liquid.

"Is any of this any good?" Lina asked, hoping she wasn't going to have to give up any of her knives. Her fears were allayed when the shop clerk snatched the pocket watch with disconcerting speed.

"This will do fine, my fine patron! Do you need a bag for your purchases?"

"No," Lina said, dumping the items back into her bag before grabbing the bundle of clothing, "that's all right. Thank you."

She had a feeling she'd been ripped off, but there wasn't much to be done about it. In her previous travels she'd been able to accrue a healthy amount of credit or currency; sometimes by plying the Necromantic trade, but in leaner times, to her embarrassment, by washing dishes and cleaning stables. Unfortunately, local economies were so varied that she tended to have to start over in every new city.

She found Alois back in the alley, along with Sebastian and Alexander.

"All right, Sebastian," she said, unfolding a pair of brown trousers, "time to put on your clothes."

Sebastian shook his head with a sound like a clicking ratchet and began to back away. Lina sighed. "Alexander, please hold Sebastian in place."

Sebastian was immediately grabbed by the zombie, something that he neither expected nor appreciated. It was not an easy affair getting him dressed.

Afterwards, she looked him over. The pants were cinched awkwardly around the part of his spinal column directly above his pelvis, and a battered pair of leather shoes was buckled on at the tightest setting to keep them from sliding right off his feet. His socks had to be pinned to his pants. A long-sleeved shirt fit very awkwardly against his ribcage and shoulder blades, but it was almost entirely obscured by an old, hooded black riding cloak that was draped over him, covering his entire upper body.

Alois looked him up and down critically. "He looks like a wandering plague victim," he commented.

"Perfect!" Lina said happily. "Alexander, you may let your friend go now."

They proceeded back out into the open air, still looking extremely strange but perhaps no longer arrest-worthy. Sebastian trailed after them, sulking.

"Where are we going?" Alois asked. "At this rate, we're going to head into the Western District."

"That's the idea, actually," Lina said. "I think they may be looking for me in the Central District by now—assuming your police forces communicate with each other—so best to be heading elsewhere."

"Looking for you? Just because of the magic? Don't worry, they wouldn't tend to bother."

"Erm, no, there was actually an incident the other day in the Northern District," she said, the unpleasant memory coming to the forefront again. She pushed it back down.

"An incident? Well, young lady, I think you'd better tell me about it. It's important that I be fully informed as to our situation."

"I... look, it's not important..." she had to stop. It was shocking to her that it was still so hard to talk about this. How could she have messed up so badly? Not only had she had to kill Alexander I, but that poor man... Sebastian had drawn even with her by now and she reached out and grabbed his hand, causing his hooded head to turn towards her and cock to the side, though his bony fingers closed around hers.

"Well," Alois reconsidered, "We don't have to discuss it if it's such a sensitive issue. Where are we going, then?"

"There's an inn I've heard about. 339 Hemlock Street?"

Alois thought about this for a moment. "That neighborhood is a tad unsavory."

"Somehow, I'm confident that the four of us will be able to handle ourselves."

The walk to Hemlock Street was indeed uneventful, though until they left the Central District they sometimes skirted down alleyways to avoid Guard posts that Alois knew were coming up.

"If they're looking for you, it will take a few days at least for your description to make its way to the Western District," Alois informed her as they slipped through yet another alleyway. "Information transfer has never been one of our strong points."

She considered for the first time then that having Alois around was not entirely without its uses. It also wasn't terribly unpleasant to have someone to talk to.

The neighborhoods they passed through began to look less and less pleasant as they made their way into the Western District. Finally, after what must have been miles, they turned onto Hemlock Street. Lina's feet ached terribly, but it was hard to ask for a rest when you were traveling with a group that couldn't get tired. Lina grabbed Alois' arm as they passed a boarded-up money lender's, stopping him in his tracks. Sebastian fell to a halt as well, while Alexander kept lumbering on until Lina remembered to tell him to stop and come back.

"You're a policeman, aren't you?" she asked Alois.

"Yes. Or, well, I certainly thought I was…"

She rolled her eyes. "Yes, well, you might be recognized here, and that would be bad for everyone. Here." She pulled a tightly wrapped bundle out of her robes and tossed it to Alois, who confusedly unwrapped it into another dingy black cloak from the second-hand store. He frowned, but dutifully put it on, pulling the hood over his head.

The four of them came down the darkening street, three of them with hoods pulled over their heads, the fourth a tall, sickly-looking man. And yet, they did not turn any heads as they entered the ramshackle building at 339 Hemlock Street, an inn and tavern that the dingy sign proclaimed to be The Foxglove.

Lina frowned. It was very poorly lit, full of circular wooden tables at which sat groups of two to six people, most of them wearing as much black as her own party was. Other than the flickering glow of a few candles, the majority of the light in the place came from an occasional brilliant flash at one of the tables, followed by a brief scattering of applause. One of them burst just as Lina stepped through the door, a short man in the corner snapping his fingers to produce a bright green burst of light, out of which flew a number of ethereal butterflies that floated to the ceiling before fading slowly from existence.

She heard Alois make a tutting noise. "I can't believe that this kind of thing is going on so openly here," he murmured. "What in Delar's name is the Western District Guard doing, if not cleaning out places like this?"

"Hush!" she said, toeing him softly in the ankle. "If they find out who you are, they won't be pleased. Besides, what's so great about your stupid anti-magic laws, anyway? They're elitist!"

"Tell it to the judg—"Alois began, but then shook his head. "Sorry. Force of habit."

Lina ignored him and headed to the bar, behind which stood a thin, middle-aged woman who was talking to the bartender. She turned as they approached, not giving the rest of her party a second glance, but she gave Lina a once-over.

"Nice robes," she said.

"Thanks!" Lina replied. "We'll take a table, please, and we'll be staying the night here."

The woman gestured to the bar's main area. "Take your pick," she said, returning to her conversation. Lina headed over to a table in the middle of the inn and the three men—if you could call them that—followed and sat with her.

Alois sighed, apparently happy to be off his feet. She actually wasn't sure if ghouls could get physically tired— or was that just force of habit again? Alexander, of course, sat perfectly still, and Sebastian fidgeted in his chair. Lina could see his white finger bones drumming against his knee, and vaguely hoped that nobody else would, though no one else seemed to be making much of an effort at hiding their magical ability. At the moment, for example, someone had turned the flames of all the candles in the building from orange to a pleasant red-violet color.

A greasy looking man ambled over to them to take their orders.

"Nothing for me, please," Alois said, earning himself a disparaging glance from the waiter.

"Do you have broiled chicken?" Lina asked. The man nodded. "I'll take that. And a glass of water."

"Hold on," Alois said, "they don't have a very good water supply in the Western District. That'll make you sick."

"Oh, all right. Then, I guess I'll take an ale."

"No," Alois interrupted again, "that'll only make you even sicker. I'd go with milk."

She sighed and turned back to the waiter, who looked intensely bored. "Broiled chicken and a glass of milk then, please."

As he walked off to put her order in, she finally pulled her hood down so she could give Alois a good glare. "I can order for myself, thank you," she said curtly.

"I'm only looking out for you, young lady."

"Well... yes, I suppose you are. Lucky for you, I'm looking out for you as well," she said cheerfully, and dug around in her robes, pulling out a cloth-wrapped package and tossing it to him. He caught it, and upon looking down he immediately recognizing the fabric pattern.

"Oh, God."

"I collected it before we left. You still need to eat, you know!"

"My, thank you," he muttered, but she noted with some satisfaction that he tucked the parcel away under his cloak.

"Will Alexander want any of this?"

"No," she said. "So, have you been to the Western District before?"

"Sure," he said, raising his eyebrow at the change in topic, "but not terribly often. It's even less reputable than the Central District."

"Where in Merund *is* reputable?"

"The Northern District is where many of the newer government buildings are, and it's quite upscale. My house is on the border of the Central and Northern Districts. And the Eastern District is where the main Church is, so that place is pretty locked-down as well."

"And what about the Southern District?"

He smiled. "There isn't one. Merund ends at the banks of Lake Heinrich at the southern end of the Central District."

"Oh," she said, far more interested in the plate of food that had just been placed in front of her than in the geography lesson. She began eating immediately.

"Where are you from, anyway?" Alois persisted.

"Not here, if that's what you're getting at."

"What are you doing here, then? And at that rate, what are you up to? What're you raising all these undead for?"

She signed. "So many questions! Sebastian doesn't give me this kind of trouble."

"Sebastian is also currently trying to eat a dog."

She looked over, and saw that Sebastian was indeed gnashing his teeth and reaching his lanky arms towards a terrified looking beagle that someone had leashed to their table leg. The owner hadn't noticed yet.

"Aww, he just wants to be like his mama and eat food. Sebastian, don't do that."

Sebastian sat back up, his arms and bony hands disappearing once again under the cloak.

"There's a good boy."

Once she finished eating, they sat awhile longer. Lina was enjoying watching the other magic users—she hadn't gotten a chance to see any real magic since she'd arrived in Merund some weeks ago. Alois, surprisingly, also seemed to find the spectacle fairly entertaining, while Sebastian mostly fidgeted and occasionally shot furtive glances at the beagle, which was hiding under its owner's chair.

Eventually, they made their way up the rickety stairs to the second floor and got a room, which contained two small beds and not much else.

"I'd probably better get my own room," Alois said.

"What? Why? There are two beds."

"Well, it might not be proper for a man and young lady…"

"Oh, come on, Mr. Alois. You could be my father."

For a moment, Alois was silent.

"Alexander, please stand at the doorway and grab anyone who tries to come in while I'm asleep, all right?"

The zombie groaned and shambled into position.

"And Sebastian, you can just sit in the chair in the corner until we wake up."

The skeleton pulled down his hood and gazed at her with a look of incredible hurt in his eyes, which was impressive when she considered the fact that he did not have any.

"Oh, fine, you can go out and walk around, but make sure no one sees any of your bones."

Sebastian happily shot to his feet and ran to the door, disappearing out of it.

"Well," Alois commented, "that seems like a miraculously poor idea."

"Yes, probably," Lina said, shrugging. She pulled the blankets off her bed and climbed in, snuggling up in her robes. She heard Alois taking off his cloak, jacket, and boots before tucking himself in as well. She shut her eyes.

"Miss Lina?" he asked.

"Yes, Mr. Alois?"

"Do you ever stop and consider the moral ramifications of animating the bodies of people's former loved ones and using them like puppets?"

Lina considered this for a moment. It wasn't, as moments go, very long. "Just now, for the first time."

"And?"

She paused thoughtfully once more before answering in a tone of finality. "I'm okay with them."

"Well, so long as you've thought about it," Alois said resignedly, and extinguished the lamp.

Chapter 7

Radcliff's eyes shot open, his just-woken mind racing with the instant lucidity granted by a sense of danger. He stared at the flickering flame floating in front of him in the otherwise dark apartment, warped and distorted by the thick glass lens of the small bull's-eye lantern being held by a seemingly spectral hand. But not really spectral, of course. The hand holding the lantern clearly did lead into the shape of a person, but the small, stuttering light barely illuminated it at all. Radcliff slowly reached behind himself, feeling for the bronze candlestick that sat on his bedside table.

"Hello, Mr. Falkenhayn."

His hand froze. The voice hadn't come from the man with the lantern, but from behind him. His brain told him not to turn his back on the man he was facing, but his reflexes ignored his brain entirely, and he spun around in his sheets just in time to see the blaze of a match being lit. The flame was traced through the air until it met the wick of the bedside candle, which ignited, casting a flickering light onto the calm face of a middle-aged man.

"I'm sorry for the cloak and dagger display, Mr. Falkenhayn. We didn't mean to frighten you, but we didn't want anyone to see us come in."

Radcliff briefly considered screaming for help. The walls were thin enough, and the faculty dormitory, where most of the faculty that wasn't very highly-paid lived, was tightly packed. The ruckus he could make would rouse half the floor. Then again, he wasn't entirely sure that any of the bastards would actually come help him. You start one accidental magical fire, Radcliff considered, and everyone turns against you for life.

"What do you want?" he said, wondering why he hadn't tried that one out earlier. It was actually, in his opinion, an extremely good question. He had nothing worth stealing and certainly wasn't important enough to murder.

"Oh, I'm sorry. We haven't introduced ourselves. My name is Thomas Schiller. This is Albert Krupp."

"Hello," said a tired-sounding voice from behind the bull's eye lantern.

"Thomas Schiller... as in, Thomas Schiller, the Magistrate of Merund?"

"Yes, that's right," the man by the candle said, as though there was nothing particularly impressive about it. "I got your letter."

"Really. I had assumed that you wouldn't read it until morning."

"Krupp and I both work late. Lucky for everyone in this case, I think."

"All right, look, let's drop this. Just go ahead and arrest me."

"I'm sorry?" the Magistrate asked politely.

"I know you're Inquisitors, or some such thing. You're angry that I didn't send the letter straight to you. Fine, haul me in, let's get it over with."

"What makes you think we're from the Church?" asked the man with the lantern, apparently called Krupp.

"I'm certain that the Magistrate has better things to do with his time than visit second-rate Wizards in the middle of the night," Radcliff responded.

Krupp laughed. "You and me both, friend."

"Don't worry, Falkenhayn," the Magistrate said. "The Inquisitorial Council probably doesn't even remember that your department exists. I, however, remember quite well, and that's why I opened your letter as soon as I saw who it was from."

"Did you really?" Radcliff asked, raising an eyebrow, allowing his suspicion to dull momentarily. "What did you think?"

"We'll discuss that in a moment. For now, let's make our way to somewhere slightly better lit. And perhaps," he said, raising his voice slightly to compete with the snoring now coming from next door, "with somewhat thicker walls."

———————————————————————————

The carriage was nicely appointed, and several lanterns hanging from the roof provided excellent illumination in the small space. Radcliff, still in his pajamas but with a cloak wrapped around his shoulders, looked at the men sitting across from him. The Magistrate had his long legs crossed, looking at Radcliff pleasantly as the horses started off with a steady clip-clop. Krupp, a handsome young man, looked fairly sleepy, and had a leather messenger bag sitting snugly in his lap.

"So, Falkenhayn. Necromancy."

Radcliff felt himself shiver slightly. To be talking about this with anyone was a thrill, much less to be doing it with the leader of all Merund. To hell with it. If they *were* with the Church, they already knew everything anyway.

"Yes, sir. Necromancy."

"Let me start by telling you everything I know about Necromancy," the Magistrate said.

"All right …"

"Necromancy is a branch of magic that deals with bringing the dead back to life. It is used to create foul shades who roam the earth, neither alive nor dead. For obvious reasons, it is an even greater insult to Delar than is healing magic, and the crime of practicing Necromancy has for centuries carried the death sentence. Of course, Necromancy has not been practiced in Merund, so far as anyone knows, for a very long time, and the Church isn't even necessarily on the lookout for it."

It wasn't much, Radcliff considered, but it was still more than most people knew about Necromancy, though most Wizards were aware of at least part of the information Schiller had recited. Necromancy was usually mentioned quickly in basic Wizarding texts when the divisions between magical schools were being explained. Past that, it did not come up again unless you chose to research it on your own at the University's extensive libraries.

Not many people chose to do this. Radcliff knew this very well, because he was able to use the library's various books on Necromancy all he wanted during his years at school without anyone else ever attempting to check out, or even look at, the texts in question.

"That's very impressive, sir," Radcliff said carefully.

"Actually, I tend to think it's rather pathetic. That's why you're here, Falkenhayn. I want you to tell me everything you know about Necromancy."

"What makes you think I know any more than you do, sir?" Radcliff asked, trying to keep his tone neutral.

"You may think that the reports which you sent me were painfully obvious, but the fact is that you'd have to know a fair deal about Necromancy to be able to so unequivocally identify it. Meanwhile, I have been Magistrate for years without ever receiving a report directly from you, and thus I know that you are not one to send out false alarms. So, please," Schiller said, smiling slightly, "Why don't you start at the beginning."

Radcliff sighed, but relented. He shifted in his seat, trying to get a bit more comfortable. How to broach such a subject?

"Legend has it," he began finally, "that Necromancy is one of the oldest magical arts, second only to the basic Wizarding schools of Conjuration and Enchantment."

Krupp snorted. "Legend has it? And what does history have it?"

"We don't have recorded history that goes this far back. The legends, though, say that humans were given the first magic, Enchantment, by the dragons."

This time, Krupp actually laughed. "Dragons? Really? Dragons."

The Magistrate smiled. "Please, Falkenhayn, go on."

"All right," Radcliff said, eyeing Krupp, "So, it's said that after a few generations of learning magic, magicians started to desire more. If they could do things like alter the minds of others, and move from one place to another in an instant, they didn't see how they could still be as vulnerable as other humans—as likely as anyone else to just drop dead one morning of a heart attack. They thought they should be immortal. And so, they started dabbling in magic to make them so. Of course, what they came up with wasn't what any of them intended... but by that time, some of them had become interested in Necromancy not merely as a means to achieve immortality, but as a kind of magic all its own. It does have many uses, surely... the ability to raise an army of willing slaves to serve you or fight in your name is the most obvious... and it *can* grant immortality, in a way."

"In a way?" the Magistrate asked pointedly.

"Well, the most powerful necromancers—and I mean only a handful of people throughout history—have been able to move beyond the lowest forms of undead, the stuff of monster stories told by children, things like horrible skeletons and lumbering zombies. They could make other kinds of undead. Undead that had the ability to think, and access the memories of their old lives."

"So they could really raise the dead?"

"Well, no, not exactly. They couldn't give life to someone who was dead. Instead, it's more like the magic becomes a substitute for life. And as I said, in rare cases, that magic can even be enough to keep the person's mind fully intact. But they're still not a human anymore. They're something else. Their bodies work differently. What I've read has suggested that they'd be stronger, more durable. Most undead require food to operate—usually human flesh. Their unnatural nature inevitably becomes apparent to others around them, which causes them to be cast out by normal society. Soon enough, it's not surprising that they begin thinking differently than humans, too. But this is all ancient. Undead like this are almost impossible to make."

"I see. Luckily, the reports we are concerned with do not seem to deal with this type of undead, so there is no reason to think that we are dealing with a particularly powerful necromancer."

"Yes, sir. But even becoming a poor necromancer takes a Wizard of otherwise high skill, sir. It is without a doubt the most difficult magical art, and it takes years to learn even the basics of it."

"And have you done this?"

"No, sir. I'm only interested as a learner, not as a practitioner." He tried not to let his disappointment show. Indeed, Necromancy was far beyond his abilities. He could only hope to try and understand it.

"I see."

"I still don't see what these purported dragons have to do with anything," put in Krupp, though he seemed to have woken up a bit and had been listening with interest.

"Ah, well, I hadn't gotten to that part yet. Back in the ancient days, when humans were first experimenting with Necromancy, it's said that the dragons were horrified by what the humans had done with the gift they'd given them. They cut off all contact with humans from then on, rejecting us for our creation of perceived abominations."

He noticed Krupp preparing another snort, and cut him off. "You must mind that this business of dragons is almost certainly only myth and legend. We must read between the lines. Whether or not there were dragons to be disgusted by Necromancy, it wasn't long before many humans took this same view, and soon it was a marginalized art, though still one practiced by many. Not uncommon in ancient history are those armies in which, if the healers could not help the wounded, the necromancers would raise them after their death so that they might fight on forever."

"Forever?" the Magistrate asked.

"Well, until they're destroyed. Plus the magic holding zombies and skeletons together tends to wear out eventually, I believe. I don't have an exact time-frame."

"Very good, Mr. Falkenhayn," the Magistrate said. "Now, on to the topic of real relevance. These two police reports—tell me about your interpretations."

"Well, I suppose the earlier one is fairly obvious…it sounds to me like an undead skeleton."

"Isn't it possible that it was merely a magically-animated set of human bones?" the Magistrate asked, like a curious student in a lecture.

"Well, yes, it is, sir, and that's what I dismissed it as at first," Radcliff said cautiously. The Magistrate seemed to know far more about magic than he would have expected.

"I don't understand," Krupp said. "What's the difference?"

"Well," Radcliff said, feeling suddenly nostalgic for his basic training at the University, "Animated objects are merely items that have been enchanted to move. Casting a spell on a ball to make it bounce across a room on its own would be enchanting an object. The object doesn't gain any form of intelligence of its own, and needs constant direction by the caster. It can't even follow orders, exactly, because it has no brain to interpret them. The Wizard instead modifies the magic which he is using in order to make the object behave in the manner he wishes. Enchanting a set of bones to stay together and then walk would be very difficult, but it is certainly possible, and has been done before."

"Hmm. And how are undead different than animated objects?" Krupp asked.

"Well, to a degree, it depends on the necromancer, as undead can vary from creator to creator. However, undead can understand and interpret orders. Some may need specific orders in order to do anything or stop doing anything, while others may be able to act partially of their own accord in what they feel are the best wishes of their creator. The main difference, I suppose, is that undead are not simply objects being made to move on invisible magical puppet strings. They are truly beings imbued with a form of semi-life, and have been given some kind of mind, though in some cases it is quite rudimentary."

"So," The Magistrate said, "you think that the skeleton destroyed in the Central District was undead because it is unlikely that a Wizard skilled enough to animate an object would then specifically order it into traffic. If it were undead, on the other hand, it could have been following some broader orders we don't know about, and been run over due to its own carelessness."

"Exactly, Magistrate!"

"Hmm," the Magistrate said evenly, locking his eyes on Radcliff's, "and yet, on the report, you originally wrote that it was merely an Enchantment incident. Why?"

Radcliff could feel himself sweating now, and wondered suddenly if the trotting horses weren't taking him off towards the gallows after all.

"Well, sir, as unlikely as it is that someone would animate a skeleton just to get it crushed, it seemed even more unlikely that we had a necromancer in town. Until I got to that second report."

"Yes," said Krupp, "the second report. I'm interested in hearing what you have to say about that one. It doesn't seem nearly as obvious as the first."

Radcliff frowned, his temper rising slightly. The first report hadn't been so obvious when they'd been asking him to explain the difference between Enchantment and Necromancy. Where the hell were they going, anyway? Couldn't they have just summoned him during business hours? He took a deep breath to calm himself, then pushed on.

"In the second case, it sounds very much as though a necromancer was trying to blend into a crowd with one of his zombies. Unfortunately for him, his zombie was a few weeks old, and presumably hadn't been allowed to eat. Zombies require the flesh of living humans in order to keep operating, and after a few weeks without eating, their drive to consume can override their orders. I think that's what happened, and that's why that poor fellow got a bite taken out of him."

"Interesting," the Magistrate said. "That's certainly plausible. But the rest of the report is where things really seem to get strange."

"Yes, I agree. The necromancer's reaction is one of the things that make me think the zombie attack was unintentional. I've read that many necromancers could channel pure necromantic energy through their hands, and use it to heal undead, just as though they were using powerful Curation magic on a human. I think the necromancer may have shot so much magic into the zombie that its system was completely overwhelmed and it simply exploded."

"But why was he trying to heal it in the first place?" Krupp asked.

"Oh, he wasn't. I think he knew very well that an overload was the fastest way to eliminate the zombie, which was no longer following orders."

"This sounds a bit theoretical," the Magistrate said. "What makes you think that kind of overload is possible?"

Radcliff shrugged. "It can happen with healing magic. Why not Necromancy?"

"It's true," Krupp agreed. "That's one of the things they teach you about healing magic in the propaganda at the elementary schools: that if they use it incorrectly, you'll explode."

The Magistrate raised an eyebrow at Krupp, who smiled bashfully.

"Of course," Radcliff added carefully, unsure whether discussing healing magic was automatically safe just because discussing Necromancy was, "such things don't normally happen accidentally. Only if a very powerful healer was trying to do it on purpose."

Krupp nodded. The Magistrate sat quietly, his eyes focused somewhere over Radcliff's head. Only the sound of the horse's hooves on the pavement pervaded the scene.

"Yes," the Magistrate said finally as the carriage was pulling to a stop. "I'm convinced. We have a necromancer in town. The question thus becomes, what are we going to do about it?"

Chapter 8

Continued: an excerpt from An Introduction to Magical History, *by Pontius Sleighman*

Chapter 7 – Magical Schools

The next two schools of magic to be discussed, Conjuration and Enchantment, are often cited as the earliest forms of Magic. Conjuration and Enchantment together are sometimes referred to simply as "Wizard" or "Wizarding" magic, because the two form the basis of a magical education, and the vast majority of Wizards who have attended University are best-trained at using these two forms. Even specialists in more specific schools like Divination typically have at least some ability in the fields of Conjuration and Enchantment. Meanwhile, these are the two forms of magic that the general public will most quickly be able to name, though perhaps only in a very crude sense.

Conjuration is typically an aggressive form of magic, and it involves the bringing into existence of substances and objects that would not exist otherwise. Both the creation of a wall of ice and a deadly ball of flame are arts practiced by the conjurer. Such arts are unsubtle and very powerful, and for this reason Conjuration specialists are sometimes considered a bit brutish by their contemporaries, who prefer to manipulate events with Enchantment or Divination rather than charging in head first with the impressive fireworks display that is Conjuration magic. Elemental processes, most notably fire and lightning, are the easiest to create using Conjuration. Liquids are a bit more difficult, and only very skilled conjurers ever manage to produce solids other than ice, which has a very low density and as such is more simple than other materials. Conjured substances are physically real, but their existence is contingent on the magic that drives them; even the most skilled conjurer's creations wear out and cease to exist within a matter of days. Conjuration spells tend to be especially draining on the mind, and it is difficult to cast the same Conjuration spell in rapid succession, which is why conjurers in battle rarely repeat the same spell. It is also worth noting here that conjurers usually have some degree of control over the movement and velocity of their creations, meaning, for example, that one could create a stone and cause it to shoot across the room without actually having to throw it.

Enchantment, which is perhaps even older than Conjuration, is perhaps the broadest school of magic. Generally, Enchantment refers to the changing of things. Any spell that alters the appearance, behavior, or nature of a person, animal, plant, or object is typically an Enchantment spell. Of course, Enchantment should not be confused with Alchemy. The difference is quite simple: Alchemy changes one thing to another, and that change is extremely real and concrete, reversible only through further Alchemy. Enchantment, on the other hand, can make only temporary changes, but often ones that are far more glamorous. Enchantment cannot make lead into gold, but it can make lead appear to be gold, and powerful spells could even make lead seem to feel and weigh as though it were gold. Further still, Enchantment can manage far more complex transformations—a dog into a cow, for instance. These spells can never last forever, though some can last for days or even weeks, and they can always be recast if the enchanter is present to do so.

Enchantment can disguise a person's true form or even make them totally invisible to the unaided eye. It can be used to influence the minds and actions of others. Perhaps the best-known form of this kind of Enchantment is the love potion. While a powerful enchanter could perhaps distill his influential magic into a sort of "love potion", it should be noted that the vast majority of love potions that are available for purchase in every city in the world are little more than a handful of rose petals suspended in rubbing alcohol—or worse.

Teleportation is a form of Enchantment as well; it changes not something's nature, but rather its location. Teleportation is an ability that most Wizards learn but that few master, and the distance over which one can teleport is also widely variable based on a Wizard's level of expertise.

By daybreak, the three men sat in the Magistrate's office, lounging in the conversation circle of chairs and couches on the western side of the room. When the girl came in with the bottle of fortified wine that the Magistrate had called down for, Krupp could only imagine what she thought when she saw them. The Magistrate of all Merund, still in his dress coat but with the top button of his shirt undone and his shoes removed, had his back against the arm of a couch, his long legs taking up most of the rest of it.

Clockwise from him was a tatty-looking Wizard with a stubbly brown beard and razor-short hair, wearing striped pajamas and sitting in an overstuffed chair that seemed to swallow his lanky frame.

And then there was Krupp himself, who needed a shave and a change of clothes, but who felt he was otherwise doing pretty well for someone who had been awake for thirty hours.

He stuck a finger in the air to catch the girl's attention, and she quickly brought him the tray, setting it down on the table next to him. He thanked her and dismissed her, then began pouring the Magistrate a glass of wine.

"I'll say again, gentlemen," Krupp said, filling the glass up and passing it to the lounging Magistrate, "I don't see that we need to go to all this trouble. I think the biting was an isolated incident. This necromancer isn't any real danger to society."

"All necromancers are a danger to society," Falkenhayn said, eyeing the wine eagerly. "What they do doesn't fit in with society. They're destined to be rejected by their peers and even by their families. After all, to practice the art requires the theft of human bodies. The necromancers, of course, would argue that these bodies are of no use to people who can't use magic to raise them, which shows that sometimes magic can lead one to forget how normal people think. If there's a necromancer in town, we will be hearing more about it, take it from me."

Falkenhayn paused for a moment before continuing. "Do you think I could have a—"

"Yes, Falkenhayn, I'm pouring you one," Krupp said.

"In addition to Radcliff's well-taken point," the Magistrate drawled softly, "need I remind you, Krupp, that practicing Necromancy is a capital offense?"

"Plenty of things are capital offenses, sir," Krupp said, passing a wine glass to Falkenhayn. "I mean, we don't go out of our way in this office to see that illegal healers are prosecuted, so why do we need to do anything about an illegal necromancer? Let the Church handle it, if they find out about it. If they don't, then who cares?"

"You may be too young, Krupp, but do you remember the burning of the Zeltarian Embassy?" the Magistrate asked.

Krupp suppressed a sigh. He had a feeling he was about to learn a lesson. "I've read about it," he admitted. "It was half a decade or so before you came into office. Religious feelings were on the rise in Merund, and the balance of power was shifting to the Church. The Zeltarian Embassy was burned by a huge crowd of religious commoners who disapproved of the Zeltarians' policies on healing magic."

"That's right. And do you know what started the religious reawakening of the commoners that culminated in the fire?" the Magistrate asked.

"I can't say that I do, sir."

"Falkenhayn?"

"Yes, sir, actually. My parents were very worried about it, I recall. It was public outrage at a dramatic increase in the practice of Curation magic. It was still illegal, of course, but the laws weren't being enforced. So, healing magic started to be a pretty lucrative trade, and soon trained magical physicians from Zeltaria began coming to Merund."

Krupp whistled. "Public outrage against foreigners *and* against declining moral values? The city was lucky to get off with just a single building burnt down."

"It didn't, unless you're not counting the hundreds of executions the Church carried out during that period," Falkenhayn said darkly. "It's also worth noting, of course, that the Zeltarian Embassy was full of people at the time it was burned down."

"Well, that's tragic of course, but they should have had their people obey the local laws."

"They did," the Magistrate said. "In fact, very few of the illegal healers in Merund at the time came from Zeltaria."

"Then why did they burn the embassy?" Krupp asked.

"Have you ever known a rioting mob to stop at the library to get their facts straight?"

"This is why I brought this information to you," Falkenhayn said, "and not to the Church."

Krupp laughed. "Are you sure it's not just because most of you Wizards have a professional rivalry with the Church, and bringing this to us was the only other viable option?"

"Well, that too."

"Whatever your intentions, Falkenhayn, I'm glad you did what you did," the Magistrate said. "I have done my best to govern with the memory of the Zeltarian Embassy in my mind. It is one of the reasons that I shifted primary prosecution of illegal Curative magic operators and customers over from the City Guard to the Church. This way, if Curative magic goes on the rise, the Church itself gets the blame."

"Well," said Krupp, "Doesn't the same stand true for Necromancy?"

"It's a foggy issue," the Magistrate said. "When the law was changed, Necromancy wasn't mentioned. Technically, it's still under central municipal administration, meaning the Guardsmen, meaning us."

"So…" Krupp began.

"So," Falkenhayn interrupted, "if the public or the Church get wind of Necromancy being practiced here, the Church will be able to blame the Magistrate and make a power grab. Meanwhile, the public will rediscover their love of arson."

Krupp leaned back, thinking. It sounded pretty bad, after all.

"Thus," the Magistrate said simply, "we'll find the necromancer, and stop him by any means necessary."

Krupp looked at Schiller, still lying on the couch, his sock-covered feet pointing directly upward. His eyes were shut, but his voice sounded awake and alert. Krupp wondered if he dared ask whether the Magistrate was allowing his religious convictions to interfere in his decision. After all, even a moderate follower of Delar was bound to find the idea of Necromancy quite offensive. Krupp himself couldn't find the drive to care. A corpse was of no use to anyone, and if some magic-addled Wizard wanted to borrow one and make it dance, he didn't see what harm that was. Nevertheless, it had been made clear that there were indeed good reasons to hunt down and stop the necromancers. And Krupp, anyway, had the distinct impression that it would be a bad idea to question the Magistrate on his religious motivations.

"We'll want to work fairly discreetly, obviously," Falkenhayn said. Krupp smirked, noting the use of "we." Apparently Falkenhayn considered himself part of the team now. The Magistrate appeared not to object, though.

"Yes. If we were to, say, announce a city-wide search to the City Guard, the information would quickly go public. I'd prefer to involve as few Guardsmen as possible. And anyway, I don't know that they're the best suited for this job."

"And who would be, sir?" Krupp asked.

"Actually, I was hoping that Falkenhayn would be able to tell us."

Falkenhayn blinked in surprise, apparently still not used to anyone, much less the Magistrate, valuing his opinion. "Well, sir, a few trained swordsmen would be useful, of course. Zombies are hard to kill with swords, but their bones are brittle and their flesh yielding, so it's easy to hack off a leg and demobilize them."

"Good. So we'll have a few Guardsmen. Who else?"

"A Wizard wouldn't hurt. Enchantment spells won't work on lower undead and the necromancer will probably be too powerful to succumb to such things, but a conjurer would be able to use magic to eliminate undead fairly quickly, as well as to immobilize or, erm… otherwise eliminate the necromancer himself. We'd want to get one of the best conjurers available."

"Naturally. We'll look into it. Now, it seems to me that an expert in Necromancy would also be a valuable asset to the team."

Krupp smirked. The Magistrate wasn't always terribly subtle. Still subtle enough for Falkenhayn, though, who was nodding agreeably. "Yes, sir. I suspect the University Librarian may have a fair bit of knowledge on the subject, and perhaps we could—"

"He means you, idiot," Krupp interjected, bringing Falkenhayn to a grinding halt. The Wizard looked at the Magistrate, who opened one eye and nodded fractionally.

"Oh, sir," Falkenhayn sputtered, "I don't think I'm cut out for the job. I've never experienced combat, and I—"

"That's what the other team members are for. You're the only Necromancy expert I trust, Falkenhayn. Well, I suppose you're technically the only Necromancy expert I *know*, but regardless. You're going."

Krupp began to get up. "Very well, sir. I'll see if I can recommend some Guardsmen who are both skilled and discreet."

"Excellent, thank you. Of course, we're still missing the last member of the team."

"We are?" Krupp and Radcliff asked in unison.

"Certainly. My eyes and ears on the mission. To keep me up to date, and ensure that everything is going on track."

"Oh, no," Krupp said, a plummeting sensation plunging through his stomach.

"Oh, yes," the Magistrate said. "So make sure that you pick some awfully good Guardsmen, Krupp, because you'll be going with them."

Part II:
The Mercenaries

Chapter 9

He wasn't a typical-looking man, but on the streets of Selan that didn't mean very much. With throngs of hundreds of people crowding nearly every important road, you could be just about as strange as you liked, and there would still be someone stranger within arm's reach.

There was nothing inherently odd about him. He was a man of medium height, but took up far more space than would another man of his size because of the massive suit of armor he wore. It was an impressive-looking thing, layers of thick metal plates on his shoulders, a breastplate strapped firmly to his chest, a bulky, open-faced helmet for his head. He clanked everywhere he went, and never seemed to go anywhere without having to make quite an effort, considering the amount of weight that his body was supporting.

He was muscular too, of course. He'd have to be, wearing that armor. Muscular knights covered in armor were not uncommon on Selan's streets either, but still, there was something odd about his physique. It showed most clearly in his uncovered hands, which were not the tough, coarse tools of a warrior. Rather they were soft and ruddy, like the hands of a scholar. He didn't carry a sword, but he had a heavy oaken spear that he used like a walking staff. A good weapon for a peasant foot-soldier, maybe, but hardly what one would expect from a roaming knight.

He strode down the streets purposefully, helmet under one arm, the sun glinting off his short blonde hair but not off his armor, which was a matte dark gray. Merchants cajoled him from their booths; many tried to sell him a sword. He ignored them, a somewhat haughty smile on his face, a mailed finger brushing a lock of blonde hair off his forehead as he pressed on towards a steeple that rose over the crowds.

In point of fact, he was a handsome man, with nice teeth and sharp blue eyes. Plenty of Selan's women knew him well, though few stayed with him for very long. Acquaintances were unsure why they left, as this man, whoever he was, seemed profitable as well as attractive, always with a bit of money to spend.

Reaching the building with the steeple, he pushed the doors open, entering into the large, dark space of a Minarian temple. He looked immediately more at home here, as many of the men inside (and indeed, they were all men) had close-cropped hair and carried vicious looking weapons. Some turned and nodded as he walked by, while others threw him disparaging glances. He did not glance back, but merely set his eyes on a leather-bound hilt sticking slightly into the aisle between the pews. He approached it a slow but determined gait, the butt of his spear thumping softly on the ground with each step.

The hilt, as Rodolphus already knew, connected to the finned head of a mace, and the mace rested next to the kneeling form of Tiberius Ursal, his hands clasped together in front of him. The contents of a small ceramic plate at his feet smoldered and burned, and a pervading haze of incense flowed from it, wisps of it filling the air and somewhat clouding the form of Tiberius.

Rodolphus slid aside the mace and plopped down into the seat it had been blocking, putting his feet up on the pew in front of him. There were more angry glances, though he made no sign of noticing them.

Tiberius's eyes did not open. "Hello, Rodolphus," he said softly.

"This incense stinks," Rodolphus noted. "What is it?"

"Thrysus root extract. It clears the mind, and brings one closer to Minar."

"There's an odd concept. Being closest to a war god when your mind is clear. I'd think bloodlust would be more appropriate."

Tiberius snorted, but his hands stayed firmly clasped in front of him. "There is a time for that, my friend. And there is a time for a clear mind, and contemplation."

"Well, I'm glad to hear that, because I've got something for you to contemplate."

"You don't say. And I was hoping you had merely wished to convert and become a worshipper of Minar. We could make a swordsman out of you yet, Rodolphus."

"You're hilarious. You interested in hearing what I have to say, or not?"

"I suppose. But I think that first we should leave here, before Luca hits you in the back of the head with his axe."

Rodolphus glanced over his shoulder at the burly man a few pews away, who was staring at the two of them and twitching with rage.

"You know he'd never get that close. What's he so worked up about?"

"This is supposed to be a silent space."

"That ain't stopping you."

"Yes, well, I believe that Minar is not too concerned with such things. And anyway, if a fight starts, people will be far more concerned with beating up on you than on me."

"And you'd escape in the havoc? Why, Tiberius, that sounds almost cowardly."

Tiberius chuckled. "Run away from a battle in the very temple of Minar? While I was at it, I might as well spit in the incense and wipe my ass on the holy tabard. No, Rodolphus, I'd just use the fact that everyone was beating up on you to my tactical advantage."

"Ah, so you'd attack them from behind, is that it?"

"I'm sorry; you seem to have misinterpreted me. I never meant to imply that I would be on *your* side in this hypothetical fight."

"I could take you. And incidentally, it might be just about time to reconsider the 'hypothetical' part of that last bit." Rodolphus glanced up at Luca, who had by now gotten up and begun striding toward them. Rodolphus caught the man's eye, smiled, and raised a hand, opening it as though he were cupping the bowl of a goblet. He said a word, and a glistening ball of flame the size of an apple appeared, floating a few inches above his palm. It cast a wavy, smoldering light on the pews around them as it rolled and contorted.

"That's close enough, oaf. It'd be a shame if I had to burn you down, together with this second-rate temple."

The man with the axe growled, but did not approach any further.

"Tiberius," Rodolphus said in a low voice, "does your religion allow him *not* to fight me?"

"There is nothing blasphemous about choosing not to fight a battle you are surely destined to lose."

"Ah, good. Because I don't think it'd be a wise idea to burn this temple down."

"Do you see that? A bit of exposure to my incense, and already your thoughts are clearing."

"Har har. I just don't like watchmen—or zealots, like you—on my case."

"Then I guess we'd better leave, before you have no choice but to begin starting fires. Or get an axe buried in your chest. I'm having an easy time picturing either outcome."

"Charming. Shall we?"

Rodolphus stood up, grabbing his spear in one hand while bringing the other arm around, pointing his palm forward, the globe of flame still suspended a few inches in front of it. He aimed it at Luca like he might have aimed a crossbow, and began backing towards a side exit.

Tiberius, moving for the first time since Rodolphus had come in, opened his eyes, bowed his head to the altar a few pews away, and slowly stood up, taking the plate of incense with him. Without looking at either Rodolphus or Luca, he walked sedately to a small table set up against the wall and used a small iron weight to extinguish the incense. Leaving the plate behind, he walked back to the pew, carefully picked up his mace, and then exited through the side door, kindly leaving it open behind him.

Rodolphus stared after him briefly. Then, with a last look at Luca, he finished his backward trek to the door. Backing over the threshold, he favored Luca with the biggest smile he could muster, then let his flame spell extinguish, slammed the door shut, and quickly flipped the latch.

"How theatrical," Tiberius said from behind him. "Next time, we really must meet at *your* place of worship."

"What, you mean the brothel?"

"Sadly, I think I do. Shall we?"

They walked down the narrow hallway, no better lit than the temple itself, and soon turned into a cramped alcove containing a winding wooden staircase, which they ascended. Tiberius' quarters, located through a narrow door on the second storey, were what one might expect, given the hallway and staircase that led to them. The single room was cramped and dark, with little more than a slim bed and a small desk fitting inside. Tiberius' few possessions were stacked neatly in any spare space available. His helmet, open-faced like Rodolphus' but with smoother angles and a crosspiece that guarded his nose, sat preferentially close to hand on his desk, with a small stack of books and papers next to it. A stack of folded clothes sat in one corner, and a chain shirt hung from several sturdy hooks on the wall. A miniscule cupboard opposite the door no doubt hid a few more items.

"Shouldn't you wear your armor to temple?" Rodolphus asked, running a finger over one of the three tapered ridges cresting the back and top of Tiberius' helmet.

Tiberius sat down and began changing his boots. "How nice of you to feign an interest in my religious beliefs, Rodolphus. No, it is traditional to bring only one's weapon. Normally one does not wear one's armor, except to battle. That last part doesn't apply only to Minarians, but to all sane people the world over."

Rodolphus sneered. "Oh yeah? And what's the point of wearing armor if you'll only have it when you're expecting a fight? I'll have you know that the majority of fights I've been in have been completely spur of the moment."

"You do tend to make enemies that are very erratic. Maybe you should try to pick fights with people who are more the duelist type."

"Eh. No one ever wants to duel with me. Something about getting an icicle shot through their eye at fifty feet."

"Verily, you are your own best advertiser. Are you going to tell me why you wanted to talk to me?"

"No. Let's go get something to eat."

Tiberius sighed and rolled his eyes, but got up, grabbing his mace as he did.

In Neylon's Restaurant a few blocks away, they settled into their seats, the waitress pushing a tankard of ale in front of each of them without so much as a word.

"Do you think they're beginning to recognize you?" Tiberius asked.

"Nah. What's to recognize?"

"Yes, silly of me. Now will you tell me what you wanted?"

"I'll think about it."

"Rodolphus, I haven't got all day…"

"Yes you do. That's why I waited until your commission expired to talk to you. So that you'd have all day."

"How did you know my commission expired?"

"Because I remembered that you were insane and signed up for two more years than I did, and I also remembered that a few weeks ago was the two year anniversary of my freedom from the army."

"Has it really been two years since we saw each other? It seems like less. Let's try for four years before next time."

"You joke, but you'd be lost without me."

"Something like that. What have you been doing with your freedom?"

"A bit of this, a bit of that…"

"Spending all your money on petty pleasures without bringing any real income in?"

Rodolphus frowned. "Who told you?"

"Minar. Maybe you should convert."

"I'll take it into consideration. Yes, I've spent most of my money."

"The army pays well, Rodolphus, but you'll find the money lasts longer if you don't spend it constantly."

"What would you know about how the army pays? You did all your service for free. There's where your crazy damn Minar gets you. A ten year stint in the army and you didn't see a dime for it."

"What do I need money for? The temple provides me with food, boarding, a small stipend…"

"Hell, you get a stipend? How much?"

"Never mind. So what have you been doing with yourself? I know that many people have a great deal of difficulty adjusting to civilian life after the army."

"Hah! I'm doing just fine. You couldn't drag me back to the army with a herd of oxen."

"Most war casters re-up after a few months of freedom—they're trained from childhood for nothing but battle, and as much as they want their freedom, when they get it, they find that war is all they know."

"Look who knows so much about soldiers, now. You'd almost think you were one yourself."

"Careful, Rodolphus," Tiberius said, raising a brow. "But rather, my knowledge comes from my position. As a religious man, many soldiers from our legion have come to me with their problems." He looked up as the waitress approached. "Ah, the fritters please, miss."

"The cheapest thing on the menu," Rodolphus snorted. "Small stipend, indeed. I'll take the lamb chop, rare, extra sauce." He waved the waitress away without looking at her.

"You will note, though, Rodolphus, that I am still getting my small stipend, and will continue to receive it. You, on the other hand, haven't made any money in two years."

"Hey, what do you know? I've made money. There are some very lucrative mercenary positions out there."

Tiberius raised an eyebrow, taking a sip of his drink. "Really? You don't strike me as the type for mercenary work."

"I don't?"

"Well, you hated the army, so why would you join a private one? And you can't work solo as a bodyguard or bounty hunter, seeing as being a war caster is a little difficult when no one is protecting your flanks."

"Ah, yeah. Well, that's actually why I wanted to talk."

"Oh, good. I might get some more praying in today after all."

Rodolphus sighed, rolling his eyes. "Don't you ever get tired of praying?"

"Oh, I don't know. Do you ever get tired of being a loafer with neither creed nor any real motivation?"

"Hey, I've got plenty of motivation!"

"Ah, I'm sorry. I meant motivation that doesn't take the form of a precious metal."

Rodolphus opened his mouth to respond. "Or food, or drink, or women," Tiberius quickly amended.

"Well, if you're going to rule out everything worthwhile…"

Plates were unceremoniously clattered down in front of them, and Rodolphus immediately attacked a practically uncooked lamb chop with his knife and fork. "All right, back to business," he mumbled, his mouth full of food. "I want to form a mercenary team, and I want you to be on it."

"A mercenary *team*?" Tiberius asked, gingerly picking up one of the fried dumplings on his plate and taking a bite of it, "What, like a street gang? Are we going to try to get shopkeepers to pay us protection?"

"No, there's not enough money in that. I mean we'd hire out as mercenary soldiers, but as a group. Instead of just as individuals."

"That doesn't make any sense. The army that hired us would just immediately split the group up. You'd go into the conjuring corps, a pikeman would get thrown in with the front-liners, and so on."

"Ah, you see, but that's the brilliant part."

"Oh, so there's a brilliant part?"

"Isn't there always? We aren't going to hire out to join up with armies."

Tiberius frowned, putting the rest of the fritter in his mouth and chewing thoughtfully. "Rodolphus, do you need for me to explain to you exactly what a mercenary is?"

"Lord, are you hostile toward new ideas. Look, once we get the team together, we'll hire out as a single unit that will act alone' to accomplish specific tasks. It'll be like hiring a bounty hunter, I guess, but there'll be a whole group of us."

"I see. Why would anyone pay for all of us when they just needed a bounty hunter?"

"Because we'll be able to do things one man couldn't. We'll be like a small army."

"Yes. An extremely, extremely small army."

"Sure, but each of us will be as good as ten normal men."

"How do you figure?"

"I'm going to get the best. We'll be the best."

"Ah, the plot thickens."

"That's right! Now do you see?"

"Am I to take it that you think I'm the best fighter in the city? Flattering, but…"

"No, idiot. You're the best healer in the city. Your ability to bash in skulls with that mace is strictly average."

"A more honest assessment. I don't know if I'd call myself the best healer, though…"

"You were at the top of your class!"

"Yes, but I'm past my prime."

"You're thirty-two years old."

"Yes. As I said, I am past my prime. Someone only beginning their military service after graduating Combat Casting School would be in better physical and mental shape."

"Yes, you moron, but they'd lack your ten years of combat experience, which would make them about as useful as a bowman without arms."

"Hmm. And I suppose you're under the impression that you're the best war conjurer in the city?"

"If I don't say so myself."

"I somehow suspect that you do say so yourself, quite often."

Rodolphus smirked, picking up his stripped lamb bone and beginning to gnaw on one end. "If I *do* say so myself, then. It doesn't matter."

"So who else would you be planning to pick up?"

"Some front-line fighter. I don't know who yet."

"Maybe Thaddeus the Axe?"

"Dead. Took two arrows in the chest at Jipon."

Tiberius frowned. "That's too bad."

"Yeah, he would have been a good choice. Are you going to finish those?"

"So you expect," Tiberius began, pushing his plate of food towards Rodolphus, "to be able to find the best melee fighter in the city, and then recruit him to your little kill squad?"

"Right," Rodolphus said, his mouth full of fritter.

"And why would he join up with us?"

"Because it's economically brilliant. Why else would I be suggesting it?"

Tiberius chuckled. "Well, because you're out of money. Because you're useless on your own and you can't stand not being in charge. This little scheme of yours is pretty much the only other option."

Rodolphus frowned slightly. "That obvious, huh?"

"That obvious, I'm afraid."

"I still think it's a good plan, though."

"I somehow doubt its viability."

"So I guess that means you aren't going to join up."

"Don't be stupid, Rodolphus. Of course I'm going to join up."

Tiberius raised his hand to block the small hail of fritter as Rodolphus began choking on his last bite.

"You what?" Rodolphus managed.

"I'm on board with your idiotic scheme."

"Why? I thought I was going to have to beg you!"

"I'll be honest. Praying isn't all it's cracked up to be."

Rodolphus grinned. "I knew it!"

"Besides, I'm a Minarian," Tiberius said, the corner of his mouth rising slightly. "We pray with our maces for one hand and our enemy's skulls for the other."

"Well, damn! This is already going a lot better than I thought!"

"Granted, we'll still need some more team members."

"Yeah. I figure we can start with one more and then pick up some others as we find them."

"All right. So, no ideas for possible joiners?"

"No one who isn't dead. Or who I don't owe money. How about you?"

"No one who could stand to spend an extended period of time with you."

"Huh. Well, do they still hang personal ads at the watch station?"

"Yes, I believe so."

"Let's go see if anyone is hiring out their services."

"Ah, yes. I'm sure the finest swordsman in Selan will have posted an ad there. 'Available: incomprehensibly skilled fighter. Fee, five Nam and one pint mead per week'."

"Don't be so negative. Let's give it a try."

"Very well. I'll call the waitress for our bill."

"Ah, about that. Do you think you could spot me on this one, Tiberius? I'm a little short."

"Just like old times," Tiberius said dryly, reaching for his money pouch.

Chapter 10

The streets only became more crowded as they made their way to the nearest watch station, and the body heat, combined with the sweltering sun, did not make for a pleasant temperature at ground level. Sometimes, Tiberius considered moving out of the most populous city in the known world. Then again, Selan was the seat of Minarian worship (as it was the seat of a dozen other religions), so it was there that he would stay.

Except, of course, when he had a mission of war to carry out. Minar would not only understand that, but be most gratified to see one of his followers taking the fight to the enemy. To Minar, after all, 'the enemy' was a vague concept, and one that tended to encompass pretty much everyone with a sword that you weren't personally friends with.

Selan was the sort of city wherein half of its residents claimed to despise it, and yet their hate was colored by affection. In that bustling, dusty, wind-swept metropolis, such people actually thrived. If one of these people were taken away from the noise and the heat and the claustrophobia, they'd become suddenly unsure what to do with themselves. Often enough they'd end up the scourge of a smaller community somewhere, as the instincts that made one competent in Selan were the same ones that made one a criminal mastermind in most other places.

As they neared the watch station, Tiberius noticed Rodolphus' back tensing, and his head occasionally turning to make sure they weren't being observed. Considering the sheer number of people around them, of course, going unobserved was not a realistic goal. Tiberius sighed, reaching out and tapping Rodolphus on the shoulder. The other man didn't notice, of course, since there were several inches of metal between his skin and the prodding finger.

Tiberius shook his head. That armor. For himself, he'd put on his chain shirt, with his blue Minarian tunic and red Minarian tabard over it. The tabard, which covered all but his arms, had the head of a hissing wyvern carefully embroidered in the center. All in all, it weighed only a fraction of what Rodolphus had on him.

"Rodolphus!" he said in what was a low voice for the crowd but would have been a yell anywhere else, "worried about someone seeing you?"

Rodolphus shot a glance his way. "Well, you never know about the watchmen, Tiberius! They're always out to get guys like us!"

Tiberius rolled his eyes. "Rodolphus, what in God's name did you manage to do? Practically everything is legal here, short of theft and murder!"

Rodolphus smiled. "Turns out we can add setting watchmen on fire to that list."

Tiberius felt a sinking feeling in his chest. "Oh, God. Why would you have done such a thing?"

"Hey, he should have minded his own business. I would have won that fight if he hadn't intervened."

"So you burned him."

"Oh, he was fine. I'm not a murderer, Tiberius. I just ruined his uniform, that's all. And maybe just a little of his skin."

Tiberius raised an eyebrow, but decided the other man was joking. It was always extremely hard to tell. "Hmm. Will he recognize you?"

"I doubt it. It was dark. Until the fire, I mean."

"Well, you'd better hope he doesn't," Tiberius said, pushing his way out of the crowd and towards the southeastern watch station, at the front of which was a lane lined with fruit sellers' kiosks only marginally less crowded than the main road. Like most buildings in Selan, the watch station was square and made of tan sandstone, coated with a layer of yellow dust kicked up from the dry city roads. The building was tall enough to provide a nice rectangle of shade, which Tiberius was grateful for, wiping his brow as they headed for the door. How Rodolphus managed not get heatstroke in that armor was beyond him.

They reached the door together, but when Rodolphus paused, Tiberius stepped in front of him and pushed through it, glad to be out of the dust and the heat. Light streamed in from two large, smeared windows, illuminating the front room of the station. It was a small, square room, with a hall leading to the north and then turning off to the right. A desk was placed partially blocking the hall. The guard at the desk, wearing dusty leather armor and a red cap, didn't look up from the book he was reading as Tiberius walked in.

As he'd remembered, the walls were covered with posters and listings. Rodolphus tentatively wandered in after Tiberius and soon had his eyes glued to a section of wanted posters. Tiberius stepped over to him and leaned close. "Expecting to find one with your picture on it, are you?"

Rodolphus growled. "No. I told you, it was dark. See if you can find any personal ads listed by mercenaries."

"Here are some," Tiberius pointed out, crossing to another wall. "'Crossbowman for hire, three years combat experience.'"

"No," Rodolphus said, coming over, "we don't need a crossbowman; I've got the whole distance angle covered."

"Your modesty never ceases to leave me awed."

"Shut up, Tiberius."

Tiberius didn't have time to reply before a sound broke the relative silence of the room, drifting in from the hall behind the guard. It was a laugh, but not a normal one. It was a long chuckle, loud and high, almost shrieked. The guard seemed to tremor slightly, but didn't look up from his book.

"What in God's name was that?" Rodolphus asked.

"Probably just a lunatic. I think they keep those in here sometimes," Tiberius murmured, eyeing the hallway uneasily. He'd never heard anything quite like that cackling before.

"You know, once we get a fighter, I'm definitely ditching this spear. I can't believe the army made me learn how to use a weapon. Waste of everyone's time."

"I've never seen you use that spear, come to think of it. Or any weapon, actually."

"What am I, a savage? Hey, here's one," Rodolphus said, moving along down the wall. "'Master fencer, skills unparalleled in all the land.'"

"'Unparalleled' is misspelled. Four ways."

"So what? A fencer doesn't need brains. Just a sword and the ability to stand between me and whoever we're fighting."

Tiberius sighed. "Whatever happened to hiring the best fighter in Selan?"

"Supply suddenly plummeted."

Tiberius frowned, but couldn't think of an argument. All the personal ads he could see were mediocre, and besides, as he'd already pointed out as they'd walked, what would a halfway decent swordsman post a personal ad for anyway?

"How about this," Rodolphus said. "'Master of exotic and foreign weapons, including the mysterious Jorngera.'"

"And what, pray tell, is a Jorngera?"

"I'm not sure. Is that one of those ones with the ball on the chain?"

"No, Rodolphus. That's a flail. Did you even attend combat school?"

"I attended the important parts."

"You know, even conjurers should have basic weapons ability. What'll happen if someone gets within your easy casting range?"

"I don't have an easy casting range; I can fry someone at an inch. And anyway, that's what the armor is for."

"That, and giving you back problems."

"God, you're negative. I should have gotten one of those silent monks to be my healer."

"That'd be quite a trick, since most curative magic requires spoken commands."

"I'll give you an extra five percent if you agree not to talk for the remainder of our time together."

"Oh, Rodolphus. I'm not in it for the money," Tiberius said cheerily, patting Rodolphus on the shoulder.

"Oh, goody."

"Well," Tiberius said, leaning in to read the small print of yet another sign, "I guess this one doesn't sound too bad. 'Master axe-wielder, willing to take on any job. Has felled forty foes.'"

"Foes is a little vague. Are we talking rabbits here, or…?"

"We could look him up and ask him. I'm sure he's a perfectly nice, stable person, and a fine conversationalist."

Rodolphus frowned. "I'm beginning to think that this may be a lost cause. Maybe we should conside—"

He trailed off as the loud chuckle sounded once again, both men turning to look at the guard, who resolutely kept reading his book.

"All right," Rodolphus said, "I have to know what that is." He turned and marched to the guard's desk, rapping his gauntleted fist against the pitted wood.

The guard slowly lowered the book and peered up at Rodolphus. He looked angry, but also tired, and somewhat pale.

"Can I help you?" he asked through clenched teeth.

"Would you mind telling us where that hideous laughing sound is coming from?" Rodolphus asked pleasantly.

"Yes, I would mind. Beat it; it's none of your business."

Tiberius was starting to get a little curious himself, and stepped around both Rodolphus and the guard, heading down the hall. Rodolphus quickly followed.

"We don't want to trouble you. We'll just go check it out ourselves," Rodolphus said, voice dripping with insincerity.

For a moment, the guard looked as though he was going to intervene, sitting up straight and putting his hand on the hilt of his shortsword. But then he sighed and slumped back down. "Fine, what do I care? I'll just count you as his visitors. The gods know he won't be getting any others."

Tiberius looked at Rodolphus and raised an eyebrow as they walked to the end of the short hall and turned into another, this one wider and leading to a dead-end. A few doors on either side probably led to offices and break rooms, and after that the stone walls became partitioned by wrought iron bars. The end of the hall had eight cells, four along each wall. It was lit only by two skylights cut directly into the sandstone overhead, casting bright light into the chamber and clearly illuminating the dust swirling lazily through the air.

A single guard, dressed similarly to the one at the desk, sat on a small wooden stool against the back wall of the hallway.

"Visitors?" he asked tiredly, looking up at them.

"Apparently," Rodolphus muttered, prodding Tiberius slightly in the back. Tiberius took the cue and began walking down the hall, looking into each pair of cells as he did. Of the first two, one was empty and one contained two wiry-looking teenagers, both sitting against the back wall of their cell. The cells lacked even beds, and each contained only a couple of ragged sheets and cloths heaped in a pile and a pail that obviously served as a chamber pot. There were no windows. A single bar of each cell was truncated near the bottom, leaving a gap big enough to push food through. Tiberius considered that a prisoner could probably grab a guard's leg through the gap if he wanted to, but eyeing the hatchet leaning in the far corner near the guard, he didn't imagine that this would be a very good idea.

The next two cells both contained older men who were asleep. One had his head resting on the rags, while the other had sprawled out directly on the stone floor. Probably drunks, Tiberius decided, a common sight for an urban jail. The next two cells...

The first one Tiberius looked into, on his left, was not only unlocked, but the barred iron gate was wide open, flush with the inner wall of the cell. A small wooden bench was resting against the back wall, and on it sat yet another guard, this one with a large crossbow sitting in his lap. A razor-sharp bolt was loaded, and Tiberius quickly noticed that the firing mechanism was taught. The crossbow was ready to fire, and the guard's finger was resting against the trigger switch. He stared at Tiberius with wide eyes.

Tiberius took a step back so that, were the arrow loosed, it would no longer plant itself firmly in his intestines. "That's bad practice," he reprimanded. "You shouldn't keep that thing loaded, and at the very least you ought to take your finger off the trigger. What in damnation are you so worried about, anyway? "

He had turned to look into the cell across from the guard, in which lurked, presumably, the threat that the arrow was meant for. It was not what he was expecting.

"What… what the hell…"

He heard the clanking noise indicating that Rodolphus was walking over to him, but couldn't bring himself to turn his head away from the thing in the cell.

"We're not sure what it is," the guard on the stool said, voice tense. "It showed up in town about a week ago. We've had word from other stations that occasionally weird creatures show up and that they usually aren't a threat, but this one…"

"I've heard of man-beasts," Rodolphus said, breathless, "but I didn't think I'd ever see one."

The thing in the cell was, indeed, some kind of man-beast. It stood on its hind legs like a man, though the legs narrowed at the bottom and bent oddly back at the knees, like the legs of a dog. The feet, broad and clawed, were padded at the bottom. A short, scraggly tail hung down between its thighs.

It was dressed as a man, with short pants that came down to the knee, a battered suit of leather armor that covered its chest, abdomen, and groin, and dingy black metal plates protecting it shoulders. Its massive, muscular arms ended in human-like hands with deadly-looking claws. Its incredibly thick neck practically burst from its armor, raising up and then jutting forward into a ferocious canine head with proud, pointed ears at the sides and a tapered snout that ended in a broad black nose. Its entire body was covered in matted brown fur, spotted with mottled grey.

It cocked its head and stared back at Tiberius, favoring him with a grin, showing a mouth full of white, pointed teeth. Without warning, it lunged forward, grabbed the bars, and shook them like playthings, causing a terrible racket and a torrent of rock dust to plume from the spot in the ceiling where the bars were bolted in. It took everything Tiberius had to stand his ground; he was able to keep his reaction down to an almost imperceptible shudder. Rodolphus, standing next to him, had managed similar fortitude, though Tiberius thought he saw a slight flash as Rodolphus cancelled a reflexively-cast spell.

The guard behind them was less level-headed. As the bars shook and the entire building seemed to shake, Tiberius heard a loud twang from over his shoulder, and knew immediately that it was too late for him to do anything about it. The bolt shot by within inches of his stomach. It went through the bars, past the beast, and stuck in the back wall of the cell, vibrating.

The thing in the cell stopped shaking the bars, though its hands stayed gripped around them, and turned its head to look at the bolt. Slowly, it turned back to Tiberius and seemed to lock eyes with him. It opened its mouth and howled out its repugnant laughter, throwing its head back and filling the air with the terrible, disconcerting chuckle.

"YEE-HEEHEEHEEHEEHEEHEE!"

Tiberius suppressed another shudder and turned to deal with the guard behind him. Rodolphus was ahead of him, having already stepped into the cell. He grabbed the crossbow from the man's limp hands, marched back into the hallway, and hurled the device one-handed through the air. Seconds later a brilliant orange ball of flame, roiling and crackling, shot out of his palm after the crossbow, overtaking and colliding with it in midair and causing it to explode into splinters of wood and metal. The debris clattered to the ground with the sound of a very brief hailstorm. The guard didn't react. He merely sat on the bench, staring at his feet.

Rodolphus turned to the guard at the end of the hall, who during the fray had stood up and drawn his sword but notably hadn't advanced at all.

"I'd love to hear some more about the thing in the cell," Rodolphus said.

"It showed up about a week ago," the guard replied unhappily.

"I know that already!" Rodolphus roared, lightning briefly crackling around his fingers. "What else?"

The guard's sword arm fell limply to his side. "It went to the Yeoman Tavern by the docks and started drinking and eating. When its tab came up it wouldn't pay for anything, and when they tried to make it... well, it brought the place down."

"It knows magic?" Rodolphus asked, his voice heavy with skepticism.

"No, I mean it physically brought the building down. Places by the docks aren't exactly well-built anyway, but that thing is incredibly strong... stronger than any man. We had to reinforce the cell before we put it in there."

"Did it kill anyone in the bar?" Tiberius asked, eying the creature. It seemed to be staring right back at him, listening intently to their conversation. One of its hands still gripped the bars.

"No, a few were hurt, but injuries were surprisingly minimal. Probably because almost everyone cleared out as soon as the thing showed up."

"Ah. How the hell did you capture it?"

"It passed out drunk in an alley a few blocks away. All we had to do was get it on a cart and haul it down here."

Rodolphus laughed. "I see. And what are you going to do with it?"

"We're trying to get it transferred to a more secure facility. The building owner at the Yeoman is too terrified to press charges for assault, so right now it's just being held because it can't afford to pay to have the building put back up. Fortunately, I don't think he'll ever have the means to pay. It's a wonder we got him before he caused any more damage. I have a feeling we got off light."

"Ahhh, lucky you. How much is the fine?"

"One hundred thirty Nam."

Tiberius winced. His stipend barely paid out that much in two years. The thing in the bars would indeed never be able to come up with such an amount.

"One hundred thirty, huh?" Rodolphus said. "All right, we'll take him."

"I'm sorry?" the guard said, frowning.

"I'll pay to get him out," Rodolphus said, digging around in the pouches hanging on his belt.

"Rodolphus, what are you doing?" Tiberius asked.

"What do you mean? Isn't it obvious? We just found our fighter."

"Rodolphus, in addition to not being human, he is a criminal and probably insane. This is a momentously poor decision, even for you."

"You prefer the 'unpuralild' fencer? This is the best we're going to do, and frankly, I think he's going to be a killing machine on the field."

"I agree. He'll kill you, and me, and whoever we're fighting, and whoever hired us…"

Rodolphus was now counting out money. "You see what I meant about you being negative? Here we are with a good thing going, and you're trying to stymie us."

"Not just trying," Tiberius said firmly. "You can't afford one hundred thirty Nam, and I'm not lending you any money. We're not doing this."

"Oh, hush. I won't even make you pay your share of him, since you bought lunch," Rodolphus said, walking over to the guard and shoving an impressive pile of coins into his hand.

"There you go, my good man. One-thirty Nam."

"But… but…" the guard stammered.

"One hundred and thirty Nam?" Tiberius growled incredulously. "What happened to you being 'a little short'?"

"Hey, when you live like I do, one hundred thirty Nam *is* a little short. And anyway, after this, I really will be broke, so I suggest you get used to the idea."

The guard was staring at the money in his hand as though it were an illusion. "You can't do this," he said quietly. "He's a menace."

"Oh, you lawmen. All he did was bring down a tavern that's probably better off destroyed anyway. Open the cell."

"No," the guard said, somehow managing to bring his eyes up to face Rodolphus. "No, I won't."

Tiberius saw the armored plates on Rodolphus' shoulders shift as he stood up straighter, a sure sign that he was getting angry.

"The law is on my side," he growled through clenched teeth. "Release him."

The guard looked pleadingly over Rodolphus' shoulder at Tiberius.

Tiberius looked back, and then let his eyes wander to the spot where the beast's cell door was bolted to the ceiling. It looked like it might not hold much longer. Suddenly, Tiberius wondered whether the thing was really all that much safer locked in here. Actually, considering the behavior of the watchmen...

"Well," he finally said, "he is right about that. There's no reason we shouldn't be able to pay to free him. You can't hold him for crimes that you're worried he *might* commit."

The guard's face sunk. Tiberius half expected the place to flood with guards to have them thrown out, but it didn't happen. The one in the cell hadn't gotten up from his seat, and the one from the front desk still hadn't appeared, even though he could no doubt hear everything. The third guard slowly unclasped the key ring from his belt, walked over to the cell, and unlocked the door, the thing inside staring at him the entire time. Tiberius braced himself, imagining that the animal would slam the door open the moment it was unlocked. Instead, it waited for Rodolphus to pull the door open, and calmly stepped out. It looked first at the guard with the key and then at the one who'd nearly shot Tiberius, its shoulders shaking with laughter that this time emerged only as a barely audible chuckling.

"Did he have any possessions?" Rodolphus asked calmly.

"Yes," the guard said unhappily, "One. We'll bring it to you once you're outside."

"Fair enough," Rodolphus said, "but we're just going to come back in for it if you don't. Tiberius, Wolfie, let's go."

Tiberius, trying not to stare at the beast, turned and walked down the hall toward the exit. A quick look over his shoulder confirmed that Rodolphus was following him, with the massive creature trailing slightly behind. They passed the guard at the desk, who had put his book down and was resolutely watching them.

"Thanks," Rodolphus said mockingly.

"Good riddance," the guard said, and his eyes didn't leave them until they were out the door. At least that, Tiberius thought, explained why the guards ended up being willing to let the thing go.

They stood around in front of the station, waiting for one of the guards to appear. It didn't take long. Someone opened the door, heaved something out, and then slammed the door shut again. On the ground in front of them was a massive single-edged sword, almost too big for a human to use two-handed. Its blade was slightly curved and surprisingly clean, and glinted in the sun. Its hilt, on the other hand, looked like two thick, crooked sticks tied together to form a T, and had been wrapped tightly with strips of white cloth.

The beast picked the sword up with one hand, swung it over its head, and slid it through two leather straps it wore around its body, so the sword was held firmly in place against its back.

Out in the streets, the three of them bunched together and began pushing their way back through the crowd. This was significantly easier than it had been before.

By the time the sun went down, they were back in Neylon's restaurant. They were sitting, in fact, at the same table they had that morning. Tiberius sighed softly. Back together for a day, and already the old unoriginality was starting to shine through. Of course, there was at least one change. An entire ring of tables around theirs was uncharacteristically empty.

Tiberius wasn't a gambling man, but he felt he had a pretty safe bet on the cause of their unpopularity. At the moment, crammed awkwardly onto a chair, the thing was holding a steak in both hands and ripping hunks off of it with its fangs. It hadn't taken very much convincing to get the waiter to bring them a raw steak.

"Well," Rodolphus said, watching the thing eat with fascination, "let's start with the obvious question. What the hell is it?"

"I've heard of non-human intelligent creatures before," Tiberius offered, wondering as he said it whether word "intelligent" was really the correct choice. "They live on the far continent. Only a few ever come here. Sometimes you can see them working at circuses and the like."

"He is one of those, then. I mean, sure, I've heard of them. Aren't they supposed to be able to speak, though?"

"Well, ours might be able to speak, too. We haven't asked him."

They both looked at the creature. It lowered what was left of the steak and stared right back at them.

"Can you speak our language?" Rodolphus tried.

It seemed to smile, then picked up its stripped steak bone, placed it in its mouth, and bit down, cracking the thing open with a sickening snap. Its teeth began making a noise like boots on gravel as it chewed up the bone, smacking its lips as it gained access to the marrow. Every now and again, it spat a bone shard onto the table.

Rodolphus coughed. "I guess we'll take that as a no."

"I think he can understand us, though," Tiberius said.

"Yes, I don't think there's much question of that, the cheeky devil."

"Of course, the issue remains of whether or not he's actually a good fighter," Tiberius said, lowering his voice and keeping an eye on the wolf. He wasn't sure how fast it would be to take offense, and he didn't want to risk making it angry.

"Of course it's a good fighter!" Rodolphus said indignantly. "You saw the way it shook that cell door, it was like the whole place was going to come down. Besides, it has a sword, doesn't it?"

"There's more to fighting than being strong and swinging a sword around."

Rodolphus frowned. "Is there? That's all that the swordsmen I know ever seem to do."

"And they," Tiberius said patiently, "probably think that all you do is wave around your hands and murmur gibberish. They don't appreciate the special training and years of work that you've put in."

Rodolphus growled. "Those bastards! You're right, the whole bunch of them have the combined intelligence of a mussel!"

"No, you're misunderstanding me—"

"I'm glad we didn't get one of those morons we used to run with, now that you mention it! This fellow here, he's better than the whole lot of them put together, if you want my opinion."

"I've nev—"

"Never wanted my opinion, yes. You're getting predictable, you know."

Tiberius sniffed indignantly. "I guess we should figure out what its name is," he muttered.

Rodolphus nodded and turned towards the beast. "Hey, you! What's your name?"

It looked at him quizzically, seeming to shrug its shoulders. The shrug turned into a rolling quake as it threw back its head, the fur on its neck bristling, black gums rolling back from its razor-sharp teeth.

"EEE-HEE-HEE-HEE-HEE-HEE!" it cackled, tongue lolling just slightly over the side of its jaw. There was a sound like a plate shattering from somewhere in the kitchen, and every diner in the place eyed the beast with trepidation. Tiberius dug his fingers into the worn wood of the table edge. This might be, he lamented, something that'd he'd have to get used to.

It was only then that it really occurred to him that signing on with Rodolphus might not have been his best decision.

"We could call it Yee-hee," Rodolphus suggested, no sign of distress in his voice.

"Yee-hee. I don't think that it really does the thing justice."

"Hurm. Well, I guess just 'the Wolf' is going to have to do for now."

"I suppose."

A waiter, quivering slightly, appeared from behind Rodolphus, placing a small tray onto the table. A teapot and three clay cups sat on it, and Tiberius reached out promptly to the pot and poured the dark tea inside into each of the three cups. As Rodolphus reached out to take one, Tiberius took another and handed it across to the Wolf, who grasped it awkwardly in one massive hand, furry fingers crossing over the top, thumb clasping the bottom.

"Drink that," Tiberius said. "It's good."

The Wolf cocked its head slightly at Tiberius. Then it threw back the entire contents of the cup into its waiting mouth.

Of course, as Tiberius had already gleaned from the temperature of the pot's handle, the tea was exceedingly hot. The Wolf howled out immediately in pain, doubling forward, furiously wiping its tongue off against the back of one if its furry arms.

"Maybe they don't do tea on the other continent?" Rodolphus suggested, sipping carefully at his own.

"Maybe not. You should be more careful, Wolf," Tiberius said, trying to put a note of force in his voice.

The Wolf seemed unimpressed, glaring at Tiberius and reaching one hand around its back.

"Hey, now, none of that," Rodolphus said. "We already paid for one bar you destroyed; we can't afford to cover this one."

The Wolf seemed undeterred, but it paused slightly as Tiberius, inexplicably, reached out again for the tea kettle, righted the Wolf's cup, and refilled it.

"Now, try it again," Tiberius said, "but sip it this time."

A slow, rumbling growl emanated from the Wolf's throat as it scooped up the cup in both hands and poured a small amount of tea into its mouth. It seemed to consider for a moment before spitting the tea out, creating a sizable stain on the table cloth.

"I guess he doesn't like it," Rodolphus said, reaching out to pour himself another cup. "Maybe they have some hot chicken broth or something in back. I bet he'd enjoy that."

"I'll bet," Tiberius said, sipping his own tea and watching the Wolf over the brim. A fan of tea or not, its anger seemed abated, and its eyes were now following a lazy black fly that had been buzzing around their table for most of the night. "Rodolphus, I seriously worry that we've bitten off more than we can chew."

"What, are you kidding? We can chew anything! And what we can't chew, I can always just incinerate."

"There are some problems, you know, that can't be solved by magic."

"Name one."

Tiberius frowned. "There are thousands. Magic can't make you happy, or bring you love, or bring people back from the dead…"

Rodolphus snorted. "Oh, come on! You can use magic to become rich and powerful, and those things bring both happiness *and* love."

"The kind that you seek, perhaps, but not the true kind."

"Oh, listen to you. You've been spending too much time in that church. You've lost your grip on reality."

Tiberius sighed. There was always the possibility, however slim, that Rodolphus was right, and that everything would be fine. Maybe a few months ago, when he'd still been on active combat duty, all this business with the Wolf wouldn't have shaken him at all. Spending all that recent time in prayer and meditation could well have altered his world-view, and likely in a way that trended away from pragmatism.

"And besides," Rodolphus continued, breaking into his train of thought, "magic can raise the dead, too. Haven't you ever heard of Necromancy?"

"Yes," Tiberius said, rolling his eyes, "but, as the great scholars before us have always eventually decided, you cannot truly raise the dead with Necromancy. You merely create shadow-things."

"More religious nonsense. I've heard that some undead retain full ability to think, as well as their memories. What does it matter what state their body is in, so long as they have those?"

"Surely even you must realize that there is more to living than a mind. Our physical bodies are important parts of us, not to be cast off so readily. Not to mention that without the divine spark of our souls, our minds would slowly warp and become twisted..."

"YEE-HEE-HEE!" the wolf chortled, causing Tiberius to start. He'd almost forgotten it was there, but now it was staring right at him, its dark, unpleasant eyes focused on his.

"Yes, that's about the response that statement deserved," Rodolphus said. "Like I said, too much time praying. That religious garbage won't save you from death."

"Well," Tiberius said, frowning and breaking eye contact with the Wolf as he pretended to analyze the clumped tea leaves at the bottom of his cup, "if you're so sure about all this, why not go find a necromancer and get yourself immortalized?"

"If you run into a necromancer, send him my way."

"Well, since you mention it, I happen to…"

"Oh, fine, fine," Rodolphus sighed, waving a hand, "you're right that I'm not entirely certain about this soul business. There's even a degree to which I'm sort of intrigued to see if there might be something else beyond this life, which isn't a curiosity I'd ever be able to satisfy if I were undead. And that'd be annoying."

"Rodolphus Plymouth, sirs and madams. The man willing to face death in order to avoid annoyance."

The Wolf howled with laughter again. Tiberius decided he'd better try to take it as a compliment.

Rodolphus grabbed the apron strings of the waiter, who was passing by and making a distinct effort not to make eye contact with anyone at their table.

"We'll take the bill, killer."

The waiter's eyes visibly tracked over to the Wolf, which had torn up its placemat and was now using its claws to pry up splinters of wood from the tabletop.

"Oh," he stammered, "it's on the house. Yes, yes, all free. But we're going to close up early tonight, so if you please…"

"Ah, yeah, time to go anyway," Rodolphus said, grabbing hold of the table for support as he forced his armor-covered body into a standing position. Tiberius followed, and the Wolf, thankfully, got up and came after them without needing to be told.

"A free meal!" Rodolphus proclaimed once they were outside, reaching his arms out and stretching his shoulders, "I could get used to this!"

Tiberius glanced back at Neylon's, just in time to see the door slam shut and hear the bolt slide into place. "I think they're trying to tell us something," he murmured.

"What was that?"

"Nothing, nothing. Where are we staying? My place can't take three."

"Your place can barely take one. We'll go to my room at Stelak's inn; I've got a few nights there yet."

"You actually paid for multiple nights in advance? That shows... unexpected foresight."

"Don't get too excited. I won the room off some jackass in a card game."

"Ah, yes," Tiberius said, shutting his eyes briefly as the three of them ambled down the street, a path through the crowd forming naturally around them. "How silly of me."

Chapter 11

The mansion seemed large and extremely ornate, though, as it turned out, only in contrast with the absolute poverty that surrounded it. Even the roads were in a state of disrepair, barely qualifying as roads so much as places where all the grass happened to be dead. The people milling about were sallow-skinned and sunken-cheeked, not straying far from the tiny straw and peat huts scattered sparsely around the valley.

Apparently, the trio riding in on the back of the hay cart was unusual enough to jerk even people as down-trodden as these into a certain state of awareness, as Tiberius was certainly noticing a good number of vacant stares directed at them as they passed. Many of the onlookers were staring at the two horses pulling the cart. Out of envy for their worth and health, Tiberius hoped, rather than out of a desire to eat them.

The Wolf, thankfully, lay asleep in a pile of hay, the wooden sides of the cart obscuring him from the view of the locals. The carriage driver had certainly found the Wolf odd enough early on, but he was from Selan, so he was used to hauling unusual passengers. Normally he brought travelers along with goods from the city, but this time there was little cargo in the wagon. The driver had told them that this was because the town had stopped sending any produce to Selan. As Tiberius looked at the people, he found himself wishing that he'd thought to bring them some goods anyway.

Granted, he would have had to sell the clothes he was wearing to pay for them. He was completely out of money, and, assuming he was telling the truth this time, so was Rodolphus. They'd sat in Selan for three weeks before Rodolphus found a job he felt was worth taking.

He certainly hoped that whatever lead Rodolphus was on to in this place paid off, because otherwise they weren't going to be able to afford to get back to Selan.

The manor house was a white, two-storey affair, surrounded by a picket fence that was somewhat dingy up-close. The wagon slowed as they approached the gate, and Tiberius gratefully lowered the rear door of the wagon, swinging out and dropping to his feet. He stretched his back and legs, yawning softly. In the cart, Rodolphus began prodding the Wolf awake.

"Do you think that's a good idea?" Tiberius asked. "We should probably leave him out here while we're talking to the governor."

"Are you crazy? He's our main selling point," Rodolphus said, poking the Wolf even harder. Its eyes snapped open, its neck cracking loudly as it pivoted its head to either side.

"Come on there, Wolfie, time to go meet our waiting audience."

It got up, grudgingly. The gate was unlocked, so the three of them proceeded up the main path to the manor itself.

"Do you want me to wait?" the cart driver called after them, eyeing the locals suspiciously. The pathetic crossroads he'd stopped the wagon at was the center of the cluster of homes which were the entirety of the town.

"Please. We have no desire to walk back," Rodolphus called back with a wave of his hand, eyes still focused on the house. The brown oaken door swung open as they reached it, causing Rodolphus to pause slightly, as though worried about poltergeists. However, a neatly appointed butler swiftly stepped into view from the side and beckoned them in. He seemed to be reconsidering this gesture when he noticed the third member of their party, but there was little he could do about it by then. The two armor-clad men and the giant beast tromped over the threshold and into the entryway, which led off into a hall straight ahead, as well as a dining room on the left and a staircase on the right. The butler, attempting to regain his composure, squeezed by Rodolphus in order to get to the front of the group.

"If you'll follow me, erm, sirs," he said, turning and heading down the narrow hall. The three followed him, clanking as they went. Tiberius took in everything, noting the grandfather clock by the door, the neatly arranged furniture in the dining room, the statuettes on a shelf halfway up the stairway. An above-average home by Selanese standards, perhaps, but truly an extraordinary one in so destitute and rural a place.

The hall led to a smaller dining chamber; Tiberius gathered that the one nearer to the front door was for entertaining guests. On one side was a small shut door that may have led to a kitchen, but the butler took them through a doorway in the opposite wall, leading into a nicely-appointed parlor.

There, resting in a leather armchair, was the man they'd come to see. He was tall and may have been strong once, though now he was clearly aging and looked to have gotten used to a somewhat sedentary lifestyle. His skin was dark brown, and his head was dominated by a mane of wild black hair that merged at his cheeks with a bushy black beard. He wore a scarlet robe of the relaxing rather than the magical persuasion, and held a glass in one hand. Tiberius was impressed to note that when the man first laid eyes on the Wolf, the only sign of surprise he gave was the rising of one of his bushy black eyebrows.

"Governor Temnos," Rodolphus said, leaning forward into a quarter-bow, which Tiberius had long ago discovered was the best he could do without the weight of his armor carrying him the rest of the way to the ground.

"We're pleased that you have made time in your busy schedule to see us."

"I'm pleased you came," Temnos said warily, taking a sip from the red liquid in his glass. "Welcome to Byara. I am impressed by your credentials. The humble money I've been able to offer hasn't attracted any private armies so far, and yet here is one led by experienced combat casters. Surely, you do the work of Yutali."

Tiberius knew that Yutali was the primary local deity, typically revered as the god of the harvest. In Selan, his worshipers were considered naïve at best and unqualifiedly stupid at worst. Comparing Yutali to Minar almost made him want to step out of the room to have a quick laugh. Instead, he nodded politely.

"Surely," Rodolphus said, his voice dripping with the false sincerity that seemed, inexplicably, to work a good deal of the time. "Well, we would be happy to assist you for the wages that you offered. Perhaps you could give us some details about the problem?"

"Of course," Temnos said, running his fingers through his beard. "Our shipments to Selan are being hijacked. Nearly nothing we send gets through anymore, no matter how many guards we assign to the caravans. And because the road is so long, it is days before we even get word that our shipments have not arrived. We are bringing in nothing. At this rate we will not even be able to afford seed for next year. These have become lean times indeed. Which isn't to say, I suppose, that we have ever had truly prosperous times. But we will not be able to survive this for much longer, I fear."

Rodolphus nodded sympathetically. "That's terrible, Governor. We'd love to come to your aid. We'll quickly find out who is robbing you, and deal with them as they deserve."

"I warn you that it may not be easy. We've lost many good people—and not a few hired escorts—to these brigands, whoever they are. I think they may be quite numerous; the gods only know why they are picking on us and not someplace more prosperous. What is the fighting strength of your army?"

Tiberius winced. Here it came.

"It's just the three of us, Governor," Rodolphus said, his voice indicating that there wasn't anything strange about that.

The Governor was mid-drink and nearly choked on a mouthful of wine, his hand clenching the arm of his chair. He managed to get it down before taking a deep breath.

"Just the three of you," he managed.

"That's right, milord," Rodolphus said. Tiberius wondered if Rodolphus really thought that such a chipper attitude was the best way to go. He also wondered why he was letting Rodolphus do all the talking. Presumably because it was his insane, indefensible idea that they were here to promote.

"Would you mind if I asked why," the Governor said slowly, setting his glass on the side table, "you are wasting my time?"

"We're not wasting your time, Governor," Rodolphus said, a note of hurt feelings in his voice. "I assure you, we are three of the most powerful fighters for hundreds of miles around. As you yourself said, we are battle-hardened magic-users, and our furry friend here is the strongest being to have ever walked the continent."

"Is he," Temnos said drolly. "He certainly looks it. For all the good it will do him, when a bandit force that outnumbers you ten to one fills him with arrows."

"You worry about farming, Governor," Rodolphus said, his friendly façade barely holding up, "and we'll worry about fighting."

"Yes, well, that would seem ideal, wouldn't it? So, let me make sure I understand. I'll pay you a fee suitable for a small army so that you can carry out a mission you're incapable of carrying out. I will then allow you to leave with all this money, either to get slaughtered in battle or else to run way with it, never to be seen again. Does that just about cover everything?"

"You listen to me, old man," Rodolphus began, and Tiberius saw that his right hand was quivering. It was a bad sign. It meant that it was time to say something.

"We don't expect the full fee up-front, sir," Tiberius interjected, cutting Rodolphus off. "We don't even need half. Just give us some start-up money to get things going, and we'll come back for the rest once we've finished the mission."

Rodolphus' shoulders slackened, though only slightly. Tiberius breathed a sigh of relief. The Wolf, oblivious, was looking around, boredom clear on its face. As Tiberius watched, it began staring out the window at a bird perched on a tree branch.

"Ah. More reasonable, yes," Temnos said, "but still a rotten deal."

"Governor…" Tiberius said, his hopes plummeting back down into his stomach. He wasn't sure how Minar would feel about his becoming involved in a martial dispute over money with a bunch of peasants, but he knew how *he'd* feel about it.

"You are right, of course," Temnos said, a note of resignation in his voice. "This is still a bad deal for me, but a little hope is better than none. And I can barely afford to upset you. I doubt you can deal with the bandits, but I'm more than confident that you can deal with me."

Tiberius' eyes darted to the Wolf. It could easily take that last statement as a request. Such would not be a fortuitous turn of events.

Luckily, it was not paying attention, its dark eyes still focused on the window.

"It's a deal, then," Rodolphus said. "As soon as you get us our 'start-up' money, we'll get on our way. It shouldn't take us more than a couple of weeks, I'd expect."

"No, I rather expect it will all be over much sooner than that. And how much money do you want, exactly?"

"Fifty Nam should do us," Rodolphus said, his cheerful fakery back in full force.

Temnos laughed. "What, are you going to pursue the bandits in a gilded carriage transporting a ton of caviar? Ten Nam."

"Forty-five."

"Fifteen."

Tiberius found his own gaze wandering to the window. This would take a while. He noted that the bird he'd thought the Wolf was looking at was no longer visible. There was, however, a peasant boy within sight not far away, hard at work with a hoe. The Wolf, he could now see, was staring intently at the boy.

"Friend of yours?" he asked it quietly, frowning.

It looked at him, and it smiled.

———————————————————

Acrid smoke burned Tiberius' nostrils and blurred his vision, curling in greasy black tendrils away from the four ruined wagons. The stench was one he remembered well. There was, he reflected happily, nothing else like it.

He shifted his mace into a two-handed grip just in time to put his back into a full-tilt swing with the bloody implement, slamming it with bone-crushing force into the shoulder of an oncoming bandit. The man probably shrieked, but the sounds of combat and the crackling of the fires were far too loud to be sure—his ears were still ringing from Rodolphus' first spell of the fight. The bandit's scimitar fell out of his hand as he collapsed, and Tiberius turned to look for his next opponent, but none were within striking range. Skirting quickly around the nearest of the blazing carriages, he came into sight of Rodolphus.

Rodolphus, as he tended to do in combat, was laughing. Or, anyway, his face certainly suggested that he was. His spear lay forgotten on the ground beside him. Blood was trailing down the front of his armor from an arrow sticking out between plates. Between his bare hands, raised over his head, a massive blob of bilious liquid appeared, suspended unnaturally in a bubble that Rodolphus slowly stretched to the size of a wagon wheel. Exhaling with satisfaction, he unceremoniously hurled the mass at a group of bandits taking cover behind a smoldering cart. The flowing orb flew with surprising grace to its targets before bursting against them, and this time the shrieking was definitely loud enough to be heard over the fire.

Tiberius turned away and stepped over a dead body emitting almost as much black smoke as the wagons, noting with pleasant surprise that most of the men who had come with them from the town, the name of which he'd already forgotten, were still alive and fighting bravely. It probably didn't hurt that their opponents, by this point, must have been remarkably demoralized. They fought with fear in their eyes, all thought of material gain forgotten as they struggled merely to stay alive.

Even that, Tiberius considered, was a futile hope. He turned his head just in time to see a wiry looking one attempting to flee the battle, and skirted into the man's path, swinging the razor-sharp fins of his mace just short of his opponent's face. The bandit, scowling from behind a gritty black beard, growled and thrusted with a long rapier.

Longer than Tiberius thought, in fact, as it slashed a deep gouge across his cheek, blood swiftly running down his face and wetting his lips. Turning his head to deflect the next gouge off the side of his helmet, he took a long step forward and swung low with the mace, shattering the man's right knee and sending him tumbling to the ground. From there, it was a simple matter of stepping on the blade of his sword and clubbing him once over the head.

It hadn't been a hard thing to lure this group of bandits into combat. After many weeks of success, they'd become so overconfident that they'd attacked the caravan with little or no scouting beforehand. They saw the seven figures, garbed in the rough-hewn hemp cloaks of farmers, and assumed that they would be little threat. When it came to four of those figures, they were mostly right. But the other three…

When the cloaks were thrown off, things changed, and the bandits were losing the fight before they even knew that they were in one.

The wind changed, blowing smoke into his eyes, blinding him. He stepped quickly aside, his eyesight clearing just in time to see another foe running toward him. Tiberius attempted to bring up his mace to block the attack, but there was no point. The charging bandit was stopped in his tracks as a storm of blade-sharp ice crystals shot past and through him, tearing hundreds of bloody cuts into his unarmored body. Saying a silent thanks to Rodolphus and looking around for more opponents, Tiberius pulled off his glove and pressed his fingers into the cut on his cheek, muttering an incantation under his breath. He felt the cut close up, leaving only blood behind. Leaving his glove on the ground behind him, he turned and went at a quick jog over the hill that the road wrapped around. The sounds of battle were now focused largely on the other side.

The Wolf, fur matted with blood, was howling balefully as it swung its massive sword two-handed like a club. Tiberius came to the top of the hill in time to see the blade smack into a bandit's stomach, slice cleanly in, and then lift the man into the air as it hit the resistance of his spine. The Wolf howled gleefully as it finished its swing, sending the body flying through the air. It was no longer in one piece when it landed.

The state of the corpses nearby was no better, Tiberius noted, and indeed, corpses were all that was left. The Wolf's massive head slowly surveyed the carnage, then turned upward to the top of the hill, eyes locking onto Tiberius. Slowly at first, its back-bent legs began carrying it up the hill towards him. Its shoulders beginning to rock wildly as it picked up speed, its great sword gripped tightly at the waist, blade hanging out to the side.

Tiberius frowned. "Hey, now!" he yelled at the top of his voice, "It's me! The fight's over!"

It showed no sign of understanding or even hearing, now mere yards away, lunging at him, sword swinging mightily towards him. He was barely able to throw himself out of the way, his shoulder hitting the dry earth moments later. He brought his mace up to defend his face, aware that his reaction was much too late, and waited for death to come.

"YEE-HEEHEEHEEHEEHEE!"

He looked up. It stared down at him, tongue lolling out of its mouth as it panted, its sword hanging loosely in one hand.

"That wasn't funny," he stammered, still holding his mace in front of his face.

It threw back its head and howled more laughter, turning its back on him and pacing away. As it did so, it threw its upper body into a wild shake, and droplets of blood flew off in all directions.

"That wasn't funny," he repeated, quietly this time, mace shaking in his hands until he remembered to lower it. He carefully got to his feet and brushed himself off, turning to look after the Wolf. It had wandered back to the wagons. Most of the fires had gone out, though the wagon that had been filled with hay was still blazing orange and red, fire licking the bright afternoon sky.

Rodolphus was leaning against one of the smoldering wagon wrecks, and three of the four men who'd come with them were looking similarly tired, cleaning off their low-quality swords against white rags that quickly became red. The fourth lay still near to them, felled by a bandit's axe.

"Did you see what that lunatic just did?" Tiberius said, walking resolutely down the hill toward the armored mage.

"You mean when he took the big one's head off? Yeah, that was messed up," Rodolphus said, sounding shaken and tired but nonetheless grinning. His face was slick with sweat and blackened by smoke, and he turned around as Tiberius approached. His hands were busily fumbling at the clasps that held his breast plate and shoulder armor on.

"Help me get this off, would you? I need you to heal my arrow wound."

"All this armor," Tiberius said, pushing Rodolphus' hands away and undoing the clamps himself, "only to have an arrow find its way through."

"Hey, you should have seen how many arrows were deflected. All things considered, I think I did pretty well."

"Yes, I'd say so. It wasn't a fair fight, of course. They didn't have any healers or combat casters."

"Nope. They just outnumbered us three to one, that's all."

"Yes, but it was immediately more like two to one after that initial thing you did."

"Those who don't want bolts of lightning shot through their chests would do better not to stand so neatly in a row."

"Mhmm. I'm sure these bandits will remember that next time." He pulled off the back section of Rodolphus' armor, then reached around and began to unfasten the breastplate.

"Speaking of which," Rodolphus asked, "did we leave any alive?"

"I'm pretty sure at least one of the ones I brought down is still alive."

"Getting soft, are you?"

"This is war, not a Sunday tournament. Minarians no more take prisoners than we expect to be given that reprieve ourselves."

He paused as Rodolphus stared at him blankly.

"Which is to say, not at all."

"Ah, right. I think I'd rather be taken prisoner, myself. So I take it you're planning to finish the job?"

"Well, no, they're out of combat now, so it would be cowardly and murderous to kill."

"Your religion is idiotic, do you know that?"

Tiberius sighed. "Why did you ask about live ones, anyway?"

"I was hoping you'd left one, so we could question him. And it's so hard to take someone alive with magic, you know?"

"With the kind of magic you practice, perhaps."

"Sorry, I should have specified. Worthwhile magic."

Tiberius smiled politely as he finally got the breastplate off. "So I guess you don't want me to heal this after all?"

"Erm. No, I think you'd still better."

"Do you."

"Fine, fine, healing magic is legitimate as well."

"See? Isn't it fun to be nice?" he walked around to face Rodolphus, grabbed the arrow, and roughly pulled it out, tossing it over his shoulder.

"Oh, gods in Heaven! You son of a bitch!" Rodolphus moaned, hands shooting to the wound. Tiberius pushed his own hands under Rodolphus' and chanted, slowly closing the bleeding gash.

"Next time," Rodolphus panted, "please check to see if the arrow is barbed before you do that."

"Don't be such a baby," Tiberius snorted, bringing back his hand and inspecting his handiwork. "That one was only sort of barbed."

"You're lucky you're not expendable, or I'd give you the acid treatment that our archer friends got."

"Ugh. No thank you—I've developed a certain fondness for my skin." Tiberius turned away and began making a slow round of the battle site, stopping at each live villager and healing up their wounds. They averted their eyes as he did so—whether in awe or fear, he wasn't sure.

"So where's the live one?" Rodolphus called, sitting down and attempting to refasten his armor without assistance. He gave up within a minute.

"I could have sworn he was right over here..." Tiberius stared at a matted place in the grass where the man with the crushed shoulder had fallen. "I thought he went unconscious, but he must have gotten up and ran off while I was distracted."

"Hell," Rodolphus said, lying back on the grass, "I thought that none of them had gotten away."

"So did I," Tiberius said, frowning. "Where's the Wolf, anyway? You know he almost took my damn head off."

"Oh, come on, you know how the heat of battle is. I nearly set you on fire at least three times today. You're lucky you're the only one with a stupid little dragon on his shirt, or I just might have."

"It wasn't during the battle," Tiberius said grimly, "it was right after. He knew I wasn't an opponent. He was doing it for kicks."

Rodolphus shrugged. "Bloodlust, you know. Melee fighters get that kind of thing all the time. What do you expect, with a combat style like his?"

"I think 'combat style' is a bit generous of a word for what he does."

"You're right. It's more like lumberjacking."

"Better. So what's our next lead, if we don't have a live one to question?"

"Hmm. Well, their hideout might not be too far from here. We'll see if we can follow their tracks. And we'll search their bodies; see if we can find any maps or some such thing."

Tiberius frowned. "Sounds like pretty slim odds, if you ask me. Do you think we need to find their hideout at all? It's always possible that we just killed all of them."

"No, no," Rodolphus said, shutting his eyes, "there are always more at the nest. They're like rats. Anyway, whoever's organizing them is probably there, and if we collect our pay and he raises a new group and starts terrorizing the farms again, we take a pretty serious bump to our reputation."

"We have a reputation?"

"We do with those three hicks," Rodolphus chuckled, waving his hand lazily towards the three townspeople that had fought alongside them. "We wouldn't want to ruin all the hard work we just did impressing them, would we? Next time they take a caravan into Selan, they'll be telling everyone about us."

Tiberius sighed. If he wasn't so sure that it had all been sheer dumb luck, he'd say that Rodolphus had taken this mission based on the notoriety gained and not just the amount of money.

"You and the Wolf will have a reputation, anyway," Tiberius said, putting a tone of mock sadness in his voice. "I'm just the little old healer."

"I agree that you're far less manly than either of us, but you do provide the valuable resource of keeping us from dying after every fight. Speaking of which, you might want to heal the Wolf. I'm sure he's covered in wounds."

"Yes, he is. Unless all that blood came from other people, which isn't out of the question."

"Well? Hop to it."

"...Has anyone ever actually acceded to the order 'hop to it'?"

"You would be the first."

"Mhmm. Well."

"...Fine, *please* go heal the Wolf."

"Hmm."

Rodolphus growled. "Is there a problem?"

"I don't know that I want to heal him, after what he pulled on the hill."

One of Rodolphus' eyes shot open. "Hey now, he's a key member of our team! He's the perfect hitting-stick. We may as well start calling him 'Cudgel.' He won't be much use to us if he bleeds out."

"We can replace him. There are others just as good."

"You know, I'm surprised at you. You can't agree to come along on a mission and then refuse to heal comrades. That's practically rule one for guys like you, isn't it?"

"Perhaps. But threatening to kill me presents something of a breach of contract."

"Don't take it so personally. He's got an odd sense of humor, that's all. But without him, we'd be back in Selan dancing for money. Our team won't work without him."

"Hmm."

"Well?"

"I suppose I will heal him. Because to do otherwise would be a breach of honor."

"Yes, it would be. Where the hell is he, anyway?"

Tiberius briefly scanned the area.

"I don't see him…"

"Well, he has to be around here somewhere."

"Ah, there he is."

"Where?"

"He's up on the hill. And he's doing something…"

"Is he walking about in circles? Dogs do that sometimes, you know."

Tiberius ignored him, walking slowly up the hill to get a better look. "Oh, God."

"All right, all right," Rodolphus sighed, sitting up, "What is it?"

"He's eating someone!" Tiberius exclaimed, throwing his hands up in the air and running up the hill. Rodolphus frowned, scrambled to his feet, and followed after.

The Wolf didn't look up as they approached, too busy opening the man's ribcage to bother with its visitors.

"Eww," Rodolphus commented.

"I can't believe this," Tiberius growled. "That's the one I left alive! He's eating the one I left alive!"

"Well, if it's any comfort," Rodolphus said, "I don't think he's alive anymore."

"We can't have him doing this. We have to get him under control."

"I agree; eating bodies is pretty out of hand."

For a moment, the two men stared at each other.

"You tell him," Rodolphus said, turning and walking casually back down the hill.

"Me? He doesn't listen to me, you jackass, he only listens to you!"

"Ah. Well, actually, I think I'm beginning to see an upside to this. We won't have to pay to feed him now. That was starting to get pretty pricey."

Tiberius frowned, staring down at the burgundy-soaked jaws of the wolf, savagely tearing away into the freshly slain body. Killing a man in combat was one thing; a noble thing, something done with honor. But this…

He shook his head and turned away, following Rodolphus back down the hill. This was not war as he remembered it.

Chapter 12

Tiberius stared upward, neck aching slightly.

"This one's bigger than the others," he said.

"Well, I'll be."

"From the top, there's probably a pretty good view of the valley."

"I'll bet there is."

"It's probably the biggest tree I've ever seen."

"Probably."

Tiberius frowned and glanced at Rodolphus, who was sitting with his back against a tree trunk, holding a dry leaf in one hand and watching as a tongue of flame slowly worked down from its center tip.

"Are you paying attention?"

"No, not in the slightest."

Tiberius barely held down the urge to start yelling. "May I ask why?" he tried instead.

"Because we're lost in this forest."

"This isn't a forest. It's a grove of trees. We entered it about two minutes ago."

"Well, fine, we're just lost. We need to get our bearings."

"That's what I'm trying to do," Tiberius growled.

"What, by looking at the trees? Something about the direction the moss grows in?"

"No, you brainless clod," Tiberius began shouting, "by climbing the tree to get a better view! But I know that the high science of 'looking around' must be completely lost on the kind of intellect that you possess!"

Rodolphus frowned, flicking away the leaf stem. "Hey, relax, Tiberius."

"Relax? Why should I relax? What's even the point of this? That abomination is just going to kill anyone we find anyway, and then we'll be back where we are now! It's a lost cause!"

"Now, look, I already told you. I specifically ordered Cudgel that he's gotta leave at least one enemy alive next time. He understands perfectly."

"I didn't sign up for this, Rodolphus."

"Then what exactly did you sign up for? Sunshine and daisies? This is war, Tiberius."

"Is it? Are you sure of that?"

"We're killing people with weapons, aren't we?"

"Yes! Yes, and then we're eating them!"

"Oh, lord. This again."

"Yes, I'm afraid it's this again!"

"Look, back in the army, the dogs used to go at the bodies on the field. This isn't any different. He's an animal. It's a natural thing."

"It's not the same. The dogs ate out of hunger. He... he eats out of..."

"Hunger, man, I'm telling you. He's just a big stupid dog with a sword!"

Hearing the insult, Tiberius quickly swept his eyes around the grove. "Where the hell is it, anyway?"

"It's probably hunting deer. Since it's an animal."

Tiberius slowly leaned forward, resting the front of his helmet against a tree trunk. He took a deep breath. "Maybe you're right."

"I'm always right."

"Battle of Trevalt, six years ago?"

"I'm usually right."

"Hmm."

"So, tree?"

"Ah, yes," Tiberius said, breathing deeply. "Tree. We need to get up it."

"I feel I should point out that if you hadn't dismissed our three villagers yesterday, we could be using them as scouts right now."

"They were never meant to be anything more than decoys. This is our job. So we're stuck with the tree."

"Enjoy your climb."

Tiberius glanced up the tree trunk. He'd have to go pretty high if he wanted to get above the other trees, and handholds were sparse, with large gaps looming between the branches. As it was, he hadn't climbed a tree in years.

"I... don't think it's going to work out."

"Join the club."

"You need to levitate me up there."

"Do I? Doesn't seem like I need to do much of anything."

"Would you *please* levitate me to the top of the tree?" Tiberius growled.

"That would be an Enchantment spell, Tiberius. Do I look like an enchanter to you?"

"You look like a Wizard to me. Do you mean to tell me you can't even cast a simple Enchantment spell? What the hell were you doing at school?"

"I'm a conjurer," Rodolphus growled. "I don't see *you* levitating yourself up there."

"It's a different situation. I was trained in a religious tradition. We only heal."

"And I only conjure! What part of this aren't you understanding?"

Tiberius opened his mouth to respond, then shut it, sighed, and sat down against the tree he'd been leaning against.

"You know what? We need to start getting more sleep."

"You *are* becoming pretty irritable," Rodolphus said. "...And I'm always this way," he admitted after a few moments.

"All right, let's think."

"Do we have to?"

"You can produce wind, right?"

Rodolphus snorted. "Of course I can."

"Right. So why don't you blow us up there?"

"I've never done that before."

"Correct."

"It sounds pretty unsafe."

"Quite so, I'd imagine."

"But I could probably save myself if things went south."

"Probably."

"Okay, I'm in."

"Good. Should we... should we go find the Wolf?"

"If you think we can go into the woods looking for him without him mistaking us for prey..."

"Let's not go find the Wolf."

"Good idea."

Rodolphus, brushing himself off, clambered to his feet and walked over to the base of the tree. Tiberius stood up.

"Uhm." Tiberius said, "I guess I should put my arms around you."

"I suppose that would be the best way," Rodolphus sighed.

"If you could make some kind of platform we could ride up on..."

"No, making things that solid is extremely difficult."

"Ah. Well, then."

He stretched out his arms and wrapped them around Rodolphus' chest, which was really quite wide, what with all the armor. He gripped a leather strap with each hand.

"All right," Rodolphus muttered, "one... two... three!"

It was somewhat akin to being hit in the chest and being sent flying—an experience that Tiberius was not unfamiliar with—except that the trip through the air lasted far longer than usual. Tiberius' vision became a blur of green, the sound of his helmet rustling and tearing through leaves permeating the air around him. He heard a loud cracking sound followed by a barked swear from Rodolphus, but couldn't see what had happened.

Suddenly they were above the tree, in the air. Without support. Their ascent began rapidly slowing as they drifted somewhat lazily just a few feet further up.

"All right," Rodolphus said, his voice tense. "I'm going to let go and stop the wind entirely. Be ready to grab on to something. If I don't make it, come heal me. I'll be the shattered carcass on the forest floor."

"I'll try to remember that," Tiberius managed, and then they were falling.

It seemed only a fraction of a second before his body hit a cascade of leaves and twigs, and immediately he shot out his arms and tried to find purchase. His hands roughly snapped through the first several branches they encountered, and fear had begun to well up in him before he finally managed to catch one arm over a thicker branch, bringing his body to a sudden and shoulder-wrenching halt.

His arms quickly began to ache in protest, and he pulled the rest of his bulk up and over so that he was sitting at the intersection of several wide branches. He sat there for a while, taking deep breaths. He removed a glove and began rubbing his finger across the scratches that the branches had cut on his face, closing the wounds.

"Tiberius?" came a gentle cry from nearby.

"I'm up here," he called. "Where are you?"

"Further down than you," the voice came back pitifully. "I think I broke my arm at some point."

"I'll heal it as soon as I can," Tiberius said soothingly. "For now, try to take a look around."

"All right."

Following his own advice, Tiberius surveyed the view. He was very near the top of the tree, and had only to move a few thin branches aside to get a good look out over the entire valley. He gripped a hand tightly over one of the branches he sat on as vertigo tugged at his senses. It was a very long way down.

"I don't see anything!" Rodolphus cried miserably. "Just the westernmost farms of Byara."

"Oh, good, then you're looking out the other side of the tree," Tiberius called. "We can get a full view." Fighting back the urge to look directly downwards, he instead let his gaze sweep out across the valley, which became gradually hillier in the north as it headed toward the great desert.

His eyes lingered suddenly on a spot in the hills several miles northeast of their position, where a small plume of wispy gray smoke stained the sky.

"I see a fire!" he shouted triumphantly. "It could be them!"

"Well, make sure you know where it is, because we're not coming back up here!"

"I'm with you on that one, Minar knows. I'm not seeing much of anything else. I guess that's our best bet."

"I can see the townspeople who were with us earlier, heading back home."

"Hah. Too bad they can't see you. I think that'd really put the finishing touch on this experience for them."

"I could make them see me," Rodolphus said cheerfully, and Tiberius heard a noise like the crackling of electricity.

"Rodolphus, if you could avoid broadcasting our presence to the bandits, I'd really appreciate it."

The crackling abruptly ceased. "Oh, fine."

"All right. Northeast to the hills."

"Right. Northeast."

"Now. How do we get down?"

"I'm going to jump. I can use wind blasts as I go to alter my speed and direction, so I should be able to land pretty softly."

"All right. What about me?

"Wait a few minutes, then jump. I'll create a cushion of air for you to land on."

"But what if you don't respond quickly eno—"

"See you at the bottom!"

"Rodolphus! Wait, Rodolphus!" He cringed as he heard a lot of rapid rustling, which receded quickly downwards until he couldn't hear it at all.

"Son of a bitch," he groaned.

———————————————————

Warm blood splattered onto Tiberius' face as the Wolf's sword cut deeply into a bandit's shoulder, then was roughly pulled out and thrust through the man's chest. The corpse fell to the ground in a heap, resting at the foot of one of the small temporary shacks the bandits had been living in, nestled here in the sparse, barren valley made by several small hills. A horse tied to a stake mere feet away bucked and whinnied as it tried to tear free of its moorings. It was a very impressive horse, Tiberius noted. It was probably a purebred, no doubt stolen by the bandits from a nobleman somewhere far nicer than Byara.

The young bandit Tiberius himself had been fighting turned and ran, stumbling over the half dozen bodies of his fellows that were strewn in his path. Tiberius ran after him without any particular grace but with at least a bit more speed. He brought up his mace and swung it into the bandit's unprotected head, sending his opponent twisting to the ground.

Tiberius leaned down and felt for the man's pulse, which was present, if a bit erratic, and laid a bare palm on the back his head, murmuring under his breath, channeling enough Curation to stave off excessive blood loss through the gash the mace's fins had cut. The man remained unconscious throughout, and Tiberius clambered back to his feet, turning to look toward the Wolf, who was ferociously exchanging sword blows with a bandit wielding a great sword almost as big as the beast's own. Another bandit, this one a huge man wearing a heavy breast plate and a full-face greathelm, emerged from a small building behind the Wolf, a large axe held in one hand. With the other, he brought up a hand crossbow and shot a bolt into the Wolf's unprotected thigh, causing it to issue a howl of rage. Tiberius began to pace toward them, leery of the giant armored man, but his attention was quickly pulled away by an obnoxious crackling sound that was growing louder and louder. His eyes searched the barren dip between hills for the source of the sound.

It was Rodolphus, his hand extended, a ball of roiling lightning like those Tiberius had seen him use before suspended over his palm. The crackling became louder and louder as, while Rodolphus chanted, the ball began to shrink, decreasing in size until it was merely a small blue orb suspended over his palm. The glowing ball bounced and rolled in place like an oversized luminescent marble, no bigger than the pommel of a sword. It was emitting a sound that was now spectacularly loud, a constant low buzzing that seemed to make the very ground tremor. When it finally left the conjurer's hand, it was not thrown, but rather Rodolphus turned his palm out to face the large bandit and the thing shot forth as though projected by a ballista, flashing across the air in an instant and colliding with the man's chest.

Everything went white, and a sound like a very nearby thunder strike exploded outward from the collision. It took several seconds for Tiberius' eyes to clear, hazy purple specters flashing in front of his vision as the bandit slowly came back into focus. His body lay on the ground. His extremities were still intact, but little more than a blackened crater remained where his chest had once been.

The Wolf was staring at the body as well, his own opponent dead on the ground in front of him, cut wide open horizontally. It would appear that while the bandit had stopped fighting during the arresting flash of light, the Wolf hadn't let a little thing like temporary blindness stop him.

By now there was but one opponent left, and he knew when he was defeated. By the time any of the three mercenaries noticed he was still alive, he had untied the attractive bay horse and was kicking it up into a gallop, heading down the middle of the valley as quickly as he could. Tiberius walked over to Rodolphus, who was panting slightly between slow chants as he lifted a hand tiredly and seemed to swat at the air in front of him, sending a bright blur of fire streaking through the air. It looked way off target, but at the last moment veered towards the man on the horse, striking him in the back of the neck. He was still near enough for them to hear the shrieking as his upper body was engulfed in flame, and he tumbled off the horse, which kept right on running.

"That's a shame," Tiberius said, licking blood off his lips. "That was a beautiful horse."

"Yeah, it was," Rodolphus agreed, short of breath. He leveled his arm in the air, pointing one finger at the diminishing quadrupedal figure. With a single utterance, a slim line of blue lightning shot out from his finger, arcing across the valley to the horse, making contact with its right rear flank.

As if in slow motion, the bay collapsed cataclysmically mid-gallop, tripping over its own legs, crashing into the ground and scraping and sliding across it as its momentum was used up on its broken body.

"Hey," Rodolphus said, grinning. "Ten points."

Chapter 13

Trevos' eyes opened slowly, groggily sweeping back and forth, waiting for the blurry landscape to come into focus. For some reason, it refused to do so. He could make out shapes, but all the edges remained fuzzy, the colors running into each other. Something felt hard against his back—was he sitting up against something rocky? He heard a sound like someone taking a pull on a whistle, only it wasn't stopping, and he had a good mind to find whoever it was and mess them up. His hand felt clumsily around his face and rubbed across his slick forehead and into his matted hair, stopping as it found a place near the back of his head far damper than the rest. He drew back his hand and saw his fingers coated in red. He stared at them, trying to figure out what it meant.

"Good afternoon," a voice said, and Trevos spun his head around to look, which was a mistake, because what had been a numb, throbbing pain quickly turned into a quick stabbing one. He winced and held his head still, letting the pain slowly recede.

"What's the matter, kid? Don't feel good?"

"No," Trevos managed, "don't feel good." He listened to the voice as carefully as he could, which was not very carefully considering how loud the ringing was getting, but he didn't think he recognized it. Come to think of it, where the hell was he?

"Hey, Tiberius, get your ass over here."

He'd been with the others...

"You too, Wolfie, time to earn your keep."

Bronson was telling a funny story about a whore and a high priest... and then something...

The blurry figure in front of him came a little more into focus. It was a man, bulky and dark. Trevos flinched away. He remembered the man now, he thought. But not well. He just remembered laughter, and fire, and screaming, and running.

"You'll have to speak more loudly," Trevos said, hoping the words were coming out in the right order, "to be heard over the whistling."

He couldn't see well enough to judge the other man's reaction. Two more figures had appeared on either side of the speaker. One was slightly smaller, the other significantly larger. If he squinted he could just about make out the face of the one in front.

"You hear that, Tiberius? The whistling."

"It's the head wound. Here, let me try to get him more lucid."

The blur on the left made a move, but the center one raised its arm.

"No, no, we don't do him any favors unless he does us some first. That's how the game works."

"He's no good to us like this. He probably doesn't even know his own name."

"My name is Trevos," he said. There was a growing feeling of apprehension in his stomach, and something in his head told him that it would have been much better not to answer.

"There, see? Sober as my grandmother. For whatever that's worth. All right, Trayvos, who's the boss? Who hired you? Where is he?"

"Trevos," he insisted, that unclear feeling in the back of his head still averring that he wasn't handling this correctly, "my name is Trevos."

"Trevos, then," the figure said, and despite the high-pitched whine he could tell that the voice had become a little darker. "Who do you work for?"

"I don't remember," Trevos said dreamily, but the urgency shot through the fog again and reminded him that yes, he did remember that much, actually.

"I don't believe you," the figure growled.

"Answer our questions," the one on the left said, "and I'll heal your head wound. You'll be able to see and think clearly again."

"Will that goddamn whistling stop?" Trevos asked.

"Yes," the figure responded soothingly, "the whistling will stop."

Trevos opened his mouth to talk again, but a little more fog cleared, and he remembered five months ago when he'd first met his employer. The man had taken him in; given him steady work when no one else would. He'd given him a home and a family of sorts, and they'd all trusted him quickly, far more quickly than he'd expected. His friends—hadn't he been with them, very recently? Some of them, at least? Where were they now? He couldn't remember.

He'd barely even had time to realize what a good thing he had, how much his life had improved. That it was banditry was, of course, a non-issue—for most of his life he hadn't even had anything worth stealing, so why should he care about people who did?

But now that was over, probably. Then again, the one named Ti...Ti *something*, seemed all right. He might make it back home after all.

"I don't remember, though," he lied, hoping it sounded true. Hoping he sounded as confused as he was.

"Don't you. He knows that the wound will heal on its own, that's what it is," the center one jeered. "He thinks he's outsmarted us, this uneducated piece of trash, this mountain-wandering peasant. This *criminal*."

"Rodolphus..." the calmer voice said, sounding tired—but also distressed.

"I don't remember," Trevos insisted, and knew it was the wrong thing to do, knew he should be getting quieter, not louder, knew he shouldn't let them see that he could care, because then he could lie as well.

"You tell us who you work for, and where he is," the bulky man growled, "or we'll cut your goddamn arm off."

It took a moment for that to register. As it slowly sunk in, the man on the left hissed and muttered something, and the central one whispered back, all too quietly for Trevos to hear. He felt his mind sharpening a bit further, but that cursed ringing was still there. Still, he was smart enough to know that the one was explaining to the other that he was bluffing.

"You won't cut my arm off," he declared knowingly.

He understood immediately that this had been a mistake. The remaining fog cleared instantly as alarm bells exploded in his head, urgency invading his brain as it tried to drive adrenaline into his weakened body. It failed to enable him to stand, though he did begin to twitch.

"...We won't cut your arm off?" the dark voice said, incredulous, amazed, nearly laughing. "Did you hear that, Wolf? He says *we won't cut his arm off!*"

"Rodolphus!" the other voice yelled, almost loud enough to cover the high, quiet sound, the sound of a blade being dragged over stone, which abruptly halted as the large figure stood straighter. Something that glinted in the light appeared over its head. The air exploded with a new sound now, one that pierced through the whistling, indeed, made Trevos forget all about the whistling. It was a loud, high chuckle, nearly shrieked, emanating from the huge thing, the thing with the sword, the thing that even his fogged eyes could see was quaking with its own mirth, its head thrown back.

"YEEHEEHEEHEEHEEHEE!" it shrieked, utterly blocking out the yelling of the other two men, who now seemed to be struggling against one another.

Neither his eyes nor his reflexes were good enough to catch or evade the blade, but his nerves could still sense the pain as his flesh was sheared, his shoulder disjointed and torn free. He could hear nothing now, but was sure that he was screaming, trying to huddle away into the rock he sat against, warm wetness slowly traveling down his tunic, coating the side of his chest.

No sound anymore, nothing, not the cackling, not the whistling, not even his own weeping. His stomach roiled and its contents flowed up into his mouth, sending him doubled over and hacking as it spilled onto the dry ground. The right side of his body felt like it was being slowly and excruciatingly incinerated.

Slowly, his eyes, which somehow could see all the better now, crept back up to his captors. The big man, covered in armor, was staring down, his mouth neutral, his eyes wide and fascinated. The other human, a few paces back, was looking at the ground. And the butcher... the butcher... he saw it, and now he remembered.

He remembered everything that had happened, and he knew that they were all dead, and that he was the last one alive, if you could even call it that anymore. He was soaked in his tears and his blood and his vomit, and he looked at the one in the middle.

"Kill me!" he screamed, "just kill me!"

He still couldn't hear, but the words the man spoke were simple enough to read on his lips. "Tell us."

"Crutchfield!" Trevos wailed, "Lord Crutchfield, of Yunder! He hired us all! Our orders come from him! Now do it! Kill me!"

"All right," the man in the armor said, and this time, Trevos' vision was clear enough to watch the sword as it swung down.

"Tiberius! Tiberius, come back!"

Tiberius shook his head, staring resolutely ahead, his boots scraping the gravel as he rounded the far side of one of the barren hills.

"Where the hell do you think you're going, anyway? We're in the middle of nowhere!"

"Home, Rodolphus! I'm going home!"

"It's a long walk."

That was true. Tiberius was almost looking forward to it. Anywhere was better than here.

The sounds of Rodolphus' footsteps became louder, and were joined by the clanking of his armor and the heaving of his breath as he jogged to catch up.

"You can't leave. We need you."

"Yes, my staying would assist you. I don't think that's what I want."

"Come on, Tiberius…"

"Come on?" Tiberius growled, refusing to take his eyes off the bland horizon before him. "Come on? You've lost it, Rodolphus. You've lost your grip on things."

"What are you talking about? I'm the same as always. It's the same as when we were in the army."

"No, it's not. It took me a while to figure it out, but it's not."

"It's exactly the same! It just pays better!"

"God dammit, Rodolphus! Don't you see? The lack of supervision… and that… that *thing*… they're changing you. It's not like it was before. It didn't used to be so… savage."

"*War*, Tiberius? War didn't used to be so savage? Maybe not from where you were standing, but I can tell you first hand that it wasn't any more peaceable than what happened back there!"

"We didn't eat bodies in the war! We didn't cut the arms off defenseless people and then murder them in cold blood afterward!"

"Don't be stupid! You really don't think the army ever interrogated anyone?"

Tiberius halted abruptly. He spun around to face Rodolphus, fists clenched tightly. "When they did, do you really think it was like *that*?"

Rodolphus stumbled over his feet as he tried to bring himself to a halt, his breath coming in pants.

"All right. All right, fine. Maybe you're right. Things got a little out of hand."

"That man had a concussion."

"Yeah, that's right. Because you hit him in the head with a mace."

"In combat, Rodolphus! He was armed and we were in battle!"

"Oh, gods, listen to you. Listen to how you make yourself feel better about what you do for a living."

"Don't do that! Don't act like it's all the same! It's not, and you know it's not!"

"Look, just calm down—"

"I will not calm down! You had that monster cut that man's arm off! You told me you weren't going to! You promised me!"

"I... I didn't think we were. It's just... he questioned us, and—"

"He questioned you? What are you now, Rodolphus? Are you a king? A god? That the very act of questioning you warrants death?"

"He asked us to kill him, Tiberius."

"Yes." Tiberius took a breath, let it out. "Yes, I suppose he did. Anything to get away from us. To get away from the trio of animals who walk like men."

"Don't be so dramatic…"

Tiberius slowly allowed his muscles to relax, taking another deep, stuttering breath.

"Listen, Rodolphus. It just has to be over for me now, all right?"

The face looking back at him was, for the first time Tiberius could remember, devoid of any cockiness or arrogance.

"But I need you, Tiberius. I can't do this without you."

"You're going to have to. I won't blame you for anything that happened. I just need you to understand that I have to leave now."

"Tiberius, please. I'm asking you, as my friend, to stay with me just a little longer."

Tiberius forced himself to meet the other man's eyes.

"Why? Why would I do that?"

"You heard what the bandit said. Lord Crutchfield. I've heard of him. He's a big-time noble. Runs his own city. This is big, bigger than anyone thought. He needs to be stopped before he gets too powerful for us to bring down."

"You can find someone else to help you."

"No, I can't. He'll figure out what happened here, and have time to prepare for us. We can't give him that advantage. We have to go straight there. There's no time for any stops."

"And that animal? You're asking me to keep traveling with it, as well?"

"You were right, I think. Bringing it along was a mistake."

"At least you… no. No, wait."

"What is it?"

"You're lying to me, Rodolphus. You're lying to my face."

For just a moment, the other man's soft, handsome face cracked into a sneer.

"And what makes you say that?"

"I know you."

"We'll drop Cudgel as soon as this thing is over, I swear."

"Your word is about as good to me as an unstrung bow, Rodolphus."

The man growled. "Then what about the bandits, huh? You're going to let them keep robbing and murdering people while you go strolling back to Selan, secure in your moral outrage? Is that going to make you feel good about yourself?"

Tiberius sighed, shutting his eyes, trying to think. For a moment, there was silence.

"We won't torture anyone else," Rodolphus eventually offered.

"That may be the truth, but only because we shouldn't need to. We know exactly where we're going."

"Well, same thing. It doesn't matter *why* we're not torturing them."

"It doesn't surprise me that you think so."

"You're going to go to the end of this with me, Tiberius. Maybe you know me, but I know you, and you can't leave this unfinished."

"Do you think so?"

"Yes. You'll stay through to the end, because neither your god nor your own honor will allow you to walk out on a battle that's unfinished, especially when it's one that you know is just, in the end."

"I see. You think I'll let that get in the way of what I've watched that monster do?"

Rodolphus paused. "No," he said eventually, "No, you'll stay with us until this is over. But then you'll leave, and I may never see you again."

"I think you're right."

"I'm sorry for losing you, Tiberius. But I'm glad I haven't lost you yet."

Tiberius opened his eyes and looked Rodolphus up and down.

"I can't tell whether you're telling the truth or not."

Rodolphus chuckled. "Another good reason to come back. To find out."

Tiberius—slowly—began walking back toward the encampment. "All right then, Rodolphus. To our last adventure."

"Our last adventure."

They trudged along in silence together, the scrub putting up little resistance to the steps of their heavy boots. Tiberius hadn't gotten all that far: the site of their battle was still clearly visible, black smoke curling away from smoldering clusters of wreckage scattered around the corpses. Rodolphus, Tiberius had long-ago discovered, tended to try to deny the enemy cover by torching every cart, structure, and even fencepost in sight.

"Crutchfield, then," Tiberius said, eventually.

"Right. Governor of Yunder, and administrator of the whole Southwestern Province."

"I know nothing of Yunder."

"I know it by reputation. Medium-sized city, borders Gravel Lake. Not nearly as big as Selan, but bigger than any of these hick farm towns we've been through. I imagine it's operating like Crutchfield's private estate, by this point. It's going to be rough."

"Rough we're ready for. Rough is just about all we can handle."

"Yes, it is."

"All right. We'll head there immediately. What's the quickest route?"

Rodolphus fiddled in one of the pouches on his belt until he located a small, folded map. He opened this out until it was the size of a page from a large book.

"There's a town pretty close. We can go there and get a carriage, and take that to Yunder. We should be able to outrun news of our victory over the bandits."

"Fine. Let's get the hell out of here."

"I'm with you there."

Tiberius sighed. "Rodolphus?"

"Yes?"

"I hate some of what has happened. But I want to apologize for a moment ago when I accused you of lying to me. You have always been a good friend, and I do believe that your word has honor. You're too pragmatic to part with the Wolf now—that's how you and I are different, and why I'm not cut out for your kind of war— but you say you'll drop him when the mission ends, and I believe you. You're a pragmatist, but you are a noble man."

Rodolphus smiled and put a hand on his shoulder.

They walked into the camp, dark now that the sun had mostly set behind the hills. The Wolf was nowhere in sight, but the young bandit he'd slaughtered was visible as a dark spot against the hillside on the other side of the encampment. Tiberius stared, thinking about reattaching the boy's arm, but he knew that he couldn't. The boy was dead, and the domain of the healer was that of life. Or at least, it was supposed to be.

Chapter 14

The rented wagon creaked under them as it was pulled over the poorly-paved road toward Yunder, the walls of which now took up a good deal of the horizon. They'd gotten the horse and wagon at a cheap rate, and would be expected to return it by the end of the week. Tiberius would be interested to see whether or not that happened. After all, they might have to leave in a hurry.

Actually, if things went according to plan, they'd definitely be leaving in a hurry.

Yunder was a big enough town that two of the three of them probably wouldn't turn any heads, but they wore their cloaks over their armor anyway. The Wolf laid on the floor of the wagon, sleeping in its usual fitful manner. Rodolphus seemed to have dozed off himself, sitting on the bench behind Tiberius, snoring softly as his body rocked back and forth with the jerking of the wagon.

As they approached the open city gates, Tiberius pulled on the reins to slow the horse. He glanced at the guards standing around the gate, but they made no indication that he should stop, and so he rode right past them. The city was clearly wealthy, neatly built and arranged, streets evenly cobbled. Tiberius guided the wagon down the wide, centermost thoroughfare. A few blocks away, it seemed to terminate in a stately plaza overlooked by an impressive cathedral to whatever gods were worshipped in this region. They wouldn't be getting close enough to it to find out which gods those were; as soon as they were out of easy view of the guards, Tiberius turned the wagon down a narrower road, taking him out of the main path of traffic.

"Wake up."

"Hmm? Are we there?"

"Yes, we're there."

"Is it time to fight?"

"I was thinking we might figure out a plan first."

"Ah, hmm. Well, we could wait until dark."

"I think we can assume that we'll go when it's dark, yes."

"And then we should probably fight our way inside, kill Crutchfield, and then fight our way back out."

"I guess I was thinking of a more specific plan."

"Do you have a map of Crutchfield's manor?"

"No."

"Then I guess we're not going to be coming up with a more specific plan."

"And how will we determine his guilt?"

"What?"

"We're working on the word of a petty bandit who was being tortured. It's a tad circumstantial."

"Ah."

"Well?"

"Well, what?"

"How are we supposed to determine his guilt?"

Rodolphus sighed. "Leave it to me. I've been practicing an Enchantment spell that will make him tell the truth."

This was unexpected. Tiberius turned back and glanced at Rodolphus, who stared back at him, mouth quirking into a smile.

"Oh, what, surprised?"

"Pleasantly surprised. I didn't notice you practicing any new spells…"

"Well, you've been so reserved and sulky lately, that doesn't surprise me."

"Ah." Tiberius turned back, looking out over the road, which was littered here and there with pedestrians crossing between the shops that lined the avenue. He turned the wagon into an alley that appeared unoccupied, reining the horse to a stop once it was settled inside. He stood and stepped carefully back into the wagon's open area, bending down and digging through their bundles of provisions for some oats.

"Look," he said, not looking up, "I'm sorry it's been like that. It's just… I haven't changed my mind. After tonight, I'm done."

"Tiberius, I—"

"No, you don't need to explain yourself; we've talked about this enough. It's behind us. Let's just try to be aware of everything we do, and the consequences. That's all. And it'll be just like the old days."

"Just like the old days, yeah."

There was something odd in Rodolphus' voice there, and Tiberius looked up briefly from what he was doing. The other man's mouth quickly broke into a grin, and he chuckled softly.

"We've been through a lot, Tiberius."

"Yes. Now help me feed this damn horse."

They waited until nightfall, at which point they headed toward the northern part of Yunder. Tying up the horse and wagon to a hitching post on a small corner with little activity, they waited several hours longer, until nearly all the house lights around them had gone out, the city lit now only by the dim lanterns hanging over the larger streets.

They drifted away from the wagon like specters, nearly silent, treading at a slow pace down a few small streets and avenues until the manor of Lord Crutchfield was visible directly across from them. The wolf padded lightly in a manner that belied its size. When it wanted to, it could be more silent than any human hunter Tiberius had known.

The manor sat on its own enormous parcel of land, an oasis of nature sitting awkwardly in the middle of the city. A white fence circled the enormous lawn, though it was low and not meant as a true barrier. Many of the windows were dark, but the grounds were still well-lit, and the manor door, a heavy oaken affair, had several armed and armored guards standing around it.

Rodolphus nodded toward it. "Shall we take the obvious approach?"

"If we start making noise this early in, we'll lose the advantage of everyone inside being asleep. Maybe better to try the back."

"All right. The ones in front will just have to come through the house to meet us."

Staying well away from the pools of light cast by the estate, they turned off the block and down onto the next one, which was lined with still impressive but slightly more modest homes. They walked down this street until they could see the rear of Crutchfield's manor looming behind the houses. Aiming towards it, they skirted through someone's property, thankful that it did not contain a dog. The three of them easily stepped over the white picket fence, and they were looking now upon the large back lawn of the Crutchfield estate. It was an impressive, rolling expanse of well-manicured grass, fringed on the edges by groves of trees and occupied in its center by a tasteful fountain made from white stone.

The rear of the estate was as brightly lit as the front. Lacking the pillars and elaborate flourishes seen on the front side, the back of the manor was a simple flat rectangle, many windows spread in rows over it. A double door, made of glass lined with delicate white wood, dominated the center of the first floor, flanked on either side by a guard holding a halberd. A smaller, much simpler door was present on the far left.

"That little door's not guarded." Rodolphus whispered. "Probably a servant's entrance?"

"Probably. And probably locked."

"As though that's really an obstacle."

"Yes... but I don't think we can approach it without those guards spotting us."

"Hmm. It'd be nice to be well within the house before they sounded the alarm."

"I suppose we could try to distract them..."

"Good idea," Rodolphus said, flicking his finger towards one of the elegant trees on the edge of the property. A slight flicker of orange rippled through the air, and almost instantaneously one of the tree's branches was on fire, casting unsteady light on the surrounding grass as the flames crackled, spreading slowly and unnaturally down the branches toward the trunk.

The guards noticed almost immediately, and both of them jogged toward the tree without bothering to check in with anyone in the house. Tiberius grinned. It didn't matter how many guards you had if they were all morons.

The trio jogged as quietly as they could toward the servant's entrance, keeping to the far edge of the yard from the fire, shaded by the trees. They huddled around the door as they reached it. Tiberius was glad that the Wolf was staying quiet and cooperative—Rodolphus seemed to have fine-tuned his control over it. As they paused in front of the entry, they both heard the clicking of quick footsteps on tile coming toward the door.

"Hell," Rodolphus hissed. "Someone's coming."

"They must have noticed the disturbance."

"When that door opens, you break them, all right?

Tiberius nodded, bringing his mace up into a two-handed grip, spreading his legs so he could put more power into his blow. As the door opened, he swung full force, adjusting his aim at the last minute to contact with the figure's head. The cracking sound was horrific. It wasn't until the body was crumpling to the ground that Tiberius had time to realize who it was.

It was a thin, slight body, dressed in black and white, a neat dress and apron now spread lazily on the grass, giving way to a bleeding, pale face bracketed by long, red hair.

Tiberius stared at the body. "No older than fifteen," he said softly.

"Fifteen year-old girls scream even louder than twenty year-old men, Tiberius," Rodolphus said grimly. "Come on, no time to lose."

"I... why..." Tiberius frowned, staring down at the body. "Why didn't I check to see who it was?"

"Because delays get you killed, man, you know that! Let's go!"

Tiberius nodded, and with a shove of encouragement from Rodolphus he found himself stumbling over the body and into the hall, which was clearly a servant's corridor. He rushed forward, hearing the heavy footfalls of Rodolphus and the Wolf behind him, and scanned the way ahead for a door. He spotted one coming up on the right, and drew to a stop as he saw it begin to open, cursing under his breath.

"I don't know what we do to deserve this kind of luck," Rodolphus muttered from behind him. "On your right."

Long experience made Tiberius throw his body to the left, just in time to avoid the startling crackle of electricity that shot from Rodolphus' extended palm. The figure who had opened the door, a male servant in his early thirties, had only the barest moment to glance toward them before the lightning impacted his head, throwing him off his feet and down the hallway, where his body crumpled against another door, twitching and steaming.

Tiberius spun on Rodolphus. "I think we can say conclusively that we're still in the servant's area, so let's try for non-lethality, yes?" he growled in a whisper.

Rodolphus held his hands up disarmingly. "As you like, as you like."

Tiberius led the way to the door, which opened into a cramped stairwell, the winding wooden stairs leading both up and down.

Tiberius started upward. "This will be the servant's stairway—it allows them access to the bedrooms upstairs so they can clear away bedpans and such. This time of night, I guess we may as well assume Crutchfield is upstairs."

Rodolphus nodded, falling into step behind. The Wolf, looking bored, brought up the rear. They made their way up quickly, making more noise than Tiberius would have liked, and on the landing two stories up Tiberius pushed open the door, peering down yet another hall, almost too cramped for either of his allies to fit in easily. Two doors were present opposite each other about ten feet down the passage, with a third down at the end of the hall.

"Here we go. These doors probably access the bedrooms. I'd bet that the one down there is the master bedroom, and these two access children's rooms."

"You'll have to tell me sometime how you became so acquainted with the layout of manor homes."

Tiberius shrugged. "We Minarians are not as impoverished as we sometimes make ourselves out to be. Most of the higher clergy live in homes like these."

"Children in these rooms, right?"

"Possibly, bu—"

Tiberius had turned, and he trailed off as he saw Rodolphus, one hand blazing with fire, hold his palm against the wall. The fire took to the wood and began to spread with shocking speed, as though his hand was sending out pulses of encouragement.

"What in God's name are you doing?" Tiberius asked, too stunned to move.

Rodolphus withdrew his hand and took several steps toward Tiberius, the Wolf following. The fire glowed brightly behind them as it continued to spread. "Children in these rooms. If there's a fire, it confuses everyone. The kids start yelping, the guards have to save them instead of stopping us during our daring escape."

"Unacceptable!" Tiberius hissed, unconscious to the flames now spreading around him. "This is not how we behave! We do not risk the lives of noncombatants this way!"

"I hate to break it to you, buddy," Rodolphus said, and suddenly his voice was totally without mirth, his smile cold, "but you broke the skull of a noncombatant not five minutes ago."

"Yes, but on instinct, and I, I—"

"Are you going to let us clear the hallway?"

Tiberius was aware that the fire was coming dangerously close, already beginning to lick at the Wolf, but he didn't care. He stood adamantly in their path.

"Not until this is settled."

"Ah, I see. Well, Cudgel, I think you win. You'd bet that burning the place would be the line, right?"

The Wolf, seemingly unconscious of the fire now singing its fur, giggled, its gums rolling back from its murderous teeth. "Yeeheeheeheehee."

"What are you talking about?" Tiberius said, his head snapping from one of them to the other. "What does that mean?"

"One second," Rodolphus said darkly, and extended a hand, placing it almost gently on Tiberius' chest. With a whispered trio of words, an irresistible force hit Tiberius like a sledgehammer, throwing him down the hallway until he buckled against the far door. He heard the wood splinter from the impact of his armor before he fell to the ground in front of it. Pain lancing through his body, he stumbled to his feet, looking up in time to see his companions pacing towards him. Rodolphus still had his hand extended, and Tiberius did not have time to react when he saw the man's lips moving again.

Another hammer blow of wind to the stomach, and the door was shattered as Tiberius flew through it. Now he lay barely conscious on a rug in the middle of an opulent bedroom, a four-poster bed dominating half of it. A picture window was mounted in the rear wall, overlooking the lawn of the Crutchfield estate.

A woman in a nightgown, nearing middle-age but still attractive and smooth of skin, was staring down at him in horror, a candelabrum in one hand.

"Out," Tiberius managed to gasp, trying to get his wind back. "Get out," but the woman did not respond, and seconds later Rodolphus and the Wolf had stepped into the room, and the woman had dropped the candles to the ground.

Rodolphus swept his gaze around before growling in consternation. "Figures. The old man's not even in here."

Tiberius managed to get to his feet as the Wolf drew its enormous greatsword, but he didn't have any time to intervene as it cut down the woman in one powerful stroke, severing her chest nearly in twain through the shoulder. Rodolphus had now turned toward the door that likely led to the main hallway—turned, Tiberius realized, to see if Crutchfield had run off to save the children. Determined to do something, Tiberius ran at Rodolphus, who was not expecting it and was easily pushed backward, fumbling to cast a spell but unable to make the correct gestures in time. Tiberius pushed harder, and with a resounding thump he had the conjurer pinned against the enormous window that dominated the rear wall of the room.

Rodolphus smiled, but it was forced, a humorless expression. "What the hell do you think you're doing, Tiberius?"

Tiberius shook his head. "Anything." He reeled back for a moment, but before Rodolphus could complete a spell, Tiberius threw all his force behind one elbow and jammed that elbow directly into Rodolphus' chest. The wonderful sound of the window shattering filled his ears, and the look of fear in the other man's eyes as he tumbled backward out of it brought him some small comfort. It was a perfectly survivable drop, no more than twenty feet, but just getting Rodolphus out of the manor seemed somehow like a victory.

He heard weighty footsteps behind him, but didn't even have time to turn before the heavy fist of the Wolf hammered the small of his back and sent him tumbling out the window himself.

Stars burst before his eyes as he impacted, and the pain that screamed through his chest suggested that he had broken several of his ribs in the last minute. Nevertheless, he forced himself to stumble to his feet, and saw that Rodolphus had done the same fifteen feet way, leering at him, rubbing at his shoulder under his armor, a maniacal glint in his eyes.

A pair of guards across the lawn were still attempting to put out the fire in the tree, as though totally unaware of the events in the home—and no wonder, Tiberius realized, for that blaze had spread with unnatural swiftness, and had broadened to lap at half a dozen other trees. As Tiberius looked up at the building, he saw that signs of the fire within had not yet spread to the outside, though from where he stood he could faintly hear yelling and rushed activity coming from within. Grimly, he turned to face Rodolphus.

"You said that things would be different." It was all he could think to say.

"I did. I said it with such sincerity that I almost believed it myself."

Tiberius stared at Rodolphus. He had managed to bring his mace down with him, but now it hung limply at his side.

"Even then, you knew you were lying."

Rodolphus grinned, and the Wolf, which by some means or another had joined them on the lawn, threw back its head and howled in delight. "Yeeheeheeheeheehee!" it chortled, no thought of silence or restraint, the horrible noise carrying far and wide through the quiet night air.

Rodolphus' grin broadened. "Oh, hell, looks like our cover's blown. Hey, Tiberius, is it okay if I do this?"

He waved a hand through the air, a large icicle forming there from nothing, and then shot his hand straight out. The thing went hurtling toward the soldiers by the trees, who by now had turned to face them. One of them quickly crumpled to the ground.

"How about this, Tiberius? Is this all right?" Rodolphus asked, hideously cheerful now, swinging his arm around and shooting a tremendous gout of flame through the servant's doorway they'd left open and deep into the manor. As the blazing jet itself slowly faded, the bright glow of multiple fires inside the house spread out over the lawn.

"Stop it!" Tiberius growled. "This isn't funny!"

"God, do you still think this is a joke? This isn't a joke, Tiberius! This is war!"

"This isn't war! I know what war is! I've dedicated my life to it!" He could hear yet more yelling now, along with the sound of furniture being overturned, from within the manor.

"No, this isn't war for *you*, Tiberius! This isn't war for cowards! This is real war! This is blood and fire! Everyone's a combatant in this war, it's just a matter of which side they're on!"

"I won't let you do this!"

Rodolphus cackled, his appalling laughter unnaturally high. "You? You'll stop me? How, Tiberius? With your little club? With your magic that can do no harm? You're powerless! You're powerless, and that's why you envy what I can do!"

Tiberius growled and brought up his mace, but that was as far as he got before one of the Wolf's massive fists slammed into his throat, sending him crumpled to the ground. He grasped at his neck and struggled to breath, staring up at Rodolphus, who walked causally over, stepping over him and kicking him savagely in the ribs.

"You're pathetic, Tiberius. Letting me lie to you like that. God, you're a hypocrite. You murder men by the dozens and then you kill a little girl and you're in tears. What the hell is the difference? Everyone living is at war, Tiberius, and we're at war with everyone. I accept what I am. So does the Wolf. What about you? You choose instead to live in a world of half-truths and pathetic justifications. You've created a system of explanations for why what you do is acceptable. But it's not okay, Tiberius. It's horrible. It's as horrible as anything I've done. The only difference between us is that I *know* what I'm doing."

"No..." Tiberius gasped. He had to get his breath back, but it stayed lost. "Not... not..."

"Yes, Tiberius! Your entire life has been a pointless web of self-deception! And now, in the end, you can't even do anything to remedy your absolutely tepid excuse for an existence, because you're just *not strong enough*. You can't help me. You can't stop me. All you can do is watch. Watch this, Tiberius."

Rodolphus began chanting: not whispering as was almost always the case in the past, but yelling, laughing out the mangled words of unintelligible Arcanic, spitting them into the air for all to hear them.

He raised his hands over his head, and in moments a massive sphere of roaring wind had formed, hovering over his palms like an oversized medicine ball. It rose softly in the air and then shot high up and over the mansion, dipping down out of sight for an instant, growing as it traveled, the size of a large wagon by the time it disappeared.

Moments later, the back of the house exploded.

Shards of wood rained out over the lawn from the massive circular hole in the rear of the manor, revealing in cross section the stories of the house, which quickly began to collapse in on each other in the absence of several decimated load-bearing pillars. Several people fell out of the ruin, landing alive in the wreckage strewn across the lawn. A few were soldiers, others were servants, and others clearly members of Crutchfield's family in their night dress. As they struggled to get up, their groans of confusion and pain turned to cries of agony as Rodolphus screamed more incantations, the ground around him bursting into flame. The blaze shot quickly outward in all directions and engulfed the entire lawn, pouring into the ruined first storey of the house, lapping and licking over those who had fallen, seeming to be fueled by their screaming.

Tiberius, still struggling for breath, waited for the flames to engulf him, but they did not come. They were everywhere, but they did not touch him.

Rodolphus would not allow him even to die.

It was only on the verge of blacking out that his wind finally returned, and he began to struggle to his feet. Fire and smoke were everywhere, horrible creaking sounds coming from the ruin of a mansion that was now threatening to rain the remainder of its tattered bulk upon the already debris-strewn yard. Even over the screaming and the sound of cracking wood, Tiberius could hear the ghastly laughter of the Wolf, who was butchering a small group of guards that must have come around from the front of the home.

Tiberius stumbled toward the Wolf. If he could just stop it... kill it... maybe some of what he'd done... help do... maybe some of it could be...

He was tossed like a rag doll as a gust of wind scooped him up and dropped him, sending him sliding through swathes of blazing grass littered with wooden shards. Now the fire did burn him. He growled in pain as the skin of his face was scorched, and forced himself back to his feet despite the protestation of a dozen shattered bones.

Rodolphus stood nearby, frowning. "So, after all this, you still think you can be the world's savior, Tiberius. You follow a god of war, and yet you think that you're a force for good. No, Tiberius. I want you to remember this: remember that we couldn't have done it without you."

Tiberius tried to run at Rodolphus, but got no further than a few steps before another blast of wind slapped him in the face, sending him stumbling back. As he did, another incantation was screamed out, and horrible pain shot through his leg. He looked down to see the fabric covering his thigh burning off, the skin beneath bubbling and hissing. He tried to brush the acid away, but it ate through his gloves and scorched his fingers, and with a sickening increase in its fizzing it ate through to the bone, ruining the muscle and sending him once again to the ground. He could barely see or think now, the pain was so great.

But he could still see well enough to distinguish Rodolphus, who had strolled over to him and was leering down at him as though he were a specimen under glass.

"God, look at you. Brave Tiberius. I can't believe I spent all that time in the army putting up with your garbage, and with the army's garbage for that matter. Freedom from the army freed my mind as well as my body, Tiberius. I don't fight for noble causes anymore. I fight for myself. And freedom isn't the only thing that taught me that."

Rodolphus' boot pressed into Tiberius' cheek, forcing his head to turn to the side. Over the raging fire, just barely, he could see the Wolf, swinging its sword, howling in glee, its tongue lolling out of its mouth.

"You could really learn something from him. I did. I didn't quite understand until we met him, but now I realize it. We're all just animals. We're all just animals, struggling against one another, and your outmoded senses of hypocritical honor and chivalry... well, look where that got you in the end, Tiberius. You'll excuse me for not sharing my epiphany with you earlier, but, frankly, I knew that you couldn't handle it. I had no faith in you, and I was right. It was funny, though, to see how many lies you'd believe. You were so willing to accept the shit I fed you. So willing to believe that it was all okay after all. It's not okay. It never is. I think you should take that to the grave with you."

Tiberius groaned. He heard the words, but could barely put them together or comprehend them. The pain in his leg, and in his head, and in his chest—it was too much to bear, and he felt himself straggling on the edge of consciousness.

No... no, I helped them get this far... it's because of me that they're here, doing this... if I don't stop them... if I can't stop them...

He rested his hand on his thigh and concentrated as hard as he could to remember the proper incantation, whispering it to himself, feeling the pain slowly begin to recede.

"Healing yourself, are you? Why? So that you can stand up and try to conk me on the head with your mace? God, it almost makes me want to cry, Tiberius. I'm barely sure why I had you around in the first pla—"

It took a moment for Tiberius' sluggish mind to realize that Rodolphus had stopped speaking, and another moment to recognize that there had been a new sound just then: a brief twang. Rodolphus coughed abruptly. A few more seconds passed before Tiberius' pain-blurred eyes spotted the small steel bolt sticking out of the man's neck, piercing through nerves and jugular. Rodolphus' eyes widened, his mouth still open to speak, but no sound came out. He collapsed onto the lawn, his own fire licking his body.

Still flat on his back, Tiberius stared at the spot where Rodolphus had been, now taken up by nothing but the sky, which should have been clear and full of stars but was instead stained and obscured by the gouts of smoke billowing into the air. He could no longer remember the words he needed to chant to keep healing his leg, which screeched with pain. The damage must have been catastrophic.

Someone else filled the spot where Rodolphus had been standing. It was a much older man, thin and pale-skinned, of average height, balding, with a neatly trimmed beard. An un-cocked hand crossbow hung limply in his right hand, and he stared down at Tiberius, eyes wide, mouth creased into a permanent frown.

"You killed them all," he whispered, only the shapes of his mouth making the words clear. "They're all dead. My guards. My servants. My... my... my family... all of them. Why would you do this?"

Tiberius stared up into those eyes, those dead eyes, and found that there was nothing he could say.

Crutchfield shakily drew a new bolt out of his pocket and loaded it into the crossbow, bringing the weapon up and aiming it at Tiberius' forehead.

"Thank you," Tiberius rasped, whether to Crutchfield or to Minar or to something else, he did not know. He heard a swish, and waited for death to come, eyes shut.

A second later, he opened his eyes in time to see Crutchfield's head roll off of his shoulders, followed quickly to the ground by the old man's slight body.

The Wolf looked down at Tiberius. And it laughed, and laughed, and laughed.

Part III:
The Necromancer

Chapter 15

Radcliff groaned, pushing a bony hand through his not-entirely clean hair. He took a long drink from his mug, trying to avoid looking at the man sitting across from him. He hadn't bargained for this. Well, to be fair, he hadn't bargained for much of anything that had happened to him recently, but still. This was the feather in the cap.

Public attitudes towards magic—that is to say, the opinion held on magic by those who could not use it—were typically a mix of mistrust and fear, though falling well short of outright hostility. Most commoners had never known magic to be particularly helpful, and so the Wizards at the University began to seem like unproductive recluses, laboring on the minutiae of magical detail while, the common people noted, there was always need of more hands out in the field.

In other lands, non-magical peoples had the best relationship with those Wizards who practiced Curation magic, for obvious reasons. However, this could not be the case in Merund, as the Delarian religion was heeded not only by the government but also by the majority of the citizens. Enchantment was out, too—though it could do some things that people found amusing, like, say, making a broom clean up a mess by itself, the more practical uses of Enchantment tended to strike people as perverse and unnatural. It ran contrary to the importance they placed on freedom of choice (ironic, considering their religious beliefs) and the natural order of things.

Divination was the most theoretical field of magic there was, and diviners rarely set foot outside the University, and so the citizenry knew little of them, though their religious inclinations tended to push them to respect the Divination school. Necromancy, naturally, would be abhorred, Radcliff thought with a smirk, but most people were not aware that Necromancy was even a real form of magic. They thought it was the stuff of nightmares. They were right, of course—but experiencing a nightmare did not always mean being asleep.

That left the Conjuration school. The flashy, aggressive school, the one that impressed other Wizards the least. Lamentably, but perhaps unavoidably, it was the one that wowed common people the most. It was exciting and substantial without seeming too unnatural or perverse. It was *real magic* as they saw it, something they could see and understand. It never occurred to them, Radcliff presumed, that short of its very highest level, its only real use was starting fires and putting holes in people's chests.

Other Wizards, as a rule, did not like conjurers. Almost all Wizards trained in Merund gained at least a basic knowledge of Conjuration, but typically they would then expand into other fields that were considered more scholarly. Radcliff himself had become interested in Enchantment, though he'd never gotten very good at it. It took a certain type of individual, on the other hand, to be so impressed by the flashiness of Conjuration in their first year at school that they stuck with it for the remainder of their time there, usually at the neglect of the other branches. Conjurers were pushy, boastful, and as Wizards went, usually somewhat stupid.

In Radcliff's opinion, the man sitting across from him was all three. Charl Reynar, conjurer. In fact, the most talented conjurer to leave the University in the past decade. This was an accomplishment that most Wizards would equate to being the most powerful rat on a rotting heap of carcasses, but nevertheless it came off as very impressive to the non-magical population. Reynar was indeed quite famous, probably the best known Wizard in

Merund—aside from perhaps the Dean of the University, who to most people was a shadowy, nameless figure.

"Boy, you sure hate him, huh?" Krupp said conversationally, sipping from his nearly-full glass. Radcliff's eyes darted to Reynar to see if he'd heard, but no, he was busily manipulating a little ball of flame to impress a pair of barmaids, who were dutifully making "ooo" and "ah" sounds.

"We have our differences," Radcliff said curtly.

"Oh, he's an asshole, don't get me wrong," Krupp said, gesturing at nothing in particular.

"He sure is that," interjected one of the other men at the table. Abstaining from his chainmail but barely passing for a civilian in his street clothes, the big grizzled man, whose name Radcliff was at a total loss for, was quite intimidating. "You know he's been calling me 'peasant'?"

Krupp shrugged. "There are plenty of unpleasant people in this world, and you'll end up having to work with quite a few of them. May as well get used to it and try to make the best of it."

"We could kill him," the Guardsman suggested, wiping a bit of foam off his upper lip.

"Do you think so?" Radcliff asked, smiling. "He's distracted now. Come, you stab him and I'll levitate his body to the attic so no one finds him."

The Guardsman grinned and slowly began to extend a meaty hand towards Reynar, who had his back turned. His fingers were just extending towards the back of Reynar's collar when the barmaids seemed to get their fill and wander off. Reynar began to slowly turn back around, and the guard's hand shot back and disappeared under the table, a complacent smile plastered on his face.

Radcliff stifled a laugh. He'd have to figure out what that man's name was.

Reynar cricked his neck and looked around the table, raising an eyebrow.

"Is something funny?"

"What could be funny, Mr. Reynar, in dark times such as these?" Krupp said, voice dripping with conviction.

Reynar sneered. "Just Charl will do, Albert. I'm sorry there are so many distractions. You know how people are around Wizards. Or, anyway, Radcliff does. Isn't that right, Cliff?"

"Yes," Radcliff forced out, "absolutely."

"Don't worry about it," Krupp said dryly. "It's best that you act the way you always do. Our group is suspicious enough as it is without us sitting here in brooding silence."

The other Guardsman assigned to the group, this one a lanky silver-haired fellow, appeared out of the crowd and fell into the empty chair, his sword clanking softly against the chair leg.

"Ah, good, you're back," Reynar said. "Any sign of necromancers in the john?"

Radcliff heard a slow hiss emerge from the clenched teeth of the big guard sitting next to him. Krupp shut his eyes and rubbed a delicate hand across his forehead.

"In spite of what I said about not sitting in silence, it would also be best if you avoided mentioning our assignment," he said, his voice remarkably calm.

"Well," Reynar said, sitting up straight and frowning, "it would have been nice to tell me that earlier."

"We did tell you that, you dumb bastard!" the big Guardsman hissed, hands still out of sight under the table. "We told you that from the get-go!"

"Now, that's hardly any way for a common person—"

"A common person! I'll wear your guts for garters, you University hack!"

"I'd like to see you try, oaf!"

Radcliff's eyes darted around the bar. It was loud, but they were bound to start drawing attention soon. He raised a hand fractionally and began chanting softly under his breath, focusing on Reynar. It would be easier to influence the Guardsman, but that would hardly be polite.

"What are you doing?" Krupp asked calmly, the tapping of his index finger against the table the only sign of his nervousness.

Radcliff didn't respond, continuing to chant, waving his hand slightly in a subtle but distinct pattern. Then it was finished.

"—going about with a sword, but I'd like to see you try—" Reynar's words cut off there, his brow furrowing as he seemed to forget what he was saying. He took a closer look at the Guardsman, who was leaning forward with a hand on the table as though he was about to lunge across it.

"You... you're beautiful," Reynar said finally, his mouth hanging open slightly.

"Oh, damn," Radcliff muttered.

Krupp chuckled softly. "What, did you do the wrong one?"

"Uhm. Maybe."

"You did actually attend University, didn't you? You didn't just, say, audit classes?"

"It's a very complex art, and I haven't done it for quite some time."

The big Guardsman seemed frozen in horror, watching with dread in his eyes as Reynar's slender hand extended to his own bulky one and closed over it.

"Ah," Reynar sighed, "how long I have waited..."

The silver-haired Guardsman, already smiling, now cracked and began laughing uproariously, nearly toppling out of his chair. The big one seemed to gather himself and pulled his hand back, but Reynar's stayed closed over it, and he didn't even seem to notice as his chest was dragged across the table as he held on.

"Oh, please, let it last a while longer," he pleaded, slowly beginning to reach out his other hand towards the guard's stubbly face.

"What the hell's going on?" the guard roared, reaching for his sword as he broke away from the conjurer's grasp and pushed out of his chair.

"This is beginning to have the opposite effect of what I intended," Radcliff said sheepishly.

"I don't suppose you could cancel the spell. You know, without accidentally turning him into a kitten or something," Krupp said, sipping from his drink.

Radcliff raised a hand and began chanting. "I promise nothing," he muttered between words of Arcanic. His hand twitched slightly, and Reynar, once again, seemed to freeze in place, mouth creasing into a frown as he tried to remember what he was doing.

Slowly, he pulled back across the table to his chair, where he sat up and brushed crumbs off the front of his tunic.

"I'm sorry, what were we talking about?" he asked distractedly, looking around in confusion.

"See? Worked like a charm!" Radcliff said, avoiding eye contact with either Guardsman.

"Oh, I'll get you for that. I really will," the big guard growled, but Radcliff was grateful to see that his mouth was turned up into a slight smile.

"Please, Leon, don't murder any Wizards until after the group's broken up," Krupp said, signaling the waitress for another round. "And *please*, let's try to nurse our drinks a little longer this time. The city doesn't have unlimited resources, you know."

"If Merund's ever at the point where a round of ales is the only thing between it and bankruptcy, you let me know," Leon said. "I'd like to be able to start rioting and looting before everyone else gets wind."

"Crossing over to enemy lines," Krupp said. "For shame!"

"I've got to get paid, Krupp my boy, one way or the oth—"

"Just come in through the door," the silver-haired guard interrupted urgently.

Radcliff responded as he'd been told, leaning back calmly and sending only a subtle glance toward the doorway. Krupp, his back to the door, didn't look at all, and Leon stretched, yawned, and slowly got up, disappearing into the crowd of people around the bar.

"Short, black robes," Radcliff said conversationally. "Fits the description. Could be our man."

"Say the word," Reynar said grimly, "and he's ash."

"He's surrounded by people," Radcliff said, frowning.

"Trust me, my aim is that good."

"Not so fast, pyro," Krupp said, readjusting his cufflinks. "Let's confirm it's our guy first. Is anyone with him?"

"No, he's by himself."

"What do you think that indicates?"

"Our target probably wouldn't go out by himself with so many opportunities for... companionship. Unless he's trying to play it safe and keep the heat off."

"Hmm. He lost control of a... pet, not too long ago. Do you think that he's been discouraged from... getting a new one?"

"No. People like him don't stop. He'll have convinced himself he can stop it from happening again. Or else he just doesn't care."

"Aww, hell," Silver-hair said.

"What?" Krupp asked, still looking for all the world like he was discussing the weather, and doing an excellent job of hiding his probably overwhelming desire to turn around and look toward the doorway.

"He just took the hood off. It's Tyril Clement."

"Who's Tyril Clement?"

"A card shark and generally a cheat all around. But no magician. Unless he's picked up some new tricks."

Krupp glanced a question at Radcliff. "Unlikely," Radcliff admitted. "Necr—pet... ownership would take years to learn, and I seriously doubt that there's anywhere in Merund you could learn it. We're looking for a stranger."

"Is it possible that our pet-owner was letting someone else pet-sit during the biting incident?"

Radcliff took a second to work that one out before responding. "That's not typical behavior. And anyway, remember what the black-robed figure was able to do when the pet got unruly. No, that was the target in the flesh, not a stoolie."

"Ah, blast. False alarm, then."

Leon reappeared from the crowd, dropping back into his seat with a loud protest from the chair's joints.

"It's bloody Tyril Clement!" he exclaimed.

"Lord, that guy really gets around," Krupp said.

"Not yet, then," Reynar said sadly. "But soon."

Radcliff sighed. That was the other problem with conjurers. Too ready to start fires. Or lightning storms, or blizzards, as the situation warranted.

"I've got to be honest with you, boss," the silver-haired guard said, "I don't think our odds are very good. There are dozens of inns in this city. I know you want to stay discreet, but it seems like a city-wide alert would be a whole lot more effective at bringing in our suspect."

"Dozens of inns, certainly," Krupp said, "but few that are as tolerant of magicians as this one. Something that I'm sure the Western District authorities are well aware of, but happily ignore provided the correct kickbacks are paid."

"Now, boss," Silver-hair started, shooting a quick glance at Leon. Both men were stationed in the Western District.

"No worries, Clim," Krupp said, "I don't care, and neither does the Magistrate. Besides, I somehow doubt guys like you are actually seeing any of the money."

"You've got that right," muttered Clim.

"However," Krupp continued, "as hiding places for our suspect go, this one has pretty high odds. There aren't all that many other hangouts where his bizarre activities and mannerisms would go unnoticed."

Radcliff nodded in agreement. "There's the Red Oak in Central, but they don't usually take kindly to foreigners. And there's also the Foxglove a few blocks from here, which we'll check out if this place turns out to be a bust."

"It's starting to look that way, Chief," Leon said grimly.

"It is," Krupp agreed. "None of the robed figures have been our mark, and we have yet to see anyone who could be a..." he sighed, but soldiered on anyway, "... a pet."

"You know," Reynar cut in haughtily, "I do have things I need to be doing. Not all Wizards are quite so adept at lazing about as our boy Cliff here."

"Are they letting conjurers call themselves Wizards now?" Radcliff countered, unable to stop himself.

"...I'm afraid that's the final straw," Reynar growled. He stood up abruptly, his chair falling back. Radcliff, beginning to shake, hastily raised a hand in front of him. Out of his periphery he saw Leon drawing a knife from his sleeve. Out of the other side of his periphery...

Clim, who had been taking a long drink a moment ago, was now doubled over, choking and hacking. As discreetly as possible considering his condition, he was shakily pointing toward the entrance.

Everyone at the table stopped just long enough to glance at the doorway.

Standing just inside the doors was what was quite apparently a skeleton dressed in human clothing.

"Holy hell," Radcliff said, forgetting about the portable incinerator currently pointed at him.

"Stay calm, everybody. Let it come in," Krupp said softly.

Perhaps too softly, because Reynar, his hand already extended towards Radcliff, spun around to face the doorway, bellowed a war cry, and flung his arm as though slapping an invisible opponent. A hail of large, glistening droplets of liquid flew forth, shooting through a gap in the crowd and impacting the skeleton. Those that missed hit the doorframe, immediately creating massive pits in the wood that sizzled and sputtered as the bubbling liquid dripped down from them, scoring long grooves as it did.

Those that hit the skeleton instantly disintegrated a good deal of the large cloak that was obscuring its torso, and the bones of a grimy brown shoulder were briefly visible. Briefly, because a few moments later, with a sickening snap, the arm broke free and dropped to the floor in a clatter, flying apart, the severed joint still sizzling.

There wasn't much chance to see what more damage there was, because now the skeleton was out the door.

"After it!" Krupp yelled over the explosive sound of the bar patrons shouting about what they'd just seen. "We have to follow it!" The five of them nearly fell over each other as they burst from their chairs and pushed towards the exit, shouldering through a knot of a dozen people as they did. Reynar was first out the door, and immediately the dark street was lit up as he projected a stream of flame out of his palm. Brilliant orange and yellow, it wound like a serpent, lancing down the street and darting to the right where it collided with a barely visible figure. As the stream disappeared, Radcliff saw the skeleton stumbling back to its feet, wearing little more now than a few rags that blazed brightly in the dark.

As the group began pounding the pavement after the skeleton, Radcliff briefly considered whether Reynar had done that on purpose, and even toyed with the idea of asking him about it later. For now, the point was largely unimportant. It was lit up like a silo fire, and they were hot on its tail. Skeletons had some initiative, but they were none too bright. It would lead them straight back to its home. Straight back to the necromancer.

Chapter 16

Alois' eyes fluttered open, his eyelids sticky, his left arm aching slightly from a night of being trapped under his body. He rolled lazily onto his back, staring up at the ceiling, clean and white, painted recently. He wondered briefly what time it was, and considered not for the first time whether he should finally invest in a decent clock. He'd have to become comfortable with the idea of paying an arm and a leg for one first, though. For now the nearest bell tower would suffice.

As though he'd portended it, the distant clang of the bell sounded. He laid there, eyes closed, slowly counting the rings, hoping it would be early enough that he could go right back to sleep. In Alois' opinion, there were few things finer than waking up early and having the luxury of dropping right back into bed.

Cong... Cong... Cong...

The bell tolled its seventh time, and he shut his eyes a little tighter, praying that it should end its course and let him get his rest.

Cong...

"Blast!"

With extreme reluctance, he rolled out of bed to see about some clean clothes.

A few minutes later, he was making his way down the stairs at a fair clip, large hand clasped firmly around the banister. He turned out of the front hall and directly into the kitchen, still adjusting his coat over his shirt and suspenders.

"Good morning, Alois. Late for work?" his wife Elizabeth asked, not looking up from the cups of tea she was pouring.

"Only a bit," he grumbled, kissing her on the cheek and grabbing a steaming teacup off the table, downing its contents as quickly as he could without scalding his mouth.

"Same as every morning."

"Maybe it'd be easier to just buy a rooster," he suggested, wiping the tea from his mustache.

"Tempting, but I doubt that would endear us to the neighbors."

"The neighbors?" he snorted. "You hate the neighbors. For all the complaining you do about them, I wouldn't be surprised if I ended up investigating a couple of murders here sometime soon."

"Hmph," she muttered, in the way she did when she was irritated. "Well, if it bothers you so much, I won't talk about it."

"No," he said, stifling a groan that would lead them into an argument, "it's fine."

She didn't respond, keeping her back turned to him as she took a tray of toast out of the oven.

"Where are the children?" he tried.

"Right here, Papa."

"Ah, good morning," he said, turning back around.

"Good morning," his daughter Cassandra said, walking into the room and reaching for a piece of toast. "Late for work again?"

"Dammit," he muttered, "yes, and only getting later. Do you need a ride anywhere? I'll probably call a cab." Alois did not have his own horse, for lack of a stable to keep it in, and for the fact the guard's station was within walking distance.

"No, dad, I'm just staying in and studying for the exam."

"Ah, right. When are they holding it, anyway?"

"It's next week."

Alois nodded approvingly. He'd taken the civil service exam himself around her age, and was pleased to see her following in his footsteps.

"Are you sure you wouldn't prefer to take the entrance exam at the Academy?" Elizabeth asked. "Maybe you could become a Wizard and enchant your father an alarm clock so he'll be able to get to work on time."

Alois and Cassandra snorted in unison. "Those snobs haven't accepted a female student in decades, and I'm ten years too old to boot," Cassandra said disdainfully. "And what good do they do down in that old building, anyway? Most of them probably aren't even good enough at magic to enchant a clock, or else the price of the things wouldn't be so damn high."

"Language, dear," Alois murmured, reaching for the tea pot.

"You need to go to work," Elizabeth said, pulling the pot away from him. He sighed, but turned and grabbed his hat off the stand by the door and exited, muttering a halfhearted farewell as he went. He strode down the front steps and up the small footpath that wound through his front lawn. Near the road, he stopped briefly and glanced down.

"Juliet? What the devil are you up to?"

His younger daughter, twelve-year old Juliet, smiled up at him. She held out her outspread palm. Alois winced when he saw the tiny spider contained there.

"Look, Papa. Want to identify his parts with me?"

"Urgh. No thank you, dear. I'm late for work. Don't bring it into the house this time, all right?"

"Okay, Papa."

"That's a good girl. I'll see you tonight, all right?"

She continued staring down at the spider as though she hadn't heard him, watching it crawl over her fingers.

"Juliet?" he tried again. He glanced down the street to look for a cab, but didn't spot any. He'd have to walk to Paulina and try to catch one there. Sighing, he turned to look back at his daughter.

"Young lady, it's customary to…"

He paused, staring down at the spot in the grass where Juliet had been sitting mere seconds before. There was nothing there. His head spun round as he searched the yard for her. He might not have normally found her disappearance so troubling—children moved quickly— but somehow, there seemed something very queer about it. He frowned. Hadn't it been brighter out, just moments ago?

"Juliet?" he called, taking a few steps into the lawn. There was no answer, but a cool wind blew gently through the yard, rippling the grass, and now Alois was sure that it was darker. Before he could think any further, the sun had disappeared completely, the sky turning the dark blue of late twilight. Street lights were glowing up and down the lane, and windows were lit up, though not those of his own home. And the front door, which he had left wide open, was now open only a crack.

He remembered this.

"What… what in Delar's name…?"

"You would speak his name, father?"

He started at the voice, stumbling as he turned to face it. There was Juliet again, sitting right where she had been. The hand that had been holding the spider was now a fist, and though there was enough light to see by, Alois couldn't seem to make out her face at all.

"Juliet?" he asked quietly, cautiously.

"You would speak *my* name, father? Do you think you still have the right?"

"Juliet… what…"

"You know what you've done. Why don't you admit it? You're glad that we're dead."

"No! No, that's not true!"

"Yes it is. You're glad we were all murdered. You're glad you've been freed from your routines. Now you're able to roam the city like a lunatic. And barely even a pretense of mourning."

"I have mourned! I have!"

"You haven't. You haven't because you're not sorry."

"I... Juliet, no..." it took all the courage he had to take a step toward her, reaching down to embrace her. He stopped in his tracks when she looked up to him and he saw the expanse of total blackness that had replaced her face, framed by her pale yellow locks.

"God can hear your thoughts, father," the dark thing hissed. "God knows everything. Not only does he know that you haven't wept for your family, he knows that you've questioned him. He knows that you've lost your faith!"

"No!" Alois yelled, as loudly as he could, trying to drown out the voice that was becoming increasingly loathsome to his ears. "No, I still believe! I only doubted for a moment!"

"A moment! What a convenient moment it was, there on the stairs! A moment long enough to decide not only that you didn't want to rejoin your family in the afterlife, but that you would pursue sinful, heretical, *evil* means to stay alive!"

"I... I..." he stammered, and now he was backing away, nearly tripping over himself, just trying to put distance between them.

"Go in the house, father! Do you know what you'll find there?"

He glanced at the door of his home, open a crack, the lights off inside

"Yes... yes, I know what's inside..."

"Go see it again, if it makes you so happy! Go see it again, if it overjoys you so!"

"No, Juliet! I loved you! I loved all of you, I swear it! I swear it in Delar's name, truthfully!"

"*Don't you say his name!*" she shrieked. "Don't you dare speak it, sinner! Blasphemer! *Murderer!*"

"No! No!"

"Mr. Alois!" a different voice shrieked, "wake up!"

Alois' eyes fluttered open. A dream. But then, why did he still hear screaming? He rolled into a sitting position and from there flung himself to his feet and marched over to the window, which Lina was already peering out of to the street below. Alois wasn't sure how late it was, but it was still dark. Outside, a crowd of dozens was gathered, their yammering voices overlapping and forming a loud buzz. They all seemed to be staring at a solitary figure, just visible down the road. It was coming in their direction and seemed somehow to be lit up, shambling down the road lopsidedly, balls of flame flying through the air behind it and bursting into small explosions on the pavement.

"Oh, no," he and Lina hissed at the same time.

"I shouldn't have let him go out!" Lina moaned. "Look at what they're trying to do to him!"

"It's not your fault," Alois said half-heartedly, still peering at the ever-approaching figure. "I should have known better as well. But how he managed to run into a law-abiding Wizard in this part of town is beyond my reckoning..."

"We have to help him!"

Alois thought about that. Did they? He was just a walking heap of someone else's bones. And, a voice in the back of his head said, a sinful one at that. He winced at the thought. Maybe this was a test. Maybe he was being given an opportunity to allow his wicked actions to be righted. If he let the abomination die, and turned himself in...

He heard an odd croaking from beside him, and turned to look at Lina. Her hood was down, and tears were streaming down her face as she peered out the window.

All right. "Let's save Sebastian," Alois said, and together they went at a run for the doorway, grabbing their few possessions as they went, Alexander stumbling after them. Moments later they were down the stairs and out the door, pushing through the small crowd of people that had gathered in the doorway to peer out. They were out in the street just in time for Sebastian to nearly slam into them.

He was in sorry shape. Where his shoulder had been there was now little more than a blackened pit; his entire left arm was missing. The cloak that had once covered his head and torso was now a ragged strip of smoldering fabric hanging from his neck. Despite his eternal smile, Alois couldn't help but feel that Sebastian looked very upset.

He grabbed the skeleton and wheeled him immediately around the crowd of onlookers and into the alley that ran alongside the Foxglove. Lina kept pace with them, Alexander stumbling slightly behind.

"What did you do," Alois growled at the skeleton, "crash a party at the University?"

It stared at him with its eyeless sockets and shook its head profusely, neither of them slowing for a minute. Ahead of them, the alley made a sharp right turn into what Alois hoped would be an exit. His heart sunk when they swung around the corner, and all that awaited them, fifteen yards away, was a dead end.

"Uhm, Mr. Alois?" Lina cried, though none of them stopped until they reached the wall.

"I know, I know!" he growled. "Damn!" Panting, he turned slowly to face the other direction, and could hear the sound of running footsteps rapidly approaching, entering the alleyway. In a few moments they'd turn the bend and be a stone's throw away. They were out of options.

"We shouldn't have gone down the alley," he said, shaking his head. "I just thought the street would leave us too open."

"It's not your fault." Lina said firmly, grabbing his arm and tugging on it. For some reason, he found it reassuring. A few seconds passed as the four of them stood there, at a loss.

"Do you have any magic at all that you can use against them?" Alois asked, though he was sure that he knew the answer already.

"Necromancy is the only thing I know," she said mournfully.

"And what about that?"

"Here?"

"It's worth a try…"

"Okay, if you think so." Before Alois had a chance to speak another word, Lina had pulled up her hood and raised her small hands into the air, holding them palm out. She was chanting softly under her breath, far too quietly for Alois to understand, especially over the ruckus of what was about to turn the corner.

"All right, boys," Alois said, grabbing Alexander by the shoulder as he pulled his saber out of its sheath, "Death or glory, is that what they say?"

The blank stares of the skeleton on his left and the zombie on his right were not reassuring, but that was all right. Alois took off at a run toward the bend in the alley, and he heard his two compatriots do likewise. He had time to briefly wonder whether Lina had mentally commanded them to ape him. Moments later, his would-be opponents rounded the corner.

The first one, wearing a set of upscale robes, was clean-shaven with shoulder-length brown hair. His sleeves were rolled up, and he yelled in triumph when he spotted them. He raised a hand over his head, and slowly a blue orb began to form there.

He was chanting what might have been the command to hurl the spell when Sebastian bent down, flexed his knees, and lunged forward ahead of the group, slamming full force into the spellcaster and sending him toppling to the ground, the blue orb emitting a fizzling sound before popping out of existence.

The next man around the corner, in mundane civilian clothes with close-cropped black hair, was shouting orders, and managed to get out "Careful, I think there may be some civilians with the—" before Alexander's substantial fist collided with his face, sending him stumbling backward into the wall, which he quickly slid down. Alois was about to point his sword and ask for a surrender when the final trio of men came around the corner all at once, two with swords drawn, the third, a wiry man with a sparse beard, apparently unarmed.

The larger of the two armed men brought up his longsword and prepared to sweep it down at Alexander, and Alois took the opportunity, slashing out with his saber and hacking into the meat of the man's shoulder. The big man howled in pain, his sword clattering to the pavement as he stumbled back.

The other armed opponent had in the meantime taken a vicious slash at Sebastian, but the sword merely made a metallic ringing sound as it ricocheted off his skull. The skeleton, still sitting on top of the Wizard, slammed its remaining fist into the swordsman's groin.

Alois did not have time to see the result of this. Something suddenly knocked the wind out of him, his legs turning to rubber, sound seeming to disappear. And yet, no one had approached into striking range, though the wiry man had come quite close to him. He could see that the man's lips were moving, and though they were not forming words that Alois understood, he heard a man's voice clearly in his head. *Put down your sword and surrender*, it said, calmly, logically. It would, Alois reflected very briefly, be terribly stupid of him to disagree with such a reasonable request. He nodded, feeling himself smile slightly, and bent down, placing his sword on the ground. The bearded man smiled in return and nodded agreeably.

Vaguely, Alois could see that Sebastian had finally been restrained by both of the swordsmen, who were holding him down with all their weight. The man with close-cropped black hair, back on his feet, was holding a hand to his face, dark red blood oozing between his fingers.

Alexander had been forced a few feet away from the jumble of so many men in such a tight space, and as Alois turned his head slightly to look, he saw that the clean-shaven Wizard had come back to his feet and, having brought both hands to bear on the zombie, was firing a roaring gust of wind into its chest. Alexander was walking forward inexorably, and as a result of the colliding forces he was largely staying in the same place. Alois smiled again, finding this quite amusing, wishing he could do something to help, but after all, he'd surrendered, and that had been the right thing to do.

Hadn't it?

The wind stopped, and Alexander began making headway once again, reaching his arms out to grab the first thing that was foolish enough to come within his grasp. The long-haired Wizard, though, was not so foolish, and moments later he swung out his hand in a rapid motion, chopping his fingers through the air. A wave of some transparent liquid, as thin as a paper fan, shot through the air from his hand and neatly burnt through the zombie's neck.

Alexander's body continued walking for several seconds after his head had tumbled off his neck and finished the considerable fall to the ground. The Wizard quickly began backing away from those rapidly oncoming and unfathomably powerful hands, but there was no real danger. The body soon lost all drive, and as the power drained from the legs mid-step, what was left of the massive zombie Alexander collapsed to the ground like the corpse that it was.

Alois frowned as he watched this, feeling a pang of remorse, and wondered suddenly why he'd surrendered, actually. He looked back at the bearded man, feeling angry now, and reached down to retrieve his sword.

Sound came rushing back as he realized what was happening. His fingers gripped the cool metal hilt of his saber, and he swung it up to the wiry Wizard, growling.

"You bastard! I'll thank you to stay out of my head!" he shouted, lunging forward. The Wizard's eyes widened as he stumbled backward, and his lips rapidly began forming words again. Alois willed himself not to listen, drawing his arm back to sweep his sword forward...

Put down your sword, and surrender!

He stopped as best he could, nearly tripping over himself as he did. Maybe surrendering *was* the right thing to do, after all. Yes, he reasoned. It probably was. After all, his comrades had been defeated, and he had no wish to kill these men, so there was little other option. He began to bend down once again, to relinquish his blade.

Yes, good! Now, where is the necromancer?

Once again, Alois stopped what he was doing, and for a moment he considered this.

Once again, he smiled. Then he rose back up to his full height, sword still in hand, and stabbed out fiercely, the blade sinking through the Wizard's thigh, eliciting a loud shriek of pain from him.

"You shouldn't have pushed your luck, University boy," Alois said, smirking. Of course, there was not very much to smirk about. Sebastian was still restrained, and the Wizard who had brought down Alexander was now staring directly at Alois, wearing a smirk of his own.

Alois brought his saber up into a guard position and considered his options. He didn't really have any. There wasn't even much use in calling out for Lina to run, as she had nowhere to go. He stood there, waiting for the Wizard to finish him off, unsure of what else he could really do.

"Hold it, Reynar," said the man with black hair, most of the blood cleaned off his face by a now almost-entirely red handkerchief hanging out of his coat pocket. He gestured toward Alois. "Who the hell are you? You're not the necromancer; I think that's fairly obvious. So you're... what? A friend and well-wisher?"

Alois laughed. "Yes, you could say that."

"Well, you can go ahead and lay down the sword, because you and I can both see that you'r—"

The man frowned, and turned his head to look back the way they'd come. Alois could hear a bit of noise from that direction, but couldn't see around the bend.

"Go ahead and what?" he asked, surprised by how polite it came out.

"Oh, holy hell," the man responded, and now he was backing away from the alleyway, though the retreat quickly ended with his back up against the wall opposite the alley entrance.

"Run! Run!" the man yelped. Wild-eyed, he turned toward Alois and ran at him. Alois, very startled himself, slashed out with his sword, cutting a deep gash in the man's cheek and sending him staggering into the wall. The dark-haired man had been the only one near enough to the corner to see down the entryway of the alley, but the noise coming from it, which was somewhere between the sound of marching infantry and stampeding cattle, had now roused the suspicions of the others. While the swordsmen were still giving their all to holding down Sebastian, and the mind-bender was still clutching his leg on the ground, the standing Wizard couldn't repress his curiosity. He backed slowly into the corner so that he could keep an eye on Alois in one direction while being able to look in the other at whatever was oncoming. As he reached the corner, he turned his head and looked.

By the time he realized just what he was seeing, it was really too late, and he'd barely begun chanting when the first skeleton collided with him. The skeleton was jet black and seemed to be covered in some sort of horrid viscous liquid, but Alois didn't have much time to figure out what that could be, as several more skeletons in various shades of brown and beige flooded into the alley after it, and after that a further mass of figures, some still quite covered in flesh, that was too numerous for Alois to keep track of. They flowed around the bend, over and past the men he'd been fighting, impassionate to their screams of protest, and within moments all that was visible was what must have been several dozen skeletons and zombies crowded into a few square yards worth of alley. Some stood, some laid, and all were pushed up close to one another. There was no sign of Alois' opponents. Lost for words, the Chief Constable could only stare.

Apparently content with their current positions, the undead stared right back.

"Delar wept," Alois said, finally.

"Wow! You were right, huh?" came Lina's voice from behind him, and he spun around to face her, looking her up and down appraisingly to ensure that she was unhurt.

"Right about what?" he asked, not sure that he wanted to know the answer.

"Right about giving Necromancy a try anyway! Who would have thought there would be this many bodies to reanimate within just a few hundred yards of here?"

Alois blinked. "Your range is a few hundred yards?"

"Sure. I mean, longer if I have more time."

Alois glanced back at the mass of undead that was jammed into the corner of the alley. "You know, I think this was just right."

As if on cue, a distinctly un-rotten human hand pushed its way out from under the mass of a mostly horizontal zombie, reaching in their direction. Showing little concern, the zombie reached out a hand and clamped it over the live one, pinning it to the cobblestones.

"They're still alive in there?" Alois asked.

"Oh, sure. They're just being restrained. Very, very well."

"That was very thoughtful," Alois said, unable to keep a smile off his face.

"Well, sure. It's not their fault they don't understand us."

"No. No, I suppose it's not."

"We should probably get going now though, huh?"

"Oh, erm, yes."

Carefully, they picked their way forward, and the mass of standing, laying, sitting, and crouching undead, with sounds of protest and moaning just barely emerging from somewhere beneath, did their best to form a path that the Constable and the necromancer could pick through.

"Oh… Lina, I'm very sorry, but I'm afraid that Alexander didn't make it."

"Yes, I know… I sensed it. It's all right. I hope I gave him a good unlife…"

"The… the best, I'm sure."

"What about the rest of these?" Alois asked as he rounded the corner, making his way finally back into a section of the alley that wasn't crowded by former cadavers.

"Oh, they all understand that they were only being resurrected for a little while. We can't take them with us and they can't be left to roam about, so…"

"Ah, yes. Right-o."

They were halfway down the alley before Lina snapped her fingers and turned back. "Oh, nearly forgot. Here, Sebastian! We're going!"

Chapter 17

"I hope you won't take it too personally," Schiller said calmly from his desk, "if I tell you that you look like hell."

Krupp groaned, not even acknowledging the remark as he crossed the office and collapsed into one of the easy chairs in the center of the room.

"What'd you do, get in a fight with a bear?"

Krupp rubbed his hand delicately over the bandage covering the angry raised gash that ran from jaw line to the bottom of his right eye, trying to avoid touching the splint that had been bandaged over his nose.

"I wish," he remarked thoughtfully. He found himself unable to stop obsessing over the fact that he'd probably have a scar there forever.

"Don't worry, Krupp. It will give your face a lot of character. Make you look older."

Krupp frowned. "Are you mocking me?"

"I'm not," the Magistrate said calmly, now at the window again, peering out of it at the darkened city below.

"Ah. Well, that's all right, then."

"Where are the others?"

"I let the guards and the conjurer go home, and Radcliff is making his way up."

"Well, what in the world is taking him so long?"

"He's on crutches."

Schiller frowned and glanced over his shoulder at Krupp. "You might have told me, we could have gone down to him instead of making him climb."

"Climbing builds character," Krupp sneered.

"That's awfully bitter of you. I doubt it's his fault, what happened."

"No, not really. Don't worry. His wound will heal, eventually."

"So will yours, enough. I really do think a good scar makes one look distinguished."

"Mhmm. You should have seen it before they cleaned the blood off, it looked positively noble."

"Yes, I remember reading that in the report."

"You did read the report, then."

"As soon as it arrived. It's quite a story."

Krupp raised an eyebrow. "You don't believe it?"

"Is that what I said?"

"No, I suppose not."

A loud creak as the door was pushed open heralded the arrival of Radcliff, who, quite out of breath, made his way slowly into the room on his crutches, keeping his left leg off the ground. He headed for the sofa opposite Krupp and collapsed into it gratefully, letting his crutches clatter where they would.

"Radcliff. Welcome back."

"Magistrate," the Wizard panted.

"So. Things didn't go well."

"They went pretty much as badly as they could have," Krupp admitted. "Not only did we not capture the necromancer, we don't even know what he looks like."

"Ah, yes. You're quite sure the man you fought wasn't the necromancer?"

"No," Radcliff said, a little more steadily. "He's not the right type at all, and anyway, he wasn't doing any spellcasting, and lord knows some Necromancy went on."

"Interesting. But it's not so that you didn't see the necromancer. Didn't it say in the report that you believe you saw him, Radcliff?"

Krupp nodded. "Yes, he told us after the fight that he spotted someone at the end of the alley, which makes sense, since the guy with the mustache was clearly trying to stop us from going back there.

"Short," Radcliff said decidedly, "in robes, which I think were sparkling."

"That was a probably a trick of the light," Krupp added.

"Well, it's better than nothing. All things considered, I think your mission could have gone far worse than it did."

Krupp laughed. "How do you figure?"

"Well, for starters, the swarm of undead that restrained you could have killed you. Or, worse, they could have killed you and then started wreaking havoc on the city, instead of becoming lifeless twenty minutes after the necromancer had gone."

"The thought had occurred to me," Radcliff said. "Awfully thoughtful of him, wasn't it? I guess he wasn't willing to do something so high profile just yet."

"Are you sure it's not that he's just the merciful type?" Schiller asked, raising an eyebrow.

Radcliff shrugged. "Anything's possible, I suppose."

"At least we know that magic works on the undead. It sounds like Reynar was a valuable asset."

Krupp snorted. "Are you kidding? That lunatic nearly burnt down the entire Western District."

"'Nearly' being the operative word. Besides, he's the only one who managed to do any damage to them. It sounds like the two Guardsmen spent most of the scuffle physically restraining a single skeleton."

"Well, Radcliff was doing a pretty good job of keeping the guy with the sword out of the fight. For a little while, anyway," Krupp said, glancing at Radcliff, who avoided his gaze.

"And you, Krupp... I suppose you supervised?"

Krupp nodded. "Yes, sir. Supervised and got punched in the face."

"I would have expected no less. Well, gentlemen. It sounds like a new strategy is in order."

"I'll say," Krupp muttered.

"Perhaps it would be best to start by laying out what we've learned. For example, we've learned that the necromancer has at least one ally who isn't undead."

"Actually, sir, I've been meaning to say something about that," Radcliff said, frowning.

"Oh? Go on."

"Well, the pallor of that man's skin, combined with his apparent strength… it's possible that he *is* undead."

"But you enchanted him," Krupp pointed out. "That doesn't work on undead, you said so yourself."

"It doesn't work on undead of limited intelligence," Radcliff replied patiently. "It's still perfectly effective on undead who think like humans."

"And why didn't you mention this before?"

Radcliff let out a sigh. "Because, as I believe I have explained, a necromancer who could make undead like that hasn't existed for centuries."

"Well," the Magistrate said, staring out the window once again, "it appears we may have bitten off a bit more than we can chew."

"What's our next move?" Krupp asked. "They could be anywhere by now. If we're lucky, they've up and left the city."

"Are you kidding?" Radcliff asked incredulously. "The potential for Necromancy here is too great. He won't leave of his own free will."

"What do you mean by 'potential'?" Schiller asked.

"The sheer number of bodies alone is overwhelming, as I think was aptly proven last night."

Krupp nodded. "Reports indicate that the undead that came to the alley emerged from sewers, basements, and, in some cases, burst right out from parts of the street."

"Which is another problem," Radcliff pointed out. "A lot of people saw what happened. Rumors will already have spread far and wide."

"Yes," Schiller admitted, "I'm afraid my brilliant scheme to hide this from the Church may not have worked out very well. Nevertheless, fifty drunks from the Western District is hardly a reliable source. The Church will make a statement sure enough, but before they really start to act they'll wait until something more concrete surfaces. We still have time to stop this."

"That's comforting," Krupp said, "but it still leaves the sticking point of 'how'."

"I think it's fairly obvious," Schiller said, finally turning away from the window and pacing slowly back to his desk. "We failed because we tried to do this on our own. We won't be so foolish again."

"Who are we going to ask for help?" Radcliff asked.

The Magistrate smiled. "Well, God, of course."

Lina had noticed the black thing that seemed to be bound around Sebastian early on in their flight from the alley behind the Foxglove, but she hadn't given it much thought. Her mind, at the time, had been occupied by more pressing matters. Now, though, as the afternoon sun traveled lazily through the sky and the three of them lay collapsed in an expensive room at an inn on the edge of the Northern District, she found it suddenly prioritized.

So, with Alois sprawled out across one of the beds, she sat up on the other and beckoned Sebastian to her. The skeleton, who looked very much the worse for wear, cheerfully obliged, ambling over.

"That's what I like about skeletons," she said. "They never let anything get them down."

Sebastian nodded agreeably, though she was aware that he probably would have done that no matter what she had said. Nevertheless, she gave him a reassuring pat on the burnt spot where his right arm had once been, meanwhile peering over his shoulder at the strange mass, which turned out to be significantly larger than she'd thought.

"Turn around, darling, let's see what you have here."

Sebastian spun about, and Lina immediately had a much better view of what it was stuck to the skeleton's back. It was, clearly, another skeleton, although it was rather less complete than Sebastian, who himself was hardly in tip-top shape.

The bones of the passenger skeleton were nearly jet black, covered by a tarry, brown-black material that might have been muscle once. This ruined flesh bridged the gaps between some of its ribs and between the radius and ulna of its still-intact left arm, making it look all together a bit more fleshed-out than the average skeleton. Its body stopped abruptly midway down the spine, where a handful of crushed vertebrae hung limply just above where its pelvis and legs should have been. Its head, lolling back away from the body as though its neck were a spring, was covered with as much of the black grime as the rest of the body.

Lina gently reached out and took hold of the skeleton, trying to guide it off of Sebastian's back. It seemed to have gotten its arms tangled into his ribcage, as though it had been hanging on to him for dear life.

She frowned. It was sad, really. It had clung on to Sebastian when they were together in the big pile of undead, hoping to go with him. Instead, it had lost its unlife only a few minutes into the journey.

She began to topple slightly as she took more of its weight in her arms, trying to slide its arms out of

Sebastian's torso. She was just about to tumble out of the bed when she felt Alois' grip on her shoulder, turning her right side up and then reaching out to help her separate the two skeletons from one another.

He laid the blackened one out on the bed, while Sebastian, still standing and now free of his load, began happily rocking back and forth on his heels.

Lina crawled to the center of the bed to inspect the blackened skeleton further, Alois looking over her shoulder.

"The poor thing," she said. "Look how crushed it got by all those other undead... even its neck is smashed. I hope they didn't all get this battered."

"It didn't look like they did," Alois said in that gruff yet reassuring way of his. "This one must have been unlucky."

"Yeah, I guess so." Lina reached over to the skull and turned it to face her. She found herself quite interested by the rotten musculature on the skeleton. Considering the state the tissue was in, it surely should have all disintegrated long ago, leaving the bone brown and dirty but relatively bare.

As the black, smiling skull was turned to face her, she gasped at what she saw. Greeting her from the front of its face were not empty eye-sockets, like those of Sebastian. Instead two big, white, human eyes stared up at her, suspended in their sockets by a matrix of dingy brown muscle. The eyes looked massive and round without any lids to cover them, and a tangle of blood-shot red ran through the white sclera of each like an intricate spider's web, joining at the bright blue irises in the middle.

"Mr. Alois," she gasped, "Do you see?"

"Yes," he said, his voice full of trepidation. "Is that... usual?"

"No," she said decidedly, shaking her head. "I've never seen anything quite like this before. Why would the rest of him decay if his eyes stuck around? It's very odd."

"Is it just me," Alois asked, his voice impressively calm, "or is it staring at us?"

"Oh, I don't know about that," Lina said, but as she looked, she couldn't help but wonder herself. Certainly the eyes had no choice but to stare... but as she looked down at them, they distinctly swiveled from her to Alois, and then back to her again.

"I think you're right! I think it's alive!"

"I thought that—"

"So did I! I don't understand how this could have happened! Oh, I wish he could tell us what's going on..."

"Your wish is my command," the skeleton sneered.

Lina shrieked and jumped backward, bumping hard into Alois' stomach. He snatched her off the bed and easily set her standing on the floor beside him.

"Ah, yes, best to run, I might nip at your fingertips," the skeleton said, its voice sarcastic and bitter and shockingly human.

"I'm sorry," Lina said cautiously, leaning back in over the bed. "I just wasn't expecting you, that's all."

"Oh, yes, I'm sure that's true," the thing said, and rolled its eyes, a very distressing sight.

"Well, why in the world should I lie about it?"

"I don't presume to guess at your motivations."

"Will you tell me who you are? What sort of undead are you, do you know?"

"I will tell you nothing, witch."

"Here, now!" Alois growled, "Don't you speak to her like that."

The skull rolled its eyes again, but was silent.

Lina stared at it, at a loss.

"You've got very pretty eyes," she tried, which might have been a true sentiment under different circumstance. The skull groaned.

"Oh, gods, what did I do to deserve this? I'm the most powerful Wizard in the world, and here I am on a nine year-old girl's bed."

"I'm fourteen!" Lina said indignantly, as she was quite sure that she didn't look as young as nine.

"The world's most powerful Wizard?" Alois said dubiously. "Someone's been in the ground too long, I think."

The skull did not respond, merely staring back disdainfully.

"Let's see some magic, then?" Lina tried, attempting to keep her voice as polite as possible.

"I'd be happy to show you some magic," the thing on the bed began, "if my entire body hadn't been completely mangled by your harem of undead minions! I can't move anything below my neck, and I can't exactly cast with my eyes!"

"Too bad," Lina said, and meant it. She did enjoy seeing other people's magic. "Are you sure you won't tell us who you are? It's not often that someone I raise is able to tell me his name."

"If you are going to mock me," the thing growled, "I shall not speak to you."

"His name should be easy enough to figure out," Alois said, ignoring it. "He said he was a Wizard, and that means he graduated from the University. They probably keep excellent records."

The skull chortled. "The banality of your expectations is matched only by the banality of your 'University.'"

Lina grinned. "I'm with you, pal, you can't learn real magic at some school."

"Fine," the skull growled, "I'll bite. If we're pals, why not go ahead and repair my body for me?"

"Oh! Well, sure," Lina said, shocked that she'd forgotten. She looked at his mangled bones, though, and had to stifle a yawn.

"Rebuilding undead material takes a lot of energy," she admitted. "I'm going to have to get some shut-eye first."

"Ah," the thing said, as though it had been expecting that answer all along. "Of course. How silly of me."

"Oh, come, you need only wait until morning!" Lina said, giving him a gentle pat on the skull. With that, Alois picked the mangled skeleton up and laid it on a small writing desk near the window.

"Rest is a good idea," he said, stepping over to the window and shutting the curtains. It was still far from dark in the room, the midday sun shining brightly outside. "Perhaps it's for the best that our sleeping cycle is getting thrown out of order. It'll allow us to travel at night."

Lina nodded. "Okay. Here's hoping things go better than last time we tried this!"

"Here's hoping," Alois said dryly. "Just make sure Sebastian doesn't get any funny ideas in his head."

Lina turned to the skeleton, who sagged his shoulders and hung his head.

"Oh, darling, don't pout, we're not angry. But I'm afraid you won't be able to leave the room at all while we sleep from now on, all right?"

Sebastian nodded sadly.

"I know you don't sleep, but you'll just have to find something to entertain yourself. There are a few books on that shelf in the corner, why not see if any have pictures?"

Sebastian nodded, more enthusiastically this time, and crossed over toward the bookcase, nearly colliding with Alois, who was heading for his bed. He patted the skeleton on the shoulder almost affectionately. Lina grinned.

"I knew you'd come around, Mr. Alois."

"Ah, well. It's as they say, I suppose: if you can't beat them…"

"Speaking of which, I've got your dinner here for you." She reached into one of her inside pockets, feeling around for her parcel of meat. Alois grunted.

"I don't… think I care to eat right now."

"Oh, come, I bet you're very hungry. You must stop being so stubborn about this. After all, the fellow it came from is hardly using it."

"Don't remind me," Alois murmured, reaching out and grudgingly taking the little bundle from her.

"We'll have to collect some more sometime soon," she said, noticing now that her own stomach was growling softly. Alois sighed, taking the package into the small dressing room. She knew he'd eat it in there, by himself.

"I suppose so," he said, shutting the door behind him. "And we'll make sure to get you something nice to eat as soon as we wake up, too."

"Good! For now, though, I just want some sleep!"

"Off you go, then. I'll get to bed shortly."

"Okay," she agreed, slipping off the bed and rounding the room, putting a few things in order before patting Sebastian goodnight. She considered doing the same for the newcomer, but thought better of it. His mood would improve in the morning, she imagined, when she fixed him up.

And then, maybe she could figure out how in the world he'd happened.

Chapter 18

The Dean of the University had been informed many times by his doctor that if he didn't learn to keep his anger under control, it would see him to an early grave. This was the reason he found it so upsetting when his sitting time in the evening, during which he stretched out in the high-backed leather chair in his study, smoked an expensive cigar, and attempted to get some reading done, was interrupted. When the blinking golden light appeared in the air over his head, he tried at first to ignore it, staring at the printed words on the page in front of him and attempting to stay calm.

It was a valiant effort, but a futile one in the end. Not long had passed before, with surprising grace, he marked his spot in the book with the intricate red ribbon laced into the spine, closed it softly, and then hurled it with all his might through the light, which seemed unbothered by the book's passage on its way toward colliding noisily with a tray of used dishes on an end table.

"What is it," the Dean growled, "that is so important that you would dare contact me in the evening?"

The little flame flickered, and there was a preternatural silence for a moment before a hesitant voice finally spoke. "I'm sorry, sir. It's just that the Magistrate wants a word with you."

The Dean groaned. "What, that sycophant Krupp? Tell him to come back tomorrow, you lackluster simpleton! And you might as well go out with him, because suddenly I don't think your services are required here any longer!"

"N—no, sir," the voice stammered, "It's the Magistrate himself. He's... he's here in the lobby."

The cigar dropped out of the Dean's mouth, rolling down his thick beard before nestling somewhere in his robe. "Schiller is here? With you?"

"Yes, sir."

"Can he hear what I'm saying?"

There was silence. The Dean's hands gripped tightly into the arms of his chair. He'd have to try to figure out the name of whoever he was talking to so that he could make him pay for this later. "Well?" he tried again, forcing the words to sound calm.

"Yes, sir, he can."

"Ah. Well, by all means, send the Magistrate in. You should have told me directly."

"Yes, sir."

The Dean waved his hand, and the little flame was dismissed, puffing out of existence as though it had never been there. He sat there glowering for a few moments before he finally noticed that his smoldering cigar had burnt through his trousers and was having a go at it with his leg. He roared and batted the thing away, pointing at the spot on the carpet where it landed and trying his best to think of the nastiest possible thing he could transfigure it into. He hadn't decided yet when he heard a gentle knock at the door.

Growling once more, he stood up and brushed himself clean of crumbs and ashes. His chambers were located high in the northern wing of the main University building. The room he was in had once been a small library, the entirety of which now served as his rather impressive study. He would not have had it any other way, though the lack of any other rooms on the floor had forced him to make a former walk-in storage closet into his bedchamber.

Marching to the door that opened onto the stairwell, he stopped briefly before opening it and did his best to remember a time when he hadn't felt an overarching need to strangle something. He had long ago noticed that most such memories came from before his appointment as Dean. He tried not to think about this very often.

It probably took half a minute, but finally he managed to get the beating of his heart back down to a level that was at least marginally acceptable. He reached forward and pulled the door open, hoping that there might be some mistake.

But no, indeed not. There stood Magistrate Schiller, still in his day suit, his tie undone and hanging around his shoulders.

"Dean Baldermann," he said politely. "I'm terribly sorry to have to bother you after regular business hours."

"Think nothing of it," The Dean muttered, stepping back to allow the Magistrate entry. The lanky man's eyes explored the study as he stepped inside.

"A very nice collection of books. Maybe we can arrange a trade sometime."

Instead of screaming 'why are you wasting my time' into Schiller's face, the Dean settled for "Yes, that's a fine idea."

"I shan't trouble you with small talk, though. I am here on rather pressing business. This is the first time I had available, and once you hear what I have to talk about, I think you'll understand why I didn't want to wait any longer."

"Ah, well. Out with it, then."

"Actually, I hate to do it, but I'm afraid I must ask one more thing before I proceed. I'll need Chairman Ludwig here as well."

The Dean stared. "Ludwig."

"Yes. That is the name of the head of the Department of Divination, correct?"

"Yes, it is. And I should like to talk to him about as much as I should like to practice lightning conjuration in the bath."

"You don't get along with him?" Schiller asked evenly, eyes still roving over the bookshelves that lined the room.

"You haven't met him, I take it," The Dean asked flatly.

"No, I haven't. Nevertheless, I'll have to ask you to call him up here."

"Heh. A lot of good that would do."

"I'm sorry?"

"Getting him out of that Divination tower is not a project that I expect you have time for, Magistrate."

"Ah, I see. Well, I suppose we'll just have to go to him, shall we?"

The Dean's heart, which was palpitating at a fair clip, sunk. "Yes, I suppose so."

The Magistrate smiled and gave a half bow. "Well, then, lead the way, unless you'd like to get changed first."

The Dean glanced down at his clothes. He was wearing blue pajamas, with a short velvet robe over them. "Just a moment," he growled, and walked over to the coat stand in the corner without waiting for a response, trading in his smoking robe for an ankle-length amber affair. He jammed his hands into its deep pockets and took a deep breath.

"All right," he said. "To the Divination tower we go, then."

It was a long trip; the University main building was palatial in scale, and had plenty of rooms that the Dean himself had never been in. They passed through the well-kept and well-traveled central corridor, past rooms that bustled with students during the day but were currently occupied by a few lone researchers, some of them producing brightly colored spectacles.

As they reached the eastern wing, things became dingier and more cramped. This part of the University had not been renovated for quite a long time. As they entered the stairwell that led up into the eastern tower, the Dean had to produce a flame to light each lantern as they came to it.

"Considering the place Divination is given in our society," the Magistrate said casually, "I'm surprised that this part of the University isn't better kept and more frequently trafficked."

"Well," the Dean responded, wondering if he could get a rise out of the man, "Maybe the Church should pay to renovate it, seeing as they seem to think that they own that particular branch of magic."

To his consternation, Schiller merely chuckled in response. "Touché," he said coolly. "About that. Do Church officials come here often?"

"They send a weekly liaison. He gets the latest prophecies from Ludwig, then takes them back to the Church."

"Interesting. What then?"

"A bunch of meditative morons at the Church spend weeks interpreting the prophecies, and then they use them to help justify old Church doctrine and establish new tenets. And of course, they trumpet them for the commoners at weekly congregation."

"You're not a believer, are you, Dean?"

"Most Wizards have what I think is a very sound policy of staying entirely out of God's business."

"That's why you don't like Chairman Ludwig."

"Hah! I don't like Ludwig because he's a spineless bastard for whom even the art of talking to himself qualifies as an advanced social interaction!"

"I can see how you might not get along with a man like that."

"No one could get along with a man like that! But don't take my word for it."

They'd come to the top of the long spiral staircase, now lit up and down by the flickering glow of the lanterns. Releasing the creaking banister, the Dean reached out and opened the ancient oaken door, realizing as he stepped into the Divination chamber that he hadn't been there in years.

The room was massive, like a cathedral, and wrought entirely of immense, rough-hewn slabs of dark grey stone. Windows high in the walls had black curtains pulled over them, leaving the large chamber lit entirely by clusters of tall candles. These were held by ornate, five-foot candlesticks of which there must have been many dozen.

Eight massive stone pillars rose from the floor to the ceiling along either side of the cavernous center aisle of the room; they were unevenly cut like the walls but roughly rectangular in shape. At the far end of the room, several long, wide stone steps led up to a simple altar.

The Dean was aware that side rooms lined the main chamber all around, though he had never been into one. The tiny doors leading to them were tucked into alcoves cut back into the stone walls, and it was from one of these alcoves that Ludwig appeared.

He was a short man, dressed in nondescript robes of midnight blue. His skin was as dark as mahogany, his head entirely bald. He wore a pair of square-rimmed spectacles, and from his chin trailed a long, curly beard.

"Yes? Yes?" he called, clearly troubled by the interruption.

"Calm down, wretch!" the Dean roared. "The Magistrate is here to see you!"

"To see both of you, really," the Magistrate said calmly. "Is there somewhere we can talk?"

"The... the Magistrate?" Ludwig stammered. "Of course! Over this way, please..."

"Are there any staff or faculty here to overhear us?"

"No, no," Ludwig said distractedly as he led them through the chamber. "We get plenty of students in the daytime, but we haven't much faculty in Divination—those with great passion for the subject usually end up pursuing more... religious vocations."

They followed him to the steps which led up to the altar, where Ludwig promptly turned and sat down, his robe pressed up flush against his bony knees.

"What, here?" The Dean asked incredulously. "What are we, juvenile delinquents, sitting on the curb and rolling dice?"

"I think this will do just fine," Schiller said happily, removing his jacket and settling down one step higher than the one that Ludwig had taken. The Dean growled, considering briefly just how much he hated them both. Grudgingly, he took a seat, fidgeting against the hard stone as he tried to get as comfortable as possible.

"So, gentlemen. Shall we proceed?"

"This had better be good, Schiller," the Dean warned. "I'm just about fed up with all this bandying about."

"Straight to the point, then. I'd like to talk to you about Necromancy."

The Dean, who had been about to say something else, succumbed to a coughing fit.

"N...n...n..." Ludwig stammered.

"Yes, Chairman Ludwig, Necromancy. I'd imagine that the Dean has already gotten wind of some of this lately. Perhaps you've seen it in your prophesizing?"

"Oh, oh yes, of course," Ludwig said, taking deep breaths. "I just wasn't expecting..."

"I understand."

"There's more to it than just rumor, then?" the Dean asked, trying to keep the true extent of his curiosity hidden. He needed to figure out what Schiller's angle was.

"Unfortunately, yes, there's more to it than rumor. We have a necromancer in town. Someone is committing the greatest sin conceivable, and in our very midst."

The Dean was unable to repress a loud, incredulous snort.

"Is something funny?" the Magistrate asked, raising an eyebrow.

"I agree that having a necromancer here is a problem for any number of reasons," the Dean said, not bothering to tread carefully, "but whether or not it's a sin, well, that I couldn't care less about."

"Don't you have any faith in Delar at all? I know we've just discussed it, but Necromancy goes against even the most basic of our religion's teachings."

"I'm the Dean of a Wizarding University, Schiller. I am not religious. We leave the gods alone, and they are kind enough to do the same for us."

"What about you, Chairman Ludwig? Are you religious?"

"Don't ask him!" the Dean roared, wishing he had something in his pocket that he could hurl at the little man to highlight his point. "He's head diviner! He may as well be the Archbishop!"

Ludwig wilted like a flower, and the Dean noted with approval that he chose to keep his trap shut.

"Ah," Schiller said, "I see. Nevertheless, it's a purely academic matter—" he paused briefly as the Dean interrupted him with another snort, shooting him a wary glance before continuing, "and I'm sorry for digressing. The fact of the matter is that we have a necromancer in the city. In addition to the fact that it has already been proven that they are a danger to themselves and others, I'm sure the possibilities of what the Church could do with this information has already occurred to both of you."

The Dean suppressed a shudder. "I'd prefer not to think about it."

"Oh, my," Ludwig said quietly, "I imagine it'd be quite like the Zeltarian fiasco."

"Very good, Chairman," the Magistrate said approvingly. The Dean suppressed a growl. "And while the good Dean here kept the University quite uninvolved during that incident, I'm sure that he agrees that the current situation could become far more serious, and perhaps quite damaging to Church-University relations."

"I had no duty to do anything about the Zeltarian affair," the Dean growled, glaring at the Magistrate. "Healing magic is well outside my jurisdiction, and you know it."

"I do, I do. But Necromancy isn't. It's hard to say just whose jurisdiction Necromancy is in, isn't it?"

The Dean frowned. The Magistrate was making a disturbing amount of sense.

"It will be whoever's fault that the Church decides it should be," he agreed darkly. "But it certainly won't be theirs, what with the religious outrage that this business will probably stir up."

"I think I've succeeded in rattling you," the Magistrate said. "So, as per why I'm here talking to you two..."

"You need help, obviously," the Dean said.

"Yes, quite so."

"Well, there was no reason to drag Ludwig away from his crystal ball for that. I'll get together some of my best Wizards, and we'll see what we can do."

"Actually, we've already enlisted the help of some of your best. Reynar and Falkenhayn, both of whom you employ."

The Dean, taken aback, decided not to bother hiding his ignorance. "Reynar didn't inform me," he said, darkly.

"I asked him not to mention his activities to anyone. I'm glad he's taking that seriously."

"Hmm. Uncharacteristic of him. The boy has as much sense as a brain-damaged tree lizard. As for Falkenhayn, I've never heard of him."

"Yes," the Magistrate said, "that sounds about right. Anyway, the fact is that the small arcane strike team idea hasn't worked out, and the brute force city-wide search idea currently remains out of the question."

"Yes," the Dean said thoughtfully. "So what does that leave us?"

"We need an edge."

"Oh, goodness," Ludwig twittered.

"Ahhh," the Dean said, "now I understand. You're going to get Ludwig here to look into the future for you."

"Yes. I thought it was awfully poetic, as justice goes."

"I care not for poetry, but I haven't seen Divination practiced in some years. Hop to it, Ludwig!"

"Erm…" Ludwig muttered, almost at a whisper, "Well, sirs… I'm afraid that it's a bit more complicated than that."

"Is it?" the Magistrate asked, voice suggesting genuine curiosity.

"Yes, milord," Ludwig continued, "there's preparation involved, all sorts of things to make ready… but if you come back here tomorrow, by then I'll have been able to forecast, and I'll be able to tell you what I've seen."

The Dean rubbed his beard. His knowledge of how Divination worked was admittedly foggy, but he wasn't quite buying this. But why would Ludwig lie? Would he really go to such lengths out of performance anxiety?

"I'd like to see the forecast myself," the Magistrate said decidedly. "As for preparation, just tell me how to help. I've nowhere to be tonight. Dean?"

"Well, Magistrate, Ludwig is the expert, and if he thinks..."

"Nonsense, nonsense," Schiller said, slowly unbending his lanky body from the step and standing up. "Come, let's get to it."

"Al—all right, yes, sir..." Ludwig murmured, slowly coming to his feet.

"I'll understand if you'd like to retreat to your quarters for some sleep, Dean. I know you're a busy man," the Magistrate said.

Under his thick beard, the Dean smiled. Actively allow Schiller to get ahead of him in the field of information? It'd be a cold day in hell first. "Nonsense," he said, "I'll hardly be able to sleep knowing that you two are hard at work! Come, let's get to it!"

Chapter 19

Alois' sleep was not terribly restful, but it was dreamless, and for that he was grateful. Fading light still flowed in through the windows when his eyes opened the first time, and he wondered what time it was. Still too early to get up, certainly; probably only a couple of hours had passed. He swept his eyes sleepily around the room, briefly startled by the foreign ceiling over his head and the unfamiliar nightstand next to him. Part of him still always expected to wake up at his home. It was, he supposed, something that he was just going to have to get used to. He was about to roll over and attempt to doze off again when he noticed the whispering, coming from just outside the door.

"...crazy, there's nothing..."

"...telling you, I saw..."

"...but how..."

"You've...stories...undead..."

He rolled out of bed immediately and tiptoed as quickly as he could to Lina's bed, shaking her awake.

"Hmm?" she said groggily, rubbing a hand through her matted hair, "is it breakfast time?"

"No," Alois hissed. "They're on to us. It's time to get out of here."

"But... but we're not ready!" Lina moaned, sitting up immediately. "Sebastian's not exactly dressed! What will we do?"

"I'll take care of Sebastian; you get all our things packed up."

"Right."

Alois spun on his heel to go get Sebastian, but found that the skeleton was standing right behind him, staring expectantly. During their escape the night before, they'd stopped for a moment and wrapped the skeleton in an old sheet to try to cover him up. His pants, miraculously, were still in basically one piece.

Alois growled and took stock of his own clothing. He decided he could make due with just his undershirt and jacket, and so removed his tunic and hastily applied it to the skeleton, struggling to get its arms and head through the correct holes.

The skull, though, remained a problem. He growled as he stared at it, black eyeless pits staring helplessly back. He paced quickly over to the closet. It was always possible that...

He harrumphed in triumph. A dingy black sack hung from the coat rack, meant to be used for dirty clothes should a guest choose to take advantage of the inn's laundry service. He snatched it from the rack and headed back over toward Sebastian, opening the bag up and throwing it over his head before he could figure out what was going on. Finding the drawstring, Alois cinched the thing tight around the neck, so that the extra, bunched-up fabric nicely hid the top of Sebastian's spine.

To finish the job, Alois pinned up the loose sleeve of the Skeleton's shirt, and shoved the Skeleton's remaining hand into the pocket of his pants.

"All right," he asked Lina, who was pulling her boots on over her bare feet, "How does he look?"

"Awful," she said, panting slightly. "It's hard to say that we should have even bothered."

"Oh, I don't think it's as bad as all that," Alois said, looking Sebastian up and down. "He just looks like a confused foreigner or something, that's all. Anyway, on the way out, you'll go first, hood down. I'll follow, and he'll come very close behind me."

"Okay, sounds good."

"All right!" Alois said, taking a deep breath and starting for the door. When his hand was on the knob and Lina wasn't right behind him, he frowned and turned to look.

"It's time to go, Lina..."

She was in the corner, attempting to pick up the half skeleton they'd left lying on the desk the night before.

"What in Delar's name are you doing?"

"I'm taking him with us!"

"Don't you think that rather defeats the point of dressing up the skeleton?"

"Well, what do you want me to do?" she asked, getting the words out with some difficulty. She successfully carried the thing most of the way over to Alois before becoming overbalanced and dropping it onto the bed.

"I take it you won't have time to repair my body this morning?" the half-skeleton asked casually, its horrible eyes staring straight up at them.

"No, I'm afraid not," Lina said breathlessly, leaning against the wall.

"Ah. Well. Silly of me to ever think otherwise."

Alois groaned. "We're hardly thrilled by how this is turning out either, sir."

"Oh, I didn't say I wasn't thrilled. It *is* all a bit funny. For me, I mean. Less so for you, conceivably."

"We have to leave him here," Alois said bluntly. "He won't fit in a bag, we have no good means of covering him, and anyway it's extra weight we don't need."

The thing didn't respond, apparently unmoved, staring steadily up at them.

"No, we can't leave him!" Lina insisted, reaching out to pick up the ribcage again.

Alois dragged a hand across his face. "I suppose it would be a bit obvious leaving an animated corpse behind... but look, stop trying to carry him! Can't we just... take his head?"

"Oh!" Lina said, as though she was an idiot for not figuring that out herself.

"Wai—" the thing began to say, but to no effect. Lina had grabbed it round the neck, and with a pair of murmured words, a brief purple flash, and an unpleasant crunching sound, the skull and a few pieces of vertebra were freed from the body. Lina tossed the head into her bag, then pushed the ribcage onto the floor and kicked it under the bed.

"All right! Let's go!" she said.

Wishing to lose no more time, Alois pushed the door open and peered out. The hallway was deserted, and so the three of them crept out of the room and down the stairs into the lobby.

As they turned the bend right out of the stairs, they bumped into the woman who had checked them in the night before. With her was a young man wearing a riding cloak, as though he were about to go out. The woman gasped, and the man stumbled against the wall to make way.

Lina nodded as she rushed by. Alois did the same. "Have to leave on short notice," he grumbled. He could feel the eyes of the two clerks burning into his back as he pushed through the door, and he could hear them begin arguing as soon as it shut behind Sebastian.

It wasn't a small task to keep both Lina and Sebastian walking calmly and casually for the first minute or so, but somehow Alois accomplished it. It was late afternoon, and there were more people on the streets than ever, all of whom would notice if they made too much of a fuss. The trio made their way down a series of alleys and side streets as Alois tried his best to remember his way around the Northern District. The people here tended to be better dressed than any of the three of them, and so it was advisable to steer clear of the larger streets to avoid standing out. With this in mind, he led them toward the main residential area. It wasn't long before he began to recognize the streets.

"Listen," he said, "this isn't working. We've been run out of two inns in as many days."

"It's just bad luck," Lina replied, "that's all. We'll find somewhere safe, sooner or later."

"I fear it will be later rather than sooner. I think... I think it might be best if we go to my house."

There was no response. Alois winced. He was going to have to convince her.

"Look, I know it seems—"

"You have a house?"

"What? Of course I have a house. Where did you think I lived?"

"I don't know... the police dormitory, or something?"

"Policemen don't live in dormitories, Lina."

"But if you have a house, why didn't we just go there to begin with?"

"Well, I mean... at first, because you wanted to go to the Western District. I'm afraid you never did manage to get to talk to anyone about magic, I suppose..."

"That's all right," she said cheerfully.

"But... wasn't that the whole reason you came here?"

"Yes, I suppose, but... well, it's not like it's going anywhere."

"Right. Well, then, after we fled there, I figured, since our attackers saw me, and since I didn't show up for work this morning, maybe someone would have connected the dots..."

"So what changed?"

"I faced reality. I'm not as well-known as all that. I don't know who any of those men last night were, but I didn't recognize any of them, and I don't see any reason to think that they recognized me. As for the Guard's Station, well, missing one day of work will hardly have caused them to raise the alarm."

"Makes sense to me."

"Does it? You don't think I'm being foolhardy?"

"I don't think you could be foolhardy if you tried."

"Well, thank you," Alois said uncertainly.

The rest of the trip to Alois' home did not take very long, and he noted with relief that no neighbors were around to witness his return home.

As he pushed the door open, he had the distinct feeling that he was returning after a long absence. Odd, considering he hadn't been gone much longer than a day. He'd left the place dark, and supposed he was lucky that there hadn't been another break-in. Then again, it hardly would have mattered much. There was little left there that held any value to him.

Lina whistled as she looked around the entryway, peering up the stairs. "Wow, this is a pretty nice place."

"Thank you," Alois responded, not sure what else he could say. "I own it, so we don't have to worry about anyone coming by and checking up on us."

"What about your work?" she asked, voice suggesting that she was only half interested in the answer. She strolled slowly down the hall that led to the kitchen and parlor, pulling her voluminous robes over her head as she went and leaving them lying in a heap on the floor behind her.

"I'll send in a note that I'm going to take some time off. They've all been telling me that I should take some leave anyway. They think that I should be crippled by grief."

"Grief over what? Getting stabbed?"

"…Yes," Alois said, leaning down and scooping up the robes, which he carried into the kitchen and deposited in a heap onto one of the chairs at the table. It was the table at which his family had normally eaten. Through the kitchen to his right was a doorway leading to the dining room, where occasional formal dinners were held.

He watched Lina, who was inspecting a set of porcelain statuettes lined up on a shelf. She was still wearing the faded yellow sundress from the day before, though now it looked a tad more unkempt, and at least a little damp. The pale material contrasted with her bronze skin, her exposed shoulders thin and girlish. It was easy, Alois reflected, to forget how small she was when she had that blasted set of robes on.

"Perhaps you'd like a change of clothes?" he asked, considering that he'd quite like a change himself.

"Oh," she said, glancing down at herself, "I guess I have been wearing this for… well, gee, must be…"

"Don't tell me," Alois said, shaking his head. "Just come this way, if you please."

He turned and led her back to the entryway and up the stairs, willing himself to ignore the faded blood stains that could still be made out in the wood. He could take solace only in the fact that most of this blood was his own. He worried that she would say something, but she either failed to notice or declined to comment.

They reached the top of the stairs and turned onto the second storey hallway, and he opened the first door they came to, leading her inside. It was his bedroom, dominated by a single large bed with a nightstand on either side.

"This is where you'll sleep," he said, stepping inside.

"Wow, really? This is awfully nice…"

"Yes, well, I think you've earned it after all the ratty inns I have no doubt you've stayed in."

"Actually, before I ran into you, I mostly just slept in graveyards."

He rolled his eyes. "My point remains valid. Wait here, please. I'll be back in a moment."

Back in the hallway, memories flashed through his mind. The hallway unlit. A body blocking his path. Whimpering coming from the room to his right. He had lived here for years, tramped down that hallways a thousand times, and yet only those last few minutes stood out to him now.

He ignored it all and carefully opened the door to the room of his youngest daughter, Juliet, at the end of the hall. There had been no scuffle here, though Alois had still avoided the room for weeks. He was sure that some of the Guardsmen had inspected it during their investigation, but their presence was not apparent.

The bed was not made; it looked as though it had been abruptly vacated. Alois suppressed a shudder, doing his best not to imagine precisely how things had occurred that night. He walked straight past the bed to the broad, white doors of the closet, opening them wide. He grabbed the wicker laundry basket from the floor of the closet, carefully emptied the dirty laundry out of it, and then, opening up the built-in dresser drawers, he dumped socks, undergarments, and everything else he found into the basket, consciously not looking. He grabbed as many dresses off the rack as he could and laid them on top of the basket, folding them over.

Back in his own bedroom, Lina was paging through one of the old books he kept on his nightstand.

"Is this yours?" she asked.

"Yes. Telphid's *Chronicle of the Southern Succession Wars*."

"It's interesting."

"Yes," he said, moving into the room and setting the basket full of clothing down by the bed, "They say at least one hundred thousand people died in it."

"Oh. And that's what you read about before bed?"

"This from someone who sleeps in graveyards. I've brought you some clothing, please take whatever you like."

"Oh, goodness," she said, kneeling down in front of the basket and flipping through the dresses.

"Some of them may be too small," Alois said, "but hopefully there will be something that fits properly."

"Where did you get all these?" she asked, skeptically considering a pair of ruffled pink socks.

"It doesn't matter," he said, and left her there. Before heading back downstairs, he took the master house key from his pocket, and locked the doors to both Juliet and Cassandra's rooms.

Since the death of his family, Alois had spent most of his time in the parlor on the first storey of his home. Located through a door-less entryway off the left side of the kitchen, the parlor was somewhat poorly lit and housed a sofa and chair, both overstuffed and overlaid in dark brown leather that was quite soft and getting to be considerably worn. Several of Alois' citations hung on the wall over the mantle, running in chronological order from left to right. Atop the mantle sat a vast model ship that Alois had spent months building a few years prior. The kits cost a fortune, and he had never been able to get a second one. Now he could barely imagine having the time or motivation.

Sebastian, at the moment, stood in front of the ship, peering at it with intense interest, frequently poking it with his phalanges, tapping against the stained wood of its hull. Alois didn't have the heart to ask him to stop, and besides had little else to offer the skeleton by way of entertainment. He wasn't really sure what its idea of fun was. Then again, he also wasn't at all sure what his own idea of fun was these days.

Now, as he often did, he laid sprawled on the couch, staring straight up at the ceiling, which was painted a consoling shade of umber. He had used to lay down every night after work with great pleasure, but it wasn't the same as it used to be. Probably, he considered, because his new body did not get nearly as tired as his old one.

He held up a meaty hand and examined it, turning it slowly before his eyes. He'd always been a somewhat pale man, and he hadn't noticed it getting worse, but now that he looked, he was sure his skin was far more pallid than it had ever been before. And yet, it was still his hand, very familiar to him. The lines running across his palm, the crags of his knuckles; they were all the same. His hands had once ached dully almost all the time; now they felt as strong and healthy as they had when he was a young man. Unlife, he was forced to accept, was not an undesirable thing.

He heard movement above him, and for a fleeting moment he imagined one of his daughters moving about in her room. But the illusion faded almost immediately; that time had passed, and besides, the footfalls were louder and less careful than those of his daughters had ever been. Even now he heard the steps thump to the staircase and then come down it, careening at a speed that Elizabeth likely would have scolded Juliet for, not that Juliet would have attempted it in the first place. Alois wondered briefly how one got to be a fourteen-year old necromancer. Somehow, he couldn't imagine that it was a happy story.

He sat up and turned to face the door before she appeared there, and his eyebrow rose slightly when she did. Her filthy yellow sundress was gone, replaced by a far more elegant dress of light blue satin, with broader straps and a lower hemline. He couldn't remember Juliet ever wearing it, though dresses had hardly ever been a concern of his.

Her dark hair, he noted, even looked as though she had made some attempt at cleaning it before tying it back. "How does it look?"

"Very nice," he nodded approvingly. "It seems to fit well enough."

"Oh, yes, it's fine," she said, nodding. "You'll probably want a change of clothes too, I reckon?"

"Mhmm," he said, "yes, I'll go see about it soon enough. Thank Delar that we have a chance to relax for a time; all that running around probably would have killed me, if I... if, well..."

"If you weren't a ghoul?" she asked cheerfully, floating over to the bookcases lining the rear wall of the room.

"Yes, that," he said. "Do I seem pale to you, by the way?"

"That's natural," she said, not even sparing a look. "Just let me know if you start decaying."

He frowned. "That doesn't... that doesn't happen, does it?"

"No, it shouldn't. But you're my first ghoul, so..."

"How terribly comforting."

"Oh, hush, you'll be fine. Are you hungry, by the way?"

"Not just yet," he said quickly, almost embarrassed that the topic still made him uncomfortable. "Anyway, I think, that, erm, I finished it all last time."

"Oh, yeah," she said absentmindedly, paging through a tome she'd pulled off the shelf, "I guess you did. I can go out and get some more tonight."

"Are you sure that's wise? The whole point of coming here was to keep out of sight."

"They've seen you, and Sebastian is… well, a walking skeleton, but they don't know what I look like. I'll wear my hood down and it should be fine."

"Ugh. We should probably do something about those robes."

"What's wrong with my robes?" she asked, voice rising defensively.

"Well," he asked carefully, "don't you think they might be a big garish?"

"I spent a fortune on those robes, you know! No one else has ones like them!"

"No one who isn't doing magic tricks at a third-rate whorehouse, anyway," came a cold, jeering voice. Lina spun on Alois, frowning. He shook his head, standing, scanning the room for the source of the sound.

His eyes fell on Lina's bag, which had ended up tossed on the leather chair near the kitchen.

"Oh, for God's sake," he said, reflexively putting a hand on his chest before remembering that he didn't have a pulse to be elevated. "I completely forgot about that thing's skull."

"Oh, goodness, such a lack of concern," the voice drawled. "I'm not sure if my feelings will ever recover from a blow like this."

"Hush," Lina said, walking over to the chair and scooping the skull out of her bag, turning it to face her. Alois was glad; those eyes made him a bit uncomfortable.

"I hadn't forgotten about you," she told it sternly, "but I still don't know what you are. I must have created you by mistake."

It cackled softly. "Funny," it said.

"Do you eat anything?" she asked, ignoring it.

"Do not waste both of our time with questions you already know the answer to, necromancer," the skull hissed. "You know very well what you meddle with."

"Fine," she said tartly, "be that way," and tossed the skull back down. It landed in the chair with a thump and rolled so its eyes faced down into the corner where the back met the seat.

Alois frowned. "Lina, didn't you say that all the undead you created in that alley were supposed to fall dead again after a short time?"

"Yes. You should be long dead by now," she said to the skull. "What's the deal?"

The thing laughed softly, as though at something that really wasn't very funny at all.

"I suppose it would be a waste of breath," it said, "if I asked you to repair my body."

"Oh," Lina said, shrugging, "Sure, I can get a start on it tonight. It'll take a long time, though…"

"Don't let me rush you," it sneered.

"Ugh," Alois grunted, "I don't know what we did to make Delar pin us with that thing."

"Who is this Delar guy that you keep talking about?" Lina asked, spinning the odd skull slowly in its place so she could analyze it. It stayed stonily silent as she did so.

"Delar?" Alois asked confusedly, never having had to answer this question before. "Delar is God, you see."

"Ah, Delar's a god. I guess I sort of figured that."

"Well, no," he tried again, "not *a* god, you see, but *the* God."

She looked at him skeptically. "Now, I *know* that's not true. Why, right before I came here, I was in Palrinya, and there they say that there are two gods, both girls. So if you're saying Delar is a god too, then that puts it at least three."

"No, no," Alois said, frowning, "those are false gods. They aren't real. Only Delar is real."

At this, the skull began softly cackling again. They both did their best to ignore it.

"I did think those gods sounded a little silly," Lina said thoughtfully. "You're saying they don't exist at all? But Delar does."

"Oh, yes, definitely," Alois said impulsively. The words left an odd taste in his mouth. "Or," he added slowly, "I thought he did. Or... I thought I believed he did."

"You thought?" Lina asked incredulously, "how can you only *think* that someone exists? I mean, either they do or they don't, isn't that right?"

"Well, gods are more complicated than that..."

"You've at least *met* him, haven't you?"

Alois snorted, "Well, I should think not. Delar has better things to do than attend to my whims."

Lina shook her head. "If you want my opinion, this whole 'gods' business is cracked."

Alois frowned. "Well, maybe Delar doesn't exist, but there must be something, mustn't there?" He wasn't sure anymore who he was asking.

Lina shrugged her shoulders. "There's magic," she said simply. "Say, have you got anything to eat?"

"Oh," Alois said, startled by the topic change, "yes, I'm sorry, I'd completely forgotten. There's bread and dried sausage in the cupboard, over in the kitchen. Erm, that way," he said, pointing.

"Oh, yum," she said, turning and heading in the direction he indicated. He let his hand drop to his side as she passed out of the room.

"Don't listen to her, ghoul," the skull said, and Alois noticed now that it had been turned so that its horrific blood-shot eyes were staring right at him. "What would she know about the gods? What could anyone alive know? But you and I, ghoul. You and I have both died, and we know what we've seen. We know there's something. Oh, there's definitely something."

"I... I didn't see anything," Alois said softly. "I only saw darkness. It was like being asleep."

"How interesting," the skull said, its eyes seeming to twitch in what passed for a facial expression. "How long were you dead before being raised?"

"Oh, I'm not quite sure," he said, having never really thought about it. "Very little time, I think. Maybe less than a minute."

"Ah," the skull said academically, "that explains it. A few more minutes, I think, and you'd have begun to see... a few more than that, and you could have begun to understand."

"How long were you dead?"

It laughed coldly. "Which time?"

"What is that supposed to mean?"

"Don't trouble your mind with it, ghoul. But rest assured, there is 'something else'. You can take my word for it, for I have seen it."

"What is it like?" He could not stop himself from asking, even though he knew he could not trust the thing.

"It's like..." it said, slowly, considerately, "Well... you know, I won't ruin the surprise. You'll find out for yourself."

"I don't imagine that's going to happen," Alois said thoughtfully, "being a ghoul and all."

The skull snorted through sinuses it did not have. "Don't be stupid. You're immortal only in the most rudimentary way. Only as much so as a zombie; immortal so long as no one decides that you're a problem. A sword through the neck, ghoul, and it's all over for you."

"What about you?" Alois asked, trying to keep the image of his own severed head out of his mind. "You're doing fine as just a head. But then again, I suppose that skeletons work differently…"

"Is that what you think I am? A necromantically animated skeleton?"

"If you're not that, what are you?"

"Maybe," it said, snickering, "you should ask your master."

Chapter 20

The Dean's lungs pumped like pistons as he threw himself at a run down the street, squinting through the night glare at the figure he was pursuing. The thin metal plates that lined his jerkin shifted with his body, the added protection slowing him down barely a fraction. As the gap between him and his prey closed, he bent his muscular arm and gripped the hilt of the bastard sword in its scabbard across his back, pulling the weapon out in one smooth motion. His legs did not ache, but felt energized and healthy as oxygenated blood cycled through his system with the efficiency of freshly wound clockwork. He hadn't been so fit since... well, to be honest with himself, the Dean had never been as fit as this. His fluttering tabard showed the purple and blue of the Magistrate's personal guard, and his peripheral vision was blacked out by the T-visor of the helmet he wore.

He spun around a corner and watched as his quarry turned into an alleyway behind a shabby fruit stand. Sometimes, it seemed like this damn city was nothing but alleys. He shot after him, clipping the ramshackle wooden kiosk hard as he passed, ignoring the sounds of it beginning to teeter and summarily crashing into the street behind him. He was briefly blinded by the intense darkness of the alley.

"Halt!" he cried in a deep voice, and within moments his eyes had adjusted. The dank walls of the buildings on either side came into focus, and the now very close figure, tiny in its billowing robes, was apparent straight ahead, still running.

It did not seem jarring at all when the sword melted out of the Dean's hand, and she found herself in the very same alley, but with the way clear ahead of her. Her small, delicate hands were clenched in fists, and she cursed her cumbersome robes, her breath rasping in and out of her chest, as she tried to keep ahead of the man who was pursuing her. She lamented that she had lost track of her friend, not sure at what point she'd become separated from him after the man chasing her first appeared outside the Bank. As the alleyway she ran down approached a Y intersection, she knew she had no idea which way to turn. Biting her lip, she threw herself down the right path, shutting her eyes against what she might find there.

When he opened his eyes, he was flat on his back, staring up at the grim stone ceiling high up above him. The sound of his own ragged breathing was challenged by the sputtering and coughing that was being produced by Magistrate Schiller, who, the Dean saw as he crawled into a sitting position, had collapsed on the opposite side of the Divination circle.

The pattern on the floor had been carefully etched there by Ludwig; a circle fifteen feet across, with a slightly smaller triangle etched inside, especially obtuse Arcanic text scribbled along its edges. Each point of the triangle had a smaller circle etched over it, just big enough for a man to stand in with his feet spread normally, and indeed the Dean had been standing in one of them. Now his back ached, telling him that at some point he must have fallen to the stone floor without even being able to soften the fall with his arms.

"Lord," he said, wiping a trickle of blood from the corner of his mouth, his lip cut by his own teeth, "now I think I remember why I decided that Divination wasn't for me."

Ludwig nodded with infuriating sympathy, and the Dean growled as he realized that the bald little man was not only still on his feet and in his circle, but wasn't even breathing heavily. The Dean felt a sudden immense gratitude that there were no other Wizards around.

"That…" Schiller gasped, holding a hand to his chest, his pulse still racing, "That was amazing! That was just, just the most sensational…"

"Yes, yes, it's quite something," the Dean said, climbing gently to his feet despite a scream of protestation from his joints. "Especially if you've never done it before."

"But Dean… how… how can you not believe? How can you not be amazed by Delar's grace, having seen what I've just seen? We've seen the plan! We've read pages ahead in the Book of Life!"

The Dean groaned. "If you could read Arcanic, Schiller, you'd know that the runes on the floor don't say *anything* about Delar. Let's not get carried away."

"And you, my friend," the Magistrate said, unfolding his lanky body and coming to his feet to turn on Ludwig, "I owe you a debt of gratitude. You've given me something far more intense and personal than any priest or Bishop has ever been able to bestow. You are a true apostle."

Ludwig averted his eyes, and might have blushed if his skin weren't so dark. "Oh, it was nothing… years of practice, you know…"

The Dean had to admit that it had been about as smooth a Divination spell as he'd ever experienced, though God knew he wasn't about to admit it. And yet, something still nagged at the back of his mind. He frowned, trying to figure out what it was.

"The Magisterial Guard!" Schiller was saying, throwing his hands wildly in the air, his face flush with excitement. "I never would have thought of it! I keep those poor fellows just sitting around with nothing to do— some of the best fighters in the City-State, pent up in the

Capitol building! What better use of them than saving our City from schism and heresy?"

The Dean nodded, only half listening. Ludwig had been initially quite insistent that the Magistrate should allow him to do the divination alone—a degree of insistence that was in truth shocking, considering the man's spinelessness. Even after consenting, Ludwig had dilly-dallied, taking longer than he needed to, dropping his chalk, mumbling incantations that the Dean now realized hadn't even been needed, as though he was hoping that Schiller might get bored and leave. And yet, the divination had gone just fine, and indeed, it had shown them exactly what they'd wanted to see, which was testament to Ludwig's skill.

The Dean frowned. So why the hesitance? Could Ludwig be in cahoots with the necromancer? But, no, the Dean rejected that idea almost as soon as he thought of it. The thought of Ludwig being capable of that kind of treason was so laughable that, indeed, he began to chuckle, and was grateful that the Magistrate was still far too carried away to notice.

"But, hmm," Schiller was saying thoughtfully, "We have no idea *when* this will happen… it'll be difficult to make use of this information without…"

"We know when it happens," The Dean said automatically. "It's standard practice for a diviner to cast spells within the divination that help determine the time and date, if they can't do it from standard cues such as the stars and the moon and the like."

The Magistrate's face lit up with fresh enthusiasm. "That's amazing. Ludwig, you know when this will happen?"

"Yes," Ludwig said miserably. "It will happen six nights from tonight, around eleven o'clock, give or take two hours."

"Amazing," Schiller said, shaking his head in astonishment. "A miracle."

The Dean, managing with superhuman force of will to suppress a groan, instead said, "So, I take it you know *where* this alley is?"

Schiller's hands dropped slightly from their places in the air. "Oh. Well, no. I don't get out of the Capitol building very often, I suppose... I wouldn't guess that either of you gentlemen might be more familiar with Merund?"

The Dean almost laughed out loud at the man. Even Ludwig couldn't stop the corner of his mouth from lifting into a skeptical smile.

"No," Schiller said despondently, "I guess not. But that's all right. I remember it well enough. And the fruit kiosk will be a big help. I've got six days to get it figured out, after all. Anyway, we know the chase started outside the Bank, so that's a good start. And..."

"Yes?" The Dean asked pointedly.

"That bit about the Bank," Schiller said slowly, "she was thinking that. We could read her thoughts."

"Only her surface thoughts," the Dean amended, "and even then, not much gets through. I believe there are other sorts of Divination that are suited for mind reading, but this isn't really one of them."

"So," Ludwig asked hesitantly, "You'll send a Magisterial Guard to the Bank to watch for the necromancer, and when she appears..."

Something clicked into place in the Dean's mind. "A girl!" he yelled, "The necromancer is a girl! And a young girl, at that!"

Schiller frowned. "Hell, you're right. Being her was so natural, I didn't even question it..."

"She isn't supposed to be a girl?" Ludwig asked curiously.

"Of course not, you twit!" the Dean said, throwing his hands in the air. "Who ever heard of a female necromancer? I mean, hell, a female magician is uncommon enough, but a female necromancer? May as well have a horse for a blacksmith!"

"Other places have many female magicians," Ludwig said, his voice suggesting an intention of being genuinely informative.

"Is that so?" Schiller asked. "Why haven't we got them here?"

The Dean laughed darkly. "Because your own holy texts forbid them, man! But I have to admit that those bastards at the Church are right on this one. Women haven't got any magical aptitude."

"With at least one exception that we know of," Schiller pointed out.

"There must be someone helping her, or something," The Dean muttered.

"So, when she comes, you'll have the Guard chase her, fulfilling the prophesy," Ludwig said, his voice carefully measured.

"Yes, yes," the Magistrate said, almost breathless with possibility. "But it would have happened even if we hadn't done this, isn't that right? Or, no, what am I saying? The future is set, so we had no choice but to do this! It's going to happen because we were always meant to see it happen here, and make it happen!"

"I don't get involved in discussions about the idiosyncrasies of Divination magic," the Dean said. "I have enough risk factors for a stroke as it is."

"But we won't do just that," Schiller said, basically ignoring him, "No, you see, the real gift Delar has given us was there at the very end. We know which way she turns, and we know that she'll barely be able to see a few feet ahead of her. There will be more guards waiting down the right path, and they'll have her mere instants after our vision cut off."

"Cute," the Dean said thoughtfully. "I have to admit, this is a better use for Divination than any of the garbage the Church does with it."

Schiller smiled. "I think we're in agreement about that. Does anyone have the time?"

The Dean dug around in the pockets of his robes, coming out with his pocket watch. It needn't ever be wound—the clockwork was powered by an Enchantment that he himself had cast on it, meaning that, unlike most of the magical watches on the market, his actually worked properly. He glanced at it and groaned.

"The sun'll be coming up."

"I guess I'd better let you gentlemen get to sleep," Schiller said, voice full of schoolboy giddiness. "As for me, I doubt I'll be getting any."

The Magistrate said his final profuse and heartfelt thanks to Ludwig, who seemed to have trouble meeting his eye. The Dean gave Ludwig a curt nod and escorted the Magistrate down the stairs and back through the University to the main entrance where his carriage waited. More people walked the halls of the school now; bleary-eyed teaching assistants entered classrooms to prepare them for the day ahead, and equally bleary-eyed researchers tore themselves away from their studies to finally head back to the dormitory.

As they approached the main doors, the Dean flicked a finger and muttered the Arcanic command that every University student learned their first day. The massive oak doors slid easily open on their well-greased tracks.

The Magistrate extended a slender hand, and the Dean took it in his and shook it. For once, he found, he was too tired—but even more so, too intrigued by the events of the night—to be angry.

"You'll keep me apprised of events?" he asked, raising a bushy eyebrow.

"My good Dean, I wouldn't dream of doing otherwise."

"Yes, excellent. Well, have a safe journey home, then."

"And a good rest to you, Dean." A spring in his step, the Magistrate headed down the stone stairs that led to the road where his carriage waited. He glanced back over his shoulder, a mischievous glint in his eyes.

"And Delar be with you, Dean! I think he is with us, tonight!"

The Dean gave him a pained smile, and shut the door.

———————————————————————————•

"Maybe you'd ought to leave the robes behind," Alois said, fingers idly twitching at the end of his mustache. "They're... a tad recognizable."

"Oh, come on! It's a big city, and I haven't been out in nearly a week. I bet they've stopped looking for me by now."

Alois shook his head. "Unlikely. Not after what you did last time. No, I think they'll be committed to finding us rather indefinitely."

"Still, we're not likely to run into them."

"She's right!" the disembodied skull called from its chair in the parlor. Alois and Lina were in the front hall, where they'd been pulling their shoes on.

"We don't need any advice from you, thank you!" Alois called back curtly.

"Oh, I get it. You won't listen to me just because I'm hoping you'll both be savagely murdered."

"Pretty much, yep," Lina said.

"He's got quite an attitude," Alois murmured.

"He's been sulky for days. He's barely spoken. He just lies there, muttering to himself."

"Mhmm. I don't think picking him up was terribly lucky for us."

"It's not his fault, really. I'd be bored too, if I was just a head."

"Granted, but I doubt much of anything could make you as caustic as he is."

"I feel bad for not recreating his body. It's just that totally regenerating undead body parts takes so much concentration... It'll take me forever. I'll get started tomorrow, though, that should brighten him up some."

"That should shut him up. I'm glad you were at least able to close up my dagger wound."

She smiled. "Oh, sure, that was easy. Sorry I didn't think to do it in the first place... I'm used to working with zombies, and they don't mind wounds."

"Hold on," bleated the skull, "Old man Alois isn't a zombie? How are we to explain the vacant expression, then? And there's the drooling..."

Alois sighed. "He's not exactly making me *want* to help him get his body back."

She shrugged. "Let's take him with us. That'll cheer him up."

Alois groaned and headed back for the parlor, where he scooped the head out of the chair. It grinned up at him silently.

"Want to come along for the ride?" he asked it, still not terribly comfortable looking it in the eye.

"My. By all means," it said.

He didn't care much for that at all, but nevertheless he tossed it into Lina's bag, which she held open for him in the hall. With that, the two of them headed out the door.

It was the middle of the night, and quite chilly. Lina stretched out her arms as she paced down the walk, her hood off and her head stretched upwards, gazing into the sky. She reached up and began tying her hair back absent-mindedly. "It's good to see the stars again. I feel like I've been in that house forever."

"It's only been... what, six days?" Alois said, shutting the door and locking it.

"Easy for you to say. You got to go on all those trips. Shopping, to the graveyard, to the police station... all while I stayed home. And, bless their hearts, I'm afraid the skull twins just aren't the best of company."

Alois chuckled. They'd by now more than learned their lesson about taking Sebastian outside. They'd set him up in the basement a few hours ago; he had access to the myriad half-full buckets of paint that Alois had accumulated over years of home improvement, and they'd hung up some old bed sheets for canvas. Alois figured it'd keep the skeleton busy indefinitely, though he didn't look forward to seeing the state of the place when they returned.

"I could hardly bring you to the station with me; I was there to tell them that I was taking some time off, not to try and explain why I had an ominous robed figure tailing me."

"You could've told them that I was your grandfather," she said severely, "since apparently I look so much like an old man to Guardsmen."

Alois sighed as they turned onto a broader street. Rush hour was long past, and it was quite vacant save for a few house servants who were on their way home for the night.

"And as for the shopping," he continued, "I just don't think it's safe for you to be out in public too often. Especially since you *insist* on wearing those things."

"Jealous," she sang, "you're just jealous."

"Anyway," he said dryly, "you're out now, so stop complaining."

"Can we go to the University?"

"What? Why in the world should you want to go there?"

"They're supposed to have one of the best arcane libraries on the continent. It's actually one of the reasons I came here."

"Ah…"

"What? What is it?"

"Well, I don't think we can go."

"Why not?"

"For starters, you're not a Wizard, and you know how it is here. Unlicensed practice of magic is illegal. I doubt they'd let us in the front door."

"But we could just say we're researchers! You can have an interest in magic without being able to practice it!"

"Well, perhaps…"

"So we can go?"

"No, I'm afraid not."

She groaned in frustration. "And why not?"

"Because," he said tiredly, "you won't find what you're looking for."

"What? How do you figure?"

"You have to understand," Alois said, "Necromancy isn't practiced here. Not at all. Most citizens think it's the worst crime conceivable. Any books the University has on it were probably destroyed or locked away a very long time ago."

There was a long pause from his side.

"Oh," she said, finally.

"I'm sorry, Lina. Maybe in a few nights we can try our luck in the Western District again, perhaps speak to some magicians."

"Yeah, maybe."

"Come now," he said, nudging her softly in the shoulder, "cheer up."

"Yeah," she said, "it's just that I think this might not be the place for me. I'm used to what I do creeping people out, but I've never been somewhere quite so hostile before."

"I'm sure it's very difficult."

"How the hell can they claim to be a Magical University if they deny an entire school of magic?" she asked hotly, throwing her hands up. "I bet this has got something to do with all that stupid 'Delar' business."

"You're not wrong," Alois admitted.

She shook her head and sighed. "You don't think I'm an abomination, do you?"

"Well, if you are, what would that make me?"

"You didn't answer my question."

He sighed. "No, Lina. I don't think you're an abomination." Hesitantly, he put a hand on her shoulder and patted it in what he hoped was a reassuring fashion.

They made their way through several residential blocks, turning one way and then another. The streets steadily became bigger, though not much busier, until they were in Merund's government district. The tower of the Municipal Armory rose high overhead, flanked on one side by the new courthouse and on the other by the state theater.

"So where's your bank?" Lina asked, gazing up at the armory's tower. It was just a hair shorter than the Capitol building down in the Central District, and most people would go their whole lives without ever seeing a taller pair of buildings. Alois wondered if, for all the places she'd been, Lina hadn't seen higher ones.

"Not just my bank, but *the* Bank. There's only the one. It's up there, on the corner."

They began to walk casually toward it, and Alois was glad to note that pedestrians were few—the area was usually fairly deserted at this time of night.

"Aren't there any local banks?"

"Not since the currency upheaval back when I was a boy. Now there's just the central state-run Municipal Bank, where you can get purchasing vouchers provided you're gainfully employed. It works at least a little better than the blasted barter system."

"I hate to mention this, but they look pretty closed."

"Of course they're closed; it's eleven o'clock at night! I just want to slip my time sheet for my last few weeks of work into the slot. Sometime tomorrow they'll cash it, and by the next day the postman should bring us some new vouchers. Which is good, considering the amount of food you consume."

"Magic takes a lot of calories to perform!"

"I'm sure it does. See there on the side wall? That's the drop box. We'll..."

The sound of running footsteps began so suddenly that they barely had time to react to it. Alois turned his head just in time to see the big man, clad in purple and blue, charging out of the shadows. He was going to yell a question, or a warning, but there was no point. By the time he had his mouth open, the man had drawn a vicious-looking sword off his back, closed the gap between them, and swung the blade down with shocking speed.

Alois stared down in horror as the skin of his chest was opened, the blade slicing cleanly into him but thankfully stopping against his sternum and ribs, drawing an ugly but largely superficial wound and leaving the front of his shirt torn open. The sword came away with a coat of thick, oozing blood coating its edge, but none flowed from the wound.

Alois realized with dawning horror that he had not thought to bring his saber with him. The swordsman took another swing, quick and without much power behind it, aiming for Alois' unprotected face. Alois blocked with his arm, wincing as he felt the blade slice through his flesh and cut a notch into one of the bones of his forearm. The pain he should have felt, though, was not there. He growled and was preparing to throw himself bodily at his assailant before he realized that Lina was no longer behind him.

She shrieked as the purple and blue-clad knight hacked into Alois' chest, and she brought her hands up to try and do something to help, though she had no idea what. She didn't have time to think it through any further; another man in the same dress, just as big as the first, had appeared out of nowhere. He bore down on her, his thick legs pounding the sidewalk, ready to lunge forward and grab her. And he certainly wasn't dead, so there wasn't anything she could do about it.

Except to run. Which she did, despite the fact that she had no idea which way to go. She shot down the street away from the Bank, pulling her robes up so that her legs could take longer strides. Her heart hammered inside her ribcage, and a quick throw of her head over her shoulder confirmed that her attacker was only seconds behind her, face hidden behind the dark iron of his helm.

Mathias Brenz had to suppress a smile when she looked back at him. She was no athlete, and she had been losing ground to him since the moment she'd begun running. He was going to catch her, and it wasn't even going to be difficult.

In a way, he considered, it was somewhat disappointing. The Magistrate didn't have them do much, and now, when he was finally employing their skills, it was to hunt down a little girl, barely old enough to flirt with boys much less fight a fully-trained swordsman. Nevertheless, Schiller had made her out to be quite a dangerous opponent. The most dangerous threat that the city has faced in years, to use the Magistrate's own terms.

The thought elicited a chuckle from Brenz. The Magistrate could be as melodramatic as he wanted; a little girl was a little girl. He didn't know what Schiller wanted her for, and he preferred not to ask. All he wanted was to do his job. He wanted to do his job because he knew he was good at it.

She was swinging into an alley now, dodging around a rickety old cart from which, during the day, an unpleasant old woman attempted to hawk fruit of dubious quality. Brenz inhaled in surprise. Schiller had been right. Brenz had thought the man was off his rocker when he'd informed them of the exact path the girl would take during the chase, but she was following it perfectly. He was glad he hadn't questioned the Magistrate's orders. If he had, there wouldn't be six more men waiting for her at the end of this alley, down the fork that the Magistrate had assured them she would take.

Brenz darted after her. At the last moment he managed to veer to one side and avoid banging the fruit cart. There was no reason to cause collateral damage, though he wouldn't exactly have felt much remorse over it. You sell people crap, and that's what you'll get in return.

Now he was closing in for the kill. He could see the fork in the alley ahead of them, and he drew his hand-and-a-half sword with an elaborate *whoosh* to goad her forward into the climax of their little trap. It was all sort of stupid, in a way. If he wanted to, at this point he could put on a final burst of speed and take her down within moments. And yet, he just couldn't resist watching the Magistrate's scheme tie itself up into a neat little bow. A new smile raised the corners of his mouth as the girl came to the fork, and he didn't bother suppressing it this time.

It turned out he had nothing to suppress. She turned left.

Left, to shoot down a small avenue and out onto a city street. Not just any street, but Trinops Row, which at the moment would be heavily crowded with workers headed to and from night shifts at the metalworking district.

Left, where Brenz had not stationed a single Guard, because the Magistrate had assured him over and over that she would not go that way.

Left, to freedom.

He growled severely, his pride wounded, his tentative trust in the Magistrate shattered. Hadn't that man done him enough harm? And now his one chance to do his city right was going to be spoiled.

No. To hell with it. He was going to get her. He put on that boost of speed, and he made that left turn and then two more sharp ones as the alley jinked back and forth, and then he was on Trinops Row. Instead of letting the little black shape disappear into the crowd, he locked his eyes on it and threw himself bodily after it, letting everything else fall out of focus.

Moments later, half a dozen workmen were lying confusedly on the ground, and Mathias Brenz of the Magisterial Guard had the girl against the cobbles, his gloved hand closed over her mouth as she struggled to get away. He heard pounding footsteps as the others came to join him, having quickly figured out that things had gone wrong.

But not, he considered happily, all *that* wrong. If anything, he was actually happy with how things had turned out. To hell with schemes. Sometimes you had to do it the old-fashioned way.

The inside of the covered wagon stank of sweat, the nine Magisterials pressed up against one another on the benches that lined its interior, forming a rough square. On the floor in the middle of them sat the girl, whose robes were torn and hands cut up, though she appeared otherwise unharmed.

Next to her was the man. Big, with a mustache, he looked like someone who might have been strong fifteen years ago, before going soft. According to the three men it had taken to bring him down, though, looks could be deceiving.

Yonts, who'd been the one to get the man's attention initially, looked like he'd had a disagreement with an oncoming stage coach. His face was covered in bruises, his right eye puffy and barely able to open. He'd pulled his tabard off and was hunched over, moaning and clutching his stomach. Brenz was suddenly pleased that he'd opted to go after the girl.

Apparently the big man had tried to chase after him, but wasn't nearly fast enough. Yonts caught up to him and gave him a few sword blows that should have brought him down, and instead ended up getting beaten to a pulp while the big guy used nothing but his fists. If Brenz hadn't left two more Magisterials behind that were able to pry them apart, he wasn't sure that Yonts would have made it out alive.

The big man had to be her father. She huddled against him, his arm wrapped protectively over her shoulder, his eyes alternating between checking her for wounds and glaring warily at the Guardsmen.

He needn't have worried. They were under strict orders not to hurt the girl unless she attempted to escape, or if she showed any sign of casting a spell. None of them were very well versed in what spell-casting looked like, so they'd let her know immediately that her head was coming off if she so much as spoke.

The ride was going about as well as could be expected until the tearing sound filled the cabin. The Guards all twitched, eyes darting from the girl to the man to each other, trying to find the source of the noise. The girl and the man looked as confused as anyone, but Brenz kept his eyes on her, and soon he saw what was happening.

She had a bag with her; a worn cloth affair, tucked under her shoulder so securely that it was barely noticeable against her robes. The noise was the bottom of the bag slowly and methodically tearing itself free of the rest. It was quite unnerving to watch. It was as though an invisible hand had made a small hole in the stitching, grabbed onto it, and from there was tearing the entire bottom away, each stitch either ripping out with a loud snap.

"Stop that!" Brenz roared, trying to draw his sword but finding it a nearly impossible task in such cramped quarters, "Stop that, or you're dead! I told you, no spell-casting!"

She stared up at him with wide, panic-filled eyes. "It's not me!"

He felt a wave of panic himself when he realized that he believed her. The bag's bottom had now dislodged from two of its four corners, and it fell open limply like a flap. The contents of the bag spilled abruptly out; a knife, silverware, a spool of yarn, knitting needles, small packages, and a myriad of items too small to easily identify poured out onto the floor of the carriage.

One item was hard to miss. Bowling out immediately and banging the wood floor with a loud thump, it was a human head, almost entirely decomposed. *Almost* entirely decomposed, except for the eyes. Eyes which, round and bloodshot, stared directly up at Brenz as the skull's mandible clacked rapidly open and closed.

His initial reaction was confusion, but that disappeared in mere moments, replaced not by fear as seemed to have taken the others but by a sort of indefinable rage. He couldn't describe how much the thing on the floor offended him. How much he hated it, hated it completely, regardless of what it was or where it had come from. He roared maniacally and pulled at the bastard sword on his back, his arm banging against the wagon ceiling as he did. Cursing, he slammed his shoulder into the Guard next to him, knocking him aside to get enough space to lean sideways and pull the sword clear of its sheath. The girl shrieked. The big man tried to push her behind himself, and the others stared at Brenz with bemusement on their faces. They were speaking, but he could not hear them. He found himself completely unconcerned with their opinion of his actions. He had never been so sure of anything in his life.

His mouth curled into a snarl of contempt as he brought back his sword and plunged it into the skull. The bone was old and rotten, and the honed metal blade splintered into it like wet timber, caving in the nasal passage, shattering the eye orbitals, slowing as it hit some ineffably tarry resistance deep within before eventually punching clean through the other side. At that moment, with the 'pop' of his sword puncturing the skull's rear, the thing's eyes rolled upwards. With a flash of preternatural red light, the skull shattered like terra cotta, leaving his blade free save for a profane black stain coating it to halfway down its length.

Suddenly sound came rushing back, and he heard stifled tears from the girl. He looked to the prisoners, and saw that the mustached man was staring at him with a mixture of derision and horror on his face. His comrades stared as well, their faces showing more confusion than anything else.

"What the hell was that?" one of them stammered, "And what'd you kill it for? The Magistrate's going to be pissed."

Brenz snorted. "I *had* to kill it, moron."

"You did? Why?'

Brenz laughed aloud now, the answer was so obvious. And yet, as he opened his mouth to give it, he found that he couldn't remember what it was.

Chapter 21

Lina held her arms tightly across her chest, hands firmly grasping her biceps. They'd taken away her robes, and it was dark and damp and very cold out as they prodded her and Alois up the impeccably decorated walkway that led to the Capitol building. The high tower loomed over them, its windows glowing with flickering orange lamplight. Beautifully manicured shrubs and trees littered the courtyard around them in careful linear patterns, but in the dark they appeared as grim specters waiting to loom forth and strike.

A constant fluttering pervaded the air: the striking violet capes of their nine escorts flapping and shifting in the wind. The men were arranged in a tight box with the prisoners in the middle, the little phalanx cutting off any possible avenue of escape, short of learning to fly.

She stumbled against a crack in the walk, and before she even had a chance to right herself she felt the point of a sword, thankfully enclosed in its sheath, jab her hard between her shoulder blades.

"Move along!" one of their captors growled. Alois' face turned even darker than it was already, and he looked ready to turn and confront the man before Lina reached out and clasped his wrist.

"It's all right," she said, trying to make her voice sound as calm as possible. "It's all right."

He nodded almost imperceptibly, and she didn't let go of his wrist as they made their way up the steps to the double doors, which slowly creaked open as though aware of the Guard's approach. The antechamber inside was no bigger than a small tavern, but all eleven of them marched their way in. The space was brightly lit, and three men stood waiting for them, eyes staring hungrily over the shoulders of the Guards in front to peer at the prisoners. On the left, a tall, lanky man with a scraggly brown beard and a crutch under one arm. Of them all, only he was staring at Alois, his face displaying a gentle sort of curiosity. In the center, a middle-aged man just as tall and thin, wearing an untucked dress shirt and peering at Lina with a look of exultation on his face. To the right, a head shorter, stood a handsome man with raven-black hair. His bright eyes seemed to bore into her.

"It worked," the man in the middle said. "By God, I knew it would, but... oh, you Magisterial Guards, you fine men, you don't know yet just what you've participated in this night."

"I didn't think it would work," the dark haired man said quietly, sounding genuinely surprised. "I guess I owe you an apology."

"Save your apologies for Delar," the middle one said happily, and now his gaze shifted to Alois. His mouth fell into a slight frown as he squinted, as if to see better.

"Alois Gustav?"

Alois growled. "Magistrate."

"You're the necromancer's assistant? I can't claim to have seen that one coming."

"That's Alois Gustav?" the black-haired man asked, standing on tip-toe to get a better look.

"Who is Alois Gustav?" the bearded man asked curiously. "I mean, other than a ghoul."

"Alois Gustav is the Chief Constable of the Central District Guard. A few weeks back he was badly hurt in a home invasion and there was a Church inquiry, but no charges were brought up against him."

"That sounds about right," the bearded man said. "They absolved him of having been healed and overlooked the fact that he happened to be undead."

"He put in for leave a few days ago," the dark-haired man said conversationally. "I guess now we know what he's doing with the time off."

"Well, do go on talking about him like he's not here!" Lina exclaimed hotly. The three men went silent and all eyes turned to her.

"Fair enough," the Magistrate said. "We'll figure things with Mr. Gustav out later. It's you who we're after. You are the necromancer, I take it?" His tone implied that he was only asking to be polite.

"I am *a* necromancer, yes," she said sharply. She'd expected an inhalation of breath from Alois at the admittance, but then she remembered that he didn't breathe. As it was, he could hardly expect her to bother lying at this point.

"I would… it would honor me to be able to speak with you, miss, if you'd allow it," the bearded man said, mouth quirked in a nervous smile. Both the Magistrate and the dark-haired man glanced at him, frowning.

"She's our prisoner, Rad," the dark-haired man said, "You can talk to her as much as you damn well like."

"Krupp's right on part one," the Magistrate interjected, "but talking to her might not be the best idea. I understand that she's of magical interest, but I think that the knowledge she carries is too dangerous for release, even to someone as careful and skilled as you."

The bearded man looked like he was going to argue, but Lina beat him to the punch. "There's nothing dangerous about Necromancy! No more than any other branch of magic!"

"You understand neither our society nor our religion, little girl," The Magistrate said darkly, "so do not presume to lecture me on matters you have no right to speak of in the first place."

She was beginning to respond when the sheathed sword gave her another sound jab in the back. Her mouth closed into a tight frown as she barely held back a snarl.

"Brenz," the Magistrate said, looking at one of the Magisterials in front, "tell me about it. Was it just as I said?"

The one called Brenz clicked his heels together as he came to attention, bringing his fist to his chest. "Yes, my lord. We awaited them in hiding near the Bank, and they soon arrived, as you said they would. I pursued the girl through the streets and down the very alley that we were told to expect."

The Magistrate laughed with such glee that he was nearly giggling. "Wonderful, wonderful. She walked perfectly into our trap, did she?"

"Ah," Brenz said haltingly, "well, no sir, not quite. It went as you said until we got to the fork, but then she turned the wrong way. I hadn't set a trap up on that end since you said not to, so I had to pursue her, but eventually I managed to bring her down." His tone picked up as he said the last. If he was expecting a pat on the head, Lina thought, he was going to be sorely disappointed. For while he was looking at the Magistrate, Lina was looking at Krupp, and the man's already fair skin had turned ghostly white in all of a second as Brenz spoke. His fingers began to clench and unclench as though he were desperate to take action but could think of nothing to do.

"Say again, please," the Magistrate said softly, lids fluttering over his eyes several times.

"Erm, yes, sir. We pursued her from the Bank to the alley, as you said we would. However, she turned left instead of right at the intersection and avoided the trap, so I had to keep chasing her, an—"

He came to a slow halt when he saw the expression that had come over the Magistrate's face. The words that the Magistrate spoke next were very, very calm.

"What do you mean, she turned the wrong way?"

"She... she turned left, instead of right, like you sai—"

"You're wrong!" the Magistrate said, loudly, almost screaming. "Don't they even teach you right from left at that worthless military academy?"

Brenz's back straightened noticeably. "Sir, I assure you, she turned left."

"It's true, sir," another of the Guards said, his voice firm. "We were set up to intercept her if she turned right, and she did not."

The bearded man, his face troubled, had crutched a few steps away from the Magistrate, now watching him warily. Krupp had moved closer, and was holding a hand in the air as if to signal him to stop.

"Magistrate, it doesn't really matter. The divination gave us as much as we needed to catch them, and here they are! The city is saved! Things couldn't have gone better, don't you see?'

"It was wrong," the Magistrate said, his voice flat and dead. "How could it be wrong? What does that mean?"

"It doesn't mean *anything*," Krupp hissed.

"We have to go to the University. Right now, we have to go there. I need to speak to the Dean, that incompetent Dean, and that little goddamn rat Ludwig. Let's go. Now."

"Uhm, yes, sir," Brenz said carefully, "We can take the wagon we arrived in, that will be faster than readying a carriage. I'll let some of my boys go home for the night so we'll have more room. What should we do with the prisoners?"

"No time," the Magistrate said, pushing through the Guards toward the still-open doors. "Bring them with us."

Krupp rushed after him, though the Guards were less inclined to part to see him through. "Magistrate Schiller! Please, please reconsider! This is insane!"

The Magistrate was already outside, taking the steps two at a time.

The Dean was stirred awake from his dreams by the blaring voice of his assistant, which seemed even whinier than usual.

"All right, all right," he groaned, waving at the little flicker of light as it looped around his head. "Shut the hell up, Reich. What's the problem?"

"The Magistrate is here, with armed men!"

The sleep drained away from the Dean's mind. "What? Are they there with you?"

"No, they didn't even come here! They barged in one of the east entrances several minutes ago!"

"Hrmm... paying a personal visit to Ludwig, I suppose. Very well. Thank you for informing me." He flicked a finger at the beacon, and it flickered out of existence before Reich had a chance to respond. The Dean strode purposefully to the rack and pulled, not for the first time this week, his scholar's robes on over his pajamas. It was at least, he considered, earlier than the last time Schiller had come to visit. The inclusion of his Magisterials was another new addition, and certainly an unwelcome one.

Shutting his eyes, he pictured himself standing at the door of the Divination chamber. He focused on the image until it was quite vivid, aided by the chant he murmured constantly under his breath. Speaking a final word, he opened his eyes upon the old oaken door at the top of the east tower stairs. Smiling slightly, he murmured a few more words to himself, a second spell settling over him like a warm blanket. A bit of protection, the Dean had always felt, never hurt anybody.

He shook out his robes and smoothed his beard before giving the door a firm push. It swung open without resistance. He stood casually, as though out for a stroll, and allowed his eyes to take in the sight of Chairman Ludwig being held nearly off the ground by two armed, armored, and well-muscled individuals. There were three more Guards nearby.

Schiller was there too, of course, as were others. A man with a crutch who definitely looked the Wizard type, along with Schiller's trained sycophant Albert Krupp. Nothing unduly troubling so far, but the Dean did have a bit of trouble with the large mustachioed man and the teenage girl, themselves huddled together with a pair of Magisterials clearly watching them very closely.

The Dean had a quick mind. Quicker even, perhaps, than the Magistrate, who stared almost dumbly for a moment or two into the Dean's dark eyes.

"If you were going to visit with Chairman Ludwig," the Dean said not unkindly, "I would have appreciated an invitation."

"Hah!" Schiller spat, glaring with contempt first at Ludwig and then at the Dean. "You'll get your turn soon enough, Baldermann. I am hardly convinced that this man's treasonous heresy doesn't course through this entire tumor of a University."

"Harsh words. Ludwig, what is it that the good Magistrate here has accused you of?"

"He—he hasn't said!" Ludwig stammered, looking even frailer than usual in the grip of the Magisterials.

"No, I haven't," Schiller said. "I was just getting to that when you arrived, Baldermann."

"My proper title," the Dean instructed politely, "is *Dean* Baldermann."

"That remains to be seen," Schiller said darkly. "You may as well stay, now that you've come. How did you get up here so quickly, anyhow?"

"Goodness," the Dean said, "It's almost as though I'm a Wizard ..."

The lanky looking fellow on the crutch stifled a snicker, which drew the Dean's gaze toward him. "And who are you, anyway?"

"Erm, it's, it's Falkenhayn, sir! Radcliff Falkenhayn!"

"Hmm. Never heard of you."

"I, I, I work in—"

"You may both shut up, I think," Schiller said softly. "I have business at hand. Captain, please restrain the Dean from leaving the chamber."

Instead of laughing as was his inclination, the Dean bowed. "Not necessary. I'm obliged to stay anyhow." To prove his point, he stepped away from the door, walking over toward the odd pair of would-be prisoners. The Guard Captain grunted.

"Right there is fine, Baldermann," Schiller said, stopping the man short of the pair. Under his bushy beard, the Dean permitted himself a measured smile. *Interesting.*

"Chairman Ludwig," Schiller was saying now, his words almost covering the soft sound of one of the Guards stepping over behind Baldermann to keep him covered, "do you know why I am here?"

"Yes!" Ludwig stammered.

There was a pause.

"Huh," the Dean said. Schiller's face suggested similar bemusement.

"You do," Schiller said finally. "I see. Why don't you tell us, then?"

"The, the prophecy we witnessed here, last time," Schiller said, his stammer lessening a bit as he gained momentum, "it didn't come true. Things went differently."

"Bold of you to admit that you know," the Magistrate said thoughtfully. "I thought this would be more difficult. So, you confess to being a charlatan? A heretic, masquerading as a diviner?"

"W-what?" Ludwig stammered, "No, no!"

"Then what in God's name do you mean by admitting that the prophecy didn't come true?" Schiller roared, looking like he might slap Ludwig across the face.

"It—it—they—they—"

"Spit it out!" the Magistrate shouted, his pale, gaunt cheeks flushed red. He grabbed at Ludwig's robe with his bony hands, shaking away at the little man.

"If I may," the Dean said thoughtfully, "I think what Ludwig must mean is that Divination is an imperfect art, and that prophecies often fail to come true."

"Hah..." Schiller began, turning his gaze on the Dean, wiping sweat from his brow with one hand, "what other explanation would I expect from a Wizard atheist? Keep your theories to yourself. It'll be your turn to confess soon enough."

"But he's right!" Ludwig managed, looking desperately at the faces of the Guards for support and finding less than none. "Divination, it... it only, it..."

"Just admit it! You're a fraud, man, you already told us so! We all saw the prophecy, we saw that when she was chased down the alley she turned right, and my Guard Captain here saw with his own eyes, not an hour ago, the girl turn left!"

Ludwig's shaking subsided just slightly as a look of confusion came over his face. "You mean... everything else went as foreseen? Goodness, what luck that is...

probably one of the most accurate predictions of recent memory…"

"Dig the hole deeper, Ludwig," Schiller said, shaking his head disgustedly. "Aren't you even going to *try* to pretend that you're an actual diviner?"

"I'm an excellent diviner!" Ludwig squeaked, doing a decent imitation of pride. "With all the possible routes that the future could take, getting such an accurate prediction is nearly miraculous!"

"Miraculous!" Schiller spat, "You think so? You think so, when the entire leadership of the Church tells us that true Divination gives us a perfectly accurate view of the future?"

"And are any of them," Ludwig asked coldly, his voice suddenly shockingly firm, "diviners?"

"Hah! You think you can turn the blame on our priests? Their view of fate comes directly from the sacred texts, the foundation of our religion and our culture! Your sins nearly run the ledger out of space, man!"

"If the Church told you that Divination was perfectly accurate, or even mostly accurate," Ludwig said softly, and now the stammering was gone, replaced with something like resignation, or even resolve, "then that is between you and them."

"I… is this… do you really think that…"

"I suppose it all makes sense, come to think of it," the Dean interjected. "I mean, magic is all about the patterns of reality, the energy fields that we exist inside of, so of course you could use it to read the patterns and detect what was *likely* to happen—but that can never account for unpredictable events. I might decide to burn everyone in this room alive, and there is nothing to stop me, but the possibility is negligible, and so Divination would probably not predict it. And yet, indeed, it *could* happen…"

The Guards shifted uncomfortably. Schiller merely stared.

"And so Divination magic can only make its best guess at possible outcomes; but a divination that looks even a few hours into the future involves hundreds of guesses. Such predictions couldn't be perfectly accurate, and would often turn out positively inaccurate. Fascinating, actually. I suddenly wish that I'd studied Divination."

"Are you so completely incapable of understanding anything outside of your base, sinful magic?" Schiller said at a bare whisper, revulsion on his face. "It is so obvious that Delar is the binding force that would allow such predictions to work without fail. No wonder Ludwig is such a failure, if he believes as you do."

"Perhaps," the Dean said, "it is your own complete ignorance of magic that is responsible for all of us being up here in the first place, instead of in bed where we belong."

"Seize him, and shut him up!" Schiller barked. The Dean spun smoothly on the Guard behind him, who had just reached out his hands. "I wouldn't," the Dean recommended softly.

"It… it might not be a good idea…" the fellow on the crutch began, but was silence by a glance from Krupp. The Dean laughed.

"Let me give you one last idea to consider, Schiller," he said, "in my sinful way, and then I promise to be silent. Is that acceptable?"

Schiller snorted. "Very well. Use your words wisely, for they are the last you will get until your trial for heresy."

"Is the Inquisition allowing trials now? My, how progressive of them…" The Dean laughed. "That wasn't what I wanted to say. No, what I wanted to say is a tad more thoughtful. Your theory, Schiller, is that Ludwig is either a deliberate fraud or an incompetent failure. Perhaps that is so. And yet, as Krupp, I think, will already know, as he does like to keep aware of all comings and goings… Ludwig does the vast majority of the divining here. The other diviners are a handful of apprentices that study under him. Nearly all the prophecies that go to the Church for interpretation are Ludwig's."

Schiller glanced at Krupp, who nodded. "That's true, yes. But I fail to see—"

"What you fail to see could fill the heavens, boy. The Magistrate, however, no doubt begins to see already. We know now that Ludwig's prophecies are inaccurate—often very inaccurate, as he himself admits—and we know that he does most of the prophesizing for the Church. We also know that interpreting those prophesies, whatever the hell that means, is reputedly one of the Church's primary endeavors. We know also that the Church claims that Divination is a perfect way of predicting the future."

Schiller's face had already fallen, and Krupp's seemed well on its way. The Wizard on the crutch gazed at the Dean with a mixture of admiration and fascination on his face.

"If the Church has been receiving totally inaccurate prophecies for years," the Dean continued, "why in God's name haven't they mentioned it? Why haven't they exposed Ludwig as the fraud he is? Unless, of course…"

"Shut up," Schiller said blankly, shaking his head.

"Unless, of course, they know as well as Ludwig that the prophecies are wrong, and their 'interpretation' is nothing more than changing the prophecies to match what has happened after the fact, in order to make the future seem preordained."

"You shut up!" Schiller screamed, "Quiet your fiendish mouth! Seize him!"

"Unless," the Dean said, roaring over the screams of the Magisterial who tried to grab his shoulder and found it as hot as a pile of burning coals, "predestination is a devious lie, a lie based on outdated, unfounded religious texts, which the Church advocates merely to cement and maintain its own power! Unless Delar, Infinite Seer, is a false God, a paltry fiction that does not exist!"

The room was full of shouting now, and moving bodies, and more hands were trying to grab him and more screams filled the air. There was the chanting of Arcanic from elsewhere in the room, and the Dean joined in with his own.

Next, there was a blinding flash.

Part IV:
The Wizard

Chapter 22

Continued: an excerpt from An Introduction to Magical History, *by Pontius Sleighman*

Chapter 7 – Magical Schools

I am sorely tempted to end this chapter now, and move on to greater things.

I am, in the end, a believer. I believe in our great City-State, and our political system. I believe in the Archbishop, the Dean, and the Magistrate, regardless of which men hold those auspicious offices. I believe in Merund. And above all things, I believe in Delar, who guides us always. Many Wizards become so obsessed with magic that they begin to lose interest in God. For me, it was different. My love affair with magic only served to increase my wonder for the creator of our world. Something so amazing, so wonderful, so breathtaking as magic speaks to a being of far greater majesty than I suspect we can even conceive.

This is why it hurts me to speak of the final school of magic. It is a misapplication. A corruption. A perversion. We should all be thankful every day that it is illegal and nonexistent in our beautiful city, and we must remain ever vigilant for its practice, as nothing could do more damage to our religion and our society.

Necromancy is one of the oldest branches of magic. The ancient myths tell us that the first magic—Enchantment—was handed down to mankind from the dragons. They saw us as their heirs to this world, the first beings to be born to it that were worthy of the art they had so perfected. Trust, I suppose, is a dangerous thing—if that trust turns out to be misplaced, it can create a wound so deep that it will never heal. So it was when mankind took the gift they had been given and changed it into something abominable. It was not long before men realized that new sorts of magic could be developed based on the Enchantment of old. Is it any surprise that within a few years, we were trying to cheat death?

Necromancy is worse than murder. Murder steals life from others, but Necromancy steals life from Delar. What crime could be greater? It is no wonder that the dragons were disgusted, and there forever ended their relationship with us. Since then they have gone away or gone extinct, leaving us alone with what we have wrought.

It is only a legend, of course. It is unlikely that dragons ever existed. Nevertheless, this story can teach us much about Necromancy and the danger it heralds. And yet, despite the cost of Necromancy, despite the fact that those who practice it have damned their own immortal souls for all time, it is an art that has never truly faded out of our world. In some dark corner of the land, there is always one so drunk with power—or so frightened at the thought of their inevitable damnation—that they turn to the worst act conceivable.

Necromancy yields pathetically little. It cannot create life, nor truly restore it. All it can do is grant a paltry unlife: a shadow, an after-image, a pathetic imitation of what we are each born with. Zombie, skeleton, ghoul, or worse, it is all the same in that it is all false. Necromancers have for centuries endeavored to bend their twisted magic toward a true resurrection. They have strived to raise the dead not with undeath, but with life.

It is a false hope, and a sad one. Let us try to forget it, and hope that others do as well.

They probably would have killed him, if he hadn't been dead already.

As it was, they crouched over him, staring. She reached out with a handkerchief and carefully blotted some of the blood from his neck, which had been torn to shreds by the iron bolt still stuck firmly in it.

"There's plenty of muscle damage, for starters. It also punctured his windpipe wide open, but it just barely nicked his jugular," she said, frowning. "It probably took an awfully long time for him to bleed out."

"Hrm," Lavine murmured. The old man ran a finger along one of the dead man's shoulder pauldrons, which might have been of high quality before they'd been so thoroughly blackened by flame. "If given even basic medical treatment, his life could have been saved."

She frowned. "Well…"

"Well, what?"

She sighed, biting her lip. "We could still save him."

"Still save him? Are you a necromancer now? He's dead!"

"Yes, definitely. But he may have passed very recently. There may not be any damage to the brain yet, which means that the only thing between him and life is his heart starting."

"And how about the fact that his arteries are just about running dry?" Lavine asked, his voice heavy with skepticism.

She couldn't help but smile. It had been a while since she'd felt challenged. "I can conjure the blood. I've never done it before, but I bet it'd work."

"Hmm," he said, clearly not willing to commit much further than that, "well, we certainly can't bring him back without clearing it with your father…"

"No, no. We have to act right away, or there'll be nothing I can do for him."

"Ais, you know that you can't…"

"Too late," she said simply, reaching over and sharply pulling the bolt out of the man's neck. The corpse's shoulders gave a brief twitch, and Lavine exhaled sharply when the bolt, which turned out to be barbed on the front, significantly enlarged the ragged red gash on its way out. Aislin tossed the thing aside and closed her hand over the remnants of the man's neck, her fingers becoming immediately wet with blood, and began to chant.

Accelerating his body's healing processes one hundred times over, she sealed up the gashes in his jugular, trachea, and muscles, new tissue growing where the old had been destroyed. To her it seemed the work of a moment, but she knew from experience that it was actually taking several minutes. Finished, she began to patch up the skin, closing the gaping wounds created by the bolt.

"Get that armor off his chest," she told Lavine, not bothering to look to make sure that he'd comply. Now came the interesting part.

Abruptly ceasing her chant, she allowed her thoughts to turn steadily red: flowing, viscous red, thrumming with life. She raised a bloodied hand to her lips and licked her fingers, tasting the coppery twang, changing the idea in her mind to match that on her hand. Just any blood, she was aware, would not do.

Satisfied, she pinched at the fresh scar tissue around his neck until she located the jugular she had just repaired, and she imagined what it was like on the inside, imagined the path it took to his heart, rejoining the web of his circulatory system. Only then did she began her new chant, carefully enunciating words of Arcanic that were less familiar to her than those she'd said previously. She could feel, though, that it was working. The creation of the blood began in her mind and ran as though through her own arteries to the tips of her fingers, which guided it into the corpse's dry veins.

Exactly how much blood a human body should have in it, she did not know any better than how much she was producing per second. However, she was still working on a time limit, and so, after spending as long as she dared on her Conjuration chant, she abruptly stopped and lifted her hand. Only now did she notice that Lavine had indeed undone the man's breast plate and moved it away. She slipped her slick hand through the neck of his shirt and rested it over his heart.

She spoke a single word, and the man's chest spasmed as his heart began beating again. She turned to Lavine and grinned.

"See? Who needs Necromancy when you've got *style*?"

Over the next hour, the man's heartbeat and pulse became stronger, and by the next morning he had opened his eyes. Captain Lajos spent the next several hours screaming at him.

Aislin lurked near the entryway of the tent, watching as the furious man shouted questions directly into the face of the stranger, who had been tied into a chair. Piercing blue eyes stared back, focused but unmoved. His mouth stayed shut, the lips drooping at the sides in an expression of total apathy. There was little change when Lajos began to strike him, beginning with slaps to the face and soon enough working the man over with his fists until sweat shined on his forehead.

The stranger, his face bloodied once again, struck more than once so hard that he fell over in his chair and had to be pulled back upright by the guards, made no sign of having felt any of it. He'd been stripped of his armor and was shirtless now, his fair skin pinkish in the sunlight coming through the slits in the tent roof. His chest was soft and not very muscular, save the shoulders. The light covering of blonde fuzz on his chest and arms made him look, in this vulnerable position, more like a boy than a man, though Aislin was confident that he was at least twenty-five, and probably older.

"Mongrel!" Lajos shouted, backhanding the stranger hard in the face, the man's neck snapping sickeningly as his head ratcheted to the side. He made no indication of noticing as a thick bead of blood trailed down from his nose and over his lips.

Finally, Lajos turned and stormed out of the tent. "Outside," he growled to Aislin as he went, and she swiftly followed. They strode through the encampment, lit brightly by the midday sun, the scent of roasted meat and burning wood heavy on the air. Lajos paced only as far as the next tent before turning on her, his grizzled face contorted with frustration and anger.

"Why won't he answer? What the hell is wrong with him?"

Aislin shrugged. "Hard to say. If there was brain damage, he might not be all there. I can't heal brain damage. No one can."

"Oh, he's in there. I can see him. Those are the eyes of a sane man, a lucid man. No, his brain is just fine."

She did not bother to argue with his purported special knowledge. "Well, the other option is that his neck is too sore and scarred for him to speak. I mean, you saw the state it was in; he was halfway to decapitated."

"Don't exaggerate. Besides, that's no good, either. If it were just his throat, he'd at least be *trying* to speak. No. No, he's just a hard-nosed son of a bitch."

"I guess that's the third option, yeah."

"You. You go in there and talk to him."

She snorted. "Me? My fists aren't quite as big as yours, Lajos. I don't think I'll have much of an impact."

"You're not going to hurt him; you're going to cozy up to him. Use those feminine wiles of yours; it's not as though it'll be the first time."

"Captain Lajos, I'm not sure I like what you're implying."

"Yeah, well, not everyone can dote on you like your daddy does. You've got a role to play here same as everyone else, so get your ass in there and do it."

She felt her nails digging into her palm as she clenched her fists, struggling to think of the meanest thing she could say in return. It was a tempting thought to call lightning down on him and watch him run, but he was too fast with his sword, and she'd be on the ground before she got half the spell out.

Besides, her father wouldn't like it.

She settled for giving him a good glare before turning back to the storage tent and heading inside, waving the guards away. She pulled the flap closed after they'd gone. It was a good-sized tent, as large as a small living area, though most of the room inside was filled with barrels and crates. A wide, clear path reached down the middle of the clutter, and at the end of it was the stranger, tied into a worn-out old reed chair.

"Shall we try this again?" she asked him, walking up close, forcing herself to look at his bruised face without turning away. His eyes stared up at her, and she knew it was not a staring contest she could win. "Let's start with the basics. What the hell was that thing that brought you here?"

"Thing" was the only way she could think to describe it, as no one who had seen it could claim to have ever witnessed anything quite so abhorrent before. Bigger than the tallest man among them, it looked like a terrible caricature of a wolf, walking on its nimble hind legs and carrying a tremendous sword with the muscular, flexible arms of a human. Its big brown eyes seemed to indicate a certain dog-like stupidity, but it was intelligent enough to wear armor.

The first of their guards to approach it now lay dead in the church, being prepared for funeral rites.

"Why did it come here, and why was it carrying you?" she demanded, and already she could feel her own face flushing with anger just as Lajos' had. "Why did it leave you here? What is your association with it?"

There was a slight twitch of his facial features, a twinge about the jaw. She leaned in closer, and while his expression was still blank, she saw that he was now tremoring slightly.

"It's all right," she said, trying to make her voice soothing, reassuring, "it's not here. It's gone. But you could help us, if you told us wh—"

She stopped abruptly when the man's face broke, his mouth collapsing into a frown. He doubled over, and she watched as he began to weep.

"I... hey, now, there's no need..."

Hunched forward in the chair, he shook his head slowly, panting out sobs.

"No more, no more," he moaned, his voice barely audible. "Just get back to it, I can't take this, just get back to it..."

"Get back to what?" she asked, leaning in closer.

Shaking, he brought his face up, and his mask of despair abruptly morphed into one of rage.

"I won't be fooled by your petty tricks!" he screamed. "I know what this is, and I know where I am! You won't fool me, or get me to lower my guard! I know what this is! *I know what this is!*"

She recoiled, flecks of his spit striking her cheek. "I… I don't understand. Listen, I don't know what you mean, all right? You're confused. You're very confused."

"No! No!" he shook his head savagely, eyes clamped shut, the force of his movements threatening to topple the chair over again. Tears streamed freely down his cheeks, and he groaned like a dying man.

Aislin did the only thing she could think to do. She stepped forward and wrapped her hands around him, holding his face against her chest, rubbing her hands gently through his dirty, matted hair.

"Shhhh," she whispered to him, as a mother to her infant, "it's going to be all right. Everything is going to be all right."

His twitching worsened at first as he tried to pull away from her, but she held him firm, whispering reassurances in his ear, stroking his face even though it was soaked in his blood and tears.

Eventually, he grew still, and silent but for his ragged gasps for breath as his heart rate slowly came back under control. Finally releasing him, she pulled out her handkerchief, which she had only just gotten clean of his blood, and used it to wipe his face. He stared at her, his eyes like ice.

"You're confused," she told him again, softly. "So let me tell you what I know, to help ground you, and remind you of what is."

Almost imperceptibly, he nodded.

"You are a warrior, who wears heavy armor into battle. Sometime in the past two days, you were attacked by an opponent wielding a crossbow, and you took a mortal wound to the neck. Healing magic could have fixed the wound, but none was administered. At this point, you probably faded out of consciousness. So far, is this all right?"

"No," he croaked, almost inaudibly.

"No? What did I get wrong?"

"Not two days. Longer. Months."

She shook her head. "No, your wound was no more than a few hours old when you were brought here, and that was only yesterday."

He frowned. "But… but… no, I'm sure…"

"What makes you sure?"

"I've… I've been counting the minutes, and…"

"You've been counting the minutes? In your dreams?"

He gazed up at her, and his expression suggested that he almost felt sorry for her. Or, was it that he envied her? In his state, it was hard to be sure.

"Not dreaming. I was somewhere. Somewhere else."

"Where? Where were you?"

She cocked her head slightly. "Could it be… the afterlife? You were dead for at least a few minutes… did you see it? Did you go to Heaven, warrior?"

"No," he said, and his gaze lowered. "No. Not Heaven. Not Heaven."

She found that she had nothing to say in response.

He laughed, and it was an ugly sound, clotted by the scarring in his throat and the bitterness in his heart. "I was only dead for a few minutes? Really. It felt like… no, not just felt like. It *was*… weeks. Months."

"That's awful," she said, aware immediately afterward how inadequate it sounded.

"What happened, after the arrow?" he asked. "You said… the Wolf?"

"Yes. You were picked up by something. A monster. It looked like a wolf, but it walked like a man, and it wielded a tremendous sword. It carried you over its shoulder like a bedroll and brought you here from wherever you were wounded. When a sentry approached it, it cut him down, laughing all the while. It threw you down next to him and walked away. It was gone from sight by the time anyone was ready to chase it, and we haven't seen it since."

The stranger frowned. "He brought me here? Why? He could have left me to die."

"Was he an enemy of yours?"

The man smiled, and the ugliness in it was only a flicker in the background now. With the tears dried away from his face, he seemed much more together. Somewhat handsome, even. "He's an enemy of all, and none."

"I don't understand."

"You needn't. Suffice to say that I'd have bet anything that he'd have left me there to die."

"I see."

"Where are we? Who are you?"

She smirked. "You first."

"My name... is Rodolphus. Rodolphus Plymouth."

"And I am Aislin Murmac. We are in Springdale, which is my father's semi-permanent settlement on the banks of the Norill River."

"Springdale," he said mechanically. "I know it. Bandit town."

"Trading company," she corrected him testily. "Our being able to defend ourselves hardly makes us bandits. We don't attack anyone who trades fair."

"I'm in trouble," Rodolphus said calmly. "Your people will hold me responsible for the dead sentry."

"Yes," she said, "but not for long. I'll vouch for you."

He furrowed his brow. "Why would you do that?"

"Because I believe you're innocent."

He stared.

Chapter 23

His eyes opened slowly, and he did not scream, though the shrieking pain of having his flesh ripped away a strip at a time was fresh in his memory. He held up a hand, but was unable to see it for the near total blackness of the tent. He settled for reaching out his other hand and feeling it carefully. He found that it was wholly intact; all the skin was still there.

He lay awake for a long time, trying to decide whether he'd just now been teleported back there, or if it had only been a dream. In his heart, he didn't really believe that either was the case.

In his heart, he suspected that he was still there, and had been all along. They were waiting; waiting for him to finally let his guard down. The moment he believed that he was free was when he'd discover that he wasn't. It was brilliant, really. It could break even the strongest man, especially if it was done repeatedly. He didn't know why they bothered using it on him. They'd broken him before the first week was out.

Though, if anything the she-devil said was true, it hadn't been a week at all. That period had probably lasted for no longer than a handful of minutes. In the end, he supposed that it didn't matter. Forever was forever, no matter how long the seconds took to pass.

From outside, he heard the gentle whinnying of a horse being walked nearby. The sound became more distinct until it was directly outside the canvas.

"Hey, Rodo," a female voice whispered, "get dressed and come on out."

Aislin, or so she called herself. Mechanically, he sat up. Any idea of resistance had been purged from his mind by this point. There was no need to dress; he'd fallen into bed in the clothes they'd found him in, fine and black, now caked with soot and dirt and dried blood. His scorched armor sat piled in the corner. There was a time when he would have refused to leave the tent without it.

Now, he got up and left without so much as a glance in its direction. It hadn't saved him, and now it was too late.

It was still dark outside, though the sky had turned from black to midnight blue in the first indication that the morning sun was approaching. Aislin stood waiting, her arm resting gently on the neck of a beautiful brown mare. Memories shot though his head when he saw it. He viewed them with a dispassionate interest, as though they were an interesting speck of dirt.

"Ugh. Didn't you see the change of clothes I got you?"

"Yes."

"When we get back, you're changing. Don't think I won't make you."

"Get back from where?"

She grinned. "To the top of Bragg's hill, obviously. That's where Tuff always sees her sunrises."

"Tuff is the horse, I take it."

"You're a clever one. Now if we can only teach you how to take a bath…"

"You awoke me for the sunrise?"

"You were sleeping?"

He frowned.

"I thought not. Come on, walk up with us." She grabbed hold of the saddle's horn and hauled herself gracefully onto the horse, squirming to adjust the positioning of her slender legs, then pushing the toes of her boots into the stirrups.

"Let's go, girl," she said soothingly, and the mare was off with at a gentle trot.

Automatically, Rodolphus fell into pace beside it, staring at his boots.

"Have you ever seen a sunrise before?" she asked, her eyes on the road ahead.

"Yes."

"A lot of people haven't. City folk sleep late, and you struck me as that type."

"I was in the army."

"Oh, that's right. A war caster, right?"

"How did you know that?"

"No weapon, no scabbard, not even a dagger. Only a caster would go around like that."

"Or a civilian."

"Civilians don't carry daggers where you're from? Besides, you wear a bit too much armor for that, I think."

"I suppose so," he said simply, and did not look up at her.

For a time, they were quiet, only the occasional chirp of an over-eager bird and the slow crunch of gravel beneath Tuff's feet breaking the silence.

"You went to Hell," she said casually, the horse making its way through a series of small foothills to the west of the camp.

He frowned. "I..."

"That's it, really, isn't it? You died, and you didn't end up where you thought you would."

"Yes," he nodded. "That's it exactly."

"And where did you think you'd end up?"

He frowned ever more deeply, trying to think back. When he finally remembered, he began to laugh, holding his stomach and falling out of pace as he chuckled hysterically. Aislin squeezed her knees to tell Tuff to stop, and turned back to watch him.

"You know," Rodolphus panted, "I didn't know where I'd end up, but I was actually... looking forward to finding out." This trailed into a chortle, and soon he was laughing uproariously once again, tears streaming down his face: tears that were not all caused by the laughter.

"If you didn't even know *how* to get a reward in the afterlife," she said patiently, "how can you have expected anything but punishment?"

"It never seemed as cut and dry as all that," he said, still giggling, accepting her handkerchief to dry his face. Despite having been washed again, it was stained pink with his blood.

"Well, it's time to remedy those mistakes. You're really lucky, Rodolphus, if you think about it. How many people can claim to get a second chance like yours?"

"Is that what I'm supposed to think this is? A second chance?"

"What do you mean, 'this'?"

"Don't be cute. I know. I'm still there. I'm still dead."

"Rodolphus..."

"I don't blame you for trying to trick me."

"You're not still there."

"Of course you won't tell me. Not until I believe I'm free."

She extended a hand, and he stared up at it, ready for it to strike him. He didn't bother flinching or trying to steel himself. He'd given up on both.

He was not ready, however, for her long, delicate fingers, the nails painted a cool indigo, to stroke his cheek.

"It's okay, Rodolphus. After what you've seen, I don't expect you to believe me."

"Good," he said tightly, "because I don't." As she drew her hand away, his aching, desperate mind screamed for him to grab it and press it back against his face, but he did nothing.

"But you've mostly played along with the fantasy that you're alive so far," she said matter-of-factly, "and nothing terrible has happened to you. So you should probably *keep* playing along. Right?"

He sighed. "I suppose."

"Good. And look, we're nearly there."

They were, and now they crested a gently winding footpath that made its way up to the top of Bragg's hill, which was not terribly large but which appeared to be the highest place around, nothing obstructing their view from the top. The sky was lightening, and Rodolphus could see all of Springdale, its tents and buildings arranged in a neat semicircle pressing up against the banks of the river. No other signs of civilization were visible. The Wolf had carried him quite a distance from Yunder.

Yunder... the Crutchfield Estate...

More memories, memories that were far more recent than they seemed. He felt himself smiling.

"There you go," she said happily. "I thought the view would cheer you up. And look, the sun is rising."

A glance confirmed this; tendrils of orange pawed at the horizon. Long ago, a chill wind bit at his face as he trudged toward the mess tent, bundled in his cloak. Tiberius fell in beside him, giving him a silent nod. Within two hours, they'd be in combat, ankle-deep in dead and wounded, totally submerged in the stink and the noise of bodies thrown against each other in anger.

His smile widened.

"Okay, Rodolphus."

"Hmm?"

"Let's figure out how we're going to save your soul."

He nodded softly. "All right."

"I don't know how you lived your old life, but would I be wrong if I said that you weren't kind to others? You shunned justice and honor? Your broke your word, you turned your back on those who needed you?"

"No," he said, barely pausing to consider, "you would not be wrong."

"Well, then it's easy enough in theory. And in practice, it's the hardest thing you'll ever have to do."

He stared blankly up at her.

She smiled. "You'll have to repent; turn over a new leaf. You've got to change, Rodo. It won't be that hard; you can get a start living with us. The people here will accept you, in time. And if you do well enough, then next time you die, you'll end up somewhere a whole lot nicer than before."

"But..." he stammered, "But if I'm only doing it to save my soul..."

"That doesn't matter. Your motivations don't matter, and neither do your thoughts. All that matters is what you do. Do good and you are good. Do bad, and you are bad. Whys aren't important."

"I... I'm not sure I can do it," he said, a bit startled by his honesty. He turned his face away from her. She fluidly dropped out of her saddle, and just as he was turning back she took a step and closed the gap between them. As he opened his mouth to speak, she gave him a quick kiss, her mouth closing over his top lip for just a few seconds.

As she drew away, he stared. "You barely know me," he said. "Plus... I've been to Hell. I don't know if you've heard."

"You're interesting," she shrugged. "And besides, would you have been given a second chance if there wasn't something that you were meant to accomplish?"

He had to admit, after all, that she had been right. He realized eventually that Hell had already had dozens of beautiful chances to pull him out of the fantasy and break his heart; if this was an elaborate torture technique, it would have climaxed already. She'd been right, too, that the others would come to accept him, a prospect he'd been equally skeptical about.

It had been easy to believe her at first, when they had walked back down the hill, the horse coming after, and she held his hand and told him about how things would be. But once he was alone again, he remembered that so far as everyone else in the settlement was concerned, he was an accessory to the murder of one of their people. Murder wasn't something that people tended to forgive; it was why Rodolphus had always been grateful that the army kept him from having to stay in one place for too long.

But because she had faith in him, the others seemed to develop a grudging acceptance for him as well. Their respect for her was far greater than he'd originally assumed. Other than the few hours a day she spent with her father helping with business affairs, she spent all her time with him, taking him around, showing him how to do all the chores that made the place run. They chopped wood and caught fish and sowed seeds in the garden together, and things weren't bad.

Sometimes, late at night, lying in bed, he bit the skin of his lip so hard that it bled just so he could taste the warm, coppery sting.

When it was dark and there was no work to be done, they sat by the fire with the others, and they talked about magic, and he told her how he only bothered with Conjuration, and she joked that if she felt the same way he'd probably still be a corpse. They'd linger around longer than everyone else, and as the embers crackled slowly she'd lean over and plant one kiss after another softly against his lips.

He imagined himself pushing her down against the bench and covering her mouth with his hand and hoping to God that she'd bite him while he took her right there, right out in the open in the middle of the settlement, her body yielding and warm and writhing underneath him.

Sometimes he'd flick his thumb and forefinger together and make a little flame, and she'd smile and laugh because she didn't know that he was imagining what the place would look like if he burned it down one night, just because he could, just to see the fire and hear the screaming and to feel again the way that war used to make him feel.

He didn't, though. He didn't do any of it, because he couldn't go back. It was far worse than any terror he'd ever felt, his fear of going back there.

The thing that made it so frightening was that it was *forever*. It wasn't anything like suffering through life, because there were always ways out. You could run away, or try to change, or just build up the courage to kill yourself and hope for something better.

But suffering in Hell was different, because you couldn't kill yourself, and if you could you'd just wake up in Hell again the next morning. It was different because you couldn't count the days until it was over, because it was *never* over, because it would last *forever*, a concept that he couldn't even really comprehend and which he tried not to think about for fear that it might drive him mad.

His urges didn't trouble him, as she had told him that his thoughts didn't matter. He took comfort in the urges, wore them like a blanket, as he tried to make his new life for himself. If being average was the price he had to pay not to go back there, then he was willing to pay it plus interest.

They were on their way to the berry grove when Aislin noticed the riders. There were six of them, lightly armored, their horses strong and fast. Rodolphus and Aislin both sat astride Tuff, who Rodolphus had found to be exceptionally fast but who couldn't be expected to perform with the weight of two riders loading her down.

He was asking who they were and whether she knew them when she began detaching the saddlebags and letting them fall where they may. She acted with admirable speed, throwing aside all the weight they could spare and tugging on the reigns until Tuff was moving at a full gallop away from the six riders, headed back over the grassy plain toward Springdale, which was miles away.

"Who the hell are they?" he said, yelling to be heard over the sound of galloping hooves and rushing wind.

"They're from Pendleton. You know how you're so fond of saying that Springdale is a bandit town?"

"Yeah."

"Well, Pendleton *really is* a bandit town, and we've been basically at war with them ever since they started taking offense that we didn't roll over when they tried to steal our shipments."

"Hmm."

"Look, believe me or not, the point is that they know I'm the boss's daughter and they'd be thrilled to kill me, or, even better, take me hostage."

"Damn," Rodolphus yelled back, "it's always gotta be bandits. And look at you, putting me in such a dangerous situation! I should tell your pop that I don't feel safe around you!"

She shook her head like he was crazy and kept driving the horse harder, swinging Tuff in a turn around a stand of skinny trees and then trying to drive her back up to top speed. Ahead of them loomed a long expanse of grassland, almost perfectly flat.

Rodolphus felt fantastic. His cheeks were flushed and his heart was pounding. He felt alive, actually alive, not just dead on his feet like all those yokels in Springdale, moving crates and gutting fish and never getting their pulse higher than a brisk jog to the mess tent.

Sure, a tiny voice in the back of his mind said, *it's all great fun, right up until you die*—but he had little trouble ignoring it. He was afraid of death, sure, but not of these dumb bastards. No, it was them who should be afraid of him.

Holding on as tight as he could to Tuff and Aislin, he turned his head to look at their pursuers. His eyes widened slightly when he saw their proximity; they'd gained a lot of ground in a mere minute. Tuff just wasn't fast enough, not with two people on her, and now they were on a flat stretch, giving the bandits plenty of time to catch up.

"You know, I heard somewhere that bandits hate lightning!" he shouted into the wind, lips pulled up into a smile.

"Where'd you hear that?" Aislin managed to bark back, her body bent forward as she tried to lean Tuff into going faster.

"Not sure," Rodolphus sang happily, "maybe a bandit told me while I was electrocuting him to death." He suddenly wished that the Wolf was there with them. He had a feeling it would have appreciated that joke.

He released a hand from Aislin's side and brought it around and back. With a few phrases of Arcanic, his hand was channeling an incredible stream of energy, crackling, dancing through the air like a snake, darting in the slimmest fraction of a second to the nearest rider, honing in on his metal helmet like a lightning rod. Rodolphus was laughing so hard by now, he almost didn't notice when the beam slammed into an invisible wall a few feet away from the man's horse and dissipated harmlessly into nothing.

"What... what the hell?"

Aislin didn't even turn to look. "They've probably got anti-magical enchantments worked on them! They have an enchanter of great power affiliated with their group."

"But... but no, no! That's not right!"

"Why do you think we're running? Don't worry, it's not much further!"

The army had employed enchanters who took care of neutralizing things like this, Rodolphus remembered. He'd almost forgotten that shield charms were possible.

He looked ahead toward the distant blur of Springdale, but he had already surmised that it was too far. The enemy was gaining, and there were still a few miles to go. It was no good.

You're going to die, the little voice said. His breath caught in his chest, and he felt like he was drowning. He could see the faces of the riders easily now, and they were smiling, just like he had been moments ago. He told himself that he wasn't afraid, because he'd been living clean, and when he died, he wouldn't have to go back to Hell. He'd reformed, after all.

"Look on the bright side!" Aislin called, an edge of dark humor in her voice. "If they kill us, according to the Minarians, we get to go straight to Heaven for dying in battle! Not bad, right?"

"Well," he laughed harshly, "I've got news for you! I died in battle last time, and wherever I ended up, it wasn't Heaven! If Tiberius is still alive, I'll have to let him know that his religion is bullsh..."

"Who's Tiberius?" she asked, having waited a few seconds but concluded that he wasn't going to finish. He wasn't listening. There was an idea in his head, but he couldn't quite get a hold of it, couldn't quite understand what it meant. Something about Minarianism. About how it was false. Their tenets, Rodolphus had found out first hand, were wrong. They thought a person got into Heaven by doing a certain thing, and they were completely, utterly...

That was it.

"How do you know?" he screamed, voice ridden with panic, teetering on the brink of lunacy. "How do you know that you can get into Heaven by doing good deeds?"

"What? This is hardly the time—"

"*It's exactly the time, now answer the goddamn question!*"

"It's just what I believe! It's what my people believe!"

His mouth, contorted into a scowl of terror and rage, slowly relaxed. His eyes closed for a moment as he turned his head away from their pursuers so that his face was mere inches away from the back of her neck as she drove the poor horse ever harder. He understood, now, finally.

"You stupid bitch," he said softly. "Do you really think that you're the first person to ever believe in something?"

She may not have had time to put meaning behind his words, because his hand was planted firmly against the small of her back, and with a murmured pair of ancient words she was engulfed in flame, fire so hot that it burned fluorescent blue, flinging her body from the horse like a broken marionette, flying yards and yards to land in a smoldering heap in the grass nearby. At the instant he struck, she emitted a piercing shriek for a sliver of a second as she experienced the worst pain imaginable. Then her body went catatonic and shut down; by the time she hit the ground, there was a good chance she was dead of shock.

He slid up into her slot on the saddle, noticing with gratification that his fire had singed Tuff's mane but done no other damage to her. He congratulated himself on his restraint and control, stroking his ego, pampering it like a neglected pet. He dug his boots into Tuff's sides and drove her faster now, the extra weight lost, not that it really mattered. The bandits were after Aislin, and by now they'd all diverted toward her body.

If Tuff noticed that she was no longer being driven by her master, she was too frightened to care, and Rodolphus turned her sharply away from Springdale, driving her as fast as she could run to the East, leaving the chaos far behind them.

Once he'd ridden her to death, he had no choice but to start walking.

Chapter 24

The row house on the corner of Ashland and Bloodhound looked patently unpleasant; its windows were black with soot and other unidentifiable grime, and the door had at least three deadbolts installed, as though the rotten wood they were mounted in couldn't be shredded by a spirited kick.

Rodolphus stood across the street next to the stairway of a nearly identical building, though this one was surely abandoned, its windows gaping, glassless holes that displayed nothing but empty rooms littered with debris. There was a time when he would have been loath to leave his back facing them, as they seemed the perfect habitat for some ethereal horror. Now, though, he had experienced far too much real terror to ever again fear what was merely imagined. So he yawned, studying the place across the street, his fingers absent-mindedly rubbing at the sleeve of his shirt.

The new clothes, all cotton, black and simple, felt luxuriantly soft against his skin after weeks of homespun cloth and years of cumbersome armor. He had left his old clothes, heavy with sweat and singed around the sleeve cuffs, in a tangled pile in the corner of a public bath stall on the other side of the city. He'd been planning to burn them, but it seemed like an awful lot of effort to go to when he had little to fear in terms of reprisal.

He'd first come to that conclusion some hours ago as his aching feet carried him along the road toward the city limits of Durkheim. By that time his adrenaline rush had long worn off, replaced with a cold lump of fear, an ever-growing ball of ice in his stomach. He flinched at every sound, ready for the bandits to gallop up and kill him out of spite. People didn't always take kindly to having their jobs done for them.

Once long enough had passed, though, the fear started to melt. There were no bands of sword-swinging horseman, nor even mobs of torch-carrying villagers, screaming after him for his blood. There was nothing but the occasional trade wagon, the drivers nodding curtly to him as they passed. In the end, the bandits must have decided not to take umbrage, and Springdale... well, they might never even find out what had really happened.

With the adrenaline pumped away and the fear evaporated, Rodolphus had time to really think for the first time since he had murdered Aislin. Now, as he navigated the unknown city, he waited for horror, guilt, and remorse to make their connections in his mind.

After two hours or so of wandering the streets, he realized that it wasn't going to happen.

He wasn't happy that he'd killed her; not exactly. And yet, he couldn't imagine any other course of action on his part. He could only hope that she understood that he he'd had to do it: she had left him with no other choice.

If he wasn't happy about what he'd done, though, why was he smiling? Why was there a spring in his exhausted step? Actually, he *was* happy. If he ever met those horsemen again, he'd have to shake their hands. If not for them, he'd still be in that hellish trading post, probably helping some backward old hick carry hay from one tent to another, all in a misguided attempt to escape his destiny. If it hadn't been for those horsemen, he might never have realized what now he knew for certain: that he couldn't know how to escape Hell, and that it was a waste of time and resources to try. It was not a guessing game that he would consent to play. There was a better way; indeed, it was now the only road left open to him, and he walked it gladly. He might have started humming, but the fact that he was already smiling made him stand out enough as it was.

It was a miserable city. Geography and climate conspired to keep the skies overcast the majority of the year, rain dampening the streets nearly every other day in the spring. The streets were out of repair and the buildings derelict. Even the pick-pockets and muggers had long since moved on to more lucrative cities, leaving only the sparse collection of figures that shambled down the streets now, heads down, making their way between shops that had long ago stopped bothering to repaint their signs. Finding somewhere to buy his clothes had taken nearly an hour. Fifteen minutes after that he managed to purchase his new brown traveling cape off a street vendor who seemed eager to do anything but look him in the eye.

Rodolphus had been the sole customer at the public bath, and when he'd given the attendant a five Nam piece, the man had looked at him with a subtle combination of disbelief and suspicion. Rodolphus had smiled. The nice thing to do, he'd always thought, was to give people what they expected. So he leaned down, reaching an arm around the boy's shoulder, and he whispered a request in his ear. The boy's wide, sickly eyes had bored into his before the response was whispered. "Number 8517, at the corner of Ashland and Bloodhound."

And so, after stopping for a hunk of charred chicken and a few glasses of beer, Rodolphus had found his way to Ashland, and walked that road until the streets grew small and residential, absent even the few people he'd seen wandering downtown.

Which wasn't to say that he might have behaved any differently, had there been anyone watching. Contented with his observation, he strode across the potholed street to row house 8517, small tendrils of electricity beginning to crackle between his fingers. He licked his lips, raised his hand, and blew out the right-side window with a simultaneous smatter of tiny bolts of lightning, allowing at the same time a gust of conjured air to take him off his feet and through the now-empty pane. He landed roughly on one knee on dingy carpeting, and scrambled up quickly. His eyes swept the room, his arm out as though he were keeping a bead on someone with a hand crossbow.

It was lived-in. A weathered leather chair sat by the cold fireplace, an end table next to it piled high with books that looked old enough to crumble apart in your hands. It was empty of people, however, and so he went forward through the cramped doorway that led into what appeared to be a small study.

The study was *not* empty. There was a man there, sitting behind a desk. Reading.

Rodolphus frowned. Was the old man deaf? He was about to show him some fire when the fellow spoke, turning the page of his text as he did.

"My, my. Conjuration. Really? Did you apprentice under a five year-old?"

Rodolphus snorted, and the fire in his hand flared far larger than he'd originally intended. He lobbed it at the old man, who somehow still was not looking up at him. When the fire spread out against an invisible barrier a few feet short of the man's head, Rodolphus frowned. When the flames suddenly flared with new life and poured directly back at him, there wasn't much he could do but dive, throwing himself to the ground and hitting his elbow hard, rolling clumsily before bumping up against the wall.

The old man stood up, finally closing his book as he turned to look down at Rodolphus.

"Can I help you, young man?"

"Cheap tricks!" Rodolphus growled. "Without that barrier, you'd be ashes on the floor!"

"Cheap tricks, are they? Shall we fight not as Wizards, then, but as men?"

The old man held one arm out to the side, the baggy sleeve of his robe rolling back slightly. Slowly, the air above and below his hand began to blur and warp as something was brought into being there. Moments later, the atoms snapped into place, and the man was holding a long, slender dueling sword, hilt and all made entirely of gleaming iron. He swung it around delicately and pointed the tip vaguely toward Rodolphus' heart.

"This is what you would prefer?" the man asked, raising a grey eyebrow high enough that it almost merged with his thinning hair.

"No," Rodolphus managed to hiss, his hands beginning to tremor as the fear came back. It wasn't as bad as before, at least—it was hard to feel really afraid when you were busy feeling so utterly, utterly stupid.

"Ah," the man said, "then maybe you'd better tell me what you do want, before I decide that I'd like to have my solitude back."

"A necromancer," Rodolphus said, gripping his belt with his hands to stop them from shaking, forcing himself to take his eyes off the shining tip of the blade that still floated inches away. "I was told I could find a necromancer here."

The man laughed softly. "A necromancer? No, you'll find no such thing here, I'm afraid."

"But you…"

"I am a Wizard. Specialization is for the feeble-minded. All of the magical arts are worth learning, understanding, mastering. Only by mastering every school can one hope to maintain a perfect defense, or a perfect offense. I could neutralize a recursive shield enchantment, if need be. You, apparently, cannot."

"You *are* a necromancer, though. If you've mastered every school…"

"Necromancy is indeed one of my many talents, yes. A favorite of mine, though I do lament that it seems to bring a deviant such as yourself out of the woodwork every few years."

The tip of the sword lowered until it was resting against the wooden floorboards, and Rodolphus felt his breathing begin to slow. "Deviant is no insult," he said carefully. "It depends entirely upon what one is deviating from."

The old man smiled. "Hmm. Just so." With a gentle fluttering of violet robes, he turned back to his desk, the sword in his hand slowly dissolving as though dropped in acid, eventually leaving no trace that it had ever been there. He scooped the old text off his desk and began heading toward the book cases against the wall. "And why is it that you are seeking out a necromancer? Romantic ideas of power over life and death, is that it?"

"I never said I wanted to become a necromancer."

"No, you didn't. Are you going to say what you do want, or will you need further encouragement?"

"I'll tell you what I don't want, old man. I don't want to die."

There was soft *thunk* as the old man pushed the book into its place in the shelf.

"Interesting."

"Can you do it? Can you help me?"

"Oh, certainly I can, but I'm afraid we're now writing the first page of a story that ends with the words 'be careful what you wish for.'"

"We live forever either way, old man. For me, it's just the choice between whether I should do it here, or someplace much, much worse."

"Wolfram."

"What?"

"You should call me Wolfram."

"Ah... all right. And my name is Rodolphus."

"I've never heard of you."

"Good, let's hope it stays that way."

Wolfram puttered over to a wheeled table in the corner with a silver tea set sitting upon it. "Can I offer you refreshment?"

"Wouldn't say no."

"Have a seat, then," Wolfram said, gesturing toward a wooden chair wedged in-between two bookcases. Rodolphus pulled it out and sat in it, wincing as it creaked with his weight. Wolfram approached at the speed of motivated turtle with two full cups of tea, handing one to Rodolphus and setting the other on his desk. He then placed his hands on the edge of the desk and swung his small frame up with what appeared to be a great deal of effort so that he was sitting atop it.

"So, Rodolphus. What is it about being a skeleton that appeals to you so? The gleaming white bones? Because I assure you, such an idea is pure fabrication, unless you'd allow me to give you a bleach bath."

"I don't think skeleton is exactly the kind of thing I'm looking for."

"And what, then, are you looking for?"

Rodolphus took a sip of his tea, wincing slightly at how sweet it was. "You tell me."

"Interesting. Interesting. You do know how to get a Wizard's blood pumping... give him free rein and a problem to solve."

"Get me what I'm after, and I'd happily throw in a woman to screw."

"Let's begin," Wolfram said, ignoring him completely, "with the basic questions. The easy ones. Do you want to be in control of your own actions?"

"Definitely."

"Well, it won't be a zombie, then, and I think skeleton will be out as well. Now, there's a variety of options when it comes to the higher undead…"

"Yes, the higher undead. Actually, I've got a question about that."

"Hmm? Yes, yes?"

"We fought some zombies once in the war, and you always hear that they're immortal. But a good decapitation seemed to do the job nicely."

"Ah. Well, you see, there's immortal, and then there's *immortal*."

"Right, exactly. So, I don't care too much about the first kind. I'm not really worried about my health, I figure I should have decades left if we're assuming I'm going to die of natural causes. But the problem is, I don't think I am gonna die of natural causes, you see?"

"Not a man who makes friends easily, I take it? Or maybe it's *too* easily. Whatever the case, I'm afraid what you're asking for is out of the realm of possibility."

Rodolphus grunted, nearly dropping the saucer. "What? You mean to tell me that with all the hundreds of bastards who have wasted their lives on Necromancy, you still can't make something that can't die? I mean *really* can't die?"

"You cannot expect what is not reasonable. If you take an animated body and, say, totally incinerate it, it will be destroyed. There's no helping that."

"I seem to recall that *you* don't have too hard a time with fire."

"So, we could make you a ghoul or some such thing, and then ward you with enchantments every few hours in an attempt to make you invulnerable to external causes of death."

"Every few hours…"

"Yes. And even then, you would remain vulnerable. It is impossible to predict every conceivable angle of attack, I'm afraid. Your foes could find some way to teleport attacks inside of your protective shell, for example, or even overwhelm your enchantments with the sheer force of their own."

Rodolphus stared into the dregs of his tea. "I... I really thought that this was going to be the answer."

"Young man. Rodolphus. I cannot grant you what you seek. But that does not mean that there is nothing I can give you."

He looked at Wolfram, his feelings tangled between hope and suspicion.

"I'm listening."

"Good. Your Conjuration magic is fierce, boy. It is. But it's not enough, not at all. Specialization is the art of fools. Specializing leaves dozens of holes in your defenses. Generalizing will leave none. If you wish to stave off death for as long as possible, perhaps the first step is to make yourself more difficult to kill. I can teach you the other schools. I can take a talented war caster and make him a *Wizard*."

Rodolphus frowned, shaking his head. "It's not exactly what I had in mind."

"And yet, it is what I am offering. I promise you, no necromancer will be able to give you what you seek any better than I can. And knowing that, what will you do? Where will you go?"

"I don't know," Rodolphus said, his heart plummeting at the realization that it was true. He did not have a backup plan. He had tried to be good, but that would not work. So he'd decided to live forever, but that was not possible, either. So what else was there? Nothing, perhaps, but delaying the inevitable.

Which, in the end, was better than nothing.

"All right. I'll stay, if you will teach me."

"Good. And yet I warn you, my dear boy… this shall not be easy."

It was at the age of seven that Rodolphus had begun to learn how to conjure, and even then it had not been easy. It had taken rigorous training, almost impossibly tiring and strict for a boy of that age. If it had not been for the determination of the instructors at the Academy, he would have washed out several times over. The War Casting masters viewed the failure of a student as a personal insult: insults that they simply refused to tolerate. To attempt to leave would have been the same as slapping one of the instructors in the face, if the act is to be measured by the consequences.

Rodolphus had learned to conjure, but at age seven it had not been easy. Three decades later, learning how to enchant was, approximately, impossible. Becoming an unequaled master of the violin at his age may have been slightly easier. His mind was not sharp enough, fast enough, could not memorize the patterns as a child's could. He spent hours repeating phrases in fluent Arcanic, performing the same subtle hand motions over and over again, and nothing ever happened. He may as well have been a deaf-mute trying to sing.

Nevertheless, Rodolphus was able to overcome the obstacle that had kept his interests far away from the other schools of magic for so many years. He had once thought that only that which was explosive and impressive was worth doing, but the last few months had taught him otherwise. Power was not always the ability to destroy a manor—it certainly *often* was, but not always. Sometimes, power was the ability to choose whether a man would live or die based on an unfathomable whim, as the Wolf had shown him. Other times, power was the ability to return a dead man to life, defying the very grip of Hell. Power was many, many things.

And, in the end, Enchantment was all about power. The power to say 'no' to reality; the power to decide that one could do better than the gods had. Power was something that Rodolphus understood; perhaps the only thing he understood. The sort of power that allowed one to bend the world to his wishes was simply too much to pass up for any reason, inability included.

So Rodolphus learned to enchant, because he refused not to. If he had to make five thousand attempts at patterning his mind before his first completion of the most basic Enchantment, then he would, and did, do it five thousand times. It was a year before he could briefly change the color of a stone. He had, he constantly reminded himself, little better to do with his time.

Things went a bit more quickly from there. Another year in, he could change the size of the stones. Months after that, he could cause them to disappear from sight completely for a few moments.

After five years, if he tried, Rodolphus could make men and women do things that they would not otherwise have done. This, though, he preferred to think of as an enhancement rather than a new ability, as it was something he'd long been able to do even without the aid of magic.

Chapter 25

Six years after he'd come to find Wolfram, the old man took him to Becket, a farming town located thirty miles from the rotting heap of a city that was Durkheim. Wolfram's teleportation was swift and clean, leaving Rodolphus with the impression that the change of surroundings had been trigged merely by a quick blink.

"You should be well on your way to teleportation, I think," Wolfram said approvingly, taking Rodolphus' arm and guiding him into the village. "But there is no rush on that measure. You have learned enough now to show me why it has been worth my while to teach you."

Rodolphus sneered. "I didn't know there would be an exam."

"I have never seen much point to an exam that one sees coming. I have the utmost confidence in you, my dear boy. Let's go get a drink."

"Say, I like this exam."

"Oh, it only gets better."

They crossed through the town, the rough-hewn hemp cloaks they wore not drawing any particular attention; they looked like traders, perhaps a grandfather and his grandson, stopping over for the night. It seemed a merry place, with a small brook constantly burbling nearby and dancing torchlight keeping the place well illuminated even after the horizon had gone dark. The tavern was large for a town so small, and crowded to match. Built entirely of pale timber no doubt felled in the large forest nearby, it was decorated with dented old weapons and armor like a warrior's ale hall, and had a massive, ancient-looking tapestry dominating the rear wall, displaying the triumph of a mighty knight over a swarm of monstrous snakes. Rodolphus and Wolfram made their way to a small table, ducking past the crowd who stood bunched up at the bar refreshing their drinks.

"Wine, my dear," Wolfram said courteously to the serving girl. "Whatever is the local specialty." She nodded and looked to Rodolphus, who gave her a wolfish grin. "Mead, girl, and keep them coming."

Upon sufficiently lubricating their throats, the two sat and talked quietly, watching the raucous crowd of laughing traders and farmers buying each other drinks, sharing stories and taking turns at a flimsy target with a training bow and some blunt arrows.

"Your exam begins now," Wolfram said, discreetly pulling his pocket watch from his vest and checking the time. "You have five minutes until pens down."

"Well, aughtn't you tell me what the exam is, first?" Rodolphus frowned, wiping hot mead from his lips.

"Ah, I suppose that would help. Your task is simple, my friend. Within five minutes, I want this place obliterated."

Rodolphus laughed. "Are you serious? Hell, I can do it in one."

"Ah, but you see, there is a caveat. You must do it without anyone fingering you as the culprit."

"…and I take it you don't mean by killing everybody."

"You are very astute, Rodolphus. Four minutes and forty seconds."

"Hell."

His eyes darted around the room. It was packed with people. Any attempt at Conjuration attacks would give him away in an instant. Which left…

He picked the biggest man he could find, who was standing near one end of the bar. Probably a farmer, the fellow was tremendous, balding and mustachioed. His sleeveless tunic showing arms firm and tan from years of fieldwork. He'd do nicely.

Rodolphus stared. He stared for just about a full minute, stretching his body up and focusing his attention fully on the man.

It did not take long for the fellow to notice, and once he had, it took him no longer to return the stare with a frown that suggested it might be on its way to a scowl.

Rodolphus began murmuring in Arcanic and gesturing delicately. He was facing Wolfram, and so it looked as though the two were conversing. His eyes, though, stayed glued to the large farmer, though the gaze was disrupted very slightly by the wink that Rodolphus threw to him.

Now the man, leering, began walking over, trying to stare Rodolphus down like he was a cornered jackrabbit. His piercing eyes, close enough now that Rodolphus could see that they were blue, were quite easy to make eye contact with, and with that his murmuring became quicker and easier, more fluid, the motions swifter and still looking for all the world like the hand gestures of a very emphatic conversationalist.

With a blink, Baldy stopped moving.

"Good," Rodolphus murmured now, still in Arcanic. The spell would do the work of getting the commands to the man in a way he could understand. "The man over there, by the tapestry. I caught him rutting your wife. She was begging him for it."

Those blue eyes widened. This kind of embellishment might not have been necessary, but gods, it was fun. Besides, giving them a reason always helped them follow through.

"Take that lamp off the table."

Baldy marched toward the nearest table and scooped up a two-foot tall double chamber oil lamp, holding it by the metal, his fingers no doubt blistering almost instantly. He didn't seem to notice.

"Beautiful. Throw it at that son of bitch."

The farmer had a good arm. The big lamp shattered against the oblivious bystander by the tapestry, cutting him and burning him and soaking him in oil that lit on fire almost instantaneously. He screamed in bewilderment and pain, turning this way and that in confusion, soon resorting to an attempt at knocking out the flames against the old tapestry on the wall, which of course took fire like it was made of sawdust and pitch.

Screams tore through the air now, shouts of bemusement and calls for water. Rodolphus had heard that water actually served to *spread* grease fires, but he wasn't sure if this qualified. Better not to risk it. He stood as though trying to get a better view of the commotion, and quickly found what he needed. There, sitting at the corner of the bar, was a massive glass pitcher of home-brewed grog, ugly brown in color and so harsh and low-quality that it was set out free for drunks to dip their cups into. It had just been refilled.

With a murmured incantation, Rodolphus made it the spitting image of a glass jug of clear water. A second later he had found someone who looked to be a trader from out of town, and with a single word and a flick of his finger, a sparkle shone in the air to the man's left, drawing his gaze. Another sparkle brought him spinning to look at the bar, and he found himself staring directly at a jug of water. It only took him a few seconds to figure out how he could make himself a hero.

The grog, it turned out, was even higher-proof that Rodolphus had expected. With its help, the tapestry and rear wall went from a contained fire to a small inferno that began lapping at the roof supports and across the oil and booze-soaked planks of the floor.

Wolfram and Rodolphus were soon standing out on the grass with the other bar goers, including the wailing lamp-victim, who was curled up on the ground and screaming now that his nerves had caught up with his burns. The apparent owner of the place, standing nearby, was openly sobbing. A pair of large men who could have been the owner's sons were meanwhile beating a figure to a pulp not far off. The figure looked to be bald with a mustache, though after having a bottle broken against his mouth he didn't look like all that much of anything.

The building was fully alight when Wolfram checked his pocket watch again. "Time," he said conversationally.

"Well," Rodolphus said, staring at his handiwork, "I don't know if I really *obliterated* it…"

"Perhaps not," Wolfram replied, "but I think it's an admirable start. Full marks!"

"Wow. I'd say this took me back to Combat Casting Academy, but I don't think I ever got full marks there."

"Hah, and what do a bunch of conjurers know about magic, anyway? But say, let us get out of here. It has become most unpleasantly hot."

———————————————————

Learning Curation magic was simpler, but not by much. Rodolphus accomplished the feat in perhaps half the time it had taken him to become adept at Enchantment. He and Wolfram had left the old row house in Durkheim, moving to a country home that Wolfram said he had purchased as a young man. Curation was less exciting than Enchantment, not very flashy at all—to practice his art, Rodolphus had to cut himself, usually with one of Wolfram's slim, silver knives, before healing the wound back up. While Wolfram had insisted that the cutting begin immediately, it had been months before Rodolphus could begin to close the wounds properly.

He graduated eventually to using his still-growing Enchantment skills to stalk silently and invisibly through the woods and take a deer by surprise, shooting a hail of icicles through its belly and then closing the wounds before the thing died of blood loss or shock. This, too, was largely unsuccessful for months, though at the very least the pair of men usually got a week of meals out of the arrangement. By the time Rodolphus was able to heal the deer, he typically killed them again anyway. No need to miss out on good eating.

Yet, Curation magic simply did not speak to Rodolphus. Nevertheless, his commitment was great; so great that he learned the art uncomplainingly for years before he finally broached the subject with Wolfram.

They were sitting at the old wooden table, supping on potato soup that Wolfram had made with the yield of the garden he spent most of his time working. Each had their face buried in one of Wolfram's ancient magical texts, but only Wolfram was actually reading. Sucking the inside of his mouth clean of soup and swallowing with a sip of water, Rodolphus cleared his throat.

"Mhmm?" Wolfram said, not looking up.

"I have concerns."

"Concerns. About your education?"

"No. Well, yes, I suppose."

"You are progressing at an acceptable rate."

Rodolphus smirked. *"Thank you."*

"You're quite welcome."

"After I'd proven that I had a handle on Enchantment, Wolfram, I asked you to teach me Necromancy."

"Yes, I remember."

"And you refused."

"Mhmm."

"You insisted that it was too advanced. That I still was not ready."

"Mhmm."

"I realize now that I should have insisted then, but no matter. I'm insisting now. I'm nearly adept at healing, and once I am, I will learn Necromancy from you."

Wolfram looked up, cocking his head. "Will you?"

"Yes. Yes, I will."

"And what is it about Necromancy that so intrigues you? Have you forgotten our talk, Rodolphus, when we first met?"

"No. I remember what you said, but I've realized—if I can't be truly immortal, so be it. But if I become a ghoul, that will be close. And with the Enchantment magic I've learned, and will eventually master, I will be an exceptionally hard ghoul to kill. It's close enough. I need to learn Necromancy, Wolfram. I consented to learn this Curation business because it can help keep me safe in my present form, but it's not good enough. This body is dying every day."

"Better," Wolfram asked dryly, "to simply be dead every day?"

"If it means being a ghoul, and most of the way to immortal, then yes."

"Tsk." Wolfram turned back to his reading. "Honestly, Rodolphus. You've gone and ruined the surprise."

Rodolphus frowned. "What? What is that supposed to mean?"

"I was going to tell you when you had mastered Curation, as a reward, but I guess if you really want to know…"

"This is childish," Rodolphus growled.

"So full of life, children. Like you wish to be. In a manner of speaking."

"*Please* tell me," Rodolphus said, forcing his voice to remain steady.

"Oh, very well. What I told you all those years ago was untrue."

Rodolphus, for once, found himself speechless.

"A complete fabrication, I'm afraid. One skilled enough in Necromancy can indeed produce an undead being that not only will never die of natural causes, but that is also entirely immune to death at the hands of others. True immortality. It is more than merely possible. It has been done."

"Why... why would you wait so long..."

"That's simple. Because I want to do it to you. Because I want to make you a lich."

"Lich," Rodolphus said experimentally, tasting the word.

"Yes. Most Wizards of my persuasion, you see, make themselves into liches in their old age, so as to live forever... but for myself, I was never quite taken by that idea. I have always thought that it would be rather interesting to see what waits in the next life."

Rodolphus snickered. "I've seen where you're going, old man, and trust me, interesting doesn't begin to cover it."

"Oh, Rodolphus. Do you really think someone like *me* would end up in the same place as someone like *you*? I think I can do a *tad* better than that."

"Watch yourself, you old—"

"In fact, your stories of Hell have intrigued me. You have first-hand information that there is something beyond this life! Death will be the start of a grand new expedition!"

"Heh. Unless mediocre old coots go nowhere when they die."

"Mhmm, but would that not be informative in itself? Assuming I was able to conceive of it in the instant of my death, and I should think that would not be too difficult for one of my acuity."

"And you really think you'll get into… what, the good place?"

"I'll go where I'm sent. Perhaps it will turn out that everyone goes where you ended up. Only seeing it for myself will satisfy my curiosity…"

"We were talking about liches."

"Mhmm, yes. Making a lich is difficult and time-consuming, and typically a Wizard can make only one. Since I do not plan to make one of myself, it would be a waste if I did not get to experience the creation of a lich before I die. Thus, I shall make one of you."

"Well, why the hell didn't you just do that to begin with?"

"Hah! Rodolphus, a lich would be my masterpiece! Do you think I could make one out of a mere conjurer? I had to make sure you were at least proficient at Enchantment and Curation first."

"You crafty old son of a bitch… I'm not sure whether to hug you, or strangle you."

Wolfram smiled sadly. "My dear, poor Rodolphus… have you ever been able to decide that of anyone?"

———————————————————————

Months later, the Curation final exam was held. Rodolphus and Wolfram carried out the standard deer practice run upon a young woman from the local village who had chanced into the forest to gather mushrooms. Upon Rodolphus' successful healing of the girl, the lich ritual could begin. There was little fanfare. Wolfram revealed that he had been practicing and preparing for it for months, and hence they could begin immediately.

Rodolphus had vaguely expected the ritual to take the form of some sort of terrible atrocity, or at least involve unmentionable deeds. He was a little disappointed.

"There's nothing inherently evil about making a lich," Wolfram said testily upon questioning, "and neither with Necromancy, nor with any magic. Spells are designed by great men who have an eye to carry out a certain task. They are usually as efficient as possible. If those Wizards make their spells with too much unneeded ritual attached, such is quickly stripped away by the Wizards who follow in their footsteps."

In the case of making a lich, even "as efficient as possible" turned out to be ridiculously complex and convoluted, if quite boring. The ritual was incredibly difficult to perform properly, and required Rodolphus to sit for days while Wolfram sat cross-legged across from him, head hung low, a constant string of Arcanic too muffled to understand streaming from his lips. Rodolphus was able to sip from a canteen, but always did so slowly to avoid breaking Wolfram's concentration. He had no interest in finding out what it meant to become a half-lich. Other than the hunger, the time was notable only for its intense boredom. Rodolphus used it to relive, in his mind, the adventure with Tiberius and the Wolf, from Selan to the Crutchfield estate at Yunder. It was, he now realized, the happiest time of his life.

Into the fourth day, Wolfram's chanting, which had become increasingly inaudible as the hours passed, finally, and abruptly, stopped. Slowly, his back straightened and his head rose.

"There," he said softly.

"Did it work?" Rodolphus asked eagerly with a parched voice, a sense of dread raising goose bumps on his skin.

"Yes, it went quite well."

"But… I don't feel any different."

"And why should you? You're still in your original body, aren't you? Physically, there is no change."

"So I'm not undead? Not yet?"

"Yes and no. This body is still alive in the normal sense, and will still die of natural causes, as it would have. At that point, instead of traveling to the afterlife, your soul will travel to the location of your new body, which will be instantly generated at the designated spot. The majority of the spell was simply empowering that effect. The new body will be immortal, and undead. It won't age, but it will rot, though very slowly. If it is slain, a new one will be created for you. Get me a glass of water, would you, boy?"

Rodolphus got up shakily and went to the pump just outside the font door, filling a glass quickly and returning with it. "Rot? Ugh."

"Please, as though you'd have let a little thing like that stop you."

"Any other unpleasant surprises for me, now that there's no turning back?"

"Well, as any dullard would imagine, sapient undead often suffer some sort of emotional change. It's hard to predict—a new manic streak, or a deadening of passions... it takes many forms. Sometimes there is no change at all."

"Hmm. I don't feel any different."

"Maybe there is no effect because you were already insane."

Rodolphus grinned wolfishly. "What about my new body—where will it be generated? I assume the designated place is right around here, yes? Maybe on this very spot?"

Wolfram took a long drink, sighing softly afterward. He looked even thinner than usual. "Hmm?"

"My new bodies. Where will they form?"

The corner of Wolfram's mouth lifted into an unpleasant smile. "Oh, did I not mention? No, I'm afraid the place of the generation is pre-determined."

In Rodolphus' mind, an inkling of dread began to develop. "Where, then?"

"It will be at the location of your death."

"Oh. Oh, then that isn't so bad. In fact, maybe I had better just go to the place that seems best and kill myself, so that I can ensure that my body gets raised in a safe location."

"Aren't you forgetting something?"

There was that dread again. "Spit it out, old man."

"Well, in fact, you've died already, Rodolphus, so the spot of your regeneration was already selected. Your body will be created in the lawn behind the Crutchfield estate, in Yunder."

"But... but that's not private enough..."

"If you're going to get yourself killed again, try to do it at night. That will help."

"They may have built something over that spot! What then?"

"The magic will work it out. Just as it will work out the fact that you technically died somewhere just short of that wretched little river settlement you told me about. In order to avoid the difficulty of locating the exact spot of death, the ritual causes the body to be formed where the mortal wound was inflicted."

"You might have told me this. There are ramifications."

"Rodolphus, I chose you for this because I knew you would be able to *deal* with those ramifications."

"How easily could someone find out that a lich's body generates where he was first mortally wounded?"

"A determined man could do it."

"Then it is not safe. Too many people know where I took my mortal wound."

"Mhmm, yes, certainly so."

"I have to kill them all."

"Yes, you certainly do."

"I'll have to look into whether they ever found out what happened in Yunder that night. Whether the Wolf left any witnesses alive."

"Anything is possible," Wolfram said, finishing off the glass of water and setting it on the floor next to him.

"I'll have to kill anyone in Springdale who remembers the circumstances of my arrival."

"Can't be too careful, mhmm."

"I have to find the Wolf and Tiberius, and kill them both."

"That should be an interesting waltz through the past for you, no? I think you'll enjoy it."

Rodolphus covered his face with his hands. "Why did you wait to tell me this? Why didn't you tell me earlier?"

"An old man such as myself takes pleasure in the small things, Rodolphus... such as surprise. There were other motives too, of course. More practical ones."

"Such as?" Rodolphus growled, his mind racing already through the necessary actions to safeguard his immortality.

"Such as buying myself a little time before you realized that you needed to kill me, too."

Rodolphus' mind whirred to a stop like a watch that had reached the end of its spring. "I... what?"

"Come, Rodolphus. I know everything about how and where you died, and I know as well as anyone living how one would go about preventing your resurrection. Further, you are hardly the sentimental type. If you could murder a girl who may have loved you and feel no remorse, what qualms could you have with killing me?"

"Wolfram, I promise you—"

"Don't waste your breath, Rodolphus. I am no Tiberius. We have lived together for a decade. You have told me everything about yourself. I know that you would kill me, and I welcome you to do so. I recommend only this…"

The old man smiled. "Don't come unprepared."

With an incantation almost too quick to detect, Wolfram disappeared, and Rodolphus the lich sat alone in the country house, staring at where he had been.

He didn't know where to start.

There was so much to do.

Chapter 26

Somewhere, deep inside the atrophied twist of ganglia that passed for its brain, the Wolf was aware that it had gotten old. Its fur had begun to turn color long ago and was now uniformly silver, pigment remaining only in a broad black stripe running down its still-muscular back. It had long since abandoned the few niceties of human society that it had once abided by; armor and clothing were, to it, most fettering, and so it no longer wore either.

It had been a long, full life, with a great many achievements—and some of them had tasted very, very good. On the far continent, the Wolf probably would not have lived this long. As it weakened its pack would turn on it, take its power and its flesh, eat it alive and by so doing become it. It was the way of things.

Not always, though. Being old did not have to mean being used-up. Either way, it was much easier to avoid all that and live here, with the humans, soft-bodied, quick of tongue but slow of limb. The old, weakened Wolf was no longer three times as strong as a young man, but twice as strong was perfectly sufficient for its needs.

If the Wolf had a better understanding of human culture, it would have realized just how much its life now resembled a twisted facsimile of human retirement. The cottage it had taken up residence in was warm and homey, like that of grandparents who had moved off to the countryside to get back in touch with nature. The Wolf had never lost touch with nature, but nevertheless it had settled down for the first and perhaps last time in its life, living alone in the cottage. Its former owners had been quite unable to protect it, and thus did not deserve it.

The cottage was conveniently located a few miles away from a small farming community, which the Wolf visited frequently. They knew it well. They had set up rickety guard towers that were amusing to knock over, and hired guards whom it was very fun to kill. It only took as much as it needed to eat. Only so much that they could still balance the good sense of fleeing against the fear of having to leave behind their homes, their crops, and their way of life. For a while, they had hired hunters and professional soldiers to hunt down the Wolf. Most demanded pay upfront, which meant that the Wolf had amassed a small fortune. With a vague and only theoretical idea that the little shiny pieces of metal had value, it kept them heaped up on a table in the main room, and sometimes sat admiring them.

In its many years, the Wolf had never once been surprised. It had no expectations of what the future held, and thus any shift of events seemed, to it, perfectly natural. Thus, it was not surprised when its home exploded around it.

The wood shards that peppered its body hurt just barely less than the blazing fire that scorched off much of its fur and crinkled its smoking flesh, causing it to howl in pain, but not surprise. Never surprise.

———————————————————

Rodolphus was not an optimist, and neither was he an idiot. Thus, as he stood on the hilltop, staring at the distant blaze of the cabin, he did not lower his arm, nor his guard. He was not waiting for confirmation that it was dead. He was merely waiting to see what it would do next.

A sick part of him had yearned to see the Wolf again. He had learned much from it... and yet, it terrified him, so he had also lived in fear of this moment. He had put it off for years. He had gone to Yunder first, where he'd confirmed that the Wolf had left no one alive to tell the tale of who had perpetrated the massacre. He did pick up one interesting lead there, but it was one he would follow-up later. Next he'd headed to Springdale, which he'd found demolished and abandoned. A quick bit of follow-up revealed that the town had been raided and destroyed a year or so after he'd left it. He wondered wistfully how the death of the chief's daughter might have contributed to such a turn of fortunes.

He had hoped that by delaying the wolf-hunt, he could avoid it all together. He'd allowed decades to pass, first learning the basics of Divination to aid him in his search efforts, and then learning Necromancy as well, thinking that it was only right to finish his education before setting out. It had been quite an education, indeed—some thirty years had passed since he had become a lich. Even now, there was still a great deal left to learn, especially about Necromancy, which made the others schools of magic look like kindergarten. After he'd tied up his loose ends, it would be back to the books.

Nevertheless, he'd finally faced that he had waited long enough. He had hoped that by now the Wolf's violent, brutal life would have come to an end. It was with an ever-increasing sense of dread that he finally followed a trail of rumor and horror story to this location, where now he stood on the hilltop, an old man, and waged war against Death itself.

What Death did next was bowl directly through one of the caved-in cabin walls, visible from such a distance only as a black spot against the blacker landscape. Rodolphus fought the urge to turn invisible. Doing so would only encourage him to run, since after all, invisibility helped little when you were the focal point of a storm of fire and ice.

The Wolf itself disappeared as it stalked out of the light of the blaze, but the grey smoke that bled from it into the night sky showed like a beacon. It was coming his way.

The hilltop was conveniently located at just about the maximum range Rodolphus could hurl a sufficient amount of fire without it ceasing to exist en route. He had estimated that it would take the Wolf about eighty seconds to run the distance. In practice, it would appear that he had severely miscalculated. The wisp of smoke was already halfway between the cabin and him, and the black splotch under it was becoming visible again.

He hurled more fire, ball after ball arcing high into the air and exploding against the ground. He wasn't sure why he was bothering, when it hadn't worked the first time. Anyway, his aim was not nearly good enough. The Wolf was covering so much ground between Conjuration and impact that it was far too difficult to predict where to aim.

Slowly, Rodolphus brought up an arm, the sleeve of his robe rolling back as he did. He made a rough triangle of three fingers and pointed at the approaching humanoid blotch, his hand quivering wildly, and muttered a new incantation. The colossal bolt of lightning that burst from his fingertips struck the core of the Wolf in a millisecond, channeling amounts of power that Rodolphus could barely conceive of into the thing's body. Sparks exploded off of it as its remaining fur was incinerated, and Rodolphus kept chanting, prolonging the spell, draining his reserves, stretching his concentration until he was on the very verge of fainting.

Finally letting it end, he dropped his arm back to his side, head swimming. Now he waited for confirmation that the Wolf, still standing, smoking more than ever, was dead.

For a moment, there was nothing. The two figures, black silhouettes against the distant blaze of the cabin, merely stared.

The silence broke.

"YEE-HEEHEEHEEHEEHEEHEEHEEHEE!"

Rodolphus *could* be surprised, but he hadn't time to be as the Wolf plunged into him like a ballista bolt. He squirmed and shook and shrieked like a rabbit, his shattered ribs crushing his heart and lungs, and the Wolf looked far more undead than he did, its fur gone along with much of its skin, its body covered in a blanket of tendon and ligament splotched red and black. Its muscles and joints twitched with the feedback of its mostly-destroyed brain. It locked its jaws over Rodolphus' screaming mouth in a lover's embrace and bit in, the man's flowing blood lubricating its corpse-dry flesh, intention joining in with tremor as its titanic neck muscles shook its head wildly back and forth.

It relished taking his flesh as he had taken its, and it sat there hunched through the night and tore strips away from his soft body, barely aware of its own wounds, its nerves destroyed and its veins cauterized. It recognized in a sense even more vague than usual that it knew this man—that it had chosen to let him live a long, long time ago. It did not regret this. The Wolf had never regretted anything. It simply *did*, and that was all.

By the time it was feasting on the contents of his abdomen, the Wolf's small frontal lobe had finished its death throes, and its hindbrain alone now drove it, though there was no apparent change in its behavior, its jaws continuing to spastically chew and fill its bloated stomach.

Once it had lost most of the rest of its motor function, it slowly crumpled up against the blood-soaked corpse, the body's warmth caressing it like the fur of a den mother. No longer able to eat, the failing hindbrain told the body to do the last thing that it could. It told it to laugh.

From the hilltop the sound carried as far as the village nearby, where men shook and bolted their doors, and children's dreams turned into nightmares.

* * *

Being born again probably felt a little bit like it must have the first time. Like drowning. He quivered naked in the wild grass, panting to fill lungs that did not and would never function. His body was young, or at least younger than it had been. Young as it had been when he'd first died, here in Yunder, in the lawn behind the manor.

He stood slowly, looking carefully around. It was still night. The manor was gone, probably demolished years ago. He was unsurprised that they hadn't built anything in its place; people got a mite superstitious when a dozen persons were found dead with no witnesses. All that remained was a vacant, overgrown lot, not a soul in sight.

He smiled grimly, swiftly cloaking himself in invisibility. Maybe he could leave a chest of clothing hidden around somewhere nearby, if the rest of his endeavors were going to go as unfortunately as his trip to visit his old friend the Wolf. Sitting carefully on a large rock, he waited a few minutes before he focused his mind and teleported himself to the site of his most recent death.

The Wolf was dead, though the occasional twitch of its ruined muscles was enough to give Rodolphus a start upon his arrival. Most of the flesh wrapping his former body had taken up residence in the Wolf's stomach—it had even gotten around to cracking open a few bones before it had inevitably perished. Rodolphus briefly considered whether it was worth trying to recover the tatters of his robe to hide his nudity, but quickly realized that the few remaining blood-soaked shreds would, if anything, make his appearance less socially acceptable than it was presently.

He stared down at the Wolf, which looked all the more alien and unnatural without its fur. He was glad that it was too dark to see much detail; the fire of the Wolf's cabin had finally died down to a low smolder. He had never fully understood the thing's decision to save his life, that day in Yunder. He had long ago decided that it must have been a snap decision, one based on only the barest fragment of thought or reason. Yet, there had to be something behind it.

The best Rodolphus could do was suspect that the Wolf hadn't killed him because it liked the world better with him in it. It saw some of itself in him, perhaps. That was not so surprising, as he had certainly seen some of himself in it. Tiberius had learned that too late to do anything about it.

The old man spooned broth to his lips with arthritic hands, blowing at the translucent liquid and watching the steam billow off of it. He sat alone in his spartan quarters, failing sunlight through the fogged glass of his windows the only illumination.

Experimentally, he took a small sip of the broth, then hissed as it scorched the end of his tongue. Sighing, he gripped the table with one hand for support as he stood, picking up the wooden bowl, turning toward the window so he could set it there to cool.

"You shouldn't heat it so much, if you don't like it hot," a voice behind him said.

The old man dropped the bowl, and it seemed to strike the floor instantaneously, the lacquered wood shearing into two parts. The broth spilled across the aged floorboards, disappearing down the cracks between them. The old man, his hands shaking, bent down. He took a towel off the counter and began to methodically wipe at the mess.

"You're not being a good host."

"That is because you were not invited," the old man said, his voice dry, rasping, scraping painfully from his larynx, the words barely understandable.

"Turn around, Tiberius."

"I don't have to. I remember what you look like. Perfectly."

The voice chuckled softly. "Yes, I know. It's a very sad story, Tiberius. I enjoyed piecing it together."

"You do not know who I am."

"You don't think so? But you know who I am, I'd imagine."

"No. No, imagining that I did know you was the greatest mistake that I have ever made."

"Such melodrama. Forty years later, and you're still making a fuss."

Tiberius, holding the counter, stood shakily back up, walking to the sink where he began to wring the warm towel out.

"Let me tell you who you are, Tiberius, and you can let me know if I get it right. How does that sound?"

Tiberius' veined hands twisted the towel, thin rivulets of liquid streaming away from it down the drain.

"After my little accident at Yunder, you went unconscious, which is not what I would call terribly surprising. Apparently sometime soon thereafter, Crutchfield was killed. I don't think I'd be taking too far of a logical jump to suggest that the Wolf did it. He says hello, by the way."

Tiberius paused for only a moment before beginning to pump fresh water onto the stained towel.

"After that, the Wolf picked me up and carried me off, leaving you as the sole survivor. Of course, what with all the fire and screaming, help came pretty soon. The mansion, obviously, could not be salvaged. You were taken to a hospital and healed. It did not take them long to figure out that you were neither a guard of Crutchfield's nor even a resident of the city. They came to the obvious conclusion: you were one of the perpetrators."

"Yes," Tiberius rasped, "the correct conclusion."

"They questioned you thoroughly. The records weren't very detailed on that subject, but I assume that it was not a terribly pleasant experience. Trust me, it was still better than what I was dealing with at the time. Fortunately for me and our good friend the Wolf, you wouldn't say a word. Literally. You wouldn't, or couldn't, speak. If you don't mind my asking, which was it?"

Tiberius hung the towel from the rack to dry.

"As you like. You languished in a filthy prison cell for a few months, barely fed and frequently beaten. Eventually, you had a stroke of luck. A citizen of Selan was thrown into the Yunder jail one night for drunkenness, and recognized you, or at least what you were. They knew at least one person in the Minarian Church, and soon enough a Minarian delegation was sent to Yunder. They successfully petitioned for your release—the records and public memory are a bit hazy on those arrangements, but I have a feeling that a good bit of Nam changed hands. You'd bet on the right horse with the Minarians in that respect. They stick together like pack animals, and once they had you loose they didn't even really want to know whether you'd committed the crime or not. War doesn't exactly breed squeamish priests, I suppose.

"Thus, things could have come to a fortuitous end, but you chose otherwise, didn't you?"

"We all do what we think is best."

"Do we? Hmm. Honestly Tiberius, I wonder if, by that point in your life, your mind was not what it once was."

"You are right on that account, but not how you think. I was saner than I had ever been. Can the same be said for you, at that time?"

"You still refused to speak, which they probably all thought was very interesting and noble of you. In fact, your stoicism impressed someone so much that it wasn't long after you were back that you were granted the opportunity to dine with the High Priest himself, an almost unfathomably rare chance for a Minarian of your level. You had a fine way to show your gratitude, though. They hadn't even served the first course when you penned a note and passed it to the old bastard. Tell me, Tiberius, what did it say?"

"It sounds like you know already."

"Yes, but I want to hear your inflection."

"'I hereby formally renounce my affiliation with the Church of Minar for all time.'"

"Mhmm. A faux pas, I'm afraid. The old man was most displeased, and promptly had you committed to an asylum. Stop me if you want to add anything."

Tiberius took a new bowl from the cabinet.

"Do you think he did it out of spite? Or was he really such a devout believer that he thought your deviance could only indicate insanity?"

"The former is why he did it. The latter is why he told himself he did it."

"Goodness, do I detect a bit of a grudge?"

"No grudge. We all do what we think is best."

"You're repeating yourself. Let's try to wrap this up, shall we? You were hauled without resistance to the asylum in the new district of Selan. The place doesn't exist anymore—condemned years back. They did keep good records, though. Sadists always do. They had you in their delicate care for thirteen years. What was it like?"

Tiberius ladled a new bowl of broth from the pot.

"The records, sadly, did not go into specifics regarding your treatment, but can I assume that it was shabby? From what I can tell, the inmates were probably a healthy mix of the genuinely, dangerously insane, and people like you who were just being swept under the rug. I bet you were exuding so much self-pity at this point, there was a serious danger that you might choke on it. That is how you spent your time in there, isn't it? Feeling sorry for yourself, hating me for what I'd done to you? When they weren't busy slapping you around, I mean. "

"You did nothing to me that I did not allow you to do."

"Hrm? You're saying it was all part of the plan?"

"No. I'm saying that I cannot blame you when I did not choose to stop you."

"I thought we all did what we thought was best?"

"That is the problem. When I was with you, I was doing what *you* thought was best. In essence, I became you."

"At some point," Rodolphus went on, "and I'm not too clear on the date—you were released, which meant being dumped on the street with nothing but a tattered tunic to your name. Poor old Tiberius dragged his body to a homeless shelter, where he met a kindly Abbott, presumably the kind who gets his kicks doting over the pitiful and helpless. You fit the bill better than a legless puppy."

Tiberius raised the half-filled bowl to his lips and slowly drank down its contents. As he did, his eyes closed with gentle pleasure.

"You joined his Order, the Pertainians. A sect which worries not over what happens after you die, but what you do while you're alive. They are best known for their commitment to kindness, charity, and especially pacifism. Some members take a vow of silence."

Tiberius set the bowl down on the counter.

"So, tell me, Tiberius. How long since you last spoke?"

Tiberius turned around and looked at the face that had followed him everywhere for four decades. "Forty years."

The lich paced around Wolfram's cottage; his cottage now, he supposed, as Wolfram had definitely not left the impression that he would be coming back. That had been so long ago—it became difficult to keep track of time, when one neither ate nor slept. This wasn't helped by the fact that he'd spent decades doing little more than reading his way through Wolfram's enormous library of magical texts. He frowned at the soot under his nails and wiped his hand once again against his shirt.

The Wolf had gone exactly as planned, more or less. In retrospect, it had probably been stupid to expect to live through that encounter. In fact, things had turned out rather well; he'd tested his immortality and found it to be everything he'd hoped for. There hadn't been even a glimpse of Hell as his soul traveled between bodies.

Tiberius, though...he had expected to find Tiberius broken, and certainly the man was, a greyed old monk on a poverty income. Rodolphus had expected more than that, though. He thought that Tiberius would be afraid, cowering in abject fear like a dog that has been trained through beating. Alternatively, he'd imagined that Tiberius might nearly welcome him, begging him to finally grant him the death that he must have so long wished for. Considering what had happened to the man since Yunder...

What Rodolphus hadn't expected was stoicism and gentle acceptance. He hadn't expected a voice dry and cracked yet strong and firm, hovering always just shy of politeness. He'd been sure that he would finally break the man's front with his cackled admission as he slid into one of the chairs: "I've come here to kill you, Tiberius."

Not even the merest ghost of surprise had shown in Tiberius' eyes. If anything, he looked mildly confused. "Well, of course you did," he rasped.

"Aren't you curious as to *why* I'm going to kill you?" Rodolphus had hissed, his teeth clenching. He would fall back on his glorious ascension to undeath to shake his opponent free of his convictions.

"The answer to that question is never one that satisfies," Tiberius said, simply.

"Fine, then. Die here in your hovel. Die as you lived, shrouded in self-pity. Will you beg for mercy?"

"No more than I would water unseeded soil."

"Save your parables!" Rodolphus had growled.

"You are young, obviously. As young, it seems, as when I saw you last. I do not know what you did, or why you did it. I am sure it seemed like the best thing to do, at the time."

"Are you ready to die, Tiberius, or aren't you?"

Inexplicably, the old man's cracked lips rose into a smile. "I am, Rodolphus. I have endeavored long and hard, and I am. Will you ever be?"

"I'll ask the questions!" Rodolphus roared, and in his rage he'd created a fireball that within seconds of roiling combustion was the size of the room. He'd barely remembered to put a protective enchantment on himself in the meantime.

Tiberius, curled on the floor ten seconds later, looked like a roast that had been left in the oven overnight by mistake. Every scrap of flammable material in the place had become part of a valley of ash coating the floor, broken with occasional hills and plateaus of scorched chair-legs and blackened book-binding. Rodolphus had stood in the ashes, staring at the charred remains of the old man in something akin to shock. It was hard to say how long passed before he heard the sound of raised voices, but when he did he quickly teleported away, confident that any records the man might have kept had been as destroyed by the fire as he was.

Standing in Wolfram's cottage, he realized that he should have done it slowly. He could have strangled Tiberius with his bare hands, forced him to beg. Cut through that façade of calm to the weeping little boy that he was sure must have been buried just beneath. What was done, though, was done.

Tiberius was dead, which was all that mattered. He crossed to the book case. There was one loose end remaining.

Part V: Lich

Chapter 27

Alfonz Samuelson had lost a calf. It was an especially troubling event, because it had only been a few weeks earlier that he had finally brought in a good enough crop to be able to barter for one. Since then, the calf had been quite placid and obedient, and as a result he had become somewhat lax in ensuring every night that it was properly secured in its pen outside the house.

He had of course immediately jumped to the worst of conclusions: that it had been stolen away, possibly by one of his neighbors, with whom he did not get along. However, a quick inspection of the scene indicated otherwise. The old chicken wire had been pushed out of its fastenings and lay on the ground, and in the mud between Alfonz's compound and the sparse little forest that the locals called the Rosewald, clear hoof prints were evident.

Still concerned but heartened by the tracks, Alfonz went inside for his hat before locking up and following the trail into the wood. The trees were spaced far apart, allowing a great deal of sunlight to shine through. Alfonz followed the trail until the ground under the canopy, dry and coated in leaves, stopped yielding any tracks at all. Nevertheless, there was an obvious path that the calf could have taken without bumping into any trees, so Alfonz chose that, and continued on.

In a few minutes he was already leaving the tiny Rosewald, and as he did he looked down at a long tract of mud that showed clear evidence of a calf's passing. The tracks proceeded on directly toward a squat home, surrounded by a rotting picket fence. Alfonz frowned, because he knew the place.

Alfonz's best friend in the village, the landlord Zibulka, had told him of the cottage. Zibulka's ancestors, all landlords before him, had kept detailed records, and Zibulka had mentioned that the cottage had been purchased by someone named Arthur Wolfram more than a century ago, back in the time when silver and gold were still used for payment. Because it was outside the town limits, the owner needed pay no taxes or other dues, and so Zibulka merely made a quick trek out every year to see if the home was still occupied; he eagerly awaited the death of whoever lived there now, presumably one of Wolfram's relatives, so that he could finally snatch it up and sell it again. Every year, though, Zibulka, standing perhaps quite close to where Alfonz stood now, saw the light of lanterns through the windows, and so shrugged his shoulders and turned back to town. He never went to knock on the door; the whole village seemed to agree upon a superstition of vague origins that said the cottage was bad luck, and farmers took such things at least somewhat seriously.

Alfonz could not read, and had to take Zibulka's word for it as to what the records said. Looking at the ancient cottage, though, he certainly believed that the place was centuries old, and he doubted it had seen even a modest renovation for decades. The picket fence had deteriorated to the point where it served in neither function nor appearance, and the wooden walls of the place showed only the faintest signs of once having been white, the paint long ago having cracked and peeled away. He wondered if Zibulka had fully thought out his plan to resell the place, seeing as the cost of fixing it up might well be more than that of building an entirely new cottage.

Alfonz had no wish to draw bad luck to himself, but he would be damned if he was going to lose a calf, so he made his way to the house, passing between a gap in the fence, and headed toward the rotten old wooden door. Taking a deep breath, he thumped on it.

"Come in," a voice said, and Alfonz found himself turning the knob and stepping into the house, not even pausing to consider. The inside of the cottage was only marginally cleaner than the outside, and the only notable items were a great multitude of oil lamps, an old wooden desk and chair, and what must have been thousands of books.

Alfonz's jaw dropped in stupefaction. The wealthiest farmer he knew owned only a handful of outdated almanacs, and Alfonz himself of course had no books to speak of. To accumulate so many of them... he could not even imagine what an effort it would take. Many were obviously ancient, the black leather bindings worn and tattered, revealing no titles. A handful looked much newer, printed on paper and bearing titles in the common print.

The lamps were all dark, the cottage instead flooded with sunlight through the curtainless windows. A figure sat at the desk, and even from behind Alfonz knew that something was wrong. The back of the head was dark and hairless, and it took him only a moment to realize that he was looking at a human skull. He tried to turn to flee, but found that his body was totally unresponsive to the commands of its brain.

The chair was slowly pushed back from the desk as the figure stood and turned. It was a human skeleton indeed, its bones blackened and tarry with what might have been the decayed remnants of muscle. Alfonz looked up to the thing's skull expecting to see vacant pits where its eyes should have been, but he instead found himself gazing into a pair of extremely bloodshot blue eyes, freakishly round with no eyelids to shroud them. The skeleton wore a tattered robe that was open in front, revealing its ribs and spinal column.

"Lucky you arrived," the thing said in a disturbingly human voice. "I had just run out of calf's blood."

Alfonz felt a tremor of fear as the thing gestured with a skeletal finger, and noticed for the first time that its hands, and the cuffs of its robe, were drenched in blood. Its reddened finger bone guided his eyes to a corner of the cabin untouched by the beams of sunlight, and Alfonz was able to turn his head to see the dismembered body of his calf, the parts piled in disorder over a large stain where the blood had soaked into the floorboards. Alfonz felt his heart plummet a little further.

"Look at this," the thing said, snatching a flat pane off the desk. Alfonz saw that it was a mirror, its surface completely covered in intricately sketched words. He had no trouble grasping that they were written not in red ink, but in the blood of his calf.

"This must be my twentieth attempt since last night," the thing said pitiably, "and nothing. Nothing. It's like he disappeared. Nothing works. Do you know that I've been doing this for… for… what year is it, anyway?"

Alfonz told him.

The skeleton paused, as though thinking. "Is that so? It was so long ago that I tied up the rest of the loose ends. I only meant to brush up on Divination before I went looking for Wolfram, but I became distracted, I suppose, and there kept on being new developments in magic that I had to make sure I was up to date on, and… has it really been ninety years, since then?"

He paused, as though he expected an answer. Alfonz nodded, hoping it was the correct thing to do.

"Hrm. No matter. What's my hurry? And it changes nothing—I would hardly put it by that old bastard to still be alive at age… gods, he'd have to be nearly two centuries old now, wouldn't he? And now I'm twice the Wizard he ever was, but what the hell is the point when I can't even find him? I bet he neglected to teach me Divination magic on purpose, you know. So that I'd have so much trouble locating him."

"Please, milord," Alfonz began, but he stopped when the terrifying eyes pivoted to him again.

"Don't beg. Are we having a conversation, or aren't we?"

"Ye—yes, milord," Alfonz managed to spit out.

"Good. I know what you're thinking, by the way. You're thinking, maybe Wolfram is dead, and that's why he's not showing up. Is that what you're thinking?"

"I... well, sir, I..."

"Of course it is. But you see, if that were the case, Divination would still be able to find the corpse. Death is no obstacle. But the way the magic is acting... has been acting for years... is that Wolfram never existed at all. I tried every method in the books he kept here, and when they didn't work I started gathering more knowledge from the great libraries, but still... still nothing."

Alfonz's shaken brain made a connection. "Arthur Wolfram, sir?"

"Hrm? Is that his first name? You'd think that'd help with the spells, but no. I guess you remember him since he used to live here? Or, no, that would have been your..." he paused, as thought it was difficult to recollect. "...great grandfather, maybe?"

"The... the landlord's ledgers, sir..."

"Ah, right," the thing said absent-mindedly, staring at the blood-covered mirror. After a few moments of contemplation, it growled and hurled the mirror to the ground. Alfonz winced as it shattered.

"Well, that's it!" the skeleton roared. "I've tried everything! What the hell am I supposed to do now, when he's still out there, and still knows?"

"Maybe, milord," Alfonz stuttered, "you could talk to someone from Merund."

The skeleton, staring down at the shattered pieces of glass and broken wooden frame, ignored him.

"We had someone from Merund visit a few years back, and they kept saying how their priests were really good at... at that word you've been using, milord."

"Divination?"

"Yeah, that's the one."

The eyes turned to him. "Merund, you said? Isn't that just a little trading town?"

"No, milord... it's a major city. Far from here, though... hundreds of miles..."

"No matter. Maybe it *is* worth a look. I think it's just about time I gave up on this mirror scrying garbage." The skeleton stood still for a moment, and then its shoulders shook slightly, as though it were trying to exhale a deep breath.

"You know," it said, more slowly, "you're completely right. It's time to get out of this rut, and Merund sounds like a good lead. It has been far too long since I voyaged into the open."

It turned its back on him, striding to a table and beginning to pick up books, reading the spines and sorting them into multiple piles. "What is your name?" it asked.

"Alfonz," Alfonz answered, his mouth moving automatically. He realized that he had said it without having time to consider it.

"Alfonz, you know the locals around here much better than I do. What would be more likely to keep them away from this cabin? For you to go back to town and explain to them what had happened here? Or for you to never be seen again, with indications left that you had gone in this direction?"

Alfonz knew which answer he wanted to give, but he realized with horror that it was not the one that came out of his mouth. "For me never to be seen again. If I told them what I saw, they might instead try to rally a mob."

If it was possible, the skeletal thing seemed to smile. "Pity."

It was night when Rodolphus arrived to the city, something that was hardly an accident. He wore only a billowing brown cloak; getting other clothes to fit his current frame was tedious, and he would not be bothered with it.

Merund was a reasonably attractive city. It was a far cry from Selan, where the dust of the perpetually dry seasons coated every building, all of which were cheap, ancient, or both. The buildings here, made most commonly of red brick, seemed far sturdier. The streets of Selan thronged with every sort of person—especially at night. The streets of Merund were largely deserted now, and those people Rodolphus did see were all of a fairly usual sort. The Wolf could walk around in Selan and only raise a few eyebrows. In Merund, they'd probably start ringing the bells to signify a barbarian raid.

He stopped briefly outside a manor and looked up at it nostalgically. Much more than Selan, Merund reminded him of a bigger version of Yunder. The weather tonight, he considered thoughtfully, was much like it had been when he'd taken the crossbow bolt to the neck. Let it happen to him again. They'd see how much it would slow him down this time.

He began making his way into the Western District of the city, and traffic on the streets increased somewhat. Before his arrival, he'd brushed up a bit on the history of Merund, which had been around for several hundred years, attaining real prominence about half a century before. His guess was that it was now likely at the peak of its power in the region, which was quite distant from the area where he'd spent his life. The Western District was one of the seedier areas, and had the highest concentration of unlicensed magic users. Thus, he went there first.

The careful regulation of magic in the city, and the forbiddance of Curation and Necromancy, tickled Rodolphus. He could only hope that his stay in Merund would be long enough for the authorities to attempt to bring him in on either charge. He had a feeling that the situation would quickly devolve into sheer hilarity.

Perhaps even worse than the city's draconian views on magic was its impressive stupidity regarding the field of Divination. While any Wizard worth their salt elsewhere was well aware of the practical limits of Divination, those in Merund, blinded by the incredible inanity of a baseless religion invented there at some point in the distant past, were certain that it could be used to accurately predict the future. Rodolphus was not even sure whether the fools knew that Divination had other uses that *actually functioned*, such as locating lost people and objects in the present. He would soon enough find out. After a bit of perusal of the city's underground magic scene, he would make his way to the bastion of ineptitude known as Merund University, and either leave as a more qualified diviner, or with a few extra lives on his scorecard.

Well into the Western District now, he turned a corner onto a larger avenue and quickly noticed that a crowd had gathered. He approached with some curiosity, keeping out of the glow of the streetlights. The crowd was dispersing;

whatever had held their attention had apparently already gone. Rodolphus listened carefully, and heard something about a walking human skeleton. *That,* he thought, *is extremely intriguing. Assuming they're not referring to me.*

He was approaching a few dawdlers and considering the best way to extract information from them when his attention was immediately drawn elsewhere. He felt a rush of energy flow over him like a slap in the face, and he stood still for a moment as he attempted to discern its nature. He quickly realized that it was a flux of magical power, seeing as no one else seemed to notice it—and even more impressive was that it was necromantic energy, spreading with incredible force and range. The caster must have been an amazingly astute necromancer, almost as powerful as Rodolphus himself.

Before his eyes, the power began to have its obvious effect: with the grim sounds of shuffling, clawing, and scraping, undead began to emerge. Several decayed skeletons slowly crawled forth from sewer vents, and a pair of zombies shambled out of the basement entrance of a two-flat across the road. Rodolphus wondered wistfully at what had caused the owners of the place to stash two corpses beneath their home. Within moments more undead were appearing out of alleyways and from around corners, and Rodolphus realized that the spell must have had an even greater reach than he'd imagined. With the number of undead arriving, he wondered whether there wasn't a morgue nearby... or was it possible that an arbitrary section of city normally contained so many bodies?

With disbelief he felt the power still increasing, and within seconds it had surpassed anything that he suspected himself capable of bringing to bear—anything, indeed, that he would have thought possible to wield. Seconds after that, something horrible began to happen: his body began to walk without his permission. He focused all his mental energies to stop it, began casting spell after spell to regain control of his body, all to no avail, and soon he found that he had been pulled to a nearby alley entrance.

As the necromantic force pushed him into the alley, he brushed up with half a dozen skeletons, and his cloak was caught and pulled away from him as he stumbled and fell forward, landing hard on the pavement. He now felt his body being dragged across the stone of the alley, with dozens of undead surrounding and piled atop him, crawling and shambling toward their destination. The group slammed into a wall before slowly readjusting and crawling around a bend, and he felt parts of his body shatter. The weight of the others on top of him caused further fractures, and as the swarm seemed to reach its goal and slow to a stop, he could see some among the undead mob standing and shambling forward, but he could not.

His body was broken, and the necromantic powers he could have used to restore it had been completely superseded. He laid there, alone in a group of dozens, mouth open in a silent scream of rage.

Chapter 28

All Radcliff could think about was how quickly everything had gone to hell. The sudden change in behavior of the Magistrate was bad enough, of course. It was extremely jarring—after all, Radcliff, no particular fan of the Delarian religion, had thought of the Magistrate as representing everything good it might still possess. The man's moderation and pragmatism in his faith had seemed quite admirable. Now, suddenly, the Magistrate was barking like the Archbishop himself, and based on a turn of events that to Radcliff was worth little more than the raise of an eyebrow.

All he could fathom was that maybe, when you stripped away all the ceremony of a religion and only believed in the most basic, principal ideal, it only meant you would be hurt even worse when that ideal was proven false.

It was worse than that, though. On top of Schiller's breakdown and subsequent crusade to the Divination tower, there was the situation with the necromancer, which itself was difficult enough to manage. Radcliff still hadn't figured out how the man Alois Gustav played into it, and he was annoyed that the necromancer, previously a figure of such urgent importance, was suddenly just being brought along for the ride. Everyone got their priorities jumbled, and he found himself unable to keep up with events.

Despite all the confusion, Radcliff had maintained at least some degree of confidence that things were going to calm down. His spirits had rallied further when the Dean showed up—order and rationality, he thought, could finally be restored, and the Magistrate's head would clear of nonsense, allowing them all to get back to business. His happiness, though, was short-lived. The situation deteriorated very quickly. Soon, he found himself faced with a dilemma.

Whose side, Radcliff wondered as he watched the Dean down one of the Guards, was he supposed to be on? He'd spent nearly the entirety of his life as either a student or an employee of the University, and even someone as marginalized as Radcliff was bound to forge a certain sense of belonging and loyalty over a period of time that long. On the other hand, Dean Baldermann had never so much as glanced at Radcliff throughout a lifetime of occasional passings in the hall, while the Magistrate, the most powerful man in the city, valued Radcliff's counsel and advice.

It was with a feeling of deep self-loathing that he realized he would do nothing. He would just sit and watch, not picking a side. *How can I pick a side,* he wondered disgustedly, *when I don't stand for anything*? The Dean, a man of convictions, would have the fight wrapped up in moments. What good could Radcliff, in his mediocrity, do for either party?

There was plenty more self-criticism where that came from. However, Radcliff did not get the opportunity to dredge it up, because at that point the stranger appeared in the room, and from there, everything got infinitely worse.

Rodolphus was glad for the darkness, for his new set of eyes had never before seen the light. The grass under him was moist with rain or early dew, and the sensation was not wholly unpleasant on his naked body. He sat up slowly, looking around, waiting for his memory to come back to him fully.

It took only a moment. He smiled, gently standing, taking a look around at his domain, the old Crutchfield estate. He considered thoughtfully that it had changed quite a bit since his last arrival. It seemed to be a park now, nicely terraced and trimmed. Short trees with coiled branches of lush green leaves and white flowers were planted in tidy rows, with paved paths curved around them. A manmade stream burbled pleasantly from nearby. No one was around. A few feet away, a stone pedestal with a flat top bore a relief of the face of old Crutchfield himself, and Rodolphus realized that it was a monument. His smile widened.

He held one of his hands before his eyes, considering it. It had been a long time since he had last seen his body with flesh on it. He stroked the familiar creases of his palm, brushed his fingers through the light hair on the back of his forearms. He hadn't at all minded losing the flesh; it meant little to him, in the end. But it was nice to have it back for a time. Perhaps dying had its advantages, providing you knew how to do it properly.

Being wrenched back to life had not been fully pleasant, but it was much better than last time. Being butchered by the Wolf had *hurt*; having his skull pierced through by the watchman's sword, on the other hand, had barely tickled. Absentmindedly, he conjured himself a black robe that draped comfortably over his body. Why hadn't he thought to do that last time, anyway? Amateur.

He strolled over to Crutchfield's monument and hopped up onto it, fidgeting until he was comfortable. From his seat he began divining the girl's new location, for at least some time must have passed since his last death. He had no physical focus for the spell, but he did know the target personally, and that made it much easier.

Very quickly, he found her, and decided to pay a visit.

Alois was only half aware of the shocking content of the accusations being shouted across the room, though in the back of his mind he realized that they seemed important. Nevertheless, he had other things to worry about, and his gaze constantly flickered from Guard to Guard, waiting for the critical moment when they'd be the most distracted. He squeezed Lina's shoulder to indicate that she should do the same; things were coming to a head, and they'd be unlikely to get another chance.

When a Guard tried to seize the Dean and shrieked as though he'd dipped his hands in boiling water, Alois decided it was time. One of the Guards who had been watching them had already started towards the Dean. The other, who had been the most consistent in keeping an eye on them, let his gaze flicker toward the conflict. It was enough. Alois' unnaturally powerful fist found the man's gut, sending him to the ground wide-eyed and sputtering. There was enough space in the back of Alois' mind to hope that he hadn't permanently harmed the Magisterial, but it was far from his top concern.

He grabbed his top concern by the hand and starting running as fast as his legs would take him for the door, planning to swing around the Dean, giving the man a nice, wide berth. He heard Lina shouting words of Arcanic in a jumbled chant as she hurried after him, no doubt attempting to call upon some sort of undead assistance. Alois doubted that any summoned minions could reach the top of the tower in time.

As Alois passed the Dean, he could swear that the man's dark eyes settled on him for a moment, and a wry smile very briefly appeared on the aged lips. Then the lips were mouthing the words to a new spell as he turned back to what had rapidly become a battle. The Dean had just begun to produce a glowing ball of energy when something much, much brighter flashed through the room, and suddenly Alois could see nothing at all. For a time indeterminate, he stood hypnotized, his eyes scorched by a blaze of absolute luminescence.

Slowly, the whiteness peeled away, the room coming back into focus. Alois saw that everyone had stumbled to a halt—even the Dean had apparently discharged his spell into the floor in surprise. A large orb of the shining white light still prevailed for a time, floating just above their heads in the center of the room, but slowly that too faded, revealing the form of a man.

He was on the younger side of middle age, with short blonde hair and bright blue eyes. His skin was pale but had a certain ruddy flush to it, and he seemed to wear only a flowing black robe, his bare feet hanging from under it as he floated in the air over them. A triumphant smile was present on his lips. Without the passing of another second, he pointed a finger at Lina, and from the finger emerged a flowing rush of sickly yellow energy. Alois tried to pull her away, tried to put himself in front of it, but he had no time to do either. The jolt hit her instantaneously, her face contorting into a shocked, confused expression as it did. She didn't fall the ground, nor burst into flames, nor any of the other terrible things Alois' grim imagination immediately predicted. Instead, she stood stock still, her face frozen in the same expression, her arms, half thrown up to shield herself, now as unmoving as those of a statue.

He reached out and touched her cheek. It felt warm, and wholly normal. "Lina?" he said at a bare whisper, hoping for any response. None came. He was distantly aware of the robed man landing softly behind her, and he managed to look over her shoulder into his blue eyes, which stared right back at him.

"Alois. You don't mind if I borrow her, do you?" The man asked grimly, setting a hand on Lina's shoulder.

Alois growled with rage, side-stepping to try and get around Lina's body so that he could face the man. The man grinned and stepped around, keeping Lina between them. As he gave chase, Alois saw that the Dean had raised his arms up and was now pointing them at the blonde man's back, murmuring under his breath. The blonde man smiled and turned, and with a wave of his hand the Dean was thrown back and smashed into the stone wall as though he'd received an uppercut from a giant.

Now the Guards were coming on, clearly confused, going in for non-lethal attacks to try and restrain the stranger, and he was laughing uproariously like he'd just heard a splendid joke. One Guard was splashed by at least a quart of some sort of liquid, conjured by the blonde man from nothing, and as the Magisterial stumbled away he covered his face in his gloves, screaming like an infant. The other Guards probably would have backed away, but they had no time to do so as the man laughed cruelly and wove flames around them, seeming to take particular pleasure in it. The Wizard on the crutch had backed up against the wall, and he seemed to be shouting words of Arcanic and gesturing quite fervently, yet with no apparent effect.

Alois fleetingly wished that he had his saber, as he'd never been one for boxing. Nevertheless, as he stepped around Lina once more he threw out his fist, using his undead strength to its fullest. The blonde man smiled and held up a palm, speaking a single word as he did. His palm caught the fist, and Alois felt all the bones in his hand shatter like he had tried to punch through steel, jagged bone fragments rending his flesh. A slop of thick blood splattering to the floor as Alois stumbled back, drawing his ruined fist away, staring at it, mesmerized.

He was steeling himself to try again, but the blonde man shook his head, as though reprimanding a child, and instead, Alois asked him a question.

"Who are you?"

The man's lips contorted into an ugly, joyless smile. "Better looking with the skin on, don't you think? Don't worry, Alois. I'm not bitter. I won't kill you."

His smooth, pale hand, still coated in Alois' blood, clamped down on Lina's shoulder. Then, with no flash, no grand spectacle, not even a word, the pair of them disappeared.

Krupp was ashamed that when the man appeared in the room, he could only stare dumbly, waiting for his brain to process this new information. Far stranger, though, than his own failure to act, was that the Magistrate, too, merely stared dumbfoundedly, as though he had completely lost control over the situation. He'd become that way the moment that things had escalated to violence. Krupp had shouted to Radcliff to restrain the Dean, but the young Wizard had only stared with a hollow look in his eyes, making no sign of having heard. They had all, Krupp thought abysmally, failed entirely at their jobs. And that was before the stranger had even arrived, after which the situation had only deteriorated further.

He wouldn't have thought that he'd have the nerve to tackle the Magistrate, but it had certainly happened quickly enough, and immediately thereafter Krupp had begun to work to get the stone altar between them and the rest of the room's occupants. He'd vaguely expected that the Magistrate would struggle, but instead the man went along with him quite placidly, brow furrowed in what appeared to be confusion.

Once they were behind the altar, Krupp had risked a glance toward the stranger, and immediately pulled his head back as fire began to fly. He cursed under his breath, disgusted by his powerlessness. Plenty of people couldn't use magic, but at least the Guards had their combat training to try and resolve the situation. Krupp couldn't contribute anything, unless one of the combatants needed his jacket taken to the tailor's.

Another glimpse around the altar, and he'd seen the writhing form of what was left of one of the Magisterials. At that point, he quickly reappraised his envy. All in all, he considered, it was shaping out to be an incredibly bad day. At the moment, he wasn't sure which he hated more: magic, or religion.

There was a sudden silence, and Krupp took another glance. The stranger was gone. The Dean was picking himself up from the other side of the room, looking quite worse for the wear. Two Magisterials lay still, unmoving. A third lie moaning piteously on the floor. Krupp could only differentiate Brenz, the captain, who seemed to be checking the pulse of one of the still bodies.

Alois Gustav was standing still in the middle of the room, staring at the place where the stranger had been when Krupp last saw him. The necromancer was nowhere in sight. Radcliff had sat down against the wall and seemed to be talking to himself softly.

The danger, Krupp realized, had passed. Which meant things were back into his domain, finally. He stood. "All right, everyone. I need status. Brenz, what's the situation?"

Brenz was shaking his head. His voice was ragged. "These two are dead. Peurtil is badly hurt. Chairman

Ludwig is unconscious, but unharmed. I think he got knocked down and banged his head on the stones."

Krupp nodded. "All right. You should go wake someone and have them run for a doctor."

"No," the Dean said, back on his feet now, walking slowly over to Brenz, one hand holding his chest. "Too slow, and he's too badly injured."

Reaching Peurtil, the Dean carefully bent down, wincing as he did. Krupp winced himself as the Dean reached out and put his hand onto the ruined, melted mess that had once been Peurtil's face. Speaking words beyond Krupp's comprehension, a faint light began to glow from the Dean's fingers, and Krupp and Brenz watched while the man's face slowly began to mend.

"Wait," Krupp said, realization dawning. "What do you think you're doing? Stop that at once!"

"Krupp," Brenz said softly, "shut up, or I'll kill you."

Krupp recoiled. Losing control of things during the combat was one thing, but now... what was his excuse now? The Magistrate was going to be furious...

...the Magistrate?

Shocked by his absent-mindedness, Krupp looked down, and saw Schiller, sitting calmly with his back against the altar, long legs folded up in front of him. Krupp crouched back down.

"Magistrate?"

"Yes, Albert?"

"Are you all right? The danger is past."

"Is it?"

"Yes, sir. Come on, we need you."

"I... I need some time to think. You can take charge in my stead, Albert."

"I don't think they'll listen to me, sir," Krupp said, as quietly as he could.

The Magistrate did not respond, and Krupp, feeling as alone as he could ever remember feeling, got back to his feet and rounded the altar, heading over to the main group. Brenz was sitting on the floor, clasping Peurtil's hand. Peurtil looked dazed, but all signs of his injury were gone, save that he was now as bald-headed as a monk. As Krupp approached, Brenz looked up at him, and the man's gloved hand moved unmistakably to the hilt of his sword.

"Look at this, Krupp," Brenz said, enunciating slowly. "You thought you saw Peurtil here get badly wounded, but you must have been wrong, because now he seems fine. You must have gotten mixed-up during all that confusion. See?"

Krupp stared down, frowning, aware of his short stature, aware of how little these men respected him and his job. The best he could do was nod, avert his gaze, and walk over to the Dean, who was now talking to Alois Gustav. Gustav hadn't moved since the stranger had disappeared.

"He knew you," the Dean was saying. "Do you know him?"

"I think..." Alois said, slowly, "I think... but, no. I don't see how it's possible."

"You just tell it, then, and I'll let you know whether it's possible."

"I think he was a skeleton that we found, a week or so ago, when Lina was summoning undead. He looked ancient, but he was intelligent, and he'd speak to us. He was mean-spirited, but seemed harmless enough. I thought he was dead—for real, I mean. One of the Magistrate's Guards destroyed him, and the skull crumpled apart, and I thought he was dead."

The Dean frowned, his eyebrows creasing into a look of deep concern.

"What is it?" Alois asked. "Do you know him too?"

"No... and yet... his face... I could swear I remember his face..."

"An old student, maybe," Radcliff chimed in dully from his seat against the wall.

"Maybe..." the Dean said, staring at the scorches on the floor as if trying to look past them.

"I have to find her," Gustav said. "It's my responsibility. But I have no idea where they could have gone."

"We can try to find them," The Dean responded. "In the meantime, let me see about your hand."

"She would have been able to fix it," Alois said dully, raising his ruined right hand, "if she were here. She told me once that Curation wouldn't work on me. Not anymore."

"No," the Dean said, "not anymore." Nonetheless, he closed his hand over the Chief Constable's, and began casting a spell. As Krupp watched, the bones began to heal and realign themselves, and pale flesh began to grow over the many small wounds. It only took Krupp a moment to understand.

"No!" he shouted, loud enough that even Radcliff looked up. "No! This is too much! I won't allow law and order to collapse like this! You can't just... you can't just begin breaking the law! There is still the law to be considered! You have much to answer for, even having the *ability* to cast spells like that!"

The Dean, who had looked up for the first few moments of Krupp's explosion, had now turned back to his work. Brenz and his companion were also ignoring him, and Gustav merely frowned, looking at Krupp with something that appeared to be, of all things, pity.

It would have been much better, Krupp realized, if they'd gotten angry, shouted him down. It would have been much better if they'd at least respected him enough to refuse him.

He finally walked over to Radcliff, who looked up at his approach. Krupp slid down next to him.

"Don't take it too hard," Radcliff said, his expression even, his face blank. "It could be worse. You could be... that." He waved in the direction of the Magistrate.

Krupp sighed. "Behold the power of my atheism. Granting me, in times of crisis, enough clear-headedness to try to take control of the situation and be universally ignored."

"Much of Delarian law has been obsolete from the moment it was created. But it seemed easier to put up with it than to try to do anything about it. But now... why keep up appearances? There are no priests here, and if there were... what would it matter? It all seems pointless now."

"Who *was* that man?"

"I don't know. But he was the most powerful Wizard that I have ever seen."

"How is that possible? He couldn't have been much older than you are."

Radcliff finally changed his expression, and surprisingly, the new one took the form of a smile. "I don't mean to disenchant you, Krupp, but I'm actually a considerably below-average Wizard, when it comes down to it."

For a moment, they sat there in silence.

"Get it? Disenchant? That was a joke."

"I got it. I was just doing you the favor of pretending I didn't notice."

Radcliff smiled again, watching as Gustav tried out his repaired hand, still deep in conversation with the Dean. "My enchantments didn't work on the other Wizard at all. I knew better than to try big ones. I did little easy ones.

Ones that should always work. They failed so completely that I don't think he even noticed them."

"And the Dean went on a blind date with the wall and is now walking doubled over. Don't expect so much of yourself."

"You, either."

Krupp got back up, offering his hand. "Come on. Let's go try to wake up Ludwig, and see if we can't get the Dean to tell us what the hell we're supposed to do now."

Chapter 29

He was called the Judge. Or, rather, he *would* be. The name hadn't caught on just yet, but Orlando—that was his real name—was a patient man. He understood that the Judge was a good name, and he knew that appearances were just as important as anything else. It had taken Orlando a few days to finally settle on the name, but he'd given the final order to his underlings a few days prior; from now on, in every interaction, he was to be referred to as "the Judge".

No expense was spared in playing the part. He'd had the old Judge's chambers in Langham Courthouse completely stripped and renovated, and now the place was oak-paneled and beautiful. The massive Merundian seal on the wall had been polished, as though to emphasize ironically all the crime that was going on right in front of it. Orlando thought it was brilliant. The morons who'd held the courthouse before him had used it as little more than a dingy, run-down hideout and goods storage facility. A total squandering of what was not merely a big, sturdy building, but a symbol. A symbol of power, and of former glory. By *holding court* in Langham instead of merely dwelling there, Orlando made himself into an enigmatic figure, one who seemed to represent a forgotten ideal of some sort of justice and refinement from out of Merund's past.

It was not difficult for Orlando to imagine others ascribing these qualities to him, as he certainly saw them in himself. He was a higher class of criminal, and even that word, 'criminal,' did not fit properly. All he was, really, was a businessman with an especially strong dedication to getting what he deserved. He fingered the length of lead pipe that he'd laid out on his desk. He'd beaten in his fair share of skulls with it over the past few years—it didn't quite fit his new image, but he was working on it. Maybe it could be his gavel.

He'd spent so much time on getting his image set up, he hadn't had much chance to actually start turning a profit. Seizing the building out of the hands of the Fifth Street Brigands had been quite costly to his organization, and his second-in-command was down at the hospital. Several others had been killed. He was short-handed, and as a result, Langham Courthouse, which he'd worked so hard to get in the first place, wasn't even very well guarded.

There was a knock on the chamber door. Orlando shook his head, shaking the specter of the future from his mind. All that he had envisioned would come to pass. For now, one step at a time. He reminded himself briefly to reprimand whichever henchman was at the door if they didn't refer to him as "the Judge".

He arranged the black gown he'd had made and taken to wearing over his ordinary clothes. "Come in," he said, trying out deepening his voice.

The doors swung open quickly, and the man who stepped in was not one of his henchmen. This man wore black robes not dissimilar from Orlando's gown, and had short blonde hair. His skin was pale, his eyes bright, and his mouth pulled up into a cold smile. The doors had opened wide, and Orlando could clearly see one of his men lying in the hallway nearby. The body wasn't moving.

"So," the blonde man said, leaning against the door frame. "You must be this Judge everybody's talking about."

Lina opened her eyes. The first thing she tried to do was scream, but no sound came out. She tried to move her arms, and found them unyielding. Aware of the lack of a hard surface under her, she quickly understood that her body was floating in the air, suspended vertically, arms hanging limply at her sides.

She was in a beautifully adorned room, wood-paneled and littered with ornate and extremely expensive-looking decorations, including four portraits bearing the likenesses of grim-faced men in black gowns. No doubt there was more to see, but she was facing away from the interior of the room, a large window about ten feet from her face.

She looked down, and saw that she was floating directly over a large mahogany desk. Sitting at the desk, leaning back with his now booted feet on the table, was the blonde man. He was staring directly up at her, smiling. She tried to kick him, but still couldn't move. She felt her cheeks flush as she realized that he could probably see straight up her robes and dress.

"Lina. Good morning."

"Who the hell are you?" she tried to growl, but again, no sounds emerged from her mouth. Indeed, she could not even mouth the words— her lips were as good as pasted shut.

"I've had my fill of fun with mysterious origins for the day, so let's cut to the chase. My name is Rodolphus. We met not long ago, only I used not to have most of the stunning body you're seeing now."

If her mouth could have moved, she would have gasped. She believed immediately what he said. In large part, it was his mode of speech, his caustic wit, his jeering tone. But more than that, it was the eyes. She'd seen those eyes before.

He gestured lazily with one hand.

"You won't be able to respond, of course. I'm no fool. When I nabbed you back at the University, I hit you with a total stasis lock effect, which is safest. But you couldn't hear me talk in that state, and I really find it therapeutic to have someone to talk to, so now I'm using some different spells instead. Don't worry—I've spent a lot of time alone recently, so I'm perfectly used to one-sided conversations. Allowing for you to speak safely would have been far too much trouble, of course. You'll find that you can't speak, nor gesture. In short, there will be no spell-casting for you, young lady. None at all."

She had already found that what he said was true. It appeared that her eyes were the only part of her body she had any control over. Deciding to focus on a single task, she tried with every ounce of strength in her body to move her right hand. She failed utterly, leaving her exhausted and frustrated. He kept smiling up at her, as though he could read her thoughts.

"You probably know this, but you're an amazingly powerful necromancer. Amazingly. Far more powerful than me, and I thought I was at least the best on the continent. When I first met you, I was sure that you'd taken control of my body intentionally. I thought that you and silly old Alois were playing with me, having a nice trick on the powerless lich. It took a pretty long time for me to finally accept that you'd actually done it completely by accident, and that in general you had no idea what you were doing. Don't get me wrong, in someone as powerful as you, intelligence and strategy aren't all that important."

Lina wondered achingly where Alois might be, and further, where she was. Was she still in Merund? When she strained her eyes to the right, she could catch a symbol on the wall that seemed to bear the name of the city. She was, then, still near to Alois. She could be found; she could be saved.

She forced herself to count out the seconds and calm down. Her situation was not so bleak; she merely needed to get herself together. After all, she could control undead with thoughts alone—it would work so long as she'd exerted control over them in the past with a verbal spell. Now she focused her thoughts on Rodolphus, commanding him to release her.

"It had never occurred to me," he was saying, "that I could have been beaten by someone like you." He laughed softly. "A victim of my own hubris. I thought I'd eliminated the sin of pride from myself, but let's face it: it's a pretty deep well."

She put more force behind the command, willing him with everything she had to just let her move her damn arms and mouth.

"I admit that I had grown lazy, passive. Misused my immortality. I mean, good gods, I've spent the vast majority of it with my nose in dusty old grimoires, barely leaving the cottage. Lord, do you realize I'm something like ten times your age? It will all be different, now. My magic can rival that of anyone alive, and the added bonus of being totally unkillable means that the only thing standing between me and ultimate authority is a bit of good old sleeves rolled-up hard work.

"I have so many questions to ask of you... but I will never be able to let you speak. Maybe we can arrange a system where you can write me messages. But, no... a hand that can write is hand that can gesture, and that'd be a risk. I am not taking risks, Lina, not with someone like you. I know the score, now. If I hadn't gotten the drop on you earlier, I'd be putty in your hands, just as before. No, I'll give you no chances. I'm afraid the source of your powers will just have to remain a mystery to me. I think I can live with that, so long as it remains a mystery to everyone else too, you know?"

Her heart pounded with the exertion of her efforts. Finally, she released a breath of air from her nose and gave up. It simply wasn't working. She was powerless. It occurred to her now, for the first time, that she was truly afraid of him.

"Once I finally realized that you had actually subjugated me *entirely by accident*, all I had to do was start practicing in order to cast spells without gestures. Have you ever tried it?"

He glanced at her briefly, as though he expected an answer.

"Most haven't," he continued thoughtfully. "It's difficult, and not really all that useful, considering that normally a skilled Wizard can make his... or her..." he smiled ironically, "gestures very discreet. Even that ability wouldn't benefit you in your current situation, since you can't speak, either. However, I had little else to do with my time, so I practiced, and meditated, and managed to learn how to cast half a dozen spells through verbal commands only. I only ended up using a couple of them when I decided to make my daring escape, of course. It was hard picking which spells to learn. Which ones would you have chosen, I wonder? Can you even cast anything besides necromantic spells? I don't believe I've seen you do so. I don't really care, either. I'm much more interested in the extent of your necromantic power, but as we've discussed, you won't be able to tell me."

Rodolphus paused briefly, as though gathering his thoughts, peering up at her pensively.

"I've thought of a test of your power," he said finally, "and I can't see any harm in carrying it out. Shall we proceed?" He looked at her mockingly, as though waiting for an answer. There was such cruelty in his look that she tried to recoil away from it, but of course she was unable to do so.

"As the lady wishes. I'll be back in but a moment."

With a gesture so quick as to be almost undetectable, Rodolphus disappeared. The chair he'd been leaning back in collapsed to the ground, empty.

She wondered if his absence would lessen the power of the spells he'd put on her. She tried again to move, to speak, to shout. She tried until tears of exertion were rolling down her cheeks. It wasn't a matter of principal anymore. She knew now that she had to get out, before he could get bored. Before he could get bored, and try to find new ways to entertain himself with her.

Far sooner than she had hoped, there was a brief popping sound, and Rodolphus was back; she could sense him standing behind her, but could not see him, her view of the room limited by the orientation of her body. She felt his hand wrap around her thigh from behind, pressing tightly through her robes and bruising her flesh. He hauled her around roughly, and now she was facing the other way, into the room, still hovering over the desk. When she saw that Rodolphus was not alone, she knew immediately where he had gone.

Sebastian the skeleton stood at Rodolphus' flank, head craning around curiously as he took in the room. Rodolphus grinned up at her and patted the skeleton on the shoulder.

"Look who I found. It's our friend, Sebastian. Don't worry, it looked like he'd found plenty of things in the basement to occupy his time while we were gone. And now he gets to take part in our test. Goodness, what a big day for him! For all of us."

The cold sweat of terror coated her back, and she did not take her eyes off of Rodolphus, who stepped abruptly toward her. He reached up and grabbed her by the hips, pulling her out of the air and flinging her hard onto the desk. The wind rushed out of her, and she lay struggling for breath, unable to open her mouth, feeling the drowning pressure building in her lungs. She wondered if she might die right then, but Rodolphus' hand gripped her chin and his fingers pushed her mouth open, and she was able to sputter for air.

"So dramatic, young girls. I'd like to say that it passes when you get older, but it doesn't. Settle down. And don't bother trying to communicate with the skeleton telepathically, either; it's not as though I didn't think of that. I've completely barred you from any sort of telepathy, and that effect will last for a long, long time." He shut her mouth and roughly turned her head so that she was facing into the room again, giving her a clear view of both him and Sebastian.

"Now," he said, backing away slowly, "let's begin. Sebastian."

The skeleton turned its head toward him curiously. It had been looking with some concern at Lina, but was clearly confused by the total lack of signals from her.

Rodolphus began chanting softly, moving his hands intricately in patterns that Lina recognized very well. He was instilling himself with a necromantic aura, giving himself the power of control over the undead. He was a quick, efficient caster, and within moments the spell was finished.

"Sebastian," he repeated, "there is a length of lead pipe on the table next to Lina. Pick it up."

Sebastian stared at Rodolphus for a long second, then turned at Lina and looked down into her eyes. She tried to shake her head, tried to do anything, but couldn't. Sebastian's glance shot down to the pipe lying on the desk in front of her, which she hadn't noticed before.

Sebastian carefully walked to the table and picked up the pipe by its end, hefting it easily in his one hand.

"Very good. Now, wield it like a club."

The skeleton adjusted his grip slightly.

"That's excellent. Hit her in the stomach."

Sebastian paused, staring down at her. She stared back up, more tears welling up in her eyes. She tried to signal him with eye movements but knew that it couldn't look like anything even remotely coherent. He stood over her, unmoving, for a long time.

Eventually, he turned to Rodolphus, and shook his head.

Rodolphus frowned. "See, this is really something. Your Necromancy, Lina, is not merely powerful. It has *staying power.* I've got you completely cloaked in fields that are blocking any magical effect you could be emitting, in addition to any sort of telepathic signals. Yet still, not only does his loyalty to you linger, it lingers even in the face of a command from another powerful necromancer."

Rodolphus shook his head and whistled, placing a hand heavily on Sebastian's shoulder. "Girl, I take my hat off to you. Sebastian, thank you for your time."

His mouth formed words that she recognized, and she immediately knew what was happening, but had no way of stopping it. The necromantic power that gave unlife to Sebastian was drained out of him with the force of a lead ball leaving the front of a cannon. His bones seemed to shatter simultaneously, as though he were a glass statue and an incredibly high note had just been wrung out. The bone shards rained to the floor with the sound of a very brief hail; within seconds it was over.

Rodolphus brushed his hand off against his robes, and smiled.

Chapter 30

Ludwig had spread the contents of the necromancer's bag on the floor and was now selecting certain items, though to Radcliff the motivation behind each choice was unclear. He'd never done well with Divination; it was a fickle art, and it wasn't uncommon for even powerful Wizards to skip over it entirely.

The Dean and Chief Constable Gustav had returned from Gustav's home moments ago with the bag in tow; Ludwig had sent them there to retrieve it.

"No operation was mounted on the girl's house," Krupp was saying. "If the skeleton's missing, it wasn't taken with the Magistrate's knowledge."

The Magistrate had left with Brenz and the other Guardsman sometime ago; they'd promised to take Schiller to his office so he could get some rest. No one knew whether it would do any good. At first the Dean had suggested rather unsubtly that Krupp should be the one to take the Magistrate off, but the man had steadfastly refused to leave, insisting that someone had to represent the government in such an important affair. In the end, the Dean had yielded.

"That leaves only one likely perpetrator," the Dean said grimly.

"What the devil would he want Sebastian for, though?" Gustav asked, frowning deeply under his mustache. All eyes in the room quickly turned to him.

"Well," he said, averting his gaze, "what do you want from me? I didn't name the blasted thing."

"These are good," Ludwig said, carefully unwinding a strand of hair from a beat-up wooden comb. "They will help. Her name was Lina, correct?"

"*Is*," Alois said testily. "Her name *is* Lina."

Ludwig either ignored the emphasis or didn't notice it, as he failed even to look up from what he was doing. "And what about her last name? It might be helpful. Anything you can tell me."

"I'm afraid I don't know her last name," Alois said uncomfortably, wringing his hands.

"Her birthdate?"

"Not that either, I'm afraid."

"How the hell do you know each other, then?" Krupp asked.

"She... well, I was hurt, and she..."

"Turned you undead," Radcliff heard himself saying. "Please, let's all just be honest about this now."

The Dean raised a bushy black eyebrow. "Do you think so, young man? I agree."

"Yes, well," Alois said, eyes lowered in discomfort, "yes, she turned me into a, erm... she says I'm a ghoul, now, and after that I did not know what was happening. I ran into her, and then I rather had to stick with her because, well, I mean..."

"She'd be far more adept in handling your situation than you," Radcliff finished for him. "Was she providing your food supply?"

"Yes," Alois said.

"There's probably some in with her things, do you want me to check?"

"No. No, thank you, I'm really not hungry."

"What does he eat?" Krupp asked, glancing up from a pad of paper. He seemed to be scribbling down notes. There was a brief silence.

"He's on a special diet," the Dean answered eventually. "And put that thing away. Any investigation save for the search and rescue of this Miss Lina is hereby permanently cancelled."

"You hardly have the authority to—"

"You know, Krupp, there's an old saying at the University. 'Power lies with those who can turn others into non-sentient organisms'."

Krupp glanced at Radcliff, who shrugged. "I haven't heard it before, but it has got a nice ring to it…"

Krupp slowly put the notepad into an inside pocket. "As you like, then."

"Ludwig, what sort of time estimate would you put on finding the girl?"

"I'll need a few hours. It's hard to say."

"Fine. As quickly as you can, please."

"I didn't know Divination could be used to find things," Alois said. He had finally taken a seat against the wall, but the constant tapping of his foot suggested his anxiety. "I thought it was only for predicting the future."

"Precisely the opposite," Ludwig said darkly before anyone else could respond. "It's quite bad at predicting the future, actually, unless you fully understand what you're looking at. It's much better at analyzing the present. It can do the past too, but that's more difficult."

The Dean nodded. "I should not have let it go this far. I was a fool to take it for granted that Divination was as the Church said. I was so involved with my own studies…. for God's sake, a five minute conversation with Ludwig would have taught me that the Church was wrong. I…"

The Dean hesitated, smoothing back his hair before continuing. "There is no excuse for how mixed my priorities have been of late."

"The balance of power between the University and the Church is extremely delicate," Krupp said, "and maintaining that balance is the key to maintaining peace in our society. It was right not to concern yourself with the affairs of the Church; doing so could have thrown the entire city into chaos."

"Well, chaos is what we'll have, soon enough," Radcliff said. "The Magistrate knows everything now, and so do all of us."

"We could keep quiet," Krupp suggested, but softly and without enthusiasm. "Things don't have to change."

"Yes," the Dean said. "Yes, they do. And all of us here shall see that they are changed, starting by revealing the fraud being perpetrated against the people of Merund by the Church. At the moment, however, I think that dealing with our mysterious assailant is the bigger concern."

All present nodded in grave agreement, save Ludwig, who was bent down on his hands and knees, wielding a small brush with which he had begun to paint a circle of runes on the stone floor near the altar.

"Who is he?" Radcliff asked, watching Ludwig work.

"I don't know," the Dean said, stroking a hand through his beard. "But suffice it to say that he is a conscious form of undead, and few who go down that path are friends to humanity. Erm, present company excluded. Whatever the case, my curiosity is roused. I have quite a few questions for both of our Necromancy prodigies. Until I have some more information, though, I think I've small choice but to side with the little girl over the man with a penchant for wanton death."

Rodolphus smiled up at her, having seen her returned to her position hanging over the desk. He felt fantastic. It was good to be in action, out in the world. It was good to be in his body, still fresh and, if not healthy, as close to healthy as the thing could get these days.

She couldn't move, but he could see the terror in her eyes. He wondered how that was possible—what, precisely, indicated her fear? He could spend all day

staring up at her, trying to figure it out. But he wouldn't—
he had to leave such spurious intellectual pursuits behind
him, for the time being. He had business to conduct.

"I came here intent on finding Wolfram," he said, both
to her and to himself, pacing over to the bookshelf as he
spoke. "But I forgot about that pretty quickly after I met
you. It's hard to worry about him at this point, even
though I know I should. He *must* be dead by now—
Enchantment can only prolong a life so far, after all—and
besides, even if he tried to stop my resurrection, he'd still
have to take me in a fight first—something I doubt he
could have handled to begin with, but now... after what I
have planned, there will be no contest at all."

He grabbed a book at random and pulled it out of its
place, impressed immediately by its heft. Spinning it over,
his face split into a grin. It was fake—a wooden block
with a book spine painted on.

He hurled it at the Seal of the City of Merund on the
wall, which it badly chipped before tumbling noisily to
the floor. "God," he said, spreading his arms. "Fake
books, criminals in the court house... if this room gets any
more allegorical, we're going to start drowning in
metaphors."

He sat on the desk, resting his head against one of her
legs as he stroked the lacquered wood thoughtfully. "I'm
going to explain what I do to you as I do it, so you'll
understand. But first, a few other things to be seen to... I
need to be ready, if your friends come for you. Old man
Alois can't find us, I think you and I can agree there.
There were a few Wizards in that room, though. At least
two, right? And one of them—one of them was a
powerhouse. Who was he, and what is his involvement?
Are we expecting him to come after you? If so, when?"

He glanced at the window. "The sun has come up."

He swung back down to his feet and glanced around for a clock before remembering that the room did not have one. Sighing, he gestured at the body of "the Judge", levitating the limp thing across the carpet toward him and into arm's reach, its limbs flopping against the ground as it went. He grabbed the man by the collar and lifted him enough to root through his vest pockets.

"Ah, here we are." He recovered an ornate golden pocket watch and flipped it open. "Just about five-thirty. I guess I shouldn't delay any longer. Daylight's wasting. It's time to get started."

He raised his hands to the girl and rapidly spoke the incantations for several new enchantments, all of them serving to further bind her in place. Time passed strangely for him while he was intoning, but he knew that with the number and power of the spells he was using, he spent at least half an hour standing in front of her, incanting in a trance.

Finally satisfied, he just gazed up at her in quiet awe. He met her eyes, dark, like her hair and skin. Her small hands and feet hung limply out from her robe, infinitely delicate; he could crush each with his bare hands, given the motivation.

He began a new incantation.

The Dean glanced toward the tower door as it swung open; Brenz strode in, his sword drawn and in hand.

"The Magistrate?" The Dean asked.

"Resting in his office. Are we ready?"

The Dean looked to Ludwig, who had slipped into a trance inside the circle he'd drawn on the floor.

"Yes, I think we're just about ready." He did a quick headcount, his gaze lingering on the young Wizard with the thin beard.

"Are you coming along? Can you help?"

"I... I don't know. My enchantments had no effect on him."

"Hmm. Either he's so powerful that he has made himself immune, or the standard enchantments simply won't work on a sentient undead mind."

"Which is it?" Krupp asked.

"I don't know. I know which one I hope it is."

"My enchantments worked on Mr. Gustav," Radcliff said, hollowly.

No one spoke, for a moment.

"I'd like to come anyway," Radcliff said, breaking the silence. "I'm sure I'll be able to help somehow."

"All right. I didn't catch your name."

"Falkenhayn. Radcliff Falkenhayn."

"Good. Krupp and Gustav, you'll stay here?"

Gustav shook his head resolutely. "No, I'll be coming with you."

"Come on, man, you're hardly at the top of your game."

"You're at least twenty years older than me, and I don't see you lingering behind."

"I'm a Wizard."

"I'm a ghoul."

"Hrmm. As you like, as you like. Krupp..."

"I think you're right," Krupp said. "I can't contribute anything to this. I'll go check on the Magistrate."

"That will be helpful, thank you. Magisterial Brenz, I hope you'll come?"

"I would not miss it."

"All right. Ah, Ludwig, you're back among us. What's the word?"

The small man removed his spectacles and rubbed a hand over his eyes, as though trying to clear them. "They're in a judge's chambers in Langham Courthouse."

"What a strange choice..."

"Not a bad hideout, if he wanted privacy," Gustav said grimly. "A civilized man wouldn't set foot in that building."

"Hrmm," the Dean murmured, "I've never been there... I'll have to teleport us to the street outside."

"I've seen the chambers, now," Ludwig said softly. "I can take us there."

"You can teleport? I didn't know that."

"What you do not know about your faculty, Dean Baldermann, could fill this building."

The Dean felt his temper flare. Who was this little man to reprimand him? Why should he have bothered to learn the capabilities of his staff? Or, he thought, glancing to Radcliff, their names...

Ludwig, perhaps, had a point. Whatever the case, now was not the time to consider it. The little diviner had already proved far more useful than Baldermann ever would have expected.

"All right, Ludwig will take us. Is the Wizard in the room with her?"

"No, she seems to be alone. She's suspended in the air... some type of binding spell."

"The three of us combined should be able to break that swiftly enough. I wonder where the devil that bastard has gone off to..."

"I'm not sorry," Radcliff said. "I'd love not to have to fight him."

"He won't let us just stride in and take her," Gustav said grimly.

"No, I'd imagine he won't," the Dean agreed. "I just wish I could recall why I recognize him... so familiar, and yet I could swear we have not met before."

"Maybe afterward," Brenz said grimly, "Ludwig will be able to divine that information out of his severed head."

The Dean allowed himself a grin. "Then what are we waiting for? Let's go expand our knowledge."

Teleportation could be disorienting to the caster, but it was even worse for passengers; the act itself involved careful meditation upon the desired location; passengers did not have the ability to see the destination in their mind, and instead simply found themselves suddenly stumbling into a completely new environment. It was advisable to make the transition with one's eyes closed, and indeed, Radcliff did so.

He opened them anew to the wood-paneled judge's chambers. Brenz and Gustav still seemed dazzled as their vision adjusted to the sudden change in lighting, though Ludwig appeared to have recovered. The Dean had already approached the desk, over which floated the form of the necromancer. She was suspended vertically in the air as though she'd been hung up on an unseen meat hook.

A complex system of runes had been scrawled on the desk beneath the girl; Radcliff did not recognize the spell. Further, more symbols had been drawn on her cheeks and forehead in some sort of blue paint. The sleeves of her robes had been torn away, and the blue patterns, crude and drawn by hand, wrapped up her arms as well.

The room was somewhat close with so many people in it. The door was shut, and there was no sign of their adversary.

"What are these runes and markings?" Radcliff asked. "I have not seen the like of them before."

"I have," the Dean growled. "Troubling… but we will deal with it later. Let us free the girl. It is no simple enchantment that binds her. This will not be easy."

Radcliff and Ludwig approached the Dean on either side, and all three turned their attention to the web of enchantments holding the girl in place. The moment Radcliff's mind fell into the right mode to process the pattern, he took a step back, overwhelmed by the complexity of the incantations holding her.

"This guy is really something," he breathed.

"Yes. She may as well be cemented up there. We'll begin with the Beliforian reverse-enchantment. I will do the main part, you two the supporting."

"Yes, Dean," Ludwig and Radcliff echoed.

Gustav, having rounded the desk, reached up to give the girl a reassuring pat on the side, grim concern written all over his face. For someone who couldn't move, the girl, her eyes wide open, certainly looked alive and distressed enough.

They began the enchantment, conscious thought fading away as all three of them allowed their full attention to be wrapped up in the gestures and words of their counter-spell. It was not easy going. They were using one of the most powerful spells available to them—the Beliforian reversal required at least two people to cast, and it was designed to strip away magical change and return something to its natural state. It was only because of the Dean's considerable power that they could cast the reversal at all.

The further into their spell they got, the more clearly Radcliff could see the effects containing the girl, imposed over her like glowing webs of light. Their efforts quickly stripped away several enchantments. All of these, however, appeared to have been redundancies, as the girl remained bound.

Sweat beaded on Radcliff's forehead as he continued chanting, and soon he could no longer see the girl or her surroundings; foremost in his vision shone the patterned intricacies of the spells holding her, floating against a black void. He was distantly aware of the Dean's voice increasing in timbre, and of his own following suit. Suddenly, another entangling enchantment was shattered, and only one remained, a bright golden mesh holding her arms and legs firmly in place. Radcliff had never seen this spell before, but it was extremely troubling that it had resisted for as long as it had; he feared that it might be beyond their powers to dismiss.

Time could not be easily measured in the trance, though with such powerful spells involved it may have been that only a few minutes had passed. His focus was slowly beginning to fail; he could feel his arms again, still making the complicated patterns required of him, but now he had to concentrate to keep them from shaking with fatigue. The room began to come back into focus around him.

The Dean's voice heightened again, and Radcliff threw himself into one last push against the unassailable force holding the girl. On the brink of collapsing, he gasped in elation as the force of their commands shattered the web. The necromancer's body went limp and plummeted to the desk; Gustav, waiting patiently the whole time, caught it with ease.

The Wizards rushed forward to him as he laid the girl carefully down on the desk, brushing her hair out of her eyes.

"Lina? Lina, are you all right?"

Slowly, her eyes opened. She shuddered slightly as she opened her mouth and attempted to speak, her cheeks wet with the tears.

"In the room," she moaned. "He's in the room."

Alois frowned, trying to understand what she meant. The awful scream from near the doorway drew his gaze back up, and then everything became overwhelmingly clear. All of them watched as Brenz, squirming as if held in place by some unopposable force, had his throat slit wide open by a pure-black dagger that seemed to float of its own accord.

Perhaps it was his ghoul reflexes, but Alois acted before any of the others. He had pushed past the Wizards, toward Brenz, the moment the blade cut flesh; he was there in seconds, but by then the front of the man's tabard was stained scarlet with blood, and Alois could only catch the body as it crumpled forward. Glad for his strength, he placed the body down and rushed past it, arms extended. The dagger had disappeared from sight. The Wizard was clearly invisible, but if Alois could just get a hold of him...

"Heel," a voice ahead of him said, almost jolly.

Alois felt his body reel to a shuttered halt.

"Good. Down, boy."

Alois' legs buckled, and he collapsed in a heap on the ground next to Brenz's lifeless body. He tried to get back up, but found his limbs unable to take commands. He roared in frustration.

"Shhh. Hush, hush. When this is over, we'll get you a nice biscuit."

Abruptly, Alois felt an intense, searing pain in his back. He was initially bewildered that the Wizard could have gotten behind him—then he realized that the knife was being controlled telekinetically.

"I know, I know, a simple stabbing won't kill you. But I figure—"

The voice was interrupted by an enormous torrent of mud that splashed over Alois' head. The mud splattered against the wall and door, but a clean, man-shaped silhouette remained. Before the clean section stood a muddy figure, not unlike a clay statue in appearance.

"There," the Dean growled. "Found you."

"Cute," the mud-covered Wizard said, sounding altogether less happy now. "Granted, it would have been more impressive if you'd found me ten minutes ago. How do you not clear the room before freeing the hostage? I hope your University gives refunds."

The Dean responded succinctly with a ball of fire the size of an ale keg. The muddy figure leapt with super-human agility, the sphere of flame passing under its legs; nevertheless, he was thrown forward by the force of the door exploding. Alois felt shards of wood bury themselves in his skin, and heard the Wizard Radcliff scream from near the desk.

The figure that tumbled into the wall before scrambling to its feet was no longer invisible. It was now a middle-aged blonde man, covered in mud and looking extremely displeased. Under the mud, Alois could see the smeared remains of runes on the man's face and wrists, painted in red. As far as wounds went, the Wizard didn't have a mark on him. Back on his feet, he disappeared anew, and the mud disappeared along with him.

Bleeding from a deep shrapnel wound in his arm, Radcliff watched in horror as the blonde Wizard appeared standing behind Ludwig, grabbing the little man by the shoulders and hurling him into the desk with bestial strength. Ludwig impacted with the horrible sound of either wood or bone being crushed, and lay motionless next to Lina, who herself appeared to have lapsed into unconsciousness.

The blonde Wizard was turning to Radcliff when another ball of flame plowed into him. Radcliff saw it dissipate against an invisible field surrounding the man, though the force of it still pushed him back. Taking the chance, Radcliff rushed toward Ludwig, preparing a healing incantation as he went. His enchantments may have been of little use, but perhaps he could still do *something...*

Miraculously, he made it to the desk alive. He crouched down and put his hands on Ludwig's limply hanging head. Mere feet away, the two most powerful Wizards he had ever encountered dueled for the fates of them all.

The Dean fired a sizzling bolt of lightning, which the blonde man deflected with one arm, discharging the blast into the wall. "More Conjuration!?" he laughed. "I started as a war caster, for the gods' sake! You can't out-conjure me!"

The Dean, oddly, smiled at this. "Fair enough," he said levelly, and the spell he cast next was unknown to Radcliff. It left the Dean's body like a writhing coil of blackness, sizzling and indistinct, darting out with incredible swiftness. The blonde man stood his ground, but a ghost of a frown flashed on his face the moment before impact.

It hit the field around him like a charging bull, shattering it with an earth-shaking boom, sending the blonde Wizard tumbling off his feet.

"What the hell kind of counter-enchantment was that?" he growled, struggling back up. He dodged aside as another black bolt blasted toward him. An odd gushing sound was left in its wake, and Radcliff realized it was the sound of air filling in the vacuum that the blackness had burned through the room. The bolt impacted the wall behind the blonde Wizard, burrowing an enormous hole straight through it.

"Not an enchantment," the Dean said levelly, and shot another. The blonde Wizard was saved once again only by his preternatural speed; Radcliff did not know if he had gained that through magic, or if it was a benefit of undeath.

"Fascinating," the blonde man said. He spread his hands and conjured a globule of roiling liquid, which he directed at the Dean. The Dean shot another of his dark bolts into it, and the entire center mass of the splash seemed to disappear, leaving only scattered droplets to rain to the ground where they sizzled furiously against the carpet.

"You're right," the blonde man said, "That's no enchantment. You're not changing things. You're just destroying them. I haven't seen this before."

"Why should you have? I invented it."

"Destruction magic. I suppose you call it the seventh school, do you?"

"Eighth. But you know that. The seventh school was invented already, and it was used here. Who taught you Transference magic?"

"So far as I know, the only man who knew how to do it. I guess he was more loose-lipped with his teachings than I thought."

"It is a dangerous magic. Too dangerous for the likes of you."

With a roar, the Dean threw out both hands, and an overwhelming wave of darkness rushed upon his opponent. The blast was too large to dodge, and his adversary did not try to. Radcliff saw him cast a one-word enchantment to drain the power away from the oncoming spell. He got the word out just before the darkness hit him.

The thing that stood there moments later was grotesque, its clothing and much of its flesh burned away. A man would have been convulsing on the floor, dying of shock and pain. The undead thing, though, stood unconcerned, leering with its lidless eyes and a gum-less mouth.

"As a conjurer," it said, "I take a sort of professional pride in showing you the error of your juvenile Destructive magic."

He raised his burnt, bloody arms over his head like a wraith, and roared the words of Arcanic to summon a ferocious torrent of fire. The Dean responded by spreading his arms and creating another intense coil of destruction, flowing towards the skeletal figure and his cyclone of flame.

The roiling explosion of fire and the crackling tendril of darkness met between the two, the destruction eating away at the fire, but expending itself in the act.

Ludwig had been healed to the best of Radcliff's limited ability; still unconscious, but cured of any concussion. Now was Radcliff's chance to end this. He brought up a hand, aiming carefully at the undead Wizard's charred head. He was not much of a conjurer, but just a bit of lightning would do...

Something grabbed his hand. He looked, and saw that it was the gauntlet of Mathias Brenz, Magisterial Guard. The man's slit throat seemed to mirror his sickening smile, though his eyes were milky and vacant. Brenz's other fist came around and slammed into Radcliff's face, sending him tumbling to the ground, his mouth flooding with coppery wetness. Brenz drew his sword and raised it two-handed over his head.

Radcliff could only throw his arms up to protect himself and wait for the inevitable, but the killing blow never came. Brenz was hit in the side of the stomach with a sizzling black tendril; this was swiftly pulled up and out through his shoulder, bisecting his body. The two parts of Mathias Brenz tumbled to the floor.

Radcliff turned to look at the Dean, who had already turned his full attention back to the fight with the blonde man.

"Mr. Falkenhayn! I will deal with this! I want you to get the others out of here, however you can!"

Radcliff nodded resolutely, ignoring the wrenching pain in his jaw. He did not have the strength to carry them out—not Gustav, at least—but by God, he was a Wizard, wasn't he?

He put a hand on Ludwig and focused, as hard as he could, on the Magistrate's office. He chanted the spell, still engrained in his memory from his studies years ago, and willed them to be there.

When he opened his eyes, he was crouched on the mosaic carpet of the office floor. Krupp stared at him dumbly from the other side of the room.

Smiling, Radcliff prepared to go back for another trip.

The Dean growled and poured more force into his spell. His incantation was more powerful than that of his enemy, but the Conjuration spell was easier to cast and empower... one of them would overcome the other sooner or later, though, and the Dean was confident that he would be the victor.

He wondered why Wolfram would have taught Transference magic to an undead being—though, perhaps the stranger had not been undead at the time. With this thought, the incredibly simple truth became clear to him, and he knew who he was fighting.

Chapter 31

It was nearly forty years earlier when Eugene Baldermann pulled on the hemp shirt and walked slowly down the stairs, stopping in the corner to take up the pitchfork that he kept propped there.

"Eugene," his wife pled from upstairs, "Please, don't do this."

He ignored her, swinging the door open and stepping out into the sun. His feet were bare, and beneath them he could feel the littered straw and dirt on the front stoop. He shut the door behind him and stepped down onto the rough dirt path that wound through the wild grass leading away from the farmhouse, past a freshly-painted picket fence and out toward the road. His departure was timed perfectly to intercept the odd procession that was making its way along the road.

There were at least twenty of them now, he knew; he did a quick head count and came out with three short of two dozen, though he might have missed one or two. They were gruesomely decrepit, in varying states of decomposition. It was with a great deal of determination that he avoided looking at the faces of those who he recognized, and indeed, he recognized more of them than not.

The man in front, the witch, was decrepit, but not decomposing. Ancient, but not dead. He stopped short as Eugene stepped out into the road. The witch's eyes had been cast down as he walked, his thick spectacles coated with kicked-up dust, and only slowly did he finally look up, mopping sweat off his brow with the sleeve of his robe.

"Yes?" he asked, softly, as though distracted.

"You're not welcome here," Eugene said, keeping his eyes on the witch, the pitchfork balanced over his shoulder. "You've been told that."

"Well," the old man said, with a ghost of a smile, "I suppose I have been. Actions speak louder than words."

"This is a community. You can't live in a community unless you're a part of it; unless you contribute to it. Otherwise, you're a leech, or worse. We welcome outsiders, and we were ready to welcome you, but we don't look kindly on what you've done."

The old man's posture straightened. His eyes were small, and hidden in sunken pits behind layers of wrinkles, but they still appeared bright and intelligent until a withered finger pushed the dusty spectacles up into place.

"Yes, yes, I'm quite aware. 'We don't hold with none of your witchcraft, sorcerer. You best be moving along and takin' your unnatural practices wit' you.' Is that about the gist of it? If so, I'm sorry to say that I've already received that speech."

"I know you did. Just before you killed Friedrich Braun."

"Oh, what are you so gloomy about? He's still up and at them, after all. Look, see?" The old man indicated one of the nearest entourage members at hand, and the thing lumbered a few steps forward. Its skin was sickly pale, but it showed less decomposition than many of the others. Its face and clothes were those of Friedrich Braun, innkeeper.

Eugene managed to suppress a shudder. Instead, he merely shifted the pitchfork to the other shoulder. "What do you want from us?"

The witch gestured at the thing that looked like Braun. "Isn't it obvious? Raw materials."

"I won't let you keep on this way."

"Your four brethren felt the same way last night, immediately prior to my murdering them."

"Those were not my kin. They were hired soldiers from Friberg."

"I hope you didn't pay them in advance, then."

Eugene felt his temper flare. His temper was getting worse and worse as he got older—and he was only twenty-three. He ground his teeth and wrapped his fingers more tightly around the wooden haft of the pitchfork.

"One last warning," he growled. "You take your black arts, and you leave us here in peace."

The old man sighed. "Or what, exactly? Why do you think I chose your awful little community for my experiments, anyway? You think I'm so absent-minded in my brilliance that I'm not aware of the petty superstitions of rural folk? I was well aware that you wouldn't take kindly to my activities, but then again, who would? So I picked a place with such pitiful resources, and so few allies, that nothing could possibly be done to stop me. You talk about Friberg like it's the big city. Son, Friberg is about a quarter the size of what I'd call a *small town*. As for this gods-awful Briksbane here, I'm forced to place it somewhere between 'hamlet' and 'post hammered into the ground'."

All at once, Eugene's restraint snapped. It wasn't the insults, exactly. It was more that he knew that everything the old man said was true. Tendons tensing in his neck, Eugene swung down the pitchfork and thrust it two-handed, aiming for the witch's throat. In a show of surprising speed, what was once Friedrich Braun rushed forward and put himself in the way of the tines, taking all four of them through the top of his breastbone. Distressingly little blood seeped from the catastrophic wounds.

Eugene pulled the pitchfork back and quickly stepped away from Braun, who was already lumbering toward him. He ducked around and saw the old man, smiling and watching from just where he'd been before. Eugene was sporting a smile of his own as once again he stabbed at the old bastard, aiming for the stomach now. Braun couldn't get in front of the fork this time, but another of the corpses was able to get to Eugene. It wrapped its arms around his body and tipped its weight backward, bringing them both to the ground. His thrust was thrown way off.

The things lumbered in around Eugene now. He struggled in the powerful grasp of the one that held him—a big man he did not recognize. He saw that it wore the remains of a chain shirt, and realized it was one of the mercenaries from Friberg. Its fingers grasped at his neck. By reflex he hammered his knee into its groin, with the results that could be expected, but he did not have time to curse his stupidity.

Muscles aching, he lost his grip on its arms and it got a hold on his neck; Eugene groped blindly and managed to grab a dusty chunk of limestone from the edge of the road. He slammed it into the side of the thing's head, and his hand came back wet. As he felt its fingers begin to crush his trachea, he hit it again, and again. There was a particularly gruesome crunch, and he felt the rock penetrate into the thing's brain. The fingers loosened, and Eugene used everything he had left to wriggle away, stumbling to his feet before the others could react, grabbing the top of the fence and hurling himself over it, his vision dark around the edges, his breath ragged in his throat.

His instinct was to run, and he did, back toward the house—but in a few moments, his head began to clear, and then stopped, turning around. The things were filing along the fence toward the gate, which was closed but did not even have a lock.

He decided to continue to the house after all. Inside, he grabbed his old yew hunting bow from where it hung over the door, along with the quiver of dog-eared arrows, which he slung over his shoulder. He took the bow with him back out onto the lawn, up which the creatures had begun to shamble. Behind them all, he saw the old man, watching from the road.

He walked again down the front path, directly into the waiting arms of the first among the corpses. Ducking aside at the last moment, he skirted to the right through the grass, running for the western side of the fence, hurtling over it and blessedly landing in a neat crouch on the road. There was just enough time to stand, nock an arrow, and aim for the old man before the wave of cadavers, turning to meet him with all the power they could muster, slammed into the fence and brought it toppling forward.

At that moment, he sent the arrow flying toward a very surprised-looking old witch.

A moment later, he had been forced back to the ground, and felt weight pushing down on every part of him, his attempts to struggle totally futile. The pressure on his head suddenly increased, and everything went black.

Eugene regained consciousness slowly over several minutes, spending most of the time trying to remember where he was. He could feel a hard surface against his back, and his wrists were bound to the wall on either side of his head. Each ankle was restrained as well.

Groggily, he opened his eyes and tried turning his head. A wave of pain shot through his skull, sending him into a brief convulsion followed by a coughing fit.

More slowly this time, he turned his head to the right to look at his restraints. He frowned when he saw that there weren't any. He'd expected straps or chains around his wrists, but for all he could tell, it looked more like someone had pasted his arms flat to the wall. The wall was wooden, and not in the best of shape. If it was rotten enough within, he thought he might be able to rock his weight back and forth and tear himself free—thought it was hard to say what would work, when he did not know the real nature of his bonds. By now, though, he remembered enough to know that magic was the likely culprit.

The idea of rocking his weight back into the wall turned his stomach and shot another, thankfully lessened, wave of pain through his aching head. It might work, but now was not the time to try it—he'd end up unconscious, which would hardly do him any good.

He took in his surroundings. He was in a barn, that was clear enough—life experience had left him well equipped to identify a barn on sight. It was in poor shape, clearly not mended or even used for a long time. The hay loft was empty and without a ladder. The foundation was stone. Several tables had been set up in the middle of the drafty building, and odd equipment was piled there—flasks of liquid, stacks of books, and a small stove, coals within glowing brightly in the dimness. A few rays of midday sun lanced into the building through holes in the roof.

He knew he could not do much; any movement made the aching in his head get worse. He stayed as still as he could. Whatever was holding him to the wall, it was doing all the work—he did not have to exert any effort in staying upright. As such, he took the opportunity to rest.

The angle of the sunlight had changed by the time the doors were thrown open, a gust of breeze from outside blowing old strands of hay across the stone floor. Two figures held the doors open; he could not make out whom, but they looked like large men. The witch entered, shuffling slowly forward. As he crossed by the table, a beam of sunlight lit his face, and Eugene could see that he was smiling.

"Welcome back, Eugene," the witch said, coming closer. He raised an eyebrow at Eugene's expression. "Your name? Don't worry; your wife is fine, if that's what concerns you. No, I dug your name out of the memories of one of our friends. Not a well-known or easy art, but certainly possible, if one desires to make the effort."

The old man smiled, went over to the table, and poured himself a glass of what looked like milk. "As you can see," he said, gesturing toward his thin chest, "I am imperforated, though not for a lack of trying on your part. Tell me, with all my grizzly friends posing a much more immediate threat, why did you go after me?"

Eugene growled. "I'm not stupid. I saw last week when Peter Kurz ran one of them through with his father's saber. The thing didn't even slow down. Hell, I halfway tore Friedrich Braun's head off, and if I'm not mistaken, I think he may be over there holding the door open."

The old man nodded, taking a sip from his glass. "Yes. Make sure to get the head all the way off, next time. So, realizing that the situation was hopeless, you decided to go after me—but you exposed yourself in order to do so. Where is the wisdom in that?"

Eugene clenched his fists and suppressed another growl, limiting himself to staring coldly at the old man.

"Dare I say that you thought killing me would rip the magic right out of their bones and send them plummeting to the ground, as the gods intended?"

"That," Eugene said tersely, "was the idea."

"Well, my friend, you were right! That's what would have happened, had you slain me successfully. And you're a good shot, at that—your arrow should have taken me right through the chest, I think. The only problem with your plan was that this morning I put several enchantments on myself to make such efforts useless. You couldn't even touch me, Eugene, unless I allowed it."

Eugene gave his back muscles an experimental flex. The pain in his head remained muted.

"I dare say you'd be more than willing to try anyway. Don't worry, it's hardly your fault—how could you know that someone with the power to raise the dead would also almost certainly be able to make himself invulnerable to physical attack? As a matter of fact, it's a bit disturbing to think how close your plan came to working. For most of my time here, I haven't bothered with protective enchantments. If any of the other dunces in this town had tried that, I'd be dead.

"They certainly made me complacent, Eugene—I never expected to find someone clever in a place like this."

As subtly as he could, Eugene attempted to pull his legs forward, away from the wall. He felt the invisible bonds pull against the wood behind him.

"You'll get no arguments from me regarding the degree of intelligence we have here," he said, holding the old man's gaze with his. "That doesn't make it right to kill folk as you like."

The old man shrugged. "Agree to disagree. Nevertheless, the fact remains that the course of events has brought us to here and now. Honestly, I enchanted myself this morning entirely on a whim. I imagine if I had ever bothered to learn Divination, I could have used it this morning and witnessed myself being shot with an arrow."

"Nice guy like you, I bet you'd see yourself getting shot with arrows pretty often."

"Indeed! But I rather think that a quiet death of old age is more likely at this juncture."

"Well. You're no spring chicken."

"Agreed; I am twice as old as any grandfather you've ever met. Nevertheless, facing death is no easier for me than for anyone else. I once had—but no, I am getting ahead of myself. We haven't even been introduced."

The old man took a step back and gave a little bow. "Eugene Baldermann, I am Arthur Wolfram, the most powerful Wizard of my time."

"Never heard of you."

"Of course not. Let's get you down from there before you do anything to the wall that you can't take back. I'm going to release you, and you're going to come join me at the table. If you do anything I do not like, I will eviscerate you."

The bonds suddenly released, and Eugene dropped to his feet. He wasn't ready, and tumbled in a heap to the ground. He was disoriented for a moment as pain roared through his head.

Eventually, he managed to stand and approach the table, where Wolfram now sat. Eugene pulled out the chair across from him and gingerly settled into it.

"Your head is still hurting, is it? I'm afraid my friends got a bit overzealous in their defense of me. You could be concussed. Here we are."

Wolfram leaned forward, and his wrinkled hand grasped Eugene by the forehead. He spoke a series of words in a foreign tongue, and the pain and fog seemed suddenly to clear from Eugene's head.

"There. Goodness, you sit here with me willingly, and even let me touch you. I am impressed."

"You said you'd eviscerate me otherwise."

"And that was the truth, but I thought you might try to run anyway."

"I shot you in the chest with an arrow. I'm out of ideas."

Wolfram smiled. "Amazing. I have lived three lifetimes, and I am still learning things."

"What do you want from me?"

"First, I want you to listen. Let me know if you need any food or drink."

Eugene sat back in his chair and shook his head, folding his arms over his chest.

"As I was saying previously, I fear death as much as the next man. Wizards, indeed, tend to be terrified of death, and the most powerful ones may circumvent the problem altogether by making themselves undead. I never had much interest in the idea; in fact, I was so willing to give up my right to lichhood that I bestowed it upon someone else."

"Lichhood?"

"It's not important; besides, you'll learn soon enough. As for my lich, I took my leave of him, for he became a danger to me the moment I'd given him what he wanted. I still have no desire to become a lich myself, and yet, part of me regrets what I've done. I may have chosen my successor prematurely. I thought my life was already over, but that was before I left that accursed cottage and finally got on the road again. I had forgotten what it was like in the real world. Everything's different. Vast new venues of exploration and experimentation are opened up. I discovered that I wasn't done with my life after all, and after protecting myself as best I could from young Rodolphus' attempts to locate me, I got back to the affair of living. I have done much in the time since. Most recently my interest in the old school of Necromancy was reawakened, and I chose this place as the site of my experiments. I have made great strides in the necromantic arts, pioneering roads never before explored. It is all written down, of course, for posterity."

Eugene shifted in his seat, but opted to say nothing. He had not been lying when he said he was out of ideas; for now, all he could think to do was hear what the old one had to say.

"So I found myself learning, doing, changing, and yet I had already chosen a successor. Rodolphus is too brash... and yet not brash enough. At first he was too hands-on, but after spending some time with me, he became a reclusive scholar just as bad as I was. At first it was only so he could gain power, but now undeath has apparently made him into an introvert. He's probably whiling away the hours over old books even now. He was supposed to represent me, but he has fallen so far behind that this is now impossible. Do you understand what I mean?"

"It is as though you had only one son to name as the inheritor of your farm and lands," Eugene said, "and in your old age you are disappointed with him, but there is naught left that you can do."

"Yes! Yes! Distasteful farming analogies aside, that is not dissimilar to how I am feeling. My time is up. I have extended my lifetime as far as it will go. My body is tired in a way that no Curation can fix. For the first time in my life, I find myself in a hurry. If I could only spare the time to teach you, Eugene..."

Eugene pushed back from the table. "Wait, that's what this is about? Me? You just met me!"

"I trust my judgment of character. You're clever. You've got native wit. You're angry, but you're not power-mad. You're far more intelligent than the average rural type, even though you were raised in a two-penny backwater where education rarely persists long enough to instill literacy. The amount of untapped potential that may live inside you is astonishing."

"Well, gosh, thank you."

"Oh, come. Living in this awful miscarriage of a place is hardly your fault."

"No. But like you said, you can't teach me. There's no time."

"No, no. And it would not work anyway. I taught Rodolphus the greater part of magic when he was nearing middle-age, but he had at least a strong foundation of magical knowledge and ability. You, on the other hand... dare I suggest that you have none?"

Eugene gave a curt nod.

"It is impossible, then. You are too old. Your mind is closed to the magical arts. I would find it tragic."

"Would?"

"Yes, would, if I didn't have a solution. Why would I bother telling you all this if I did not have a solution?"

"Wait, now. I don't consent to become—"

"Eugene, let's not insult both our intelligences by pretending that you have a choice in this matter."

Eugene slowly shut his mouth. His hands gripped the edge of the table.

"Lesser Wizards talk obsessively of the five schools of magic—that is, Conjuration, Enchantment, Divination, Necromancy, and Curation—as though to find some mystical sixth would be a great feat. They don't really understand anything. When one has invented as much magic as I have, one begins to see things that stop fitting neatly into schools. Would I call my Transference spell a part of some 'sixth school' of magic? Oh, perhaps. But that doesn't really matter. What matters is that I have it. Rodolphus does too by now, I have no doubt—all the notes he would need to learn it are in my cottage."

"Transference?" Eugene asked, frowning.

"Yes. That's how we're going to do this. I'm going to give you my power. All of it. My memories, too, but that's merely incidental. You won't need to learn a thing. Though, my boy, I do hope that you will go about educating yourself once I've given you the means to do so."

"You... wait; I don't think I understand..."

"It doesn't matter. Soon, you will gain my knowledge of the magical arts. Which, if I do say it myself, is considerable. I'm afraid I'll be leaving you a bit of a blind spot in Divination, though... I've never been any good at it, oddly enough. You can fill in the blanks on your own, if you care t—"

Eugene shot to his feet, the old chair clattering to the ground behind him. He swiftly scooped a glass beaker, full of red liquid, off the table. As he was bringing his arm back to throw it, his body froze in place, his muscles flashing into rigidity.

"Now, now," Wolfram said testily, "it is far too late for that. I don't blame you, though. As I've said, you simply haven't had the upbringing to prepare you for something of this magnitude."

Wolfram walked around the table to Eugene and plucked the beaker from his hand. Dipping a finger into the thick red substance, he began to smear it across the tabletop, drawing a large glyph of some kind.

"My soul will not be bound with you. It will be set free of my body, to go..." his glaze flickered upwards, to the hole-filled roof. "Elsewhere, and there is only one way to find out the exact destination. The explorations are only just beginning for me, I think."

Wolfram stepped over to Eugene and began drawing some sort of pattern on his face and forehead with the red sludge, then rolled up his sleeves and marked his arms as well. Setting the beaker down, he picked up a similar one, this full of a blue liquid, and began adding to the glyph on the table.

"I *could* use the spell to transfer my power only, leaving me alive but without my magic—but to Wizards, life without magic could hardly be called life at all. Thus I will give you my entire self, and you will be all the more powerful for it. Worry not, though; I am not conquering your body. Your soul will remain the one and only inside of you, and my memories will be a secondary set that will settle into the back of your mind, to be recalled when needed. Nevertheless, my knowledge and power are bound to cast a sort of shadow of myself on to you. Or, at least, I suspect as much. When you follow me on my final voyage, a long, long time from now, I hope that we will be able to discuss it.

"An added bonus to all this is that—and again, I can really only speculate—the fact that my life essence will route through you before moving on should greatly confuse any Divination spells that are used to locate me. It will drive Rodolphus insane. He can consider it my parting gift."

Wolfram now took the blue substance and began smearing it onto his own face. On each cheek, he drew a complex symbol with many bends and angles. On his forehead, he traced three fingers down, creating a triple strike mark that came halfway down the bridge of his nose and his eyelids. He then rolled up his sleeves and applied further markings to his forearms.

Wiping his fingers clean on his robe and stepping around so that the large glyph on the table was between himself and Eugene, Wolfram smiled broadly and began to trace intricate patterns in the air with his hands. "Make me proud, son."

The Dean watched as his destruction slowly ate closer and closer to Rodolphus. It would be simple enough. He would kill the lich here, and then go kill him again as he was raised in Yunder. He could then disenchant the resurrection site, and the matter would be finished.

"It's over, Rodolphus!" he called over the crackling of the spells raging between them. "Yes, I remember you now. Wolfram told me all about you. Remember Wolfram, Rodolphus? Your best and only friend?"

"Wolfram?" The lich snorted. "He wasn't my best friend. I *killed* my best friend."

The Dean frowned, but supposed he should not be surprised.

"I wonder," the lich called back, his voice oddly devoid of concern, "did you ever learn much Alchemy?"

The Dean frowned again at the odd question, but did not worry himself over it. Let Rodolphus waste his breath if he wanted. The coil of destruction was crawling toward him, inch by inch.

He expected that there may be a grand explosion to finish things, so he was relieved when he saw Radcliff finally crawl over to Alois' body and teleport away with it, finishing his work and clearing the room.

"No," he responded to Rodolphus. "What's the point?"

"A common sentiment! And let me ask you this: what would you do if someone threatened to drop you in a lake of acid?"

The Dean could only snort.

"It's tough, right?" the lich continued. "A conjurer can make a small amount of acid, and so can an enchanter, but in either case one could defend themselves with a simple shield enchantment. A standard shield enchantment would quickly be overwhelmed by total emersion, though. You could make yourself immune to acid, but a spell like that takes a long time to cast, and wears off within a few days. Who goes around with such a thing prepared? So, yeah, a lake of acid would be rough. But those don't occur naturally, do they? I love acid, but the damn stuff is hard to get in quantity."

"This is an interesting way to be spending your last few minutes!" the Dean shouted, keeping his eyes ever on the war of magic that he was slowly winning.

"I thought you'd think so! Well, here's the kicker— I've had a lot of time to study things, being immortal. Even the newfangled things that old pompous bastards like you think are superfluous. Things old Wolfram couldn't have taught you, since they were after his time. Things like Alchemy. And what's interesting about about Alchemy is, you can get really, really good at it, but since people only used it to make precious metals, and managed to destroy the economy within a few years, no one ever really bothered. No one but me. And the thing is, old man, the thing is... it turns out that with Alchemy, you can really make substances in quantity... and I'm not just talking about gold."

The Dean watched as the lich pulled one hand out of his spell and pointed it straight up, making a series of gestures that the Dean did not recognize, but the purpose of which he could guess. His gaze strayed upward, and he watched as every atom and molecule currently composing the ceiling and walls of the room—the carbon of wood, the ferrite of iron, the silicon of glass, all of it—was converted into pure hydrofluoric acid. Gravity did the rest.

Chapter 32

Radcliff's foray into teleportation had gone very well, but things fell apart as he tried to make his final trip back to the courthouse.

For starters, no matter how hard he focused, he couldn't get himself there— quite a discouraging fact, as previously he'd done it with surprisingly little difficulty. Soon he began trying to think of different spots in the room, perhaps ones he would be able to visualize more clearly. This did work, finally, as he pictured the white marble fireplace set into one wall.

He opened his eyes in time to see the fireplace sweep past him as he plummeted through the hole that used to be the floor. He fell well past where he expected there should have been another floor a storey beneath, and, looking down, watched in horror as a jagged mess of splintered wood piled on the ground below loomed closer and closer.

At the last moment he was able to get enough of a grip on himself to cast an enchantment.

Carefully, he floated the remaining handful of yards to the ground, where he splashed into a puddle. His boots immediately began to hiss furiously, and he quickly stepped out of the liquid and up onto the mass of debris that seemed to occupy the entirety of the room he was in. He realized that the wreckage must have been the remains of the floors which he had noted earlier as conspicuously absent. The hissing did not stop, though it lessened—the wood itself seemed to be totally saturated by the virulent liquid, whatever it was.

He forced himself to take several deep breaths to slow the racing of his heart. Finally, he found the focus to renew his enchantment, and began to float over the debris. His boots hissed still, and finally he kicked them off, wincing as they landed with a splash in another puddle. He realized now that the ground beneath him was less a group of puddles than a shallow pond that had islands of wreckage jutting out of it.

The rest of the building was hardly in better condition. Though the stone outer-shell seemed strong enough, the wooden walls around him looked decayed and decrepit, creaking and groaning horribly. Merely being off the ground was no guarantee of safety, and he began looking frantically for the nearest exit.

His eyes strayed to something lying among the debris, notable for being bright red in a sea of muddy brown. He levitated over to it, and felt his stomach turn as he recognized what it was.

A human hand, striped nearly entirely of flesh, revealing bone and musculature that was wet and bloody and sizzling. Could the Dean's Destruction magic have done this? He hovered closer, moving around to bring the rest of the body into view.

His hopes plummeted when he saw that the ruined body still had something of a beard left, largely its only recognizable feature. He felt his heart sinking, and he reached desperately toward the body, though he could not bring himself to touch it.

If the Dean was dead... where was the undead Wizard? Was he lurking invisible nearby, merely biding his time before he descended upon Radcliff with his full arsenal of unfathomable arcana?

If so, Radcliff realized, he would be powerless to stop it. If the Dean could not do it, what hope was left? He stared at the horrible thing that had once been a man, and reached out again. He could not leave him here, surely— he had to take him away from this...

His fingers brushed the remains of the thing's robe, and a booming voice filled his head. It was inhuman, and buzzed as though created entirely through vibrations.

"MR. FALKENHAYN."

With a start he hovered quickly back, but the voice continued, unabated.

"I SUSPECTED THAT YOU WOULD BE BACK. THIS MESSAGE TO YOU WAS COMPOSED IN MY LAST MOMENTS. ALREADY THE DAMAGE IS MORE THAN I CAN HEAL, BUT PERHAPS THINGS ARE NOT IRRECONCILABLE YET."

Radcliff was familiar with this spell, an enchantment that imparted a message upon a physical object. It interpreted the intention of the caster at the time of casting into words.

"I... how did he do this?" Radcliff stammered. "What are we supposed to d—"

"THE WIZARD'S NAME IS RODOLPHUS," the voice sounded over him, echoing inside his head as though inside a cave, "AND HE IS A LICH. EVEN IF SLAIN, HE WILL BE REBORN AT THE SITE OF HIS DEATH. FOR RODOLPHUS, THIS IS CRUTCHFIELD PARK, LOCATED IN THE CITY OF YUNDER."

"How do you know that?" Radcliff managed to get out, but he did not know if there was much point.

"THE SITE MUST BE DECONSECRATED. YOU WILL FIND THE RITUAL FOR DOING SO IN THE OLD BOOK TITLED *THE UNSPEAKABLE CODEX*, HIDDEN BEHIND THE BOOKS ON THE TOP SHELF IN MY OFFICE. YOU MUST DO THIS, AND THEN KILL THE LICH."

"I... but surely you can't expect that! How in God's name am I supposed to do what you couldn't?"

"I AM SORRY, MR. FALKENHAYN, THAT WE WERE NOT ABLE TO GET TO KNOW EACH OTHER

BETTER. THAT IS MY FAULT. I DO NOT KNOW
WHETHER WE SHALL MEET AGAIN, BUT IF WE
DO, THAT IS THE FIRST OF MANY MISTAKES
THAT I SHALL REMEDY."

Radcliff waited, but there was nothing more. The
sudden silence in his head was somehow even worse than
the booming voice. Gradually he was able to make out
sounds again, and he realized quite suddenly that the
groaning of the building around him had gotten worse.

Above him, the marble fireplace tore free of its
foundations and plummeted down to the ground, crashing
into a pile of wood. The wall it had been mounted in
groaned and sheared down the middle. The rest of the
building began to tremble, and did not stop.

As Radcliff teleported out, Langham Courthouse was
collapsing around him.

Alois had regained the ability to move the moment
he'd been taken from the courthouse. He took a moment
to get a grip on his surroundings. Quickly he spotted Lina,
lying on a velvet couch, eyes shut, brow furrowed. Albert
Krupp stood over her as though unsure what to do.

Alois mirrored the sentiment, but approached and
tentatively felt the girl's forehead. She fidgeted slightly,
and he realized that his hand must be very cold. Her head
was hot, but he was gratified at least that her breast was
rising and falling in a pattern of fairly regular breathing.

"Lina?" he whispered softly. She did not stir. Taking
his hand away, he pulled her robe off as carefully as
possible, revealing a light green dress that he had
provided from Juliet's things.

"What's wrong with her?" Krupp asked finally, hand
tapping anxiously on a tabletop. "What did he do?"

Alois shook his head. "I'm not sure. He had her strung up... strung up like a damned hanged-man, but I don't know what he was doing to her."

"I hope she comes along soon," a soft voice said from over Krupp's shoulder. Alois turned to look, and saw the Magistrate of Merund standing before the large window mounted in the far wall.

"I believe I owe her an apology," he continued.

"Yes," Alois said, "I should think that you do. You're sure you don't still want us thrown in jail?"

"I do not expect you or anyone else to forgive my stupidity, Chief Constable Gustav. But I... I have reanalyzed my priorities, and I hope that you will allow me to help you."

"We may not need help—the Dean may be solving our problem for us as we speak," Alois responded.

Krupp glanced past Alois. Turning, Alois saw that the Wizard Ludwig was seated in a chair several yards from the couch, looking quite the worse for wear.

"Ludwig has come to," Krupp said. "Ludwig, do you know what's going on in the Courthouse?"

"No. The Dean was fighting the other Wizard ... I was attacked by... by Brenz."

"That's not right," Alois said. "Brenz was dead, for starters."

"Death is not proving the obstacle to violence that it once did," the Magistrate pointed out.

"Yes," Krupp said. "In addition to being undead himself, the Wizard must be a necromancer."

"That explains why he was able to keep me from moving," Alois said. "Only I would not have thought he could have controlled me, with Lina so near... but none of us know anything of this."

"No, I'm afraid we don't," The Magistrate agreed. "Ludwig, I suppose you're the only Wizard in this city who *doesn't* secretly study forbidden magic?"

Ludwig blushed slightly, but nodded.

"Why did Radcliff leave, anyway?" Krupp asked testily. "He'd already rescued everyone."

"I went back to help the Dean," Radcliff said from behind them, startling Alois yet again. He found himself wishing that people would start announcing themselves more formally. Radcliff had materialized near the door. Oddly, he wore only socks beneath his short robes.

"I guess that was a stupid idea," Radcliff said, walking into the room and toward the desk. His face was drawn and forlorn, mouth set into a frown. He carried a leather-bound tome under one arm. "I'm not sure what I thought I would be able to contribute."

"Well?" Krupp asked anxiously. "What happened?"

"The Dean is dead. The lich killed him, and brought down the entire building in the process."

Krupp groaned, and the Magistrate briefly shut his eyes. When they opened again a moment later, he said, "The lich?"

"That's what it is. The other wizard. When I went back, the Dean had left a message for me. He told me that it was a lich, a sort of undead. It... well, it's all here in this book."

"May I?" The Magistrate asked, taking the book gently from Radcliff's clutching arm and laying it out on the desk. He walked to the other side and sat, opening the book to where the marking ribbon had been placed. His brow furrowed. "The spelling here is very archaic, but I think I can manage."

"The lich," he read carefully, "is the most powerful and most difficult to create of the undead creatures. Only the most powerful sort of Wizard can create a lich, and even then, only one may be created in a life-time. Most truly great Wizards will thus bestow lichhood upon themselves so that they may live forever. It is true immortality, for the lich can die neither of age, nor of disease, nor even in battle. Should its body be destroyed, the lich will be reborn at the site of its death."

"For Delar's sake," Krupp groaned.

"It was long thought," the Magistrate continued, "that a lich was thus unstoppable, but in ages past the power of the liches soon became a great evil for the living world. It was at this time that the High Wizard's Cabal of Selan joined together and created a ritual for desanctifying the death site of the lich, thus disabling his rebirth and turning him into little more than an empowered ghoul, able to be slain. Long guarded, this ritual is as follows..."

"Well?" Alois said, once the pause had begun to linger.

"This is... beyond my expertise," The Magistrate said. "Radcliff?"

"Not really my angle, either," Radcliff said, peering over his shoulder. "It's ancient Arcanic, instructions for the ritual. I'm not terribly familiar with this form of the lexicon..."

"I am," Ludwig said, his small voice tired but resigned. "Bring the book here, please."

The Magistrate closed the book and carried it to Ludwig, setting it gently in his lap before opening it back up. The Divination Chairman's dark eyes quickly went to work, scanning back and forth across the pages.

"Can you do it?" the Magistrate asked eventually.

"With Falkenhayn's help," Ludwig murmured, "yes... yes, I can do it."

"All right. Constable, will you be joining them?"

"No," Alois said, surprised. "No. I'll stay here with Lina."

"Of course."

"I'll go, then," Krupp said.

The Magistrate's brow rose slightly.

"Of course," he repeated. "You should all make haste. I will stay behind with Chief Constable Gustav and his young charge... I have made enough of a mess of things as it is without causing further problems."

Alois frowned. There was no reason to assume that the Magistrate's remorse was genuine, and yet already he found it difficult to condemn the man. Radcliff seemed to agree.

"It's all right, Schiller," Radcliff said. "You've made a long career out of being cool-headed and useful. You were long overdue for a screw-up."

The Magistrate allowed a wry smile to show on his slim face. "Yes. Well, I suppose I'm glad it's out of the way, and I hope it's another fifty years before the next one."

"However," Radcliff continued, "I don't think this is going to work. Yes, we can deconsecrate his death site— that is, assuming he doesn't sense our presence there and slaughter us before we can. But what is the point? I can't think of anything we can do to kill the lich. I'm sure he will have some way of reconsecration, and then he'll hunt us down, and there will be nothing that we can do about it."

"You are suggesting what, then?" The Magistrate asked.

"I don't know. Maybe he's got what he wanted and now he'll leave. Is there anything to be gained by provoking him further?"

"We should not make assumptions about his motives. What if he is here to stay?"

"Then it might be best to run."

"I agree with Radcliff," Krupp said. "We don't have a chance. But... I think we should try anyway, because...

no one else even knows about the threat. We've been saddled with this responsibility. As little hope as there is, there's still less if we run."

"Yes. But I do not presume to force anyone to do anything," the Magistrate said.

"I will go to Yunder and try to disenchant the site," Ludwig said quietly.

"Then I will go with," Radcliff said, grim finality in his voice.

"Yunder's hundreds of miles from here," Ludwig said, finally closing the book. "I can divine in order to teleport us, but I have not been there and it will be very slow unless I have a connection to it, or to someone who lives there."

The Magistrate managed another smile. "You know, I think I may have just the thing."

Rodolphus felt as good as he had in ages. After all, he'd killed the most powerful Wizard within hundreds of miles. The city was his oyster; the game, virtually won.

It *was* a game, too—he'd realized that somewhere along the way. He'd come to find Wolfram, but right now he found that topic extremely tedious—it was all but a foregone conclusion that Wolfram was dead already, after all. Enough of that. He'd spent too long trying to protect his lichhood and had totally neglected just being a lich. What was the point of being immortal if you weren't going to do anything with it?

He was reformed. He had seen the light. He smiled to himself as he thought about the game, the same one played by barbarian chieftains and tyrant warlords the world over. The goal of the game was to be king. The only rule was that there could only be one king at a time per locality.

He was pretty sure that the king of Merund, a Mr. Schiller, lived in the enormously tall building in the East, so that's where he was going.

He was willing to admit the possibility that he did not look as good as he felt; that bearded bastard had certainly gotten a good hit in. Most of the tissue had been stripped away from his arms and face, leaving bones coated here and there with chunks of charred black sinew. It was a good thing, he mused, that he hadn't had this much trouble hanging on to his skin back when he was a man.

He'd been prepared for a great deal of necromantic aptitude when he sucked out the girl's powers, but still, he was surprised by how much power there was. Granted, he hadn't really gained any new abilities—it was rather the case that he could use them more swiftly and more expertly than before.

Before, for example, if he'd wanted to raise an army of undead, he'd have had to go to the cemetery. Now, that wasn't strictly necessary. The cemetery would come to him; hundreds of members of its community were now on their way to rendezvous at the tower.

Himself, he could have flown to the tower, or chosen from a variety of other methods of speedy travel, but what was the rush? It had already been a delightfully productive night. He liked a walk.

It was still dark, though the sky was getting lighter. Only a few people were out on the street. Those that got a good look at him screamed and ran. He was hoping he'd get to kill some guards soon.

He paused briefly somewhere in the northern Central District when he noticed that the enormous building he was passing by was a hospital. He raised his hand and strummed at an iota of the girl's power, incanting in Arcanic, fingers outspread.

He lowered his arms again and waited. In a moment, screams began sounding from inside the hospital as some of its former patients got up to come and join him.

A walk was certainly all well and good, but a walk with company—well, now he was really on to something.

Ludwig had sketched out a circle on the carpet in chalk—Krupp had thought about pointing out how expensive the carpet was, but had decided against it. The chalk, apparently, was kept by Ludwig on his person at all times. He'd sketched a large rune inside the circle, and was now sitting cross-legged atop it, mumbling under his breath. In front of his ankles sat a model sailing ship, made of wood with sails of real lacquered cloth.

"Why do you have that thing?" Krupp asked the Magistrate.

"The Governor of Yunder gave it to me, the one time I met him. Six years ago, I believe. He was on a diplomatic tour, though I am shocked that he came this far east. I think he was after a reliable supply of fine glass—we do still send a few merchants out to Yunder each year, thanks to his visit."

"Okay, but why did he give you a ship?"

"He makes them, apparently. Gives them out like candy to justify making more."

"Strange man."

"Everyone must have a hobby."

"What's yours, then?"

"Administering the city."

"Gentlemen," Alois Gustav said from the window, "there may be a problem."

Frowning to each other, Krupp and Schiller joined him, gazing down onto the main thoroughfare. An orange glow gathering in the east suggesting that dawn was threatening to break. The street was shockingly crowded for this time of day—Krupp tried to do a quick estimate, and figured that there must be at least four hundred people filing into the plaza below.

"Who the hell are they?" Alois asked.

"Is Rodolphus one of them?" Krupp said, squinting down. It was impossible to be sure. They were high up, and besides, it was still dark.

"He'll be out there," a small voice from the couch said.

They all turned, and Alois rushed forward, kneeling down so he could get a better look at the girl.

"Lina! How are you feeling?"

She grimaced, and shook her head.

"What's the matter? Are you sick? Radcliff may be able to help you."

"No," she said, "he can't help me."

"Why? What's the matter?"

"My powers. They're gone. He took them from me."

"I…he can do that?"

"That's impossible," Radcliff said.

"Not anymore!" the girl shouted at him, rising into a sitting position. She gestured at Alois with a skinny arm. "Not anymore! I can't feel any of them, now! Not even Mr. Alois! Ro…Rodolphus told me he was going to take my powers, and I didn't believe him, but he did! He's taken them all! That's why he let you get me down; he knew I couldn't do anything! He thought it was funny to leave me alive when he'd taken it all away from me!"

"Then those are all undead," the Magistrate said levelly, still staring out the window.

"Yes," Lina said. She came shakily to her feet, Gustav quickly rising as well as though he might have to catch her if she fell.

"If you can't feel the undead anymore," Radcliff began, "how do you kno—"

"In this instance, Radcliff," the Magistrate said, "I believe she is merely connecting the dots."

"I told you that we should have called the City Guard here to protect us," Krupp said, shaking his head. He felt a strong wish that he'd gone against Schiller's wishes and done it anyway.

"What would be the point? How many could we have mustered in time? Not enough to stop that many zombies, and whenever a Guardsman died, this Rodolphus would raise him up to join his ranks."

"Yes," Gustav agreed, "I know better than anyone that they're not trained or equipped for something like this. They couldn't do anything but die."

Krupp opened his mouth to say that their deaths could still buy them some time, but instead he said, "Well, we have to come up with some kind of plan. We should all go to Yunder. He won't know where we went, and he'll waste time searching the tower."

"Don't you remember, Albert?" the Magistrate asked. "The whole point of deconsecrating his death site is to kill him. We should be happy that he showed up. This is part B of the plan."

"Part B is supposed to come after Part A, you know."

"Ideally. But no, just the three of you will go… and the rest of us will try to deal with this."

"…How?"

"Oh, I still have a trick or two up my sleeve. Besides, the way leading up here is narrow, so it's not as though the whole of his horde can get to us immediately. Unless he can do so with magic," he added, looking at Radcliff.

"Not easily," Radcliff suggested tentatively.

"It is finished," Ludwig said, standing from the circle at the other side of the room, dusting chalk from his robes.

"Then it's time," the Magistrate said. "Good luck, fellows. I'm afraid there is no time for long good-byes."

Hesitantly, Krupp stuck out his hand, hoping the Magistrate would get the idea. He did, taking the hand and shaking it warmly.

"You know, sir," Krupp said, "administering the city really shouldn't count as your hobby. That's your job."

"Hmm, you're right. I suppose my hobby is having existential panic attacks, then."

Krupp glared. "I'm glad you're already willing to laugh about this."

"Who's laughing?"

Krupp, Ludwig, and Radcliff gathered together. Radcliff gave a small smile to the girl.

"Close your eyes," Ludwig reminded them, and Krupp quickly did so. He heard Ludwig incanting next to him, and in a moment they were gone.

It was pitch black when they emerged on the other side. Radcliff tried to wait patiently for his eyes to adjust, but it didn't seem to help much. He heard movement near him, and a moment later a whispered curse that sounded distinctly like Albert Krupp.

Radcliff quickly incanted a small light, the glowing diode floating gently in front of him, casting pale luminescence about the room. Massive burgundy curtains explained the darkness. It was a fairly large bed chamber, though most of the space was taken up by an intricately carved four-poster bed. A man in the bed wearing silk pajamas was sitting up and staring at him in what could only be abject terror.

Krupp cursed again, and as the man opened his mouth and cried the first syllable of a call for help, Radcliff hissed Arcanic and motioned sharply with his hands. The figure went sliding back down against the headboard, eyes drooping shut.

"Just our luck that he's a light sleeper," Krupp grumbled, making his way toward the window and drawing the curtains open. The glass panes behind them stretched from floor to ceiling, revealing a carefully manicured lawn. They looked to be two stories up.

"If we were assassins, he'd be in trouble," Ludwig commented thoughtfully. "I wonder if this method of infiltration is used in places where powerful Divination magic is available."

"Knowing the ingenuity of humankind when faced with the prospect of turning a profit, I'd say almost definitely yes," Krupp said distractedly, fumbling with the window latch. He pushed the windows wide open, then glanced at Radcliff expectantly.

"Well? Make us float, or something."

Radcliff sighed and cast the spell, and the three of them were able to step out of the window and drift gently to the ground.

"All right. We're looking for Crutchfield Park, right?"

"Yes. What's the exact location within the park?"

"I have no idea."

"Once we're close enough to the site, the first part of the spell will locate the exact position for us," Ludwig interjected.

"Great. So where's the park?"

"How should I know?" Krupp asked.

"I thought you said you'd found a city map?"

"No, I said I *didn't* find one."

"Hrm. All right. We'd better get looking, then. I hope it's not a very big city."

Chapter 33

Alois stared down at the assembled horde of undead in the plaza below, splayed around the fountain as though they were there to watch the Magistrate give a speech from the top of the tower. Granted, from up here he'd have to yell very loudly...

"Well?" he asked, "what's the plan?"

"We need to buy time," the Magistrate responded from his desk, where he had just finished packing a shoulder bag. "I doubt we can hope to beat him without Radcliff and Ludwig, so we need to keep Rodolphus busy until they can finish disenchanting his resurrection site. Then we can all try to kill him."

Alois winced as he saw a flash of bright light below. Briefly, timber rained down on the front of the plaza. "I think he just blew the door open."

"All right. Time for us to make our escape, I think."

"Are you crazy?" Lina asked, turning to face Schiller. "If we go down there we'll run right into them! Are you under the impression that I still have some of my powers? Because let me tell you right now..."

"No, young lady, I'm aware that the three of us are functionally helpless. But I wasn't planning for us to go down by the main stairway."

Schiller made his way over to a closet against the wall, opening out the hinged doors. Shelves beginning about three feet up were stacked neatly with bound collections of records. Schiller bent down very low to the bottom of the closet. Though the wall there looked uniform enough, he reached out and pulled part of it to the side, revealing a dark opening.

"This way, please."

Lina looked at Alois, who shrugged his shoulders, but made his way over. The Magistrate had already crawled through.

Alois waited until Lina had gone through the opening before making his way through himself. It was something of a close fit.

"Make sure to close the closet and door behind yourself, would you?" Schiller's voice said from somewhere below him. Alois felt stone under his hands now, and turning around he reached out to pull the closet doors shut, though he could not close them quite all the way. He then slid the trap door back into place, plunging them into darkness.

"You can stand," Lina said from behind him. He carefully did so, relieved when his head did not impact the ceiling.

A brief flash of light appeared below them. They were on a small stone landing before a circular stairway that wound downward. Schiller, just visible before a bend in the stairs, was using a match to light a lantern hanging in a wall bracket. He took the lantern and proceeded on down the stairs.

"Make use of the banister, please," he remarked as an afterthought.

"I thought that we were supposed to distract him to keep him from doing any harm to your city," Lina said, scrambling down the stairs after him. "If he finds the office empty, won't he just leave?"

"No, no. We weren't so very subtle. The lights are all on, for starters. He'll waste a few minutes looking, but he'll find this stairway quickly enough."

"So we're just delaying him a few minutes?"

"Not just. We're going to the basement. It will be much easier to hold them off from down there."

"I didn't know this building had a basement," Alois said. He watched Lina scramble down the stairs in front of him and wished that they could slow down; someone was liable to break their neck.

"There's no reason you should. This is the only way to get to it. The Guards don't even know about it."

"How is that possible?"

"It's old. It predates this building—goes back to the founding of the city."

Alois nodded in approval. "His little army is going to have a hard time with all these steps. He might decide to leave them behind and go on without them. That'd be a great help."

"He's got to get them *up* the other flight of stairs, too," Lina said, a slight sneer in her voice. "I don't envy him that. They're probably falling all over each other."

The stairway was dank and every corner was thick with cobwebs—the metal banister was unpleasantly cold and slightly moist. They kept going for quite some time, and Lina and Schiller were both breathing hard by the end. Alois was sure that they must have been at least several stories below ground level—and possibly quite a lot more.

The stairway ended somewhat anticlimactically with a simple wooden door, very ancient and decrepit in appearance. Schiller turned the knob and swung it open, forcing a rusty squeal from its hinges.

The chamber they stepped into was immense. Wrought from the same large blocks of grey stone that made up the stairwell, the place was at least as large as the downtown Police station that Alois had worked out of—four stories high, and perhaps one hundred by one hundred feet in area. A thick layer of dust coated every surface. The vast chamber was empty, bearing only two distinct features: the first was a dozen great torches hanging from the wall in evenly-spaced brackets. Their flickering flames glowed pale blue.

"I wish the Dean were here to tell us more about these torches," Schiller said. "I understand that for conjured flame to still be burning after hundreds of years, the creator must have been extremely powerful."

"Was the city founded by Wizards?" Lina asked, sounding very doubtful about the idea.

"In part, actually, though you won't find that in the official history," Schiller said, strolling forward toward the room's second distinctive feature. It was a wooden portcullis fit for a castle, rounded at the top and bracketed by great strips of black iron, held up by a system of heavy chains connected to a large manual winch that looked like it would require several men to drive. A symbol had been scrawled on the door in scarlet paint, glowing fluorescent in the blue light. The character looked like a jumbled, hastily scrawled star with too many points. Around the outer lines there was writing, though it was not in a language that Alois could understand. As the three of them neared the door, he guessed that it might be Arcanic.

"Can you read that, Lina?"

"No," she said, "I can't actually read Arcanic, remember? I just have some phrases memorized."

"They say," the Magistrate said, "That Arcanic is the ancient language of the dragons, who taught magic to mankind at the beginning of our age."

"Come, Schiller, don't speak nonsense," Alois said. "I've certainly been introduced to some odd things over the past weeks, but I can still say with solid confidence that dragons do not exist."

"What do you think, Miss Lina?" Schiller asked, still looking up at the symbol.

"I guess he's probably right," Lina said, shrugging. "I know the far continent has produced some pretty weird stuff, but…"

Schiller set down his bag and spread it open, pulling out its contents. A sheathed short sword came first, which he wove into his belt to hang from his hip. He then withdrew a pair of fine long daggers that bore the crest of the Magisterial Guard, handing one to each of them. Finally, he dug into the bag a last time and pulled out a large leathern flask.

"Water?" Lina asked hopefully.

"No, I'm afraid not," Schiller said, uncapping it. He approached the enormous gate and began splashing the contents of the flask onto it, seeming to make particularly sure to soak the wood that had the rune scrawled over it.

"What exactly are you doing?" Alois asked cautiously.

"Take a step back, please—I think it will become obvious enough."

They quickly fell back, and Schiller lit a match and thrust it into the drenched wood, quickly igniting the liquid—some kind of oil, apparently. He set down the lantern and stepped away. All three of them watched the flames spread across the front of the wood, crackling merrily as they burned through the oil and then began consuming the ancient material beneath.

"I don't suppose you're going to tell us why you did that?" Alois asked, watching the runes melt and burn away.

"Yes, by all means," said an echoing voice from the far end of the chamber, "I'd be quite interested to know."

They all turned, startled, and by the stairway door stood something halfway between a man and a skeleton, all cooked flesh and bloody tissue and stained bone, a black robe perhaps hiding the worst of it. He leered at them from fully intact eyes suspended by tissue in their bony orbitals. Around him stood a group of a dozen skeletons, their bones ranging from bleached white to jet black.

For a moment, there was silence. The fire crackled behind them, dying slowly, the moldy wood unable to maintain a good burn.

Slowly, Rodolphus spread his arms. He had just enough feature left to his face to adopt a look of consternation.

"Well?"

"Excuse me, sir," Krupp asked the night watchman, feeling the blood flowing to his face. "Could you... tell me where to find Crutchfield Park?"

"Park's closed, this time of night," the cloaked watchman replied, holding up his lantern and considering them skeptically.

"Yes, sir. It's just... erm, we're vacationing here, and my wife told me she lost her purse there today."

The guard took another look at them, and did not look any less cynical. Nevertheless, he held out his arm and pointed.

"One block that-a-way."

Lina couldn't move. When she'd first seen him, she had clutched the hilt of her knife, pressing so hard that her knuckles must have turned white, and she felt an insane desire to throw herself forward and try to kill the thing that had so quickly found them.

Her logical mind assured her that this was not a sound way to behave, and in that moment of hesitation her anger was swiftly replaced by fear as she realized the hopelessness of it all. They could do nothing. Mr. Alois with his strength might have been able to deal with a handful of Skeletons, and the Magistrate, if he was skilled with his sword, may be able to fight one or two. She would be useless. Without her magic she had nothing, and could contribute nothing. None of them had anything like the ability needed to fight the lich himself.

He was going to kill all of them. If they were lucky.

"I'm waiting," Rodolphus said, beginning to stride slowly forward, his entourage of skeletons—twelve of them, Lina saw—following in his wake, their naked grins leering.

"Of course," Schiller said, freakishly calmly. "Perhaps a few moments ago you overheard Mr. Gustav saying quite firmly that dragons do not exist. He is, of course, completely correct."

"Well," Rodolphus jeered, "excuse me if I'm less than floored by this revel—"

"With one notable exception," Schiller finished.

Rodolphus stopped where he was, about halfway across the chamber from them. Slowly, Lina turned to look at Schiller. Alois, had stepped to her side at some point in the last few moments, was staring as well.

Schiller began speaking, very loudly, and it was not in the common tongue. Lina could not understand the words, but she knew Arcanic when she heard it.

The last few words were muffled beneath a terrible crash as the gate behind them exploded outward. Lina found herself being pulled to the ground by Alois. She could hear the hail-like sound of fragments of wood being littered across half the room.

She pulled herself up into a crouch, Alois groaning beside her. She put a reassuring hand on him as she looked up toward the ruins of the gate. Something was coming through it.

It was enormous and grey, coated in curved, diamond-shaped scales. Its snout housed a prodigiously long set of jaws, its brown teeth menacingly jagged. A lithe tail whipped behind it. From its back rose two sets of colossal bat-like wings, and each of the four presented, at its apex, a three-fingered claw with brutally curved talons.

Its right eye was clouded milky white, and from just above it emerged the decaying leather-bound hilt of a large greatsword. A horrible red scab closed the catastrophic wound and climbed the rusted blade of the sword halfway to the hilt.

Its left eye was shiny black, like an orb of jet. No intelligence or mercy could be found there.

The thing's head swept quickly across the room, and its eye landed on Lina herself, but moments later a sizzling bolt of electricity collided with its head, and with a terrible roar it shifted its attention to Rodolphus.

It was, Rodolphus considered, remarkable that a 150 year old lich master Wizard could still behave stupidly based on animal instinct. The dragon shook its head as though the electricity were only mildly irritating, then threw its horribly jagged body forward with startling grace.

Rodolphus threw out his hand and his skeletons rushed into its path, for all the good that did. The beast's first set of wings shot forward, the pseudo-hands at their apex grabbing hold of a skeleton each. The wings summarily shot open, releasing the skeletons to send them hurling to shatter against the stone walls. Like a jack knife the second pair of wings shot out over the first and repeated the maneuver. Meanwhile, the thing grabbed a fifth skeleton in its mouth and crushed it to dust. The swinging of its head as it did so was enough to knock another two prone.

He would not have shot it if he'd been thinking more clearly. There was no reason to assume that Schiller could actually control this thing—in fact, now that he looked at it, the beast looked quite beyond anyone's control. This was bad news. It was notoriously difficult to mind-control animals, because they did not have any higher faculties to pervert or confuse. And a *raging* animal—well, that was just about a lost cause. He wondered briefly if he should teleport away, but reasoned that if Schiller *did* somehow have control, leaving might only make matters worse. He'd likely have to kill the thing one way or another, and there was no time like the present.

As he considered his options he threw shield after shield onto himself, all of them designed to block brute physical force. He considered trying to use Alchemy, but he would prefer to avoid it but as a last resort—a place like this could collapse on him if he changed too much of its structure.

By now the dragon had dealt with the majority of his minions, and he sent his last skeletons rushing forward, sending them practically diving into the thing's mouth as he tried to think. He watched its enormous wings unfold yet again, and found his inspiration. Chanting and signing, he sent a torrent of gale-force wind at the beast, hitting it dead on and sending it hurtling into the air. Lifted by its two pairs of enormous membranous wings, it was sent slamming into the stone wall over the gateway.

He kept the wind going, manipulating it, spinning it until a funnel cloud was formed. He might be able to kill all his birds with one tornado, if he managed things correctly.

He noticed the oncoming sword just in time. The King—or whatever his actual title was—had stridden right through his kinetic barrier, which was after all supposed to stop *brutal* movement, and had nearly cut what was left of Rodolphus' throat wide open. Rodolphus managed to stumble backward at the last moment, but his spell collapsed, the dragon falling in a heap to the ground, roaring in either agony or rage.

Schiller lunged forward again, but Rodolphus was ready this time. He caught the blade—literally, holding it in his hand, ignoring the sensation that was the closest he could feel to pain, and tore it free of the man's grasp, tossing it over his shoulder. Schiller smiled sadly and, amazingly, threw a punch. Rodolphus parried the arm with his own and grabbed the man by the throat, lifting him off the ground.

"Pretty good trick with the dragon, Schiller. But a trick is all it was. Tell my buddies in Hell that I say hello."

With his free hand he shot a slim thread of lightning through the man's gut. He brought his palm up to send the second one through his head.

The pain sensation shot through him again as a blade was plunged into his stomach and torn upward toward his chest. He roared, throwing down Schiller and kicking out in fury, sending Alois Gustav stumbling away from him.

"Roaches! Like roaches!" he growled, instantly taking control of the ghoul and locking his legs together and his arms to his sides. He strode forward and gave the man a push, sending him tumbling over like a log. "Just for that, dear Alois, the girl is going to get far worse from me than death."

He would not make the same mistake twice, however, and did not allow himself to be distracted further—there was still the girl to lunge forward and stab him, as seemed to be the popular thing. Meanwhile, the dragon was not finished either. It had regained its feet and was galloping toward him. He smiled.

It was like old times. He couldn't enchant. He couldn't use Alchemy. This was a job for Conjuration. Fleetingly he wished for Tiberius and the Wolf at his side.

He raised a hand and greeted the thing with a blaze of fire, and was impressed when it took it full on, howling in pain, its four wings reaching out around and grasping for him. He did a quick speed enchantment and sidestepped, blowing one claw out of his path with a sizzle of lightning and burning away another with a splash of acid.

The dragon was fast, though. Too fast, and he found a set of claws squeezing around him, bringing him in toward the thing's mouth. He'd recently seen exactly the effect that those jaws had on a human skeleton.

One arm was pinned to his side, but with the other he conjured, as quickly as he could, a brutally sharp longsword, composed entirely of steel. As he neared the thing's mouth, a smile raised the tattered muscle around his mouth. If he hadn't been immortal, he might have been afraid.

"I like your sword," he said to it conversationally. "I think you should make it a matching pair."

As he was plunged toward the dragon's mouth, he thrust his sword directly into its good eye. Its scream made the noises it had made previously seem meek by comparison.

He was sent tumbling to the ground. He could have done that in a dozen much safer ways, but he'd opted for the fun way, and that always turned out to be the best choice. The dragon, roaring in despair, was stumbling around the room blindly, groping for him. He gave it a wide berth, watching it rear up and howl in frustration.

But, where the hell had that girl gotten to?

"Behind you," a small voice said, and he turned. Indeed, there she stood.

"Well. I'm afraid you're just about out of allies, little girl," Rodolphus said, walking slowly forward. "You know, I used to be like you. A one-trick pony. One school of magic, and that was it. I learned the hard way, just like you, that if you can't use that one school, all of a sudden you're worthless."

"You must know a lot about being worthless," she said, but he could hear the tremor in her voice.

"Hah. Little girl... you really do remind me *so much* of myself. I did not understand. You never will. I'm going to decorate Alois with your innards before I finish him off, but that won't be for quite some time. No, no, there's no rush at all, with Schiller taken care of. I won the game. Did you even know that we were playing?"

He spread his arms and mock inhaled. Air whistled through the multitude of holes in his throat.

"Gods. Victory's even sweeter than I was expecting. I hope ruling with an iron fist can compare." He reached out a hand and took another step forward. "Come on. Let's you and me go somewhere a little more private."

She reached her own hands out. One held a knife. He raised his brow as she sliced her palm open, blood flowing out from the wide wound easily, running down her wrist, dripping to the floor.

"Suicide is a decent choice," he said. "but I'm afraid you're doing it wrong."

"It probably has trouble with your smell," she said.

He frowned.

"It probably has trouble with your smell," she repeated, and she flicked her hand, splashing more blood out, some peppering the hem of his robe. "You being undead, and all."

He heard the pounding of clawed feet against stone, and he had exactly enough time to look over his shoulder as he was drawn into the fanged mouth.

Lina watched as Rodolphus, who had been standing directly between her and the dragon, was crushed to splinters in the beast's enormous jaws. He went silently, without screaming.

Holding her burning palm against her dress to try and stop the flow of blood, she jogged away from the spectacle to Alois, who had just climbed to his feet, looking in a daze.

"We have to get Mr. Schiller and get back to the stairwell," she told him quickly, and his look of confusion cleared into a resolved nod.

Mercifully, the dragon showed little interest in chasing them. It lay on the floor and licked the rotten bits of lich out from between its teeth, crowing softly in something like despair.

Being born again probably felt a little bit like it must have the first time. He opened his eyes and cursed his stupidity, but so it went. This was why, after all, he'd gone to the pains of becoming immortal. He stood.

This was odd. There were men gathered around him— men that he recognized. Two of the Wizards he'd encountered earlier, as well as a dark-haired young man. They didn't seem to notice him, even though they were all hunkered around him, staring at something on which he stood.

He frowned. What was this? Was he invisible upon rebirth? He didn't remember Wolfram having said anything about that.

Whatever it was, he'd deal with it later. He pointed his finger at the older Wizard and shot a jet of acid through his forehead.

Or, he tried to. Nothing emerged from his finger. His frown deepened. What the hell was going on?

"That's it," the older Wizard said.

"Yes? It's finished?" the younger responded.

"Yes. The bond is broken."

"What? Look up, you goddamn lunatics!" he roared, and he shouted the phrase to engulf them in fire, just as he'd done to Tiberius a lifetime in the past. Nothing happened. He held up his hand, and it seemed less solid than it should have been—slightly translucent. He looked down, and realized that he was standing on a rune. An extremely advanced cancellation rune.

Beginning at his feet, he began to disappear.

"No," he said.

The three men stood up. They shook hands. They turned and began to walk away.

"Come back here, you sons of bitches!" Rodolphus screamed, his legs vanished, his abdomen slowly fading from existence. He tried to eviscerate them, incinerate them, pull them apart, but his hands were impotent. He tried to lunge at them and pound at their faces, but he could not move from the spot. As he realized he could do nothing, the anger drained away, and he remembered what it was to be afraid. A moment later, the lich was dead.

Chapter 34

Alois laid Schiller down in front of the stairs; the man was alive, but his breathing was badly labored. His wound, cauterized upon creation, did not bleed.

"I don't know if carrying him up all these stairs is going to do him much good," he said grimly. "It might be better if I went up to get help and brought it back down."

Lina nodded, though she was still staring out the door and into the large chamber. She'd insisted that they leave the door open; Alois was at least relieved that there was no way the dragon could fit through it. It had begun moving toward them, belabored. It crawled as though it had lost control of the rear half of its body.

"It can still smell you," he said.

"Do you think so?" Lina asked. "I wonder if it isn't just sensing that this is the way out."

The beast did not make it all the way. With a final groan it collapsed forward, raising a cloud of dust from the stone floor. Spined lids slid over its eyes, Rodolphus' sword having disappeared. It lay motionless.

"Do you think his attacks killed it?" she asked distantly, "or did it just give up, finally? I wonder how long it was back there, trapped."

"A very long time," Schiller managed to wheeze from the stairway.

"Come on," Alois said, putting a hand carefully on Lina's shoulder. "We need to go get help."

"No, it's all right," Schiller moaned. "I hear footsteps above us. Someone's coming."

Alois nodded, and when he turned back he found that Lina had slipped away, back out the door. He ran quickly after her.

"Lina, I really don't think it's safe…"

"It's dead," she said sadly. Approaching it, she gently patted its enormous scaled head. "Dragons are supposed to be intelligent beings," she said. "I think this one must have been, once."

"Maybe," Alois said.

Lina reached forward and wrapped her small hand around the hilt of the ancient sword buried above the dragon's right eye. It was a massive weapon, fit to be wielded in two hands by an enormous man. She wrapped another hand around the hilt, and pulled.

The sword did not budge. It had remained in place so long that it was practically a part of the dragon's body, and all her might could not influence it. Her head turned to Alois, and she looked up at him.

"Fathe—"

She paused, blushing softly. "Mr. Alois," she started again, "will you help me?"

His eyes widened, and he reached over her and grabbed hold of the sword, pulling as he never had before. The blade first gave slightly, then wiggled in place, and then finally released its hold. He pulled it free and let it clatter to the floor. Several feet of the blade were black and corroded beyond recognition.

Lina gently ran her fingers over the awful wound the sword had left in its wake. Behind them, Alois could hear voices.

"Who is it?" he called, turning, squinting in the dim light.

"It's us," the young Wizard Falkenhayn said, walking into the room. "We finished the deconsecration... The Magistrate said the lich was killed, though we're not quite sure which happened first. Do... do you think it's over?"

"Yes," Lina responded, "it's over."

"How can you be sure, though?"

"Because," she said distantly, "I got my magic back."

Alois saw suddenly that she was not merely stroking the wound in the dragon's head. The wound was closing. The scab was receding.

"Lina…"

"It will be all right. He can't hurt us, not anymore."

The wound closed, showing no sign that it had ever been there, but her hand remained in place, a faint blue glow highlighting it as her Necromancy delved deeper into the thing's ruined brain.

Radcliff approached and stood by Alois' side. "Ludwig and Krupp took Schiller for medical help; he was beyond my means to heal," he told them softly. Alois nodded, his eyes on Lina and the dragon.

Eventually, Lina drew her hand back.

Slowly, the dragon's eyes opened. The one on the right was black, perfect and smooth; so too was the one on the left, the damage inflicted by Rodolphus having completely vanished.

The beast's four great wings unfurled, stretching to their full breadth before telescoping closed again. Its eyes traced over the three of them warily. Suddenly, in a great voice that was half broad-chested old man and half hissing snake, it began to speak. Alois could not understand the words.

Radcliff responded to it in the same language and it nodded slightly. "Yes, human. I do speak your common tongue. What has happened to me? I cannot remember… or, I do remember, but I wish I did not. Have I been… reanimated?"

Lina nodded hesitantly. "Yes, my lord. I hope that the stories of dragons thinking Necromancy an abomination are not true."

Startlingly, the thing laughed, a deep, rumbling noise. "An abomination! Only, perhaps, because you humans managed to think of it first. No, my young lady... I am grateful..."

"Where did you come from?" Radcliff asked it, breathlessly.

"My name is Delar," it rumbled, and Alois might well have fainted had he not been a ghoul. "I ruled this place once, very long ago. Humans—your ancestors, perhaps— overthrew me, and imprisoned me here. That was... I think it may have been a very long time ago. I was not a kind ruler, and was not surprised that they would seek to slay me... I find myself wishing they had done so, rather than... this. I suppose it would be difficult for humans to understand exactly the nature of the hell that they condemned me to."

"You're Delar!" Radcliff said incredulously, waving his hands. "Astonishing! You know that today you're worshipped as a God here?"

The dragon laughed again. "Is that so? My people worshipped me as such long ago, but I never imagined that those who overthrew me would continue the tradition. They knew better than anyone just how finite my power was."

"Did you ever claim, my lord," Alois asked carefully, "to know the future?"

The dragon considered him, then shook its great head. "No, I never made such a claim. Would you mind, comrades, if we left this wretched place? It has been a very long time since I was able to smell the air."

Radcliff glanced warily at Lina. Alois knew he was worried about what the dragon might do when it was free, but indeed, there was little worry at all. Now that it was a ghoul, Lina could exercise complete control over it if the need arose.

Lina nodded, and so Radcliff laid a hand carefully on the dragon's nose, and indicated that Alois and Lina should take hold of him.

Moments later, they found themselves in the great plaza that, Alois realized, must have been many stories directly above the ancient chamber. The sun had risen and filled the morning with early light. The dragon roared in exultation, sending pigeons fluttering in every direction. It stretched its enormous wings and flapped them mightily, though it did not takeoff. It smiled at them, if a dragon could smile.

"We do not fly, as your people have always insisted. We are quite adept gliders, however. When I wish to fly, first I shall have to climb." He craned his neck up to look at the great Magistrate's Tower. "Kind of your people to build such a nice, high place. I always bemoaned the lack of mountains in this region."

Alois smiled to himself when he saw several stunned townspeople, the bright-and-early type, staring in stunned silence at the dragon. Many turned and ran. A Guardsman was striding hesitatingly into the plaza, and Alois turned to go and meet him. If they thought that this was surprising, there was still a great deal more in store.

For instance, he had a feeling that hundreds of corpses had been relocated from the graveyard to the interior of the Magistrate's Tower. That was only for starters.

Magistrate Schiller died the next day, lucid and in high spirits. His magically-inflicted wound was beyond Radcliff's skill to heal, and no highly skilled healer could be found in time. At his request he was taken to the roof of the Municipal Bank, where the group that had averted the conquering of the city stayed and rested. The doctors said that Schiller must have been in great pain, but he refused drugs for it and, if anything, behaved as though a weight had been lifted from him. He spent many of his last hours conversing with the dragon, conversations to which both Krupp and Radcliff listened with great interest.

"I was told that a dragon vanquished at the founding of the city was trapped below the tower," Schiller had explained, "And reasoned that destroying the rune and then calling out in your language to get your attention would bring you out. I did not know, however, the true circumstances of your capture and imprisonment... it would appear that even the secret histories are rather dubious."

"I can hardly blame your forbearers for that," the dragon had responded. "I myself did not allow the Merundians of my day to write down *anything*, much less the truth."

As his last act as Magistrate, Schiller rescinded the ancient laws forbidding the practice of Necromancy and Curation.

"There will need to be regulation," he said, "but you're mad if you think a dying man should be saddled with that sort of bureaucratic tedium."

"This may not go over as easily as we seem to be assuming," Krupp said grimly. "Once he gets past the yelling and screaming phase, the Archbishop is going to try to veto this."

"Of course, but both the Dean and the Archbishop must veto a Magisterial act to be successful."

"Unfortunately, Magistrate," Radcliff said, "The man who will take over as Acting Dean until a new one can be appointed is not likely to be entirely cooperative with us."

"What, you mean Assistant Dean Herbst? Don't be ridiculous, Radcliff. He's not the Dean. You are."

Radcliff sat in stunned silence through the series of back-claps and handshakes that followed.

"But... but Ludwig..."

The old diviner rubbed his bald head, smiling. "Sorry, my friend, I already made the Magistrate promise that he wouldn't put me in that soul-crusher of a job. It's all yours."

"And Krupp will replace me as Magistrate, naturally," Schiller said, as though it was a foregone conclusion. Krupp gave a modest bow, though he could not seem to wipe the grin off his face.

"You can just appoint him like that?" Lina asked.

"I can with Radcliff's support, luckily. And Radcliff's appointment is allowable thanks to the presumed posthumous wishes of Dean Baldermann... a tad shaky, but legal nonetheless. Though, the two of them could still use some more supporters. I would recommend Mr. Gustav for some nice position involving the City Guard or the Army, if he's planning to stay here in our fair city."

Alois smiled. "I go where Lina goes. It's not right, you know, a young girl not having a parental guardian."

Lina was sitting cross-legged under one of the dragon's wings, an open book laid on her lap. She wore a new set of robes, garishly inlaid with silver.

"I was actually thinking it would be nice to stay here, at least for a time. Do you think I could take lessons at the University?"

"We'll have to ask the Dean," Alois said.

"Of course," Radcliff laughed. "I think the faculty is going to be in such an uproar anyway, they won't even notice that we've started letting girls in."

"I may stay here for a time as well," Delar rumbled, "If I might be permitted to do so."

"Absolutely," Krupp nodded. "I was going to ask you to stay. Your presence will do a great deal of good in convincing the citizens of Merund's true history. The first thing I plan to do as Magistrate is see that a revised official history is published, and distributed."

"A noble effort," Schiller nodded, "but do not forget about the Church. The struggle will be brutal, and it is not likely that it will be bloodless."

"So be it," Krupp said solemnly. "I think the Church has had enough say in how Merund is run. Maybe a visit from our friend here will help convince them of the new way of things."

Delar laughed heartily. "Somehow, when they speak of *meeting Delar the Forever Seer*, I do not think that I am what they have in mind."

A few nights later, Alois woke in a cold sweat. He realized he was not alone. His arm was touching something warm and wet. He understood immediately that next to him lay the butchered body of his wife.

In the hall he found the body of Cassandra, which he picked up and laid on the bed next to her mother, as he'd done before. It was with some trepidation that he then approached Juliet's room.

"But it's not my room anymore, is it, father?" the grim voice of his daughter sounded from behind her bed. "You gave it to her. You gave it all to her. Our bodies were practically still warm when you began replacing us."

Alois slowly rounded the bed and saw here there, Juliet, or at least the thing that looked so much like her, its face obscured by a perpetual shadow.

"You're glad we're dead," it hissed at him.

He recoiled. "I'm sorry…"

"If you're sorry," it told him, "kill yourself. Put right the wrong you have committed. Return to God's natural order."

He stood silently, for a moment. Finally he took a step forward, and reached out his hand. The thing looked at it as though confused, and finally he took it gently by the wrist and pulled it to its feet.

"I'm very sorry that you died, darling," Alois told her, "but I have discovered that I am not sorry that I did not die that night. I am glad that I did what I did. I am doing my very best to try and be happy. I hope that you and your sister and your mother are happy too, wherever you are."

"You... you're glad we're dead, you had wished for us to die—"

"Juliet," he said softly, "if you are real, and not only a dream, please tell your sister that I love her."

And he turned his back on her, and walked away.

When he passed the doorjamb, the house faded, and he awoke. He did not dream of Juliet again.

Epilogue

In the far Eastern part of the city, overlooked by a domed chapel that loomed over everything for miles around, there was a meeting room. It was brightly lit and splendidly ornate, the walks bedecked with silken tapestries and gilded lamp fixtures. The men and women sitting at the table were equally resplendent, draped in the vestments of the highest offices of the High Church of Merund. They were renowned as the most religious people in the city. About half of them believed in God.

"I still don't understand why we didn't have the dragon killed years ago. Didn't anyone suspect that this could happen?"

"And how does one go about killing a dragon reliably, anyway? Besides, who could have predicted that Schiller would release it?"

"I could have. It's a travesty that we allowed him to come into the position of Magistrate. We should have blocked it."

"We tried."

"We should have tried harder."

"Please, gentlemen, let's not cry over milk that was spilt so long ago."

"And the Dean? Baldermann was never a friend to us. Maybe the new one…"

"I doubt it. Baldermann was indeed no friend, but he knew how to play ball. This one was hand-picked by Schiller on his deathbed. We can be sure that he'll be difficult… and controversial."

"So what are we supposed to do?"

"We'll do what we have to."

"We could lose a lot of public support. Isn't anyone else worried?"

"What's changed? People have always had to choose between religious faith and observed fact. If the latter is increasing in strength, we need only increase the former."

"Besides, Schiller is dead. We should be happy. Krupp is practically a teenager."

"Exactly. This isn't a time to worry about losing our position. No, quite the opposite. Our position has long been unacceptably marginal. These events are a blessing. Necromancy has been legalized, for God's sake. How many commoners are actually going to approve of that? Popular sentiment is going to be on our side. Let's use it. Let's remind the Wizards and politicians where the real power lies."

"I agree with the Cardinal. We will adopt his ideas. Does anyone oppose this?"

The room, for once, was silent.

To be continued in 2013

A note from the author

A sequel to *Ghoul* is in the works. If you would like to be sent an email when the sequel becomes available, you can sign up with my mailing list at the following URL: http://ralphmcgeary.tumblr.com/

I am honored that you chose to read *Ghoul*. Having read it, please allow me to ask a great favor of you: would you consider reviewing it on Amazon, or on another site where literature is reviewed? The more reviews Ghoul has, the more readers will be able to find and enjoy it, and the more feedback I'll have to work with.

Thanks for reading!

Acknowledgements

My sincere thanks to my four early readers: Kevin McDonough, Alex Schwab, and especially Jim Gies and Andrea Nelson. It's unlikely that this book ever would have been finished without their ongoing encouragement.

Thanks too to Kevin not only for his excellent work on the cover and maps, but also for graciously allowing me to borrow his pet Wolf. In that line, thanks to Dan McNerny for giving me and Kevin a guided tour of the Pits.

Thanks to Mom, Dad, Helen, Jerry, Erin, Aunt Maureen, and Stacy, all of whom provided all the help and support I could have hoped for and more.

About the author

Ralph McGeary lives in Chicago, Illinois. He holds degrees in History and Anthropology from Loyola University Chicago. *Ghoul* is his first novel. —

Made in the USA
Charleston, SC
29 November 2012